UNTIL THE DAY YOU DIE

TINA WAINSCOTT

St. Martin's Paperbacks

This is a work of fiction. All of the characters, organizations, and events portrayed in this novel are either products of the author's imagination or are used fictitiously.

UNTIL THE DAY YOU DIE

ISBN: 0-312-94163-3
EAN: 978-0-312-94163-5

Printed in the United States of America

St. Martin's Paperbacks edition / July 2007

St. Martin's Paperbacks are published by St. Martin's Press, 175 Fifth Avenue, New York, NY 10010.

10 9 8 7 6 5 4 3 2 1

To my great-uncle Bill Copestakes, who left us too soon

What I wanted most was to close my eyes and make it all disappear. But I couldn't look away from all the blood.

— MAGGIE FLETCHER

PART ONE

PART ONE

CHAPTER ONE

He stood inside a nearby shop window, waiting for her. Just as he did every day when she left work. As he did every morning when she arrived. Quaint buildings with shops and boutiques lined Market Street in the seacoast town of Portsmouth, New Hampshire. They offered plenty of places from which to watch her. He ostensibly perused a rack of biographies in the bookstore while looking out the window. Mostly he saw tourists, bored teenagers, women loaded with shopping bags, and portly men puffing their chests as they inhaled the sea air.

All the while he watched for her.

Six months ago he had begun his possession of Dana Mary O'Reilly when he'd dropped into the Mystic Café, the new-age coffee shop where she worked. Her watery smile, shifting eyes, and defensive posture had aroused his instincts. He smelled insecurity, loneliness, weakness. So he'd investigated, scoring her on the pertinent points on his checklist: no boyfriend or husband; no friends; no kids. A steady schedule. A house surrounded by foliage. All the things that made her an ideal pet. The only negative was the sister, but he could handle her.

He'd begun the saturation phase, following Dana, taking pictures and taping them to his dresser mirror, the bathroom wall, his car dashboard. Wherever he looked, she was there, frozen in a moment—crossing the street, chewing on her fingernail—his for as long as he wanted her.

Then he'd moved into the infiltration phase, playing the guileless suitor in front of her coworkers, bringing puerile gifts like stuffed animals bearing hearts. She'd spurned him, awkward, stuttering, barely meeting his eyes before darting back to the counter. Like any respectable guy, he'd backed off. But they had a secret, he and Dana. He was much more than a naïve schlub with a crush.

Movement caught his eye. His prey. She hovered just inside the café door, searching for him. It had become a game. Their private game. *Where, oh, where could he be?*

A couple walked into the café, and the man held the door open for Dana, forcing her out into the open. Apprehension and frustration filled her brown eyes. He liked the fear. He liked it a lot.

Today her usual Gothic ensemble included long, flared sleeves, long black skirt, and black Converse sneakers. Her thick, dark hair needed brushing. She pulled a cigarette from her pack and lit it with shaky hands. She walked with shoulders hunched and chin tucked in, her body static but for her legs. He wished he'd made her walk in that insecure manner, but she'd come that way. She reminded him of a mouse now, taking several steps and stopping, searching, everything but sniffing the air and twitching her whiskers. *That* was his doing at least.

He'd violated her safe little world, all the way down to the panties she wore. It gave him a powerful thrill to know he'd touched the fabric that now shielded her most private parts. While she was at work, he sprawled on her rumpled bedsheets, rubbed her panties over his body, used her deodorant. Then he left subtle clues to let her know he'd been there. That she had no privacy now. Letting her know by degrees that she was never alone.

As she was everywhere in his world, he was everywhere in hers. Most important, he was inside her mind. Even in her dreams, if her thrashing and crying out were any indication. He smiled. She couldn't escape him, even in sleep.

With her free arm tucked around her waist, she walked toward the High-Hanover parking garage. He moved so that when her gaze flashed past the bookstore she would see him. She stiffened, sucked hard on her cigarette, and then walked faster. Acknowledging their exchange wasn't necessary. Being there, watching her, was enough. She tripped on a raised brick and caught her balance seconds before slamming into a parking meter. Her cigarette went flying, rolling under a car. An old man looked at her with both concern and puzzlement. She glanced back toward the bookstore window. He wasn't there.

She had already been unbalanced, as evidenced by the array of prescription drugs in her medicine cabinet. He had pushed her to the edge. Soon, very soon, she would break. The Red Hot Chili Peppers song "Breaking the Girl" played in his mind. He liked watching the pieces of his pets' souls splinter away.

She walked into the garage and aimed the remote key fob at her car as soon as she approached it. The chirp echoed off the concrete. Her fingers wrapped around the car handle but paused. The folded piece of green paper awaited her on the driver's seat.

She snatched open the door, crinkled the paper, and dropped down into the seat as though her bones had liquefied. She started the car and sped out of the garage. A few minutes later he pulled up next to her at a red light. His dark windows prevented her from seeing him. She chewed her fingernail while she waited. Glanced at the seat beside her. Forward. Then back to the seat. Then reached over. He smiled as she wrestled the ball of paper open. He shoved aside a fast-food bag, a dog-eared paperback thriller, and packs of soy sauce to find his camera on the seat beside him. With his other hand he lowered his window and recited the words as she read:

"*I live in her mind,*
Her thoughts,
Her soul,

Under her skin.
Though she denies me,
I am already a part of her.

"*She dreams of me,*
When she sleeps,
So fitful through the night,
As though sensing I am there,
Her guardian angel,
Watching over her.
Always."

She balled up the note and threw it with an angry scream. Then she looked his way. He snapped one last picture, capturing her shock and indignation. Beautiful. The light turned green, and she burned rubber through the intersection.

He took his time. He knew where she lived.

He had gone much further with Dana. He had not only slipped into her home; sometimes he'd also been there when she'd arrived home. He could smell her, as he watched from his place in the closet or the pantry. The prospect of getting caught tantalized him.

Maybe she would catch him tonight. Maybe he would make sure she did.

CHAPTER TWO

"Ms. Fletcher, you're one busy woman," my client said when my cell phone rang for the umpteenth time.

I smiled another apology as I glanced at the incoming number. I'd told the two men I was showing million-dollar homes to that I had to make sure it wasn't my nine-year-old son, Luke, who was at his best friend Bobby's house. In fact, the number on the screen represented my bigger concern: Dana.

"Sorry, I've got to take this."

I ran to the foyer to get as far from hearing range as possible. My fingers went right to my worry curl. "What's wrong?" I answered, the way I'd started answering my sister's calls lately. Forget *hello* or *how are you?*

"He's been here," came her strained voice.

My heart dropped. Earlier Dana had called from her car to tell me about the latest poem, terrified that it meant he was watching her sleep. The thought totally creeped me out.

She didn't wait for me to respond. "I went shopping. Then I got stuck in traffic for an hour, an accident. I felt safe, 'cause he wasn't around. Then he called my cell phone, playing that song that sounds like Enigma, about a heart going boom, boom, boom whenever he thinks of her. Nothing threatening. Probably a nice love song he's made ugly.

"It was dark when I came home." She had an edge in her

voice at that; she hated being out in the dark. "The closet door was open. I know it was closed when I left, Mags. These are the games he plays with me. Little things to let me know he's been here. The bed was made. And he left a pair of my panties out again, too. He's *touching* my panties. I know that's what his 'Silk' poem was about: 'The silk and cotton slide against my fingers. I have touched what now touches her—' "

"Stop! Stop memorizing those icky poems."

"I can't help it! They keep bouncing around in my brain, like a jingle you can't push out. But I'll show him. I bought new panties today. They're big and ugly, like the kind Mom wears."

Dana had only just bothered to tell me, the person closest to her, that she was being stalked—*stalked,* for God's sake! He'd appeared five months earlier. At first she'd been embarrassed about her discomfort over her suitor. Her co-workers thought Colin Masters was sweet, if a bit overeager. Dana had finally told him she wasn't interested. On the surface he had taken it well. He didn't come in as often and no longer brought gifts.

But, according to Dana, his actions had actually become more sinister. He watched her when she arrived at work, was waiting when she left, and the poems had started arriving. At first he left them on her car window and then inside her locked car. That's when she'd finally told me, three weeks ago. The poems weren't threatening, but they were creepy in a warped-love way. The gifts he'd given her reminded me of the kind gawky teenage boys give their girlfriends, except this guy was in his midtwenties. Was *he* warped or was Dana, in fact, being paranoid? Besides, stalkers usually chose celebrities or ex-lovers. Didn't they? Not someone quiet and barely noticeable like Dana.

I got especially concerned when Dana started talking about the "evidence" of Colin's presence in her home, despite that her house was secured. The more hysterical she got about that, the more my stomach twisted. *Paranoia will destroy you.* Wasn't that an old Kinks song? I remembered one called "Acute Schizophrenia Paranoia Blues." I hated thinking it, on multiple levels. My doubts felt like a betrayal. And if she was imagining things, her mental state had deteriorated to a whole new level. That scared the hell out of me.

I shoved those thoughts aside. "What we need is proof that he's breaking in. We changed the locks, added another dead bolt. Was there any sign of forced entry this time? How about the windows?" I had installed double locks on those, too. Every time I'd run over to Dana's house, we'd found nothing tangible. I'd so wanted to.

"Just like always. He's a damned ghost!"

I had never seen him, even when I purposely arrived at the café when Dana did or left when she left. I wanted to talk to him, get a feel for what this was really about. Was he deranged or was Dana misinterpreting? She had once pointed out his beige sedan with dark tinted windows as it slowly cruised by. I had held up my hand in a "wait" gesture while running up to the car, but the driver had continued on.

I felt twisted, not sure whether I wanted to believe Dana or not. Which was worse, insidious stalker or mental disease?

I'd done research, and yes, stalkers did target ordinary strangers. Sometimes all it took was a polite smile to engage one. I convinced Dana to go to the police and file an incident report. In all one chunk I had to admit it sounded even more paranoid, but Detective Thurmond took her information and ran it through his software program. He'd explained that he was learning threat assessment procedures, though the department didn't have an official stalking division.

The problem was, the subtle behaviors Dana had described—deodorant in the sink, for goodness' sake—didn't match the stalker typologies, particularly the naïve pursuer that Colin seemed to be. Her impassioned observations didn't help: *His eyes touch me. When he looks at me, I can feel them on my body.*

When Thurmond warned us that the person filing a restraining order must face her stalker in court, *No, no,* and *absolutely not!* was Dana's immediate response. I hadn't pressed. I'd read that restraining orders sometimes incited a stalker into violence. When we left, Dana was sure the detective was at that moment laughing at her. Another sign of paranoia.

After a pause she said, "You saw his car that one time, but you haven't actually seen *him*. You don't think I'm making this all up, do you, Mags?"

I took a breath, needing to get this right. "I believe you're afraid of this man." But I wasn't sure that he was stealing into her home to move things around. If he were some sicko, he'd leave creepy gifts like chicken hearts and jars of semen. "And I'll do everything I can to help you. But I wish you'd see Dr. Reese, and no, not because I think you're crazy. I think he could help you to cope with—"

"No. He put me on those drugs, and I felt muzzy. I have to be on alert."

I squeezed my eyes shut in fear and anger. How long could this go on before she cracked? How long could I? "First thing tomorrow I'm calling a security company to have cameras and an alarm installed."

"Okay," she said on a breath.

"Do you want me to come over?"

"Are you with clients?"

"Yeah. I can't run over right this minute. Serena's had a couple of complaints from clients annoyed that I abandoned them." To look at an open cabinet or a made-up bed.

"Serena's your best friend. She understands, doesn't she?"

"Yes, but as the broker of her own real estate company she's got to make sure the clients are happy. And it's the beginning of busy season. We've been straight out at the office for the past few weeks."

"I'm sorry, Mags. I know how much being a good real estate agent means to you. I'll be fine. If he was here, he would have come out and slashed my throat already."

Jeez. She'd always been a morbid drama queen. "I'll call you in a bit. If you feel in danger, promise you'll call the police. And you're welcome to stay with us." Though I knew she wouldn't. She treasured her sanctuary and privacy too much.

"Mags, you're the only person in the world I can depend on. I know I put a lot on you. I always have. Mom wrote me off as being born under a black cloud. But you never did. I want you to know how much I love you for that."

My throat thickened. "I love you, too."

Dana hung up, leaving me with a knot in my stomach. I'd known her for twenty-seven years and still didn't really know her. We were nothing alike. I took after our Irish dad, with his sprinkling of freckles, curly light brown hair, and quick laugh. Dana took after our mother, with her sturdier body, striking features, and serious demeanor. I had somehow taken responsibility for trying to draw Dana out of the shadows. Even as far back as when I was four and she was two, I could remember working to make her smile. Oh, the joy of seeing that rare, brief smile.

The more I saw my mother distancing herself from Dana, the more I moved into her vacated role. Mom did the necessary things, like buying Dana's clothes and helping with her homework. I put her hair into tails every morning; I heard what was between the lines and coaxed her feelings and fears from her. I gave her hugs just because she looked like she needed them.

I felt I needed to make up to her that I was capable of happiness and she wasn't. I would never forget a night when I was a teenager, laughing in the living room with my friends. I caught sight of Dana lurking in the hallway. I tried to put her out of my mind. My friends didn't like her, and Dana didn't like them, either. When they'd gone home, I went to her room and found her on the floor. She'd tried to overdose on vitamins. While I had been laughing. Even now, when I was having a good time, I sometimes thought of Dana, alone and in shadow, and found my laughter fading.

Only minutes after I'd stumbled all over myself apologizing to my clients, the phone rang again: my boyfriend's number. Marcus and I had no plans to cancel or modify, so I let it go to voice mail and tuned back in as the men nitpicked everything.

"Would you be interested in buying a historic home with

the intention of restoring it?" I asked them. "I know one that's a steal. I'd buy it myself if I had the resources."

I had a fascination with home restoration. I was addicted to *This Old House* and didn't miss an episode of *Extreme Makeover: Home Edition.* Marcus and Luke teased me about my crush on Ty Pennington. There was no point in denying it, so I just gave them a sly smile.

The men tossed around my suggestion but, unsurprisingly, couldn't come to an agreement. "Too messy," the tall, skinny one said with a dismissive wave. "All that dust, those construction types loitering about."

"But think of preserving historical integrity," the shorter one said, and then with a leer, "and all those construction types loitering about."

"Let's move on then, shall we?" As I continued to show the house, guilt nagged at me. Was it my mother's voice? *A good mother would put her child first, work second.* Oh, gawd, it *was* her voice. She'd been a stay-at-home mom, but that hadn't made her a good mother. But I *had* been working too much lately. At first it had been the occasional evening showing and then finalizing a contract on the weekend. When cancer ate away my husband Wesley's life three years ago, our part of the medical costs depleted our savings. It wasn't greed that drove me but a deep need for financial security. And Luke's college fund. I hated the thought that college would come before we both knew it.

"Gentlemen," I said when I could break into their debate about elongated versus round toilets. "I'd love to stay longer, but I'm already late to pick up my son."

As soon as I escaped, I called Bobby's mother, who happened to be my boss and friend, Serena Reese.

"Did they finally make an offer?" she asked after I identified myself.

"No, another wasted evening. I have this terrible feeling they're just looking at homes to pass the time. And drive some poor, unsuspecting real estate agent crazy."

She laughed sympathetically. "Hang in there, girl. I've heard what a bulldog you can be."

"Bulldog? Who said that?"

"The Millers. They told me how you were ready to walk away from the house they were in love with unless the seller updated the plumbing. They were horrified . . . until you got your way. Now you're their idol." She chuckled. "Listen, the boys are already asleep, worn out by their tag football game. How about you pick Luke up in the morning?"

"No point waking him up, I suppose." We said good-bye and hung up. I felt even less like a good mother. But I could still be a good sister. I dialed Dana's number. "Just making sure you're all right. Want me to come by?"

Her voice sounded light and thready when she said, "No, no, that's okay. I'll talk to you later."

"Hey, wait. If you're in trouble, say the word"—I scrambled for something—"'banana.'"

"I'm fine. Just tired. I'll talk to you tomorrow." She hung up.

I found it odd, yet odd and Dana often went together without meaning anything ominous. "Banana?" I uttered, shaking my head. Next I tried Marcus's cell phone, trying to score good girlfriend points, but he didn't answer. He had only left a cursory "call me" message, typical of the "nonphone" person he'd warned me that he was.

When I met Marcus Antonelli at the Pirates' Treasure cancer benefit a year ago, my heart did a stone-across-the-water skip. He was tall, with a full head of short, dark hair. Mostly I was attracted to his easy confidence. I was afraid of loving and losing again, but I was also ready to embrace happiness. Marcus gave me the comfort and emotional security I craved. And he was good for Luke. Marcus understood Luke's dyslexia, since he had it, too. The best part was when we all spent time together. Sometimes I muted my laughter just to hear the two of them guffawing together.

And yet I felt darkness hovering at the edge, heard the rumble of thunder like an approaching storm. I found myself counting my sins—worse, in my mother's voice—fearing which one could bring down my world again. Premarital sex (but with a man I loved). Calling that guy who'd pulled out right in front of me a dirty word (at least Luke wasn't in the car). Both sins I was pretty sure my soul could get away with.

I drove into Wellwood Manor, which had been an older community of family Cape Cod and Colonial homes when Wesley and I moved here. It was undergoing yuppie revitalization, for better or worse. Elaborate play sets replaced swing sets; SUVs replaced minivans. Even the bird feeders had become fancier.

Two restaurants and a bar had sprung up, inviting nightlife and mixed reactions from residents. I'd recently bought a bungalow a couple blocks away from my house and let Dana live there for a hundred dollars a month. I'd had to convince her I was merely holding on to it for an investment, not as a rental property. She didn't want charity, but she couldn't afford her own place on her salary without a roommate, something Dana detested. So, as her surrogate mother, I made sure Dana had a home of her own.

I passed Chubb's Pub, where live music drifted out into the air. People wandered down the sidewalks, happy to be wearing light coats and sweaters on this early-summer night. After the long New England winter, residents celebrated the first hint of spring.

A block away, things quieted again. It was still too chilly for sitting out on front porches, a favorite pastime for our area. A couple on one side of the road huddled close as they headed away from the activity. On Dana's block, a lone man stumbled toward the restaurants, crossing the side street with his head ducked into his jacket. I slowed in front of Dana's bungalow and glanced at the clock: 9:45. My fingers went to my worry curl, a gesture so automatic, so ingrained, I'd never get rid of it. My finger wound the curl tighter and tighter as I stared at the entrance to the driveway.

The house was shrouded in foliage, a feature that Dana wouldn't be persuaded to eliminate, even for security reasons. Lights glowed from behind the dark curtains. All looked well. No one lurked, no beige sedans were parked in the vicinity. I thought about calling again, but she'd been pretty definite—no banana. I continued down the road toward home. On her next day off, I was going to take her out for lunch and to the salon. Just the thought lifted my spirits; I knew it would lift hers, too.

The prospect of an empty house loomed before me as I walked in, even as I told myself I should be relishing the time alone. Not completely empty, I realized, when Bonk, our brown Lab, bounded up to me. Luke gave Bonk the moniker when, as an unnamed pup, he kept sliding across the wood floors and bonking his head on the wall. I knelt down and petted him, and a minute later he was through the dog door that allowed him access to the backyard. Even happier about the warm weather than I was, Bonk was continuously racing in and out.

I eyed the knitting needles and jumble of pink yarn that would become a blanket for Serena's coming baby. I found knitting relaxing and giddily feminine, even though I wasn't very good at any of that stuff. I'd always been too much my dad's girl to be girly, being into sports and hanging out with the guys at the car dealership. For a long time I'd seen being a woman as being chaste and subdued, like my mother. It was only when I grew into womanhood that I realized that wasn't the case. I embraced my femininity.

I fingered the weave of soft yarn. No angel would grace the corner of this one. Most of the blankets I knitted were for the hospital, to swaddle stillborn babies.

In the end, the rare opportunity to soak in my Jacuzzi tub won out over anything productive. I wandered through the too-quiet house decorated in a mixture of contemporary and nine-year-old-boy styling.

I took a Dove dark chocolate out of the bag in my nightstand and unwrapped the foil. The little message printed inside read: *You're allowed to do nothing.* Ah, appropriate. I popped the piece into my mouth. When good health meant eating a piece of dark chocolate every day, I embraced the notion.

I sank in with a groan and then had to catch several Batman figurines swirling around in the bubbly water, since Luke preferred my tub to his. Even as I lined them up on the ledge, I knew he'd tease me about the preciseness of their alignment. I skewed them on purpose.

Lulled by the sound of the jets, I drifted off. I wasn't sure what woke me, but my eyes opened with a start. I pulled myself from the water, dried off, and trudged into the kitchen for a glass of water. I blinked idiotically at the clock: 11:30. I'd been in the tub for an hour and a half?

I was surprised to hear the cell phone beeping. Hadn't I taken it into the bathroom? I'd meant to, in case Marcus called back. When I retrieved the message, the hairs on the back of my neck shot up. A sob, I thought, but couldn't be sure. Then a squeak. I had to play it twice more to figure out it was Dana saying my name in a voice so filled with anguish that tears sprang to my eyes. That was all, just a sob and my name. She'd called an hour ago.

I fumbled with the numbers. The phone rang until the machine picked up. Dana's droll voice instructed, "Hope you don't hate these things as much as I do. Leave a message."

"Dana, it's me: Maggie. I'm sorry I missed your call. I was in the tub and didn't hear the phone. I'm coming over in about ten minutes unless I hear from you." What had happened? I'd never heard her sound like that and it terrified me.

I phoned Mom next. She would be tuned into the Sky Angel network until midnight.

"Mom, it's me," I said when Angelista answered in a gruff voice.

"Amen," she said before greeting me. "You must have some sixth sense when you decide to call me. You always call during prayer."

I caught myself feeling guilty and stopped. "It's just dumb luck—"

"Or Satan trying to use you to interfere."

"Then don't answer the phone! That's what the machine I bought you is for." I took a quick, calming breath. I loved my mother because she was my mother. But I didn't like her much. "Have you talked to Dana tonight? She left a disturbing message on my machine an hour ago and now she's not answering."

"She only calls me a little more often than you do," Mom said in a plaintive voice. "And speaking of which, I tried calling you earlier, too. What have you been doing all this time?"

"I got home at ten, got into the tub, and fell asleep."

"Goodness, working until ten." It amazed me that Mom didn't actually have to chastise me to . . . well, chastise me. "And falling asleep in the tub, very dangerous. The reason I was calling was that the youth pastor mentioned he hadn't seen Luke in three weeks."

I reined in my impatience. "I'm not going to force him to go." *Like you forced us,* I didn't say. My childhood had been saturated with religion. It was only after I'd moved out that I learned not every Christian denomination believed in harsh punishment and rules. Though Mom considered me a lazy Christian, I was comfortable in my faith. She should have been glad I hadn't been turned off altogether. "We'll talk about it later. I've got to check on Dana. Bye." I hung up and ran into the bedroom to dress. I had a tight feeling in my chest that had nothing to do with Mom, and everything to do with Dana.

I pulled into her driveway a few minutes later. Her car was there. The lights were still on inside. Everything seemed normal. When I knocked on the door I thought I heard a *thump* inside. I knocked again.

"Dana! It's me!"

After a few seconds, I rummaged in my purse for the key tucked in a crevice. I had convinced her to give me a spare key, which I promised to only use in an emergency. Did I think she was going to do something crazy like take her life? she'd asked. I'd said, *No . . . well, maybe.* Dana detested meaningless platitudes and suspected concealed motives, so I used neither. It was much easier on both of us.

Did this count as an emergency? Damn right it did. I used my key to let myself in.

Hang in there, Sis. I'm coming.

CHAPTER THREE

A decent sort of fellow would call an ambulance. But he wasn't decent. And it was better if she died anyway.

His pet was still on the bed where he'd dumped her. Her breathing was raspy. Blood covered the pillow and crusted her nose. Bruises marred her face like an outbreak of mold. She stared at the ceiling to avoid looking at him.

"I wouldn't have been so hard on you if you hadn't screwed everything up," he growled. "Do you know how hard I worked on you? You think what I do is *easy*?"

They never appreciated how much he put into stalking them. They never saw his side of it. Women always complained that men never paid enough attention to them. Well, he did. And still they complained.

"Everything was going along just perfectly. Then you had to go and spoil it. You proved yourself unworthy of my honor."

Instead of revealing himself in a spectacular way, he'd allowed rage to consume him. He had to admit it had felt good. Before the shame of not being able to control it set in, it had felt very good.

This wasn't the first time things had gone wrong. His first pet disappeared before he'd finished with her. His second pet's bully of a brother had complicated matters, but he still

got great satisfaction knowing that as she spoon-fed her
brother and wiped his ass she thought of him. Yes, she thought
of him every day. The third . . . well, the gun had ended things
prematurely. A shame, that.

He looked down at Dana and felt no stirring. The drug of
her had worn off. He'd never had such a sweet opportunity
to withdraw from the woman who had occupied his mind
and body so thoroughly. To purge her from every cell in his
body. The obsession was a drug addiction.

The ringing phone jarred him from his thoughts: a woman's
voice on the machine in another room. Then silence. He had to
finish cleaning up. One hair could place him there, irrefutable
evidence.

He slid the bloody length of chain into a plastic bag and
placed it into his duffel. The Baggie containing the soggy
condoms was already inside. Then he pulled out his portable
vacuum. Her eyes twitched at the sound of the machine as it
ran over the carpet. He tossed a blanket over her, dismissing
the act as an afterthought.

Already the feeling of restlessness and emptiness settled
into his bones. He was only happy when he had a purpose,
an obsession to fuel his one other pleasure: his art. In that
sense, real life fueled his fantasies. And sometimes his fantasies fueled his real life, too. Next time he would make sure
it ended on his terms.

Just as he finished cleaning, he heard someone knock on
the door. A woman called out.

He peered out the peekaboo hole Dana had recently
installed. Because of him, no doubt. He imagined her asking the salesclerk about the different models . . . thinking
of him.

The porch light illuminated the woman. The sister. He'd
seen her around when his pet had tried to convince her that
she had a stalker. The sister had corralled his pet to the police station. Obviously not to file charges. He smiled, imagining again how it would have sounded as she detailed his
supposed menace.

The sister looked uptight as she brushed her shoulder-length curls from her face, only to have them bounce right back again. Usually she looked professional and put together. She reminded him of a doll a neighbor girl had when he was a kid. The doll's name was Suzy, though he didn't remember the girl's name. She was always brushing the doll's brown curls and pretending to have conversations with it. It was such a cute dolly. Wouldn't he like to hold it?

He'd ripped off Suzy's head with his teeth. The girl's screams echoed pleasantly in his head.

The woman knocked again. He liked watching her, even with the distorted view. She was short, like her sister, but petite instead of stocky, with a heart-shaped face and Cupid's bow mouth. He had never targeted sisters before. Usually he moved on to a new area and a completely unrelated woman. It could be interesting, going after the sister who had to deal with the mess he left behind. And this sister was feistier. He usually chose the weak, but it was time for a challenge. He even admired her for standing by her sister when what she was hearing must have sounded insane. So for her devotion she would be rewarded.

With him.

His groin tightened at the prospect. The cute-as-a-dolly lady started going through her purse as though looking for something. A key? Couldn't take the chance. He grabbed his bag and wedged himself into the coat closet near the front door.

The door opened and, through the wooden slats, he saw her take a cautious step inside.

"Dana? It's Maggie. I'm coming in."

She locked the front door before flooding the living room with light. Her dolly face creased with worry. She looked at the two wineglasses on the coffee table and tilted her head quizzically.

He smiled. She had locked the door thinking to keep him out. If she only knew that he was less than three feet away. He could reach out and grab her. Could smell her lilac soap.

He would leave it up to fate. If she didn't discover him, he would make her his next pet. If she opened the door to hang up her sweater coat . . .

He had to keep himself from letting out a low, rumbling chuckle. *Oh, come on, dolly. Come on. Open the door.*

CHAPTER FOUR

I swore I felt heaviness in the air, beyond the reek of cigarettes, beyond the darkness of the walls and brown furniture.
I had once sensed that Luke was down by the lake, somewhere he was forbidden to be. He was. Right now I sensed
something being really, really wrong. Both maternal instincts, I thought.

The two wineglasses on the coffee table, along with the
empty bottle of merlot, confirmed it. Guests were an invasion of Dana's sanctuary, she said. With her eerie Dalí
prints, I hardly considered it a cozy retreat. The only normal
picture in the room was one of her, Marcus, and me on her
mantel. We were celebrating Dana's last birthday, getting
toasted on watermelon martinis at my favorite waterfront
restaurant. She'd been happy then, and it had warmed my
heart to see her laugh.

Dana had chosen "desert pottery" for her walls. "I'll bet
the guys at the paint manufacturer call it dried poop," I'd
teased when we'd rolled it on. She'd stuck out her tongue at
me. Shrouded windows only added to the cavelike atmos-
phere. Oprah picks, full of angst, and Anne Rice's vampire
books dominated Dana's bookshelves.

I slid out of my sweater coat and headed toward the closet
door. The door Dana claimed Colin left open. I told myself it

had nothing to do with having the creeps at that thought, as I flung my coat over the chair instead.

"Dana?"

The kitchen was dark, but I peered in anyway, remembering how she used to sit at the table in the middle of the night. *Just thinking, Mags.* No sign of her.

The washing machine was chugging away. I peeked into the small laundry room, the smell of Clorox burning my nose and eyes. Why was she running a load of laundry now?

I turned on every light in the house. I saw no further evidence of the guest, but Dana's closed bedroom door made me hesitate. Any possible romantic relationship was hampered by her belief that letting a man into the sanctity of her body was a violation she couldn't fathom.

The hairs on my neck prickled to attention. I turned around and looked into the living room. Nothing. At the same time I heard a groan coming from Dana's bedroom. Not a sexual kind of groan. Then I saw what had alerted my sixth sense: the front door was unlocked. I knew I locked it behind me. Fear gripped my heart in an icy hand.

I turned the bedroom doorknob, slipped inside, and locked that door. My heart pounded as I turned around.

What I saw didn't make sense, not at first. Something was on the bed, something grotesque, misshapen . . . not human. My body stiffened even as my thoughts clicked into place. It *was* human. And if it was, then it had to be—

"Oh, my God, Dana!"

I stumbled toward the bed, falling to the side of it. I couldn't say anything else, could only take in the sight of her. The swollen skin around her eyes left them as slits through which tears streaked down. Her face, upper chest, and neck were mottled with red and blue marks. Her nose, her mouth, misshapen. She looked like a monster in the old late-night movies we used to watch as kids. A blood-splattered blanket covered her from the chest down. I could see her trembling beneath it, curled into a semi-fetal position. There were no sheets or pillowcases on the bed. And most odd, she was wet.

I grabbed for the phone and dialed 911, my brain cells finally realigning. "I need"—words wouldn't push through my constricted throat—"I need an ambulance. My sister . . . she's been beaten."

"Is the person who assaulted her still there?"

I hated that the woman was calm and businesslike. *But no, that's her job. She gets calls like this all the time. She has to be calm. Unlike me, who can freak out once help is on the way.*

I thought of the unlocked door again. He'd been here. In the house when I'd come in. But he'd left. The unlocked door meant he was gone. "He left right after I got here. We're locked in the bedroom."

She verified the address. "We'll send the police and an ambulance right away. Is your sister conscious?"

"I think so. But she's hurt . . . bad." Those words clogged my throat.

"Try to get her to respond, but please stay on the line."

Numb shock had turned into automatic action. I set down the phone and turned to Dana, wanting—needing—to do something for her.

"They're coming. Hang on," I told her, seeing no response in her glazed eyes.

She was breathing through her mouth, necessitated by a nose that was clogged with dried blood. I sat gingerly on the bed beside her. "Can I get you anything?"

She only stared.

"Who did this to you? Blink once if it was Colin Masters."

She did blink. Was it an answer? She tried to speak. First only a garbled sound. And then one word huffed out. "I . . ."

I leaned closer, holding my breath. I didn't know whether to encourage her to speak or not. She wanted to say something, though, so I waited. I wanted her to tell me who had done this to her. I wanted to hear his name.

"I . . . d-d-deserved it."

"No." That took me by surprise.

Her eyes closed on my protestation. I panicked for a moment, afraid she was dying. But her chest rose and fell in a steady but shallow rhythm. "Dana, you didn't deserve this. Do you hear me?"

I picked up the phone. "Where's that ambulance? Dammit, get it here already!"

"They'll be there in approximately two minutes." She asked me questions about Dana's condition. As I answered, I took in the room, seeing the broken chair and shards of her porcelain lamp lying on the carpet. Blood was splattered across the headboard and wall. Not in life-threatening amounts. Just a little . . . but all over. God.

Only then did I think of the biggest violation a woman can suffer. I searched Dana's face, down her bruised neck and shoulders until the blanket blocked my view. I couldn't handle finding out if . . . no, not yet. She was naked, though, beneath the blanket. Her clothes were on the floor, in shreds. My stomach clenched, and I swallowed back my nausea.

As the sound of sirens penetrated my consciousness, I noticed something: though specks of blood were everywhere, I saw none on her except the accumulation in her nostrils.

Wet. No blood. I shivered at the deduction: he had bathed her.

The police arrived first. One officer checked the house and the other took photographs of Dana and the bedroom. The woman tried to explain that it was necessary so that the scene could be preserved before the medics disturbed the evidence. I felt Dana's humiliation with each flash, one right after the other, even if she gave no indication of it.

As soon as the medics arrived, one of the responding officers escorted me from the house and started questioning me. Before he'd asked more than my name, a tall man in plain clothes approached us. His bulbous eyes took in the scene as though he were taking pictures with his brain.

"This is the vic's sister, Maggie Fletcher," the officer told him. "She found her."

I knew it was human inclination—and laziness—to shorten words, but I still bristled. I shook hands with Detective Antoine Armstrong, who specialized in sexual assault cases. With him was Detective Steve Lanier, whose fish-belly white skin was a stark contrast to Armstrong's dark chocolate skin. Lanier stepped back as Armstrong took charge.

"Colin Masters did this," I said before he could even ask one question.

"Hold on; let's start from the beginning," he said, though he did write down the name.

I couldn't keep my gaze from the front door, wanting to be with Dana but knowing I'd just be in the way. When medics wheeled her out of the house on a stretcher, I insisted on accompanying her in the ambulance. I wasn't sure if Dana was conscious, but I couldn't let her wake up without me being there.

"There won't be room for you," Armstrong said. "Let me drive you. We can talk on the way. The more information I can get, the faster I can apprehend this guy."

"Drive fast."

"You seem sure this Masters guy attacked your sister," he said as I followed him to his vehicle.

"He's the son of a bitch who's been stalking her." It came out in a mindless rush of words on the way to the hospital— the open doors, the bed being made, Dana's blink, and the diary I knew she kept. I was only cognizant of one thing: being very certain about not repeating what Dana had said.

Armstrong escorted me to the emergency area and waited while I asked about my sister's condition. No news yet, and no, I couldn't see her. I knew that, but I'd had to ask. I dropped into a chair, feeling like a bag of bones, and finished telling Armstrong about Dana.

He'd written everything in small, neat script. "I'm going to need you to come down to the station and give a taped statement. But we can start with this."

When he stood, I sank into dark thoughts, imagining what Dana had gone through. I caught a glimpse of her in the back area and heard Armstrong talking to the nurse about questioning Dana while they waited for the X-rays. I was surprised when he asked me to accompany him.

"It may help her to talk to me."

In the fluorescent lights, Dana's injuries looked starkly brutal. But her eyes were open, and I saw a change in them when she saw me, a flash of relief or gratitude maybe.

"Hi, honey," I said, giving her a smile that felt ridiculously empty. I wanted to touch her, but I was afraid to hurt her. "This is Detective Armstrong. He needs to ask you a couple of questions. Remember how you blinked when I asked if Colin attacked you?"

Armstrong took over. "Dana, I want to get this guy. Blink once if you understand me."

After a moment's hesitation, she blinked.

"Good. Do you know the person who assaulted you?"

Another hesitation, but she blinked.

"Was it Colin Masters?"

She blinked again.

"Okay. That's good. That's what we need to bring him in." He kept his gaze on her eyes, never letting it drift to her damaged body. I was grateful for that. "I know this is tough to deal with. You've been through a lot already. But we need your help to lock this guy up. We don't want him to do this to anyone else. You can stop him, Dana. And we'll help you every step of the way. Do you understand?"

Dana didn't blink. In fact, I saw terror in her eyes, which she shifted to me.

"You just scared her."

"Be a lot scarier if this guy gets away with this because she won't testify. Happens more than I care to contemplate." His nose was flat, his nostrils big enough to fit marbles into. I noticed that they'd flared as he said that. He flipped his notepad closed and slid it into his jacket pocket. "I'll see you later."

I gave Armstrong a cursory response, but my focus was on Dana. "We're going to fight this together. Through that and whatever comes afterward. I love you, Sis."

I couldn't say any more; my throat had tightened, holding

back the tears. A nurse approached and asked that I return to the waiting area. I kept my gaze on Dana until she was out of sight. Only when I saw all those strangers in their own states of agony did I think of Marcus and Mom. I slumped into a chair in the corner of the room and called them. After I hung up I stared at the yellow walls. Was yellow for hope?

I did have hope. That Dana would pull through this in one piece. That Colin would go away for a long, long time— without Dana having to testify. I couldn't imagine her on the stand.

Marcus arrived at the hospital first, and when he pulled me into his arms I collapsed under a wave of tears. Before he could extract what had happened, Mom arrived. I had to tell her about not only the attack but also the stalker. Dana had made me promise not to tell Mom.

"I could have been praying all this time if I'd known." Mom pulled her sweater tight around her, stretching the woven red yarn, and sat several chairs away. I felt anger and hurt radiating from her, but it paled in comparison to my guilt.

If only I'd taken the phone into the bathroom with me. I was sure that Dana had called to tell me about some suspicious sound she'd heard. I could have gotten there in time to save her from most of this. And worse . . . what tore into my heart was that I had doubted her.

Marcus made me sit down and took the seat beside me, holding my hand. He'd thrown on one of his starched shirts, though his hair was tousled.

Mom started praying in a rapid-fire whisper, just as she had when my father was here after a construction accident. I had prayed with her until my mouth had gone dry, but he'd still died. *Everything happens for a reason.*

I kept staring into the back area and then, when I couldn't stand it anymore, I looked at the scuff on my white shoe that I hadn't noticed before. I quelled the urge to spit on my finger and rub it out. I went back to my worry curl instead.

A few minutes later the doctor, who looked a lot like June

Cleaver, walked into the waiting area. Marcus and I stood in unison, though my knees barely kept me upright. "Mom," I called, rousing her.

Dr. Jameson gave us the gentle look meant to soften bad news. "Right now Dana's resting under sedation. She's suffered broken and fractured bones, including two fingers and her right elbow; several contusions; a possible concussion; and severe bruising and swelling. Her nose was shattered. No severe internal injuries. Oddly enough, no defense wounds. Usually we see evidence of a woman putting up her arms to protect her face, skin beneath the nails where she scratched the assailant. But here, nothing."

I couldn't breathe yet. "Was she . . . ?"

The doctor slowly nodded. "This . . . was the most vicious sexual assault I've ever seen." Even she seemed to have trouble saying it, but not as much trouble as I had hearing it. "She was raped, both anally and vaginally. The trauma was severe enough that it tore through the vaginal wall. She gave me nonverbal permission to collect evidence for the rape kit."

Mom broke into tears. I'd forgotten she was standing beside me.

As I stroked my mother's arm and tried to hush her, Dr. Jameson waited before continuing. "Physically she'll recover. The emotional damage will take longer. We've done what we can for now. We'll continue to monitor her. You can go in and see her if you'd like, but only for a few minutes."

It all twisted my stomach so badly I nearly gagged. I'd already thrown up twice reliving those minutes in her house. There was nothing left.

"Maybe it's God's punishment," my mom whispered. "She slipped away from Him. She worked in that heathen new-age place."

"She didn't do anything to deserve this," I growled, making my mother wince. Dana's words, though, echoed in my mind. *She* thought she deserved it. Why? I'd get the answer soon. "Bad things happen to good people. Haven't you heard that expression? Good things happen to bad people, too. Why does it always have to be punishment with you?"

But I knew. When Mom was a girl, she had stolen a doll from the general store. The next day a stray bullet had killed her father during a robbery when he returned the doll. Suddenly she believed everything her mother had been telling her about sin and punishment. Mom never let that belief go. For every tragedy she tried to analyze our sins and then save our souls.

Mom's legs were wobbly as she walked toward Dana's room, but she didn't look back at me. I let her go alone.

More inane platitudes bounced around my brain as I waited for Mom to come out. *Too much of anything can be a bad thing. Time heals all wounds.* I didn't believe either of them.

An older couple nearby got news that made them cry in relief. The woman hugged the doctor and wouldn't let go until the man pried her away. *Good for them,* I thought, trying to bury my resentment at not getting good news like that.

Raped. The word thumped down hard on my chest. Raped both ways, making the crime even more degrading. Oh, jeez. I couldn't help but think about it, imagining the pain, the torture. A cry escaped my throat, and I pressed my face into Marcus's sleeve. "Make Colin Masters pay for this."

I could tell Marcus that. He was Rockingham County's Attorney. Never before had he been so much my knight on a steed.

He stroked my cheek. "They have enough to bring him in for questioning. Just having a suspect puts us farther ahead than most rape cases. I doubt there'll be any problem making an arrest. I'm sure something will place him at the scene. Then hopefully he'll confess and it'll be all over."

But I'd heard the stories. Marcus had once said that rape cases were the hardest to work. There was often a lack of hard evidence. The victim had to deal with so many layers: guilt, shame, trauma. Sometimes she refused to testify, and without her testimony, the case often fell apart. Dana wouldn't testify. She wasn't strong enough.

Sometimes justice wasn't served. That was the most harrowing thought yet, that Colin could get away with this.

The thought cramped my insides, doubling me over in pain.

"Are you all right?" Marcus asked, putting his hand on my leg.

I raced to the bathroom.

CHAPTER FIVE

"I don't like leaving Dana."

Marcus squeezed my hand as he drove. "Your mom is there. She'll call if anything changes. Nothing should at this point."

No. The worst was over. I ached for what my sister would still endure.

The Portsmouth Police Station sat high on a hill, a former hospital that had been renovated to house some of the city's civil services. We went to the second floor, an enormous room that seemed to house a hundred desks. Detective Armstrong led us to an interview room. It seemed strange, being there in the predawn hour. It was quieter than it had been the last time I was here, though the smell of burnt coffee was just as strong.

Marcus sat next to me, holding my hand as Armstrong asked questions. The camera was on a tripod, ready to take my formal statement. How was I going to say I'd been dozing in the tub while my sister was being brutalized? Or that I'd been at her house and decided not to stop in? Fear, anger, and guilt swirled inside me. Anger towered over the other two.

I still felt clear on not telling anyone, even Marcus, Dana's words about deserving what Colin had done to her. For all I knew, I'd misheard her. I didn't want anything to be misconstrued.

Armstrong leaned over and fidgeted with the camera. "Ready?"

My voice trembled as I recounted the night's events. "I called her, I guess it was a little after nine. She was fine. *Too* fine, I thought." The wine? I laughed, shook my head. "I even told her to say the word 'banana' if something was wrong. She didn't."

No defense wounds.

I deserved it.

I was at the part where I had driven past her house when something popped into my mind. "I saw a man."

"What?" both Armstrong and Marcus asked.

"I saw a man walking down the sidewalk, on the same block as Dana's house. He looked tipsy."

Armstrong leaned forward. "Did you see his face?"

I tried to picture him, but it was a memory I'd tucked in my "insignificant data" file. "I don't remember. Except that he was walking *away* from Dana's house. But, for all I know, he may have seen my car and pretended to be going in the other direction. Maybe that's why he looked off balance." I tried to recall the image. All I could see was a guy with his face averted. *Hiding?* I now wondered. I shook my head. "I do remember he was tall, maybe a medium build, though it was hard to tell in the coat."

"That's not going to do us much good if you didn't see him."

After I was done with the video, Armstrong continued with his questions. "Maggie, had you ever seen Masters following your sister?"

"I saw his car once. I walked up to it, but he wouldn't stop."

"Did you see him inside the car?"

"The windows were darkly tinted."

"So . . . you never saw the guy lurking around?"

"She saw him. He'd wait for her to go to work and then to leave. She was always looking for him. Paranoid." I rushed on. "She's clinically depressed but not . . . acutely schizo-phrenically paranoid." I didn't want to share the doubts I'd had about her observations. "She was scared of him."

Armstrong leaned back, a troubled look on his face. "But *you* never actually saw the guy?"

"No," I said in defeat, unable to pussyfoot around the question anymore. "But she blinked. That counts as an accusation, doesn't it?"

"It's enough to bring him in for questioning. Maybe enough to get us a search warrant, but that'll be trickier."

"Why?" I asked.

Marcus said, "New Hampshire lives by its motto, *live free or die,* and it fiercely defends the Fourth Amendment concerning search and seizure. From your sister's injuries, though, it looks as though her assailant used a chain." I quivered at that, and he gave me a sympathetic grimace.

Armstrong said, "That's what we're basing our request on, to find that chain along with any evidence of his stalking her. To go farther, though, we'll need more. She's going to have to point him out and say he did it." Armstrong looked over the notes again. "The two wineglasses bother me."

"They bother me, too," I blurted out.

"Was she dating someone?"

"No."

"Have friends over?"

"No."

"Ex-boyfriends?"

I nearly laughed at that. "No one in a long, long time. No one seriously. She's been clinically depressed since she was a teenager." I felt as though I were bad-mouthing my depressed, friendless sister. "There'll be fingerprints on the glasses. You can run them through the system, right? Find who they belong to?"

Marcus said, "Actually, it's pretty rare that we get a full, clear print, despite what you see on television. Then there has to be a suspect or a print in the database to match it to."

Armstrong said, "Was there a chance that she had a change of heart about Masters—"

"No. No way would she let him in. I was with her two weeks ago when she found one of his poems. If you'd seen the fear on her face . . . no, it's not at all possible."

Armstrong referred to his file. "This the poem?" He held up a square of green paper in a cellophane wrapper. The text was printed in a computer font that was supposed to look like handwriting.

All I want is to crawl under your skin,
Like a parasite, to snuggle into your blood and muscle,
And suck your essence,
So that it will be mine, too.
Think of me whenever you scratch,
A vague itch on your body.
It's me, worming my way through your veins,
Making everything inside you mine.

I shuddered. "Yes, that's the one."

"None actually threaten her," Armstrong noted after he read the other poems in the file.

"He's very clever," Marcus said, trying to position his long legs in the limited space. He finally crossed one ankle over the other. "He uses words like 'parasite' and 'blood,' but in a warped-love-poem way. He never makes a direct threat."

Naturally Marcus and I had discussed this before.

"It's like he knows how to skirt the line," I added.

Marcus had a habit of curling his hand into a fist and pressing it against his mouth. He usually did it when he was deep in thought or concerned about something. His voice was muffled when he asked Armstrong, "What do we know about this guy?"

Armstrong leaned back in his chair with a teeth-jarring squeak that he was obviously used to. "Seems as though Masters walks that same line in his behavior. On record, he's just an overeager suitor who has never so much as touched or overtly threatened the objects of his obsession. He's had two restraining orders filed against him. It seemed he backed down and moved on. I say 'seemed' because the victims still complained that he was stalking them, though there wasn't any evidence. No witnesses saw him hanging around, and he didn't leave notes. Or poems."

"Did they report things in their house being moved?"

Armstrong drummed his long fingers as he checked. "Yes. One even said her car was in a different spot."

"Sounds a bit paranoid," I said, guessing what the reports probably implied. "And totally like something he'd do."

"It's why nothing was done. Why nothing could be done. Interestingly, each victim was in a different town. Now that we're digging deeper, we've found inklings of . . . possible violence. I need to investigate further before I say anything."

I glanced at the report, following his finger: a woman who lived in Boston named Marisol Vasquez. When he saw me reading, he lifted the paper to deter my nosiness.

"We've finally located his address, an apartment in Stratham, not far from here. We're working on a search warrant. I suspect he's also renting a place locally, as he's done before. We'll find that, too. And hopefully some hard evidence. It's possible he'll 'fess up once we have him in custody. It's happened before. Depends on how crazy the guy is."

I'd read about stalkers who were delusional, like the one who believed Madonna was his wife and the woman who thought she was married to David Letterman. Colin Masters wasn't that kind of crazy. Not if he'd played the game so skillfully, pretending to be one thing when he was another. Not when he'd walked the line so he wouldn't be arrested. Not when he'd taken pleasure in tormenting Dana.

That sneaky son of a bitch was much, much worse than crazy.

As Marcus and I headed toward the police station's entrance, I heard someone calling my name. I was surprised to see Detective Thurmond loping toward us. Thurmond reminded me of someone who might have lived with the Munsters, with his rail-thin body and long, melted-wax face.

"Maggie Fletcher," he said breathlessly, then introduced himself to Marcus. Thurmond turned back to me. "It's been bugging me since you and your sister came in. Especially when I heard . . . I'm so sorry about what happened. If we'd only known."

"Known what?" I asked.

His forehead was flushed and beaded with sweat. "I knew there was more to this guy. Kinda a hunch, know what I mean? So I kept digging. Looking at other departments', even other states', stalker assessments. I found a new way of categorizing stalker typologies. That's where I found Colin Masters." He was waving papers in triumph. "The checklist came out to ninety percent when I inputted what your sister and the two women who filed restraining orders against him reported. If only I'd had this when you came in." He looked torn over that.

"If we had known . . . what could we have done?"

"The only option would have been for her to go into hiding. Stalking duration: long term. Victim perception: helplessness and fear. Victim risk: high. Ability to intervene: low. Victim selection criteria: none apparent. Motive: control." He'd obviously memorized a list.

I felt chilled. "What is he?"

"The most cunning type of stalker. The most dangerous. The most likely to keep coming after his victim, even years later. A sadistic stalker."

Marcus and I headed out, somber after hearing Thurmond's characterizations that fit exactly what Colin had been doing. Now I knew that I wouldn't have been able to save Dana from the beating. Colin would have probably done the same to me. I was damned lucky that he left the house after I'd arrived, though it still made me uneasy. Why had he spared me?

When we walked out of the police station, two reporters were converged on a police spokesman, throwing questions about a high-profile businessman who'd just been arrested for fraud.

"That's all I can say at this time," the man said before turning away.

As the reporters did their wrap-up, I walked over. I didn't think about it, didn't give myself a chance to second-guess. I turned toward the blaring lights behind the camera that was aimed at me, amazed at what I was doing. "*I've* got something to say. My name's Maggie Fletcher. Colin Masters stalked and terrorized my sister for five months. Tonight he brutally attacked her. He's stalked women before; he'll do it again. Colin, if you're out there, turn yourself in. You need to pay for—"

"The case is still under investigation," Marcus said as he hustled me away from the cameras.

I heard one of the journalists saying in his on-camera voice, "That was County Attorney Marcus Antonelli. We'll follow up with more as we learn details."

I held my tongue as Marcus marched me to his car, helped me inside, and then got in on the driver's side.

"What was that all about?" we both shouted at nearly the same time.

"You have no business making accusations that aren't founded yet." He scrubbed his fingers through his hair, a clear sign of agitation. "I know you want Masters arrested. So do I. But you have to understand, I'm in a precarious position here. I'm the one who will be overseeing this if it goes to trial. I don't want any allegations of tampering, and I don't want anyone thinking I'm making statements about a suspect's guilt. I've got to be careful. Especially since we're involved. That puts a lot of pressure on me, Maggie. Everything I do will be under scrutiny. I don't want to jeopardize the case."

I let out the air in my chest, understanding his position.

When he saw my anger melt, he released a breath, too. "We'll get this guy. For now, we need to remain low-key about accusing him."

A thought occurred to me. "You'll tell me everything, won't you? Don't hold anything back, Marcus. I swear I won't go off half-cocked again. But I need to know everything."

His gaze held mine. "I'll tell you everything I can."

I didn't like it, but it would have to do. Then I felt vaguely guilty for not telling him about Dana's strange utterance. "I need to get Luke," I said, my mind skipping to the next order of importance. I wanted to go right to Serena's house, hold my son, and make sure he was all right.

"You'll scare the hell out of him and the whole household if we barge over there now. I'll call you at ten thirty and make sure you're awake. That gives you a few hours to conk out. You're going to need it."

He was right, of course. I felt as though I'd been dragged fourteen miles strapped to a panicked horse.

When we got to my house, Marcus peeled off my clothing and tucked me into bed. Bonk poked at my hand with his cold, wet nose and I stroked his head.

I said to Marcus, "You should get some sleep, too. You look ragged."

He tilted his head. "I will. I want to stay on top of this right now."

Then I remembered. "You called me tonight. Last night." I shook my head. "Whenever it was. I couldn't get hold of you."

He hesitated. "It's nothing. Nothing that can't wait until we get through this."

"But . . ."

He kissed me on the forehead, which felt oddly father-like, and left before I could try to pry it out of him. Honestly, I wasn't up to any more problems. I was already stretched so thin a harsh word could shatter me.

CHAPTER SIX

MAY 18, 2006

Luna looked into Eroz's eyes, glistening tears streaming down her cheeks. She couldn't speak, not with the steel spike he'd driven through her tongue. Still, he could see her thoughts playing out in her huge eyes: Don't kill me, please! I didn't mean to hurt you.

Eroz circled her, where she was tethered spread-eagle to the table. He still limped from where she'd stabbed a steel spike through his thigh. Soon it would be healed, leaving another scar on his sculpted Greek-god body.

She had meant to hurt him. Not only with the spike but also with her sweet smiles and gentle caresses. She had pretended to love him. Then she had turned on him. Luna was a cannibal witch. She'd thought she could defeat him—and then eat him. Ingest his strength and intelligence, his cunning and courage.

She'd been wrong.

She was still trying to use her charms on him, but he was way past that. He now saw her fangs, her red-devil eyes. The mirage of her perfect body had faded to reveal a wretched, flabby woman. The 40DDD perky breasts with nipples the size of saucers had been for his temptation. Now they were shriveled like deflated balloons.

"I found your sister," he said. "Is she a conniving bitch like you?"

Luna's eyes widened, then hardened.

"Since you won't tell me, I'll just have to find out for myself, won't I?"

Eroz positioned himself between her legs. Her eyes bulged when she saw the spike gripped in his large, muscular hands. The same spike she'd tried to drive through his heart. Only his lightning-fast instincts had saved him from death.

Her mouth trembled, sending a drop of bloody saliva shimmering down her jaw. The spike still glistened with his blood. It was lethally long and sharp.

He smiled. "Back at ya, babe."

The final frame was filled with her scream.

Colin painted those letters of agony in bloodred gouache and fell back in his chair with a sigh. His fingers were cramped, his eyes bleary, and his heart felt . . . heavy. Satisfied and yet not. But the story of Luna was finished. Usually he let a story sit for a day or two. Not this time.

Young graphic-novel artists might think he was arcane, using the old-fashioned mediums of colored pencils and paint. His love for the textile kept him in the dark ages. The feel of the lead scraping across the paper, the eraser crumbs clinging to his palms. The glide of paint, the scrape of blade across dried paint to create special effects, and mixing water and gouache to just the right shading and consistency. He had no intention of giving that up to look at a screen.

That came later, when he scanned in his work to post on his Web site. Only then did he use software to tweak color and glitches. Several advertisers and 842 subscribers paid his bills as they perused the site, wandered through the archives, and waited for the next installment of the two ongoing story lines. He posted them in serial format, since whole books took up too much disk space. Subscribers could view them online week-by-week as he posted them or download them chapter-by-chapter or as completed books.

Colin never participated in the forums, but he monitored them regularly, enjoying the accolades and zapping the criticisms. Their harsh words crackled along his skin like an electrical current. Nobody criticized him. One particularly "vocal" fan was kicked off the site forever. Even Colin's grandma, the only person who ever loved him, learned not to criticize his work. After witnessing his quick rage, she'd *suggested* he tone down the violence and sexual content.

Most of his subscribers fed his ego, building him up to monstrous, mysterious proportions. They guessed why he didn't publish in a traditional way. He wanted the money for himself. Another poster argued that he'd make more money by getting published. He was deformed, socially or physically, and didn't want any interaction with a publisher, one guy posited. Only one person got it right. Colin simply didn't want to conform to the rules of publishing. Only so many frames per page, only so many pages, too much of this, not enough of that. He wanted complete control, wanted to go by his own rules, which were strict enough.

One of the story lines was the usual: busty broads kicking ass in a futuristic world, having wild sex, with themselves and others, and generally being bad.

Then there were his stories featuring Eroz, a male superhero. In every novel Eroz encountered a different woman. She pretended to be sweet and virtuous, then began a domination game with Eroz, and finally revealed herself to be wretched and evil. All loosely based on Colin's pets.

Colin rubbed his eyes as he started scanning in everything. Luckily, he only needed about four hours of sleep per day. He'd worked in a frenzy throughout the last day and night. He didn't have much time. The police had already found his apartment in Stratham, and with the sister's public appeal, they'd find this place, too. His damned driver's license picture was splashed on the news and in the newspaper, wanted for questioning. He used chopsticks to push a stray picture into the crackling embers in the fireplace. There would be no trace of Dana here, other than as Luna, and there weren't enough tangible links to make a case.

The finished pages adorned his walls. He wouldn't take them down. They only proved what a talented artist he was. And the violence? Well, the women always got what they deserved.

As the sun began to rise, he packed up his laptop; his comprehensive notebook of character histories, settings, and sketches; the scanning equipment; and anything that might lead the police to his Web site. He only let in whom he wanted. He didn't want cops sniffing around.

He packed up his knives in their carrying cases, models for Eroz's weapons. He surveyed the apartment. Piles of laundry. Sealed bags of garbage, shoes, books. Nothing incriminating. The chain he'd used on Dana was scraping along the bottom of the Piscataqua River.

"You." He eyed the ratty dog looking at him from beneath the pillow on the couch with its one eye. The damned dog. Why couldn't he get rid of it? His grandma had bought it for him when he'd gone to live with her at the age of ten. He'd scorned it, a stupid thing that couldn't ease the pain of rejection. He'd tossed it in the trash several times but always ended up pulling it back out and jamming it beneath his pillow. So he told himself it was his good-luck charm, even as its presence embarrassed him. He didn't want the cops to find that, so he crammed it into his duffel bag.

After loading everything into his wonderfully generic Buick sedan, he headed to an air-conditioned storage facility rented under another name. He stored his equipment where he kept much of his years' worth of art. He thumbed through the storyboards, taking them in with a long gaze, memorizing them. It might be a while before he could return.

Whenever he chose a pet, he knew there was a risk of getting caught, though he was smart enough to cover his ass. The need for obsession was stronger than the fear of getting caught. It was probably a good thing his grandmother had died before he'd made stalking his vocation. Then again, her death had intensified that empty place inside him, turning his voyeuristic tendencies into his obsessive desire to people-watch. Soon watching wasn't enough. He wanted to control someone, just as he controlled his characters. His pets *became* characters to him in a story line much more exciting than any he could create. Real fear. Real blood.

He had started with a woman who lived in his neighborhood. He was amazed at how easy it was to follow her, staying only a few feet away for hours. The serious fun began when she did notice him. When he approached her. When she started becoming frightened.

After she'd disappeared, he knew he had to branch out. Choosing more than one woman in his town would raise flags. He started renting efficiencies in other cities so he could experience new environments and new people.

His portable drawing table and sets of mechanical pencils sat on the passenger seat. He patted them as he got in. As long as he had these, he would be fine.

His mouth spread into a smile. Oh, but he'd be fine anyway. Yes, everything was going to work out quite well.

CHAPTER SEVEN

MAY 18, 2006

I awoke like one who wakes from a nightmare, gasping for air, heart thundering, and body covered in sweat. Another night had passed. So much could have happened. Maybe they had Colin Masters in custody. Or maybe he'd crept into the hospital and made sure Dana couldn't testify. He was good at that kind of thing, creeping, sneaking, like a snake. Even knowing that a cop was posted at her door didn't allay the panicky feeling as I dialed the hospital number, just as I had the previous two mornings.

"Dana O'Reilly's room, Nurse Pickford speaking."

"How's my sister?" I asked, forgetting to be polite.

"She's still in an unresponsive state. I'm afraid we're going to have to feed her intravenously if she continues this way. Dr. Jameson was going to talk to you this morning."

"I'll be right there," I said, already clambering out of bed.

The house was unnaturally quiet without Luke. Serena had graciously offered to let him stay at her house during this trying time. The dog, too. I didn't want Luke to see his aunt like this. Or to see *me* like this, for that matter. I called Serena as I dried off.

"The boys and dog are outside," she said. "How are you holding up?"

Answering would bring on tears, so I ignored her question.

"How's Luke doing?" I'd seen him several times and it had been harder than hell to hold it together.

"He's fine. Worried, but fine. Bobby's keeping him occupied. Any news?"

"The investigation is moving along," I said, just as Marcus had told me many times. They were pushing the evidence through much faster than usual, eager to nail Colin so the public wouldn't panic about a rapist.

"David will be glad to talk to her if you think it would help." Serena's husband was the psychologist who had counseled Dana six months ago, to no avail.

If only she'd talk. To him, to anyone. "I think that's a good idea. I'll try anything."

"I'll check with him and see when he can stop in. Luke, want to talk to your mom?"

"Hey, Mom," he said a moment later.

I felt a rush of love and gratitude that he was all right, even as I picked up the sulkiness in his voice. "You doing all right?"

"Someone at school said Aunt Dana was, well . . . raped. They said you were on television, saying some guy did it."

I knew I should have been up-front with him about Dana's attack, but I couldn't get the words out when I'd tried. I took a deep breath. "She was, and I was."

"Are you trying to protect me, you know, like you did with Dad, not telling me stuff?"

"No. Yes." I gave a watery laugh. "That's my job, to protect you. It's in the parental contract. Right there next to being able to kiss you anytime I want."

"Mom," he said on a whine.

"You're right. I'm sorry you found out that way."

"Is she . . . okay?"

I started to give him an upbeat, vague answer but stopped. "No, she's not." My throat tightened and my mouth stretched into a frown. "She's hurt pretty bad. Inside and out."

"She'll be okay, won't she?" he asked, concern in his voice. He wasn't particularly close to her, but she was family, after all.

"I hope so," I whispered. "I'd better go. I'm going to see her at the hospital. When she's a little better, you can come, too. But not yet."

He didn't protest about me protecting him again. "Okay."

"Are you all right staying over there? If you want to come home, just say the word."

"We're having fun. It's kinda like having a brother."

I found a smile in that, tinged with bittersweet. Wesley and I had talked about having another child. Right before the diagnosis. "I love you," I said, and not expecting any answer, added, "Bye, sweetie," and hung up.

My cell phone rang immediately afterward. Another call from my two prissy male clients that started with, "I know you're rather preoccupied right now, but did you get a chance to talk with that architect?" Through gritted teeth I reminded them that I'd already given them the man's name and number so they could speak directly with him. Phone calls from clients rankled, especially the ones who knew what was going on. At the moment I hated being on call. Hated being a real estate agent. Hated the day-to-day stuff that still had to be done. That included eating. The only thing I had an appetite for was salted peanuts—salt to replace what I'd lost in my tears? I wondered.

Remember how much you love selling, I told myself. *Remember how, when you were a kid, you washed cars at Dad's Toyota dealership, filed paperwork, and even made your first sale at fourteen. How you realized you loved selling stuff.*

Unfortunately, my thoughts turned grim. *Remember how Dad died in a freak accident when you were seventeen. Inspecting the construction site for his dealership expansion, even wearing his hard hat, when a crane collapsed on him. Remember that?*

Oh yeah, I remembered. At least with Wesley, there were warning signs. His fatigue and pain and lump in his left testicle. The tests, the devastating diagnosis, and a guess as to how much time we had to settle his affairs. With my father, it was sudden. One morning he was kissing me good-bye and by dinner he was gone.

As I wallowed in my grief, Mom sold the dealership I was supposed to take over someday. She had never been a fan of how Dad made his money, claiming it promoted materialism and debt. I still resented her for that, but mostly I resented her blaming Dad's "greed" for his death.

When I graduated, I had still had the love of matching up people and cars, only working at a dealership would have been too painful. So I went into the business of matching people and property instead.

The problem with being a real estate agent was, as I'd discovered during Wesley's illness and after his death when I was a zombie, I couldn't take a leave of absence. I had too much going on, and clients called me direct. The worst clients were the ones who tried to soothe me by saying, *You're young, cute* (which I hated being called). *You'll find someone. In the meantime, could you find out what's taking the bank so long?*

Now, as then, I hated the feeling that I was letting Serena down.

It was nearly nine when I left the house, my hair damp and a granola bar in hand. Couldn't live on peanuts, after all. I called Marcus on the drive to the hospital.

"I was about to call you, honey," he said. "I—"

"Have you found him yet?" I was being rude, but I didn't have enough spare energy to be polite these days.

"No, but thanks to your outburst on the news, we found the studio he was renting in Portsmouth. Looks like we just missed him."

"Damn. Damn, damn!" I added, since one wasn't enough. "We have to *get* this psycho. He shouldn't be out there another *minute* while Dana lies in the hospital!"

"I know," Marcus said in the tolerant way he always responded to my rantings.

I took a calming breath. "And you found?"

"They've just started going over the place. Why don't I tell you when I see you?"

"I know you have this aversion to talking on the phone, but tell me now."

I figured Colin would have pictures and notes that would

prove he was stalking her. I'd seen it in the movies, those creepy shrines made in honor of the victim, pictures of her eyes and mouth cut out and pasted on a bloodred wall.

"They're still processing everything from both his apartment and the studio. There wasn't much at the apartment. His grandmother raised him there, and according to the Stratham investigator, it doesn't look like he's changed it much since she passed away five years ago. Sounds like he was involved in a few teenage incidents of voyeurism and fights, but nothing on record, of course.

"We know more about him based on what we found at the studio here in Portsmouth. He's crazy about sushi; we found a trash can full of take-out containers and chopsticks. At both places we found an odd mix of historical books and babe magazines. He appears to be an artist; there were supplies, drawing boards and stuff. He left drawings from what looks like an adult comic-strip story. Violent stuff, busty women. He burned a bunch of pictures in the fireplace, though a few surveillance-type pictures of Dana fell behind the grate and didn't get completely destroyed. We found remnants of what looks like a journal."

"Are the pictures proof that he was stalking her?"

"We'll need more than that to make a case, unfortunately. If we'd found more, we could establish a pattern. Two shots taken at the same time showed Dana walking down a sidewalk, probably leaving work. Defense would argue that Colin was just taking random pictures."

I blew out a breath of frustration. "What about the journal? Was there an entry for the night of the attack?"

"Don't we wish? The only legible pages were from January. He refers to her as 'D.' If we find one conclusive thing we can nail him on stalking."

"*On the stalking?* Marcus, you've got to get this guy for what he did to her. The stalking was bad enough, but he has to pay for the assault, too."

"I'm sure we'll get more. We did find something interesting, but nothing we can use. The woman in Boston that Armstrong mentioned . . ."

Marisol Vasquez, I remembered.

"Masters was brought in for questioning after the woman's brother was beaten so badly it left him brain-damaged. She fingered Masters because he'd allegedly been stalking her, though she hadn't reported it until then. Guess the brother took matters into his own hands by having his homeboys threaten Masters. Problem was, the police didn't have enough for an arrest, so we can't use it."

I was still processing the kind of beating one would suffer to sustain brain damage. I couldn't help picturing Dana's battered body. "I've got to stop this animal." My fingers tightened painfully around the steering wheel.

"Not you; we've got to stop him. I don't want you involved."

"I *am* involved. He mauled my sister."

"I know. What I mean is, I don't want you involved in trying to find this guy. I don't want you hurt. You've got to remember the legal system sees him as innocent until proven guilty."

"Dammit, Marcus, don't give me that crap, not in this case. Have they processed the . . . the rape kit yet?" I hated even saying the word "rape."

"Don't get your hopes up on that. You were right; he did bathe her."

I shuddered. "To wash away any evidence?"

"Probably. So any trace of bodily fluids is gone. They didn't find any hairs in the drain or anywhere else that didn't belong to Dana, which makes me think he shaved his body. Early indications are he used a condom. They didn't find any skin beneath her nails." *No defense wounds.* "They're still combing over the evidence taken from her house. But so far they haven't found much—"

"But the creep's been in her house several times!" I believed that now. I believed everything Dana had told me. "He had to have left something."

"I'm sorry, hon. I hate to say it, but the bastard's good. He even threw the sheets in the wash and doused them with chlorine. We're guessing he vacuumed the bedroom."

"Well, dammit, what *did* they find?"

"A partial fingerprint on one of the wineglasses that wasn't hers. She did have wine with someone."

That took me so off guard that I blew a red light. Luckily the light had just changed, so I only got wailing horns as my punishment.

He continued. "The police are questioning and finger-printing her co-workers."

I'd already been printed, for elimination purposes. "It wasn't me. And it wasn't Colin. You didn't see how scared she was of him."

She'd said she deserved it. If she'd invited him in, maybe to reason with him . . . no, I couldn't see it.

Marcus said, "She probably had someone over, just casual and insignificant."

Fear pressed against my chest as I pulled into the parking lot. "No evidence at her house. He wasn't arrested for that guy's assault. And he's never acted violently toward his stalking victims, that we know of anyway. My God, he'll get away with this if Dana won't testify." My voice was shrill.

"I'm going to do everything I can to make sure he doesn't."

"He can't, Marcus. He can't get away with this." I wanted to believe Marcus; I really did. "I'm at the hospital now. Dana's still not eating or talking."

"I know."

"You do?" I turned off the engine but remained in the car.

"I'm here now. That was why I called you. Armstrong brought in Detective Marianne Jones. She's trained in sexual assault cases, got a reputation for being gentle and support-ive while getting information. But that's only if Dana's re-sponsive. I thought you might want to be here."

"You bet," I said, disconnecting and opening the door.

I left my meeting with Dana's doctor twenty minutes later feeling numb. Armstrong and the woman I assumed was Jones were standing outside Dana's room. I nodded to them but went in to see Dana even as they tried to engage me in conversation. I knew they had more questions, and I was willing to help. But I needed to see my sister first.

The sight of her shocked me all over again. With the bruises in full bloom now, she looked even worse. Her eyes were open—as much as they could open, anyway. Anger nudged away the numbness. Why had he done this to her, of all people? She was already so weak emotionally. Damn him for picking her! I imagined scratching his eyes out—no, gouging his heart out. I had only seen his driver's license picture and I imagined that face begging for mercy, crying in remorse—I halted those thoughts. I was clenching my jaw, probably grimacing in rage.

It scared me to see her like this, day after day. I'd held her hand through some dark times, but I'd never seen her so . . . hopeless.

"Dana, what's this I hear about you not eating?" I began in my best big-sister voice.

I sensed, more than saw, the detectives hovering near the door. I pushed aside my annoyance at their intrusion and said, "Dana, dammit, come out of there. I know reality hurts, but I'm here for you, just like I've always been. We'll get through this together, you hear me?"

The tear that slid down her cheek startled me.

"You can hear me," I whispered, my own tears starting. "Why won't you talk to me?"

She shifted her gaze away. I knew she hadn't sustained brain damage, nor had her jaw been broken. Dr. Jameson said either it was psychological or Dana simply didn't want to communicate. The way she'd looked away from me, I thought it was the latter. But why?

I lowered my voice to a whisper. "Dana, you did nothing wrong, understand? And you didn't deserve this, dammit. There's nothing you could have done to deserve this."

She still looked away from me, tears tracking down her face. There was nothing more I could say. I trudged toward the door. The detectives waited patiently; I gave them credit for that.

"How is she?" Armstrong asked.

I could only shake my head, thinking he looked too rested to be working very hard on Dana's case. He introduced me to Detective Jones, a woman in her forties with a head full of curls thicker than mine. I wondered if she'd developed the round-faced, chubby look to appear softer and kinder. I said, "I hope you can help her. And I hope she can help you, too."

"I'm going to do my best."

Armstrong wasn't as gentle. "She needs to cooperate so he can't do this to someone else." The sheen of oil on his tight curls caught the light when he moved.

"I don't think she'll handle being up on the stand, especially not with Colin sitting right there. You're going to have to make your case with evidence, I'm afraid. Marcus said you found someone else's prints on the wineglass."

"The mystery guest. I don't think they're Masters's, either. We've compared them to common prints found at his apartment and studio. We've already ruled out her co-workers. Now that the shock has worn off, have you remembered anyone she might have invited over?"

The shock hadn't worn off yet. "No one."

"A man she might have casually mentioned? Male neighbor perhaps?"

I shook my head. He was reaching. But I noticed he was specifically suggesting a man.

"She wasn't, er, promiscuous, was she?" he asked.

"She didn't even like the idea of sex." I furrowed my eyebrows. "Why are you asking? Whoever it was probably didn't have anything to do with her assault, since we know that was Colin. Why does it matter if she shared a glass of wine with someone?"

The two detectives exchanged a look before Armstrong focused on me again. His nostrils flared. "They shared more than a glass of wine. We found semen around her mouth and on the living room floor. And it doesn't match Colin's DNA."

CHAPTER EIGHT

Colin sat in the waiting area with his face buried in a newspaper. He was sitting yards—freaking *yards*—away from the cops while they were out looking for him. Damn, he loved it. The cop who'd been posted at Dana's door had gone for a break when the big shots arrived. Colin knew he was taking a risk, but he looked nothing like the picture on his driver's license.

Besides, they obviously didn't have anything on him if he was merely wanted for questioning. If they did find something? He smiled. He wasn't too worried.

He chewed his thumbnail, extracting a sliver of crescent-shaped nail that scraped at his tongue as he moved it around his mouth. Maggie-the-dolly rushed in and into the arms of Marcus Antonelli. Her damp curls bounced with her movements, brushing against her shapely shoulders. A sweat suit covered the curves Colin knew she had, though the pants highlighted her sweet little ass. What a lovely performance she'd given on the news. Impassioned, angry, at least until her boyfriend had reined her in. Her boyfriend, the Rockingham County attorney. Imagine his luck.

At first Colin had been pissed that she'd accused him, just like Marisol had done. Then he realized Maggie's accusations would only make it more fun—more justified—to turn his attentions on her. He wanted to start the discovery process but had other things to focus on at the moment.

Marcus had to run. He was sorry, boo hoo, but he'd be in touch. Another hug, meaningless assurances, and then he departed. As Maggie headed toward her sister's room, a doctor called her name. Maggie followed her to an office down the hall, her fingers manically twirling a curl at the curve of her shoulder. The detectives spoke, though Colin wasn't close enough to hear them. What he did know was that Dana was a zombie. He had succeeded in breaking her down. But what she'd done had probably helped push her over the edge.

Colin stood, stretched, and ambled to the elevators. Marcus was still waiting for the car. Colin rode down with him.

Fifteen minutes later Colin kept his hat low and his back to the camera in the lobby as he slouched in the phone booth. A nurse answered.

"I need to speak with Dana O'Reilly please."

"She's not taking calls. May I help you?"

"Actually, you can help *her*. My name is Dr. Robert Mitchell. Her psychologist, Dr. Reese, suggested I give her a call. I'll be consulting on the case." Colin had seen the doctor's name on her prescription bottles. "I know her situation is severe. Unfortunately, I'm hung up in another emergency right now. Could you do me a favor? Hold the phone to her ear for a moment. I just want to let her know who I am and that I'll be coming to help her soon."

"Well . . ."

"I think it'll help prepare her," he pressed.

"Hold on, please," the nurse said, probably going to check the paperwork. "All right, here she is," she said a minute later. "Dana, this is an associate of Dr. Reese's, who's scheduled to see you this afternoon."

He heard a rustle of sound. "Dana? Dana, can you hear me? It's your friend from the other night. If you tell anyone it was me, I'll tell them what you were doing. I'll tell them what utter, despicable trash you are. No one will stand by you as you sit on the stand and relay what I did to you. No one will think you're the poor, innocent victim. Will they, Dana? And that's because you're not."

I'd heard the expression "you could have knocked me over with a feather." I'd never actually experienced anything like that until now.

"There has to be some mistake," I said.

Armstrong said, "We double-checked in light of what we knew about your sister. There's no mistake."

I heard a ringing phone, the tangle of voices from the nurses' station down the hall, and even someone softly crying. It all became a buzz in my head.

She'd been with a man. Sexually. I couldn't begin to process it.

"Was there semen in her . . . her . . . ?"

"No," Jones said. "This was a foreplay situation probably. Heavy petting, as we used to call it."

Then I heard a heart-wrenching cry from Dana's room. Nurse Pickford came running out, her wild eyes looking for me. No, not me . . . the detectives.

"He called her, the man who did this to her! He said he was referred by Dr. Reese. I held the phone up to her ear. She listened for a few seconds. Then she screamed."

Armstrong said, "Find out where the call came from."

She nodded and ran off. I was already on my way to Dana. She was now curled up in a fetal position. I was horrified to see her thumb in her mouth. Her eyes were wide open, but she didn't see me. Didn't seem to hear me. She kept whimpering, terrible animal-like sounds that made me think of baby rabbits being attacked by a wolf.

The nurse came back, assessed Dana, and gave her an injection. "To calm her."

"Did you hear what he told her?" Armstrong asked.

"No. Dammit, he sounded so professional. So convincing. He knew her doctor's name."

"He is." I watched Dana's contorted body slowly relax, though her eyes remained open and stark full of fear. I closed them, like one who respectfully closes the eyes of the dead. I didn't like the analogy, but that's what it felt like.

A man stepped into the room a few minutes later. "I traced the call. It came from inside the hospital. The lobby."

I nearly lost my balance and had to hold on to the side of the bed. Oh, God, he'd been here. Right here. I started trembling, too. With fear. Anger. Armstrong and Jones raced down the hall. I wanted to go with them, to act on the fantasy I'd had earlier. But I couldn't leave my sister and I knew he wouldn't be there anyway. I leaned close and whispered, "He can't hurt you again."

Colin prowled around the kitchen, finding pots and pans perfectly lined up, spices in alphabetical order. She kept her personal papers in her office, neatly labeled for his perusal. Perfectionists made it so easy.

The problem was the boy. Colin had suspected that she had a child when he saw the framed Batman poster and stacks of Yu-Gi-Oh! trading cards on the table. He found a huge roller coaster in the basement made of K'Nex pieces. Posters of roller coasters in his bedroom. The boy—Luke Fletcher—was nine. Nearly the age Colin had been when he found his father hanging in the garage.

The boy invoked one of Colin's rules: never choose a single mother. The boy had suffered enough tragedy, after losing his father to testicular cancer three years before. At least the man hadn't taken the coward's way out, not considering who might find his limp body hanging above a puddle of piss.

Pictures all over the family room attested to a once happy family. Dad seemed like an okay guy. Looked a little pale and thin in one picture of the three of them at Disney World. The last picture Dad was in.

Still, Colin investigated. He lay on Maggie's king-size bed, stroking the silky comforter. He smelled her sweet scent on the squishy pillow. He went through her bathroom cabinets. Not much in the way of prissy girl products, but the woman took good care of her feet. She had a whole drawer of lotions, pumice stones, and clippers. An extra-large T-shirt hung on the bathroom hook next to her robe, proclaiming: *Relay for Life*. In one drawer she had practical undergarments on the left, sexy, frilly ones on the right. Those were probably reserved for the Rockingham County attorney.

Colin touched a framed picture of a teenage Maggie with a man who must be her father. He traced her face and the line of her nose. Already he had invested himself. What he'd do with her he wasn't quite sure yet. But he would figure it out.

He picked up a picture, tucked it in his jacket pocket, and left.

On the way back from grabbing lunch I stopped in the restroom to splash icy water on my haggard face. Everything was cold in this restroom, but it was quiet. Peaceful, even, when no one else was there.

Three hours had passed since the call. Surveillance video had revealed only a man wearing a cap over his face, all too aware of the security cameras. What we didn't know was what he'd said to her.

Dr. Reese was scheduled to arrive in an hour. I held on to the hope that he could help her. I felt the same frustration Detective Armstrong felt. I wanted Dana to say the words "Colin did it." I wanted her to communicate. But she was worse than ever.

When I headed back, I saw a nurse dashing into Dana's room. Had she come around? I caught the sense of urgency as I sped up. A doctor I didn't recognize and another nurse blocked my view as they bent over Dana.

Then I saw the blood. Just a glimpse between shoulders and arms as the three moved in frantic motions. They shouted out words I couldn't understand. It felt like a dream, where things don't make sense. I had trouble moving my feet, as though I were walking through mud. I felt invisible as I slogged to the other side of the bed.

Blood puddled on the floor. One woman wound gauze around Dana's wrist. Why was there blood? Had Colin gotten back in? No, I'd just passed the cop posted at the door on my way in, the one who also stood watching in confusion.

Dana's face looked gray. Eyes blank. Then I saw the other wrist, bandaged as well. Blood seeped out to stain the white. A stretcher was brought in, and Dana was shifted onto it in one smooth motion and carted out. I stood in a daze. Stared at the bloody puddles. Two of them. Smeared by shoes, red footprints fading as they led out the door. Room empty. The cop was talking to the nurse.

A man in a doctor's coat came in. His words floated to me from some great distance. I couldn't focus on his face. Dr. Jameson wasn't in. He was very sorry. They couldn't save Dana. She had no will to live. No fight.

No defense wounds.

I tore my gaze from the blood on the floor then to look at him. "What . . . what are you saying?" The words seemed to stick to my tongue.

"I'm very sorry. Your sister committed suicide."

Marcus had been three towns away when I'd found the voice to call him. Overseeing thirty-seven police departments and his staff had him on the road a lot. My mother and I had been sitting in the hospital waiting area for an hour by the time he arrived. He didn't say a word, just pulled me into his arms and held me. He even reached out and squeezed my mother's shoulder. She was as numb as I, but much more solemn. I knew she was thinking what suicide meant for a person's soul, according to the Bible. Thankfully she hadn't said anything. I was too destroyed over what had happened to Dana's body to contemplate her soul.

Dana had broken a glass vase. Taken a shard. Cut her wrists. She'd waited until she knew I'd be gone for a while. I'd even given her my timeline: *I'm going to get something to eat, sweetie. I'll be back in an hour.*

I don't know how long we sat there in silence while I

mentally replayed everything I'd said to her. Had I not been here enough? Not been supportive? Marcus's cell phone rang, shattering those ruminations. It was after five o'clock, but he was usually on call. He mouthed the word *Armstrong* before answering. I felt his muscles tense just before he shot up straight.

"Yeah? . . . You're kidding. . . . We're coming in." He disconnected and turned to me. "Colin just walked into the police station. He wants to cooperate. Without a lawyer."

Only then did the life return to my blood. I surged to my feet. "He's got to pay for what he did. For what he made her do."

Mom pushed to her feet more slowly. "That won't bring her back."

"I know. But it's the one last thing we can do for her. The one thing we can make right."

CHAPTER NINE

It was over. That's what I kept thinking as Marcus and I sat in a conference room at the police station. Several empty chairs surrounded the long table, making me feel small.

I still hadn't processed what Dana had done. I should have seen it coming. The despair was clear in her eyes. I had worried how she would handle this when life itself seemed insurmountable. I tried not to let myself feel anything. I couldn't handle those emotions yet, not when I had to keep my cool. But my body couldn't contain them. I trembled. My teeth chattered. My stomach ached.

Marcus and I sat catty-corner at the end of the table, our shoes touching in silent support.

For the tenth time, he stilled my hand on my worry curl. "Sorry, but it's driving me crazy."

So was my compulsive cleanliness as I picked up the sugar packets and stir sticks and dabbed up every grain of sugar on the faux wood table with my finger.

He pushed to his feet and paced again. I could have told him that made *me* nervous, but I held my words. He was here with me, feeling every bit as tense if his pacing was any indication.

"It's a good sign that he's been in there so long, isn't it?" I asked.

"Yes. And a good sign that he's still not asked for a lawyer.

That's when everything stops and the answers are much harder to get."

I'd wanted to sit in that room you see on television, the one behind the two-way glass. I wanted to see Colin Masters spill his guts, cry in remorse. I pictured him under the glaring light, good cop and bad cop playing him, threatening, cajoling . . . breaking a kneecap. I had a hard time seeing his face, though. His driver's license picture looked scruffy, his thick hair nearly obscuring his features.

Marcus stood and stretched. "I'm going to get more coffee. Want some?"

"No, thanks." I stood and stretched, too, and then stepped into the hallway. I allowed my fingers to slip to my worry curl. Ants marched down my veins, or at least that's what it felt like.

Marcus had stopped to talk to a uniformed officer on his way to the break room in the adjacent hallway. I used the restroom and walked to the water fountain. I'd heard about interrogations going on for ten or more hours. The only thing that kept me from pulling my hair out was that Colin would be in prison.

As I leaned over the spout and tried to catch the tepid stream of water, a low voice behind me said, "She never even fought back. Wanna know why?"

Even as the words spilled down my back in icy rivulets, I couldn't believe I'd actually heard them. I spun around, water dripping down my chin. A man with the stature of a wrestler stood close to me, his light blue eyes slicing right through me. His shaved head set off the sharp angles of his face and strong nose. But those words . . .

"What?"

His blunt mouth stretched in an eerie Mona Lisa smile. He leaned toward the fountain to take a noisy drink. I stumbled back and looked for Marcus. He was stalking toward me, wearing a hard look of concern. The bald man stood and wiped the back of his hand across his mouth the way a boy does. His eyes held a smug gleam. His gaze seemed to wrap around me. And there was something else about them.

He stepped away and walked over to Armstrong and Lanier as Marcus reached me. I saw the man say something congenial to the detectives, smile, and walk toward Lanier, who began to escort him out.

Marcus took hold of my arm. "What did he say to you?"

The man walked slowly, taking his time and looking at me. His clothes looked as though he'd unearthed them from the bottom of the laundry basket.

"Who is he?" I asked vaguely, my gaze as locked to the man's as his was to me. There was something about the way he was looking at me. . . .

"Colin Masters. I'm sorry; I didn't know you were out here."

Colin. Oh, God, Colin. He flashed a smile at me just before he walked through the doors. I looked at Marcus, my whole body growing cold. "That was . . ."

"I saw him talking to you."

It took a few moments for my brain to process the information. Colin Masters had been standing next to me. He'd spoken to me. And now, now the words made sense in an appalling way. I could hardly push them out. "He said . . . Marcus, he said she never fought back . . . asked if I wanted to know why. He was talking about Dana. He was talking about what he'd done to her." Marcus tried to pull me close, but I pushed back. "He's bald."

"He shaved his head and his chest. And probably his body hairs. We suspected he'd done that when we didn't find any hairs at the crime scene."

"Isn't that proof? Of something at least?"

He shook his head. "Bodybuilders sometimes shave their bodies. He even cooperated by removing his shirt. There were no abrasions, no signs of defense wounds Dana might have inflicted."

No defense wounds.

"That's because she didn't fight back." I was still staring at the exit. But why?

That's when it really hit me. I gripped Marcus's arm. *"He just walked out of here. No cuffs."*

Marcus pried my nails out of his skin. "He didn't cop to the crime. When I reached the break room, Armstrong, Lanier, and Masters were just coming out. Marcus went for a drink while they filled me in on what had transpired."

"They let him go?" The words roared out this time, catching the attention of everyone around us.

Armstrong walked up to us with a sober expression. "We had no choice. Our only hope was either getting him to confess or tripping him up. We tried everything: the sympathetic we-understand-you tactic, the bully tactic. He admitted to having a crush on Dana and that he'd taken pictures of her. The remnants we found in the fireplace indicate he took a lot of pictures, but he said only a few were of Dana. He claims he was home the night of the attack, and denied ever following her. And he acted utterly appalled that we'd think he'd broken into her house. Either he's innocent or he's the coolest damned criminal I ever saw. I'm betting on the latter. He didn't flinch, didn't give anything away. Not even those little gestures that indicate nervousness. He acted sad about what had happened to Dana but said he'd moved on when she'd told him she wasn't interested."

"But he hadn't."

"We can't prove that. That's the hell of it, we can't prove a thing."

I was staring at the door where the arrogant son of a bitch had casually sauntered out. I knew what the smile had been about. He'd been laughing, laughing because he was walking out right after letting me know he'd hurt Dana.

Marcus told Armstrong what Colin had said to me, and I saw anger and frustration on his face. His nostrils flared wider than I'd ever seen them, an emotional barometer.

"That's proof, isn't it?" I asked, feeling an overwhelming sense of desperation blanketing me.

Armstrong shook his head. "Hearsay. Unless someone else was close enough to hear it."

"He said it low, just for me. I wasn't even sure I'd heard him right."

It hit me then. This was a game for Colin. He had taunted

Dana by doing things she couldn't prove. He was playing a game with the cops, pretending to cooperate. Now he was playing with me. That's when I realized what it was that had struck me about his gaze. Dana's words floated back to me: *His eyes touch me. When he looks at me, I can feel them on my body.*

That's exactly how it had felt.

Just like that day when I'd stood in front of the cameras and accused Colin, a crazy thought jumped to mind. I held in the words, though, rolling them around in my head for a moment. I had to do this right. I was going to do this. Was I? Could I? My heart was thundering now, blocking out the men discussing the case. The futility of the case. Colin wasn't going to be arrested for the assault. He wasn't going to be arrested for stalking. He was going to get away.

No, Maggie, you can stop him.

For Dana. I wasn't able to help her before, but I could help her now. I was going to do it mostly for Dana. A little for me. And for the next woman Colin would target.

I sucked in a breath. "Oh, my God." I hated starting out with the name of God, but that's what had come out. I now had their attention. I touched Marcus's arm. "The shaved head. I didn't . . . wasn't . . ."

Marcus looked at me with concern. "What, Maggie?"

I focused on him, clutching his arm even tighter to keep my balance. My knees really did buckle at the weight of what I was about to do—had to do. "Colin is the man I saw walking away from Dana's house the night of the attack."

CHAPTER TEN

It was I who spent the next hour being questioned in the conference room, with Lanier, Marcus, and Armstrong. They didn't believe me. No, no, that was being paranoid. They were skeptical. Of course they were. They should be. It just meant I had to answer the question *Are you sure?* several times.

Yes, I was sure. I hadn't suspected it was Colin that night because the man I'd seen was bald, and Dana had described a man with thick, brown hair. *You said you couldn't see his face.* Ah, but I had seen his face. I just hadn't remembered seeing it. Colin had triggered the memory. Yes, he'd been walking away. Perhaps, as I'd guessed when I first mentioned him, he had turned around when he saw my car.

Armstrong, with his feet up on the table, looked at Marcus. "Do you think it'll fly?"

Marcus looked pale. I hated putting him in the middle of this. In that moment I'd decided to do this, I'd also decided to keep up my lie to him, too, to keep him clean. It was bad enough, me doing this.

"The defense attorney will jump all over it. She 'suddenly remembers'"—he put finger quotes around those words—"when she sees Colin at the police station and knows he's walking? She's the victim's sister, desperate for justice."

I was desperate, no doubt about it. Okay, and for a little

revenge, too. If no one else could make him pay, I would. I tried—and failed—to keep from twirling my worry curl. I knew it looked like a corkscrew gone awry.

Armstrong said, "What about what he said to her?"

"What he supposedly said," Marcus added.

"He didn't *supposedly* say it," I clarified, even though I knew how all of that "alleged" business worked.

"Does it make her statement stronger or weaker?" Armstrong asked. "If we enter what he said as evidence, it's only hearsay. She didn't recognize him *until* he said it. That weakens her eyewitness account. I think it's stronger if she recognizes him without it."

"Plus, it could always be argued that she misheard him. No, let's leave that out to be safe," Marcus said.

Armstrong looked at me. "Are you absolutely sure of this, Maggie?"

"I am." I'd never lied like this before. Little white ones. *I love that hairstyle! I'm doing great, thanks.* I'd sometimes lied to Luke to protect him from the world's cruelty. "And I'll stand up to a defense attorney's badgering. I know what I saw." And what I didn't.

Armstrong looked at Marcus. "We can bring him right back and book him." Armstrong wanted that. It was written all over his face, in the way his fingers clenched and his nostrils flared.

I saw a scared-rabbit look cross Marcus's face. We were all looking at him, anxiously awaiting his word.

"I won't waver," I promised. "I won't change my mind."

"There's only one problem," Lanier said, breaking up the tense moment. "The mystery DNA. Someone else was there that night."

"That's my concern, too," Marcus said, and I swear I heard relief in his voice. "It leaves a gaping hole of reasonable doubt. I'm not confident we'll get a conviction."

Armstrong said, "We've got to track down the mystery donor. But we all know it was Colin who assaulted her. He was stalking her, though our proof is sketchy. He was lying about his whereabouts the night of the assault. I think that, with Maggie's testimony and all of the circumstantial evidence, it may be enough. It might be all we ever have."

If I'd felt a tremor of a doubt, that statement eradicated it. We would likely not get anything more. Armstrong wanted to believe me. Lanier, always the quiet one, wanted to as well. Marcus was a surprise, but I knew it had something to do with his job. Conviction rates or percentages or whatever. It annoyed me that he would put that ahead of getting this man.

"And," Armstrong added, "we'll run down the women he's stalked in the past, get them to testify. That would help the stalking case."

Marcus slowly nodded. "We'll do our best."

"Put Stewart on it," I said. "He's the best you've got."

Stewart Cooper was the deputy attorney, Marcus's assistant. And a friend.

I signed my statement, Armstrong went to get the arrest warrant, and Marcus and I left. Serena was going to drop Luke off on her way to a meeting, so that gave Marcus and me a little time alone.

He was quiet as we drove. I felt the weight of guilt on my shoulders, but I couldn't turn back now.

"It's going to be a hard case," I said at last, unable to take the silence anymore.

"You don't realize how tough."

"You don't think the jury will believe me?"

He wasn't looking at me, but since he was driving, I didn't take it personally. "It's going to be tricky."

That's all he said, and then we were at my house. When I opened my front door, he didn't move to come in. I felt a trill of alarm in my blood. Even though I'd intended to send him home after a short while so I could be alone with Luke, I hadn't expected Marcus to leave right away. Not after everything that had happened.

"I've got a lot of work to do," he said.

We stood facing each other, our expressions grim.

"Maggie—"

"Do you—"

We'd both started talking at once; both stopped. But neither of us laughed.

I'd been about to ask if he believed me. I wasn't sure, though, if I was ready to hear his answer, especially when I saw the doubt etched on his tired face.

"Do you want to come in for a few minutes?" I asked instead.

"Maggie, I understand why you're doing this."

"Doing what?"

He gestured, looking for the right words. "Thinking you saw Colin that night. It's not too late to tell Armstrong you were mistaken."

"I'm not mistaken." I knew Colin had done this terrible thing and that he wouldn't have an alibi that would clash with my testimony.

"Revenge isn't worth perjuring yourself on the stand. And if the jury doubts your identification of Colin, they might doubt everything else you're going to say. You could jeopardize the whole case."

So there. Marcus had said it: he didn't believe me. I wasn't sure why I felt so hurt. I was lying, after all. "Is it your career you're worried about?"

He covered his mouth with his fist, hiding part of his face from me. "It's the case."

"What case is there without my testimony? That maybe he was stalking her? That's it, isn't it?"

I saw the defeat in his eyes, but in typical attorney fashion he still argued. "At least that's a more solid case. We have the pictures and journal fragments. We have her diary."

"And what would he get, if convicted? A couple of years? Probation? Slap on the hand?"

"Dammit, Maggie, you don't know what you're doing."

"And it'll look really bad on you if you don't win."

He shook his head. "It's not about me. It's about you. About your sister and what she deserves."

That last bit startled me. Marcus didn't know what Dana had said. But that was not what he meant, I realized. "My sister deserves justice."

"Sleep on it. You'll realize that you only thought it was Colin. It was dark."

"And if I don't?"

His answer was to turn and leave.

I forced myself to close the door but didn't have the strength to do more than lean against it. Something about the dark, quiet house felt different, but I couldn't pinpoint what. Bonk wasn't there, of course. Nor was Luke. I chalked it up to that.

I heard a horn beep out front and opened the door. Luke was running up the drive, backpack hanging off one shoulder. I waved to Serena, who blew me a kiss before driving on.

I couldn't believe how perceptive my son was when he paused in front of me and asked, "Something happened, didn't it?"

I could only nod as I backed up so Luke could come in. "How did you know?"

"Serena was acting funny. All she'd say was you called."

I looked at my son, who seemed so small and vulnerable as he waited for me to tell him. His blond hair came from Wesley, and the texture was an unfortunate mix of his thick hair and my curly hair. Sometimes it fell in between, ending up shaggy. I couldn't help trying to tame it as I searched for the right words.

"Dana died this morning." That wasn't the hardest part.

"Mom, what happened? I thought she was going to be okay."

I knelt down to his level. "Sometimes . . . people feel overwhelmed by what life throws at them. Dana wasn't strong like you and me. She didn't have the will to live."

Okay, I hadn't been completely honest.

"Mom . . ." He hugged me. Comforted me. I had to struggle to keep from bawling.

"There's something else you should know," I said, needing to move off that subject for now. "I saw the man who attacked Dana at the police station. I remembered seeing him near her house the night he hurt her. I'm going to be testifying against him."

"Will he go to jail for a long time?"

"I hope so." I looked at him. "I want to keep Open Doors, okay? About Dana's death. About everything."

He nodded.

I'd learned the opening-up process from the counselor I'd gone to for help in dealing with my father's death. Wesley Fletcher was younger than I'd expected, and he made me laugh . . . like Daddy did. I don't suppose it was a big surprise that I fell in love with Wesley. I knew it was unethical, though, so I didn't tell him, even when I stopped seeing him. A year later we ran into each other at a tire shop. Not particularly romantic, but I felt that same rush. This time I sensed the chemistry coming back at me, and the rest, as they say, is history.

Therapy hadn't helped Luke as much when Wesley died. I did learn, though, that Luke was afraid to love me too much because he might also lose me. That had just about broken my heart. And it was something I understood well. Hadn't I felt the same way about Marcus? So Luke and I had started doing Open Doors. I'd tell him what I was thinking. He'd tell me. A nonconfrontational way to open lines of communication.

We had popcorn for dinner, neither of us particularly hungry. He took his shower and went to bed early. I prowled the house, anxious and restless. The rubber flap of the dog door was slightly skewed, allowing the cool air to seep into the kitchen. I kicked it back into place and for the first time realized a man could conceivably crawl through. Our first dog had been much bigger.

I poured myself a glass of wine. My hands were trembling. I saw myself in the window above the sink, a hollow-faced woman with smudges beneath her eyes and hair a curly tangle with a corkscrew. I was too numb to care.

I unwrapped a Dove chocolate and popped the whole piece in my mouth. When I read the "fortune," I nearly swallowed it: *Do what feels right.*

A sign? Yes, I'd take it as one.

My footsteps echoed on the tile floors as I clutched my glass and walked to my bathroom. The scent of perfume saturated the air, and I found one of my bottles lying on its side with the cap off. A puddle of perfume pooled at the bottom of my shell sink. A drawer was open a few inches. Even in a hurry I felt compelled to close drawers completely, the annoying ingrained habit of a perfectionist. Lately, though, I'd been living in a haze.

I hadn't even made my bed properly, I realized. A corner of the pillow was peeping out beneath the jade comforter. The closet door was askew.

I thought of Dana, then. Her paranoid observations. I still couldn't be completely sure that she hadn't imagined all of that. And I didn't blame her. Now I was noticing the same things. I felt a twinge of paranoia. I hadn't been home most of the day, after all. He'd been free most of the day.

I closed my eyes and let it wash over me. Fear, paranoia, the ache of not being able to trust my perception. I'd become Dana. Now I knew how she'd felt.

I sank to the floor and cried.

Colin let himself into his Portsmouth studio and frowned at the mess the police had left. Ashes were scattered all over the area rug where they'd been digging in the fireplace. Dammit, why hadn't he checked behind the grate to make sure everything had burned completely? Not only had the picture given them possible evidence for stalking, but it had also been a violation of his privacy that they'd read one of his journal entries. Faint evidence, but it could prove troublesome.

He wasn't worried, though. They couldn't touch him.

He called for a delivery from Su's Garden. While he waited, he thought of Maggie. The look on her face at the police station was precious. He could have fun taunting her about Dana. Firing up Maggie's pain, her frustration that he was going to walk free. He could allow himself that much without violating his rule.

The knock at the door came too fast to be dinner. He looked at the two officers with what he knew was a dumbstruck expression.

"Colin Masters?" one said, though he obviously knew that's who he was. "We have a warrant for your arrest."

"On what charges?" Okay, they were going to try to stick him with a stalking charge. Big deal.

"Burglary, aggravated felonious sexual assault, stalking, and anything else we can throw at you." The young man gave Colin an Elvis sneer.

Colin hid his surprise. No, this couldn't be. If they'd found something at Dana's house, they would have arrested him earlier.

They took great pleasure in cuffing and marching him to the patrol car to the amusement of the nosy neighbors. He gave no indication that he was worried. He wasn't. Just annoyed.

They kept him waiting in the same room he'd been in earlier, while his stomach betrayed him by growling every few minutes. They didn't let him call Su's to change the delivery destination.

Then the tall black detective finally entered, along with his quiet partner, whose job seemed to be observing, assessing, and perhaps trying to intimidate the suspect with his dogged stare. Colin had perfected that look much better than the pasty-faced cop ever could. And in fact, when he did meet the guy's gaze, he was the first to back off, not Colin.

"Anything else you want to tell us about that night?" Armstrong said as he slid into the chair opposite Colin. "Coming clean now will help you later."

Sure it would. "Not a thing."

But they had something. The officers had read him his Miranda Rights. It was official. No more of that gooey talk about understanding his need to stalk women.

"We've got a witness that places you in the vicinity of Dana O'Reilly's house at the time of the attack. Saw you walking down the sidewalk in the block her house is on. That means you lied about your whereabouts."

Colin stiffened, unable to believe what he was hearing. He'd never been on the sidewalk. He'd parked at the restaurant, woven along backyard property lines until he'd reached Dana's yard. "The witness is lying. I wasn't there."

"I think you're the one who's lying."

"Besides, it was dark. There wasn't even a moon out that night. I remember that. I was sitting out on my balcony and couldn't see anyone's face from there."

"She saw you beneath one of the streetlights."

She. A neighbor? No, the backyards were as dark as a well. A couple of dogs had barked, but they couldn't tell on him. So who had told? More important, who had lied?

Only one person came to mind. Maggie Fletcher.

Anger burned in his veins. The detective's voice droned on like the hum of a generator, drowned out by Colin's thoughts. She was lying to get back at him for what he'd said at the station. The bitch was lying. She was going to get him, too, drag him through the system and into court. He still had a backup plan, but this was going to complicate things.

He smiled as a thought occurred to him. She was lying. That meant he could break his rule about choosing a single mother. All bets were off.

"I want a lawyer," he said as Armstrong was asking him what was so damned funny.

Colin's smile grew even wider. *Magdalena Ruth Fletcher . . . welcome to me.*

CHAPTER ELEVEN

"Magdalena Ruth Fletcher, you are lying."

I sat on the prim, flowery couch and tried not to shrink under my mother's accusing glare, made more intimidating by her beak nose. I hated my full name, the first of many religious things my mother would push on me. But I really hated that she'd seen through me.

"I'm not."

When I'd arrived that morning, we'd hugged and cried again. Then I'd told her what happened at the station. What Colin had said to me and my sudden recognition of him. I was going to have to get used to telling it, perfecting it. I'd already decided I would tell no one the truth about my lie.

But my mother had seen right through me, as she'd always done. I should have remembered that.

"What does Marcus think?" Mom asked from her well-worn easy chair. It was flanked by end tables stacked with magazines and books about faith and worship.

Her question took me off guard. I realized it would be a bad idea for them to be in the same room anytime soon.

"He's worried about the case not being strong enough. But my identification of Colin is the only thing that's moving things forward."

I hadn't answered her question exactly. She knew that.

The lines on her forehead and between her thick, dark eye-brows furrowed with disapproval. "Lying is against one of the Ten Commandments, Maggie. Don't you know you'll go to Hell for that? And on the stand yet! You'll have to put your hand on the Bible. You'll have to swear to tell the truth, and nothing but the truth, so help you God."

I wanted to tell her that maybe God had put Colin next to me, that He'd had Colin say those despicable words. That He'd put the idea into my mind. And given me the Dove message: *Do what feels right.* It had felt divine. But that would be admitting the lie, and I couldn't do that.

My mother was crying now, soft sobs that racked her large chest. She pressed a ragged, crumpled tissue to her nose. I thought she was crying over Dana again, so I came close and put my arms around her.

"My daughters are lost to me. I won't see them in Heaven. Please, Lord, intervene."

I pulled back, anger nipping at my nerve endings. This was how she often manipulated me, and I was embarrassed at how many times I'd given in. I turned away and stared at a framed print of Jesus holding an infant.

My mother must have gotten the hint. She contained the tears and said, "I know you always felt responsible for Dana. You mothered her more than I did."

"That's because you weren't there for her."

"I know," she said on a ragged breath, surprising me with the admission. "I could never connect to her. I prayed over that. I felt awful. But no one could reach her. No one but you." She smiled faintly. "I knew you switched those hamsters. You were afraid she wouldn't handle her hamster's death well and you switched them. You were a good child." *Who'd turned bad,* she didn't say. "It's not your place to make things right this time."

"There's nothing that can make it right," I said in a low voice.

"That's what we're taught," she said, looking at a muted Pat Robertson. "Let God punish that man for what he did. Give it into His hands."

I couldn't do that. Colin wasn't about to confess. He'd go on to terrorize some other woman. Perhaps even kill her. Maybe then he'd leave something behind and get caught. I couldn't let that happen, not when I had the power to stop him.

I left, as Marcus had done to me last night. I knew he felt the same frustration. Only my sense of justice was stronger. And I needed to be strong. I headed to nearby Brentwood, where the county's courthouse complex was located, to meet with the Rockingham County attorney.

The vultures stared down at me. Ten, maybe twelve of them. Four stories up, perched on the two peaks of the brick courthouse. They reminded me of gargoyles, stonily watching those who went up and down the granite steps. If I were looking for signs, well, they weren't a good one. Obviously others took them as a bad omen, too, men and women in suits with their gazes trained on the turkey vultures with apprehension.

I had to clear the metal detectors before I could take one of the sets of granite stairs down to the ground level. The receptionist behind the bulletproof glass directed me down the hall after making a call.

When I walked into Marcus's office, Stewart Cooper announced, "There's our star witness!"

He was balding, nervous, and had perpetual sweat stains under his armpits, which he seemed unaware of as he hugged me.

Marcus's expression was far less enthusiastic. I could tell that he was hoping I'd changed my mind.

"I won't let you down," I said in answer to his unspoken question, taking a seat in the area where a love seat and two chairs were crammed around a coffee table. Marcus was leaning against the front of his desk, and Stewart was in one of the chairs, with his feet on the table.

"Good," Stewart said. "I want to nail this son of a bitch."

"You're prosecuting?" I asked hopefully.

"You betcha. I liked Dana. I feel terrible about what happened." I knew he'd called Dana a few times to ask her out, but I was sure she'd turned him down.

Marcus felt terrible, too. I knew that. It made this so much harder.

They filled me in on the process that would continue from here. Colin would be arraigned that day in Portsmouth's District Court, but the case would be entered in the state's Superior Court since it was a felony. There would be a Probable Cause hearing, and then the Grand Jury would hear the case. After another arraignment, it would finally go to trial.

"That sounds like it'll take forever," I said, hearing a whine in my voice.

"Normally it could take as long as a year," Stewart said. "Marcus is calling in favors to move things up."

I gave Marcus a look of gratitude, but he glanced away before asking, "How's Luke taking all this?"

It touched me that Marcus asked. He might not care how I was handling this, but at least he cared about Luke.

"It hasn't been easy for him. Losing someone in his life is hard, even if he wasn't that close to Dana. I couldn't bring myself to tell him how she died, not yet." I shifted mental gears, away from a subject that was still too tender. "Anything new on the case?"

Stewart dropped his feet to the floor and reached for a bottle of water. His double chin convulsed as he drank. "We've got a case, but barely."

Marcus said, "Just remem—"

"You can indict a ham sandwich, I know." Stewart waived the unspoken *but you can't necessarily get it convicted.*

"No confession once he was arrested?" I asked.

"He lawyered right up. When they questioned him the first time, they played it so he wouldn't clam up. Detectives sometimes try the soft approach. Once the questions become incriminating, they have to Mirandize him, and that puts the suspect on the defensive. But the fact is, he doesn't have to say a damned thing. He'll be arraigned later today."

"But you think we have enough to convict?"

Stewart ran his hand over his head, and I wondered if he realized how often he did that. "I think we've got a chance."

I looked at Marcus. "You're awfully quiet." I could tell by the nervous glance between them that Marcus had mentioned his doubt about my testimony. So I saved him by saying it aloud. "He doesn't believe me. Or at the least, he doubts me."

Marcus wasn't bold enough to come out and say it. He wasn't as good at personal confrontation as he was at professional confrontation. "We have a shaky case, and you're a shaky witness. I'd rather wait until we have something concrete to move ahead with."

Stewart, my champion, said, "But that's probably not going to happen. Nothing turned up at Dana's house. Nothing concrete at either of Masters's residences. And the past stalking victims aren't turning out to be a big help, either." He turned to me. "The woman he stalked in two thousand three was the first we have on record. She filed a restraining order, but proof was a problem in pressing charges. She told friends that he was still stalking her, moving her car around, and then it was stolen a month later."

"She won't testify?"

"More like can't. She disappeared."

I felt my stomach tighten. "On her own?"

He shrugged. "Her friends said she'd worked herself up to such a state, they think it was her own doing. They questioned Masters but didn't have any evidence. Besides, this happened six months after the restraining order had been filed—and had never been violated, as far as the police were concerned."

"What about the one whose brother was beaten? Please tell me she's still around."

"Is but won't testify. She claims he still pops up from time to time. She's scared to death of him."

Another turn of my insides. "Wasn't there a third?"

"Two thousand six, filed a restraining order, Masters appeared to back down, victim didn't think so, the same old no-proof story, and then . . ." He looked at me, and his face grew red.

"What?"

Marcus said, "She committed suicide."

I felt my bones dissolve and I slumped into the love seat. Tears pricked at my eyes, but I blinked them away. I'd already cried so much. As I gathered my wits, I looked at both men. "Could that be what Colin wants, to drive them to suicide?"

"I've discussed this with Detective Thurmond, and . . . well, it's a possibility. From what we can see, he seems to choose women who are fragile."

"And he drives them mad," I said. "Thurmond's testifying?"

"He's willing to. We're going to try to interview Masters, get a psychological profile. But I doubt he'll agree to it."

I got to my feet, and Marcus walked over. I thought he'd take my hands in his, but he didn't move to touch me. "There's something else you should be prepared for. Dana's diary will be entered into evidence. The defense will likely make a motion for discovery, which means they'll be able to read it."

The diary. I'd forgotten about that. "And?"

"I read a copy of it this morning. She sounds . . . paranoid. Hysterical. Despondent. She identifies Colin by name, which is good. But I'm concerned how she'll come off to the jury. The defense attorney will probably play that up, that Dana was unbalanced. It'll be public record. Are you prepared for that?"

He was trying to talk me out of testifying, but everything he told me only made me more determined to go ahead. "I am."

Stewart did take my hand, a gesture that made my eyes water again. "There's something else that may happen. The attorney may also play up Dana's promiscuity."

"What? She wasn't promiscuous!"

"Just the opposite," he muttered.

Marcus said, "Just because she wouldn't go out with you doesn't make her a cold fish, either."

Stewart blinked. "No, of course not. She blew me off, true. But when I saw her at the market a few weeks ago, she was much friendlier." He raised his hands. "So no hard feelings. I gave her my card, said if she ever wanted to get together . . ." He shrugged.

Could it be that Stewart had stopped by that night? One night the three of us had gone to Dana's house on Stewart's suggestion to invite her along. She'd declined. Stewart did know where she lived. I didn't believe the mystery man had assaulted Dana, but he may have seen something. Maybe he was afraid of Colin. Or of being blamed.

Marcus said, "Thing is, the jury will only hear the relevant evidence. She gave oral sex to someone no one else knew about. It doesn't look good."

"It opens up the suspect pool," Stewart added. "If it weren't for the blinks, it seems much more likely that the mystery donor assaulted her."

I took a deep breath. Let it out. And met Marcus's eyes. "I know you'll do your best to make the case stick. I can handle everything else." I bent down and retrieved my purse from the floor. Then I looked at Marcus again. "Are we still on for tonight?" We'd planned to go to a local sports-themed restaurant. "Luke's looking forward to it."

I wanted life to be as normal for Luke as possible, and I knew how much he treasured spending time with Marcus.

"I can't," Marcus said. "I've got to work on this case."

A turn of the knife in my heart. And he'd thrown it onto my shoulders. I only nodded and walked out after a whispered good-bye to Stewart.

Luke had gone home with Bobby after school. Getting to see Luke forty minutes later was a salve for my soul. Serena invited me into her model-home-neat Tudor in an upscale neighborhood. When she gave me a hug, her distended belly grazed mine. "How are you holding up?" she asked quietly as Luke gathered his belongings from the enormous family room.

I could only shrug.

Serena's curtain of black hair grazed her shoulders. Even five months pregnant, she looked beautiful and dressed exquisitely. "I'm here if you need me. But—and I hate to mention this now—I'm starting to get calls from your clients."

"I'm sorry. As soon as I'm ready—"

"I'll try to take on as many as I can."

"Thank you. There's going to be publicity around the trial. About Dana. And me."

"We'll stand strong."

She was the closest friend I had, and her support meant everything to me, but I didn't want her hurt, either. She'd been through a lot. She'd lost her home and everything in it to Hurricane Andrew, and she'd lost two babies since Bobby.

I noticed Luke's jerky, terse movements as he snatched up his Game Boy and threw it into his duffel bag. He passed me by and walked to the car without so much as a glance.

"He's mad because he feels left out of things," Serena said. "Or that's what I gathered."

I nodded. We'd had a similar disagreement when Wesley had died. I hadn't told Luke the details, and I'd made the excruciating decision to stand by Wesley's wishes that Luke not see him in those final days when pain racked his body and soul. Luke still resented that, but he'd only been six, too young to see his father waste away. Right after the terminal diagnosis, we went to Disney and all the other parks in Orlando to create memories that would have to last a lifetime. Wesley and I didn't tell Luke about the cancer until we'd returned.

As I got into the car, I realized it was a never-ending cycle, parents doing something that their child resented and someday that child doing something that his child would resent.

I turned around and opened my mouth to say something, but Luke beat me to it. "Dana killed herself."

I blinked in surprise. "How did you hear that?"

"A kid at school said he saw it on the news. Is it true?"

I, with my impulsive plea on the news, had made the attack more newsworthy. I leaned against the seat. "I sort of told you."

He snorted. "Sort of? Mom, I'm growing up. I can handle knowing . . . stuff."

"The truth is, I'm not always sure if you're grown-up enough to handle certain . . . stuff. It's my job to protect you from the ugliness. And I was going to tell you, but I wasn't sure how."

I let him have his indignation. More would follow in the next few years; might as well get used to it.

"How did she do it?"

"She slashed her wrists with a piece of broken glass."

I knew he was imagining it as he stared at the dashboard. "But the doctors were right there. Couldn't they save her?"

"They tried. She lost too much blood."

"But why? Why would she do that?"

I touched his cheek. "I wish I knew."

He let that settle in for a moment. "When is Marcus coming over?"

"He's not. He's working on Dana's case. I'm sorry."

My cell phone rang as we waited in line at McDonald's, a bribe to cheer up my son. He hadn't wanted to go to the sports restaurant without Marcus. Not that I blamed Luke.

When I saw Marcus's number on the screen, I cheered up. Maybe he'd changed his mind. "Hi."

"I've got some bad news," was how he started, without a greeting or any warmth. "Masters was granted bail. And he posted it."

The smell of French fry grease balled up in my stomach. "No, it can't be."

"Actually, it's not all that unusual. The good news is that he's waiving his Probable Cause hearing, so we're going to move directly to the Grand Jury."

That wasn't good news. Good news would be Colin confessing so there wouldn't be a trial. I tried to digest my anger. "Will I . . . will we see you this weekend?"

Marcus hesitated, and I saw Luke perk up from the backseat. "No. Maybe next week, when things settle down."

He meant with himself, not with his work. I didn't want to lose him over this. Every time that possibility edged into my mind it made my stomach clench. I loved him. Didn't he love me enough to understand why I had to do this? *Let's just get through this, Marcus. Then we'll be okay.*

Please let us be okay.

I was sprawled on top of the sheets watching the minutes tick by. I'd cried twice, blowing my nose and splashing my face and telling myself that I wouldn't do it again. But I could feel more tears, coming as inevitably as high tide. The crazy thing was, I wasn't even sure why I was crying. Dana? The possibility of losing Marcus? The pressure of my life? Maybe it was everything crashing in on me.

A sound in the house stemmed the tears. I listened, hardly breathing. There, a small sound, maybe coming from the living room. I slipped out of bed, thinking that I'd catch either Bonk up to something or Luke snacking in the kitchen.

The dog, however, was nowhere in sight. Maybe he'd gone outside. The dog door was slightly askew again. It was only lately that the flap was getting caught. I knelt down to figure out what it was catching on—and saw a shoe on the step outside.

I yelped and fell to the side when I lost my balance. Then I lurched up, my gaze fixed on the pane of glass. I saw nothing. No one. I turned on the backyard light, but that only created shadows in the hedges surrounding the yard. My heart thundered in my chest. Had I imagined the shoe? I bent down again but saw nothing that could have looked like a shoe. I took several deep breaths to calm my racing heartbeat. The house was quiet again. I leaned down and fixed the flap.

I never went back to sleep.

Colin watched Maggie's widened eyes scan the backyard. Somehow she had heard him. Probably hadn't gotten to sleep. Her conscience pestering her, no doubt. He had only just fought his way through the dog door when he heard footsteps on the tile. There would be other opportunities. He had to be careful, though. Didn't want to mess up his freedom.

Maggie finally turned off the lights and returned to her bedroom. He saw the television go on, or at least the glow through her curtains. Through a crack he could just make out the edge of her bed. Many women who lived alone didn't open their bedroom curtains and rarely noticed the slight shift he created. Then the light went on. As he shifted, he saw a scrapbook lying on the tangle of sheets. Old photos of two girls. Maggie and Dana. He heard crying. Maggie's voice. He strained to hear what she was saying. Words. Angry words.

". . . Dana. How could you . . . ? I know you were scared . . . scared, too." Damn television kept cutting into her dialogue. Then he smiled when he heard her say, "I'll get him, baby sister. I'll make him pay."

After Maggie had blown her nose, she doused the light and walked to the window. He edged to the side. She looked out for a few moments and then closed the curtains tight, obliterating the crack.

He'd made her nervous. Good.

That was only the beginning, of course. He had a lot more to look forward to.

A lot more.

CHAPTER TWELVE

Two weeks dragged painfully by. My mother had arranged a small memorial service at her church, her last effort to appeal for Dana's soul, I guessed. Five people showed up, Luke, Marcus, my mom, the preacher, and me. Marcus's presence had touched me, given me hope. His hasty departure had hurt, though. It had hurt more to see Luke's disappointment at that. I hadn't told my mom about the rift between me and Marcus, nor had I told her about my going back to church—my church, not hers. I contributed to every charity that sent me a letter or called, and I left piles of cash in the donation box at church. Atonement. I couldn't get past what I had been taught growing up: I was what I'd done.

Now, on a Monday morning, Luke and I were having breakfast. He was eating; I was sitting in front of my bowl of soggy Frosted Mini-Wheats watching him. His shaggy hair that he hated kept falling into his face, but he'd resisted when I suggested making a salon appointment.

He looked up at me. "So now this guy goes to court, right? Like on TV, where people testify and a buncha people say whether he's guilty or not."

I was trying to keep the details vague, but Luke wanted facts. Unfortunately, he wasn't talking much about his feelings. "Something like that." The Grand Jury had indicted

Colin on burglary with intent to commit the crime of aggravated felonious sexual assault, and aggravated felonious sexual assault. They didn't have enough evidence to nail him on stalking; they were afraid if the jury didn't buy that, they wouldn't buy the rest. What the Grand Jury had was a man who had an unnatural interest in Dana, diary entries that showed he had stalking tendencies, and my testimony putting him at the scene. He'd waived the formal arraignment process. The court had reassessed the bail, but Colin had managed to post it. He was still free.

Luke sank back into thoughts that made his forehead crease.

"Open Doors," I said, trying to ignore what open doors had meant to Dana. "I'm sad."

Luke looked up, his face so much like Wesley's it hurt when I was least expecting it. His strong chin and blue eyes. "Mom, I don't want to do that right now."

"I do. I want you to talk to me, too."

"Is Marcus mad at you?" he asked instead. "I thought he'd be here more. For you. For us."

That innocent question jabbed at my heart. How could I explain? "It's tricky because he's in charge of Dana's case. It's called a conflict of interest."

"He loves us. He should be here with us."

I could only agree and try to hide my frown.

When the phone rang, I forced a cheerful tone into my voice. "Maybe that's him now." I picked up the phone. "Hello."

"Maggie," a gravelly voice said. "Do you know what happens to little girls who lie?"

It took me three tries to smash the off key. *Him.* It had to be him. Calling. Taunting me.

"Who was that?" Luke asked.

I managed a shaky smile. "Wrong number. Let's get going."

As he finished, I looked at the caller ID screen. No incoming number.

"Mom, you look funny," he said as he put his bowl in the dishwasher. "You okay?"

My heart ached to protect my son who was too eager to become all grown-up. Sometimes that meant lying. As much as I hated it, it was necessary. "I'm fine. Just fine."

Later that day I passed the absent secretary's desk as I headed to Marcus's office. His door was ajar, and his voice shot out through the crack. "You think you can pull that crap on me? Celine, that's not the deal we made. . . . Yeah, you do that. I'll fight you every inch of the way." I flinched when the phone crashed down and the word, "Bitch," poisoned the air.

I'd never heard Marcus utter profanity. He was always the epitome of grace and good conduct. I tapped on the door and edged into the office.

He was digging the heels of his hands against his eyes. Surprise turned to shame. "You heard me, I suppose," he said, not asked.

I made sure I had no trace of incrimination in my expression. "Exes can do that to a person." I closed the door and sat down. Marcus and Celine's divorce two years ago gave him partial custody of his thirteen-year-old daughter. "Something's going on with Celine. That's what you wanted to talk to me about the night Dana was attacked, wasn't it?"

"She's trying to take Tawny to Chicago. That's where her boyfriend lives. I'd just found out that afternoon."

"Oh, Marcus, I feel awful." And now I was dumping so much more on him. "I'm sorry. If you want to talk . . ."

He shook his head. "I've got it under control." By his haggard face and bloodshot eyes, he didn't.

And he still didn't want my support. I hadn't been there when he'd needed me. I felt myself shrivel. "Marcus . . ."

He picked up a paper and moved right into business. "We've had an interesting turn of events this morning. Jerry Crawley called; he's Colin's defense attorney." Marcus even remained behind his desk, keeping a professional distance between us.

"Crawley? He's good, isn't he?"

"Best scumbag money can buy. They want to go to trial without jury. That means we can schedule the trial sooner. And this will be over sooner."

"Why would he want to do that?"

"Speeds things up on his end. Less cost. It's good for us, too. You don't have to live with this hanging over your head for a year."

I nodded, wondering if he knew just how much weight did hang over me. I suspected he did and that's why he was distancing himself from me. If I crumbled, I could drag him down with me. The feeling that I was beginning to lose him reminded me of the early days of Wesley's illness, when the signs started showing. When we couldn't hope it was a misdiagnosis. My stomach ached; my heart screamed, *Go back; tell the truth!* Admitting that now would only make things worse between us.

He shuffled papers, glancing down but not really looking. "Some good news: you can clean out the bungalow. We're done with it."

Good news wasn't that I could remove the bloodstained carpet and bed and pack up my dead sister's belongings.

"I'll start on it this week." I was hoping he'd offer to help or even just be there, but I would never ask. Not now. I wanted to tell him about the phone call, the one I was sure Colin had made, but his accusation would open up the unspoken accusation on Marcus's mind, too.

There was something else I wasn't going to tell him. I'd left a message for Marisol Vasquez of Boston over the weekend, begging her to testify. She hadn't returned my call.

"Crawley filed a motion for discovery, as we knew he would. And he wants to depose you. That means he's going to grill you on what you saw that night."

I swallowed hard. "I'll make myself available." Our exchange was eerily sterile. I stood. "Thank you for coming to Dana's memorial service."

Finally the ice mask softened. "How are you holding up?"

I felt tears tickle my eyes but blinked them back. "It's still hard to believe." When he didn't say anything else, I walked to the door. "Will we see you this week?" It was more important that Luke see Marcus than for me to see him alone.

"I'm . . . not sure."

I tightened my mouth and gave him a quick nod before leaving.

On the way out I signed up for ten rolls of wrapping paper on the form on the secretary's desk. To support her son's band trip, I assured myself, not out of guilt.

Yeah, right.

I was in a deep, exhausted, and dreamless sleep that night when I heard my cell phone ringing. I scrambled out of bed and tracked down the phone right after the call went to voice mail. It was two in the morning.

I dialed in and found no message. As I began to trudge back to bed, it rang again. I hoped it was a wrong number as I punched the talk button.

The gravelly voice chilled me as it wrapped around my name—my legal name. "Magdalena Ruth, I have a question for you: Is a lie worth dying for?"

The line went dead. My fingers clutched the phone. Was Colin threatening to kill me if I went ahead with my testimony? My hands shook as I viewed the incoming number, but the screen said: *Restricted*. I could report it. Threats were against the law. What kept stopping me was a simple fact: what he was accusing me of was true.

"He's just trying to scare you. Don't let him." Except my trembling words gave me away. So did the way I was sucking in jerky breaths.

As I stood in my kitchen wearing only my long T-shirt, I had the eeriest feeling that he was outside in the yard. I snapped off the light and waited for my eyes to adjust.

Hulking shadows moved in a night breeze; the prickly edges of holly bushes scratched against the windows. "You can't scare me, Colin. You can't. . . ." I ran to my room and closed the door. Oh yes, he could.

• • •

My mom had called Wednesday morning, one last effort to save me from destroying my eternal future. Despite that, I told my big, fat lie at my deposition, even as a voice in my mind chanted, *Liar, liar, pants on fire.* Not my mother's voice, of course, but that of some child on a playground long ago.

Jerry Crawley sat across from me, giving me a glimpse of what I'd be facing on the stand. He was a birdlike man in his fifties, lean to the point of bony, and curiously tanned.

"Mrs. Fletcher, in your initial statement to police, you said you couldn't see the man. He was, in *your* words, walking *away* from you. Away from Dana's house. Explain to me what changed."

"I did see the man's face, obviously. I just didn't remember seeing it. And then, when I saw Colin, it clicked."

"Clicked. Yeah."

Crawley made me draw a diagram of the street along with locations of my car and the man. "I'm going to drive down that street tonight to see what can be seen. I'm going to *measure* the distance from where you say your car was and where the defendant *supposedly* was."

"You do that."

When I stepped out of that room, I felt as though I could breathe for the first time in hours. Once I'd given Stewart the blow-by-blow, he asked, "Is everything all right between you and Marcus? I figured he'd be here for moral support."

"He's feeling a lot of pressure. Because of his connection with Dana."

Stewart gave my arm a squeeze. "I've got to get ready. . . ." He nodded toward the room I'd just been in. "Oh, and . . ." He pulled at a lock of my hair. "You've got to work on this."

My corkscrew, undoubtedly sticking out from the rest of my hair. I fluffed it with my fingers.

When I was ready to leave, I turned the corner and came face-to-face with Colin. He was also there to give a deposition. The sight of him stole my breath. Big. Rumpled. Smug. Crawley hustled over and tried to usher Colin past. He was twice Crawley's size and didn't budge.

Crawley was probably worried that his client was going to say something to me, and in the presence of others, no less. I hoped he would. But Colin said everything with his eyes. He stood there looking at me, and then . . . he smiled.

"You can't scare me," I said. "Not with your calls or your stares."

Jerry's eyes bulged. "Colin, we should go—"

"I think you are scared, Maggie Fletcher. Despite your tough façade, you're a scared little girl hiding behind your lies."

Only then did he continue walking toward the room where I'd just told my lie. Where he would tell his.

I took a deep breath only after he'd gone. I wanted to throw up, to purge his words from my head. He looked too confident. He was being so damned cooperative. Was he so sure his attorney would break me down? Colin didn't have to testify, but I did.

As I reached my car, my cell phone rang. I answered in my professional realtor voice.

The muffled voice tingled along my skin. "You've gone and done it, Maggie. Now you'll have to pay."

The sound of the disconnect shot me into action. I ran back into the building, determined to find someone who had seen him on the phone. People looked at me as I huffed past, obviously out of shape. I approached the room but looked everywhere for Colin, expecting to find him returning from wherever he'd slunk away to make the call.

He was sitting in the deposition room, laughing with his attorney. The sight was a double jab in my stomach. The woman who had transcribed my deposition was still there ready to take down Colin's version of events.

A secretary who had just come from the room asked, "Can I help you?"

I pushed past her into the room. "Colin just called me. Threatened me. Surely you heard him?" I said to Jerry.

He looked at me as though I'd lost my mind. "He's been sitting here with me since we got here."

"No. You left him alone for a moment. Or he stepped into the hallway."

Jerry shook his head. "Sorry, but he didn't."

The stenographer subtly agreed.

It couldn't be. And I knew Colin wouldn't have made that call in front of anyone.

Stewart walked up, cell phone in one hand, cup of coffee in another, clearly surprised to see me.

Jerry said, "We're about to start. You'll have to leave."

I waved away Stewart's puzzled look and stepped out of the doorway. I watched through the window. Just then Colin looked up at me. He winked. Then Jerry closed the blinds.

That evening I went to Dana's bungalow for the first time since that terrible night. Alone. I'd spoken with Marcus the day before, when he'd advised me that they'd managed to get a June 18 trial date. We made small talk, an excruciating exercise. He wasn't bold enough to come out and say, *Last chance to back down.* I hadn't been bold enough to ask for his company tonight, either, though I'd mentioned I was going to be here. I had determined long ago never to be needy.

I hoped we could get past this. I loved him. Luke loved him. I knew he loved us, too. I would not crumble and let him down under cross-examination, and Colin would go to prison. Then we could resume our lives. I desperately needed to believe that would happen. It was the only thing getting me through.

I hauled several flattened boxes from the trunk of my Lexus, along with a packing-tape dispenser. I'd had no idea there were cleaning services that specialized in crime scenes. They'd torn down the yellow tape, taken out the carpet and bed, and cleaned all the fingerprint powder. When I walked inside, it looked so normal, as though Dana were there, perhaps in the kitchen fixing a cup of tea. I ached at that thought. Swallowed a wad of grief.

The house also felt cold and empty. The sun hadn't quite

set, but it was already dark inside. I turned on light after light, chasing away the shadows. I couldn't chase away the ones inside me.

Luke had offered to help, and I'd been touched and awed at the gesture even as I'd refused. This was too glum a task for a boy, especially if his mother burst into tears once in a while.

I turned on the smooth electronica satellite channel, the ambient and mostly wordless music fitting my mood. I could have gone morose and chosen alternative rock or blues. Picking something upbeat seemed wrong.

I reassembled the boxes and labeled one: KEEP. I didn't think Dana had much that I'd actually want, but I had to keep some things from her life. I would put them in my closet, next to memory boxes containing items belonging to my father and Wesley. Now I would think of her, too, when I walked in to choose my clothing for the day. I could be angry that she'd taken herself away. And yes, I was a little. But I knew she'd felt she had no choice.

I spent an hour packing her clothing into boxes for Goodwill. They would think these had come from a costume shop for Goths, the dark medieval-style skirts and dresses. Continuing in the clothing vein, I walked to her long dresser. I was unnerved to find her underwear drawer open, the only drawer that *was* open.

The hairs from the back of my neck all the way down to my forearms prickled. I turned around. The closet door was ajar, the small space now empty. It moved ever so slightly, as though something unseen had just walked past. As I watched, frozen in place, the door kept moving. I looked up at the ceiling fan that spun around and released a breath. Just air currents.

I turned back to the open drawer. Maybe the investigators had left it open, though I couldn't imagine why they would have opened it to begin with. This was how Dana lived. In doubt. Fear. "Oh, Sis," I whispered. "I'm so sorry."

Dana hadn't been kidding about buying underwear like our mother's. I threw it all into the trash box, hating Colin for what he'd done to her. Yet it was something that had given her a small sense of triumph. I closed all the drawers, wanting no reminders, and went into the living room. Serena had suggested that I rent out the bungalow, and though I hadn't given it much thought, it made sense. I could afford to let Dana live in it, but it made no sense to let it sit empty.

I went into the kitchen and packed up all the foodstuffs. I found a bottle of Strawberry Hill wine, the kind I used to drink when I was a teenager. I poured it into a glass, along with a few ice cubes, and took a swig. I shuddered, then took another swig.

It was late by the time I finished in the kitchen. I was tired, but I wanted to push on and get it done. Then I could collapse into my bed and sleep. I plodded into the living room, now carrying the bottle with the last of the wine, and slumped down on the area rug. The one-piece stereo system seemed inadequate for Dana's large collection of CDs. I dumped a container of cassette tapes into the giveaway box. Dana liked older alternative rock bands like Orgy, The Cure, and Depeche Mode. Some bands I didn't know, like Massive Attack. I sorted the CDs into ones I might listen to because they'd remind me of Dana and ones I'd never listen to.

I looked at the cover of the next CD to be considered. Enigma. They'd had a couple of hits in the nineties. Then I remembered the song Colin had played for her on the phone. She'd said it sounded like Enigma and they sang about a heart going boom, boom, boom. I turned the case over to read the song list. My chest tightened at the title "Boum-Boum." I inserted the disk into the stereo and forwarded to track 5. Chills skittered down my spine as I listened to the words, the same ones Dana had described.

Why did she have this in her collection? If she'd found the song, she would have mentioned it to me. If she already owned the CD, she would have recognized the song. And that left . . .

"Uh-uh."

Colin had *not* crept in here and left the CD for her to find.

Or would he? That would be one hell of a mind game, and he was good at that sort of thing. The idea gave me the chills all the way down to my nerve endings.

It was during that unnerving thought that I heard the noise. Knowing I was in full paranoia mode, I still turned down the stereo. I barely breathed as I listened. A soft thump sound, coming from the coat closet, where I'd hung my sweater coat earlier. My heart skipped a beat for a second and then thundered on.

I stood, though my knees felt jellied. That was where Colin had been hiding the night of the assault, or at least that was my guess. Was he there now? I crept to the kitchen and grabbed a knife from the butcher block.

I'm crazy, crazy, crazy, I thought as I walked toward the closet door. *I should call the police. Then I'd sound . . . well, crazy. Like Dana did.*

The louvered slats would reveal my approach and my weapon. I slid my hand behind my back; my fingers ached as I clutched the knife handle. I walked as though I were going to the front door, but my eyes probably gave me away. I was sure fear was etched all over my face. Still, I played my part, curling my damp fingers over the doorknob. I took a breath. One. Two. Three!

I swiveled, threw the closet door open, and held the knife aloft. Nothing. Well, at least I hadn't stabbed the two coats hanging in the closet. See, how sane that was? My sweater coat lay crumpled on the floor where it had fallen. That's what I'd probably heard.

I laughed then, more like a throaty giggle. I was wielding a knife at coats. I made the *Psycho* motions and sounds, chiding myself. Now I really knew how Dana had come up with her beliefs about Colin sneaking into her home. How easy it was when you were on edged.

I left the door open, though, and returned to my place on the floor. I checked the dead bolt, to make sure it was still locked. I took deep breaths and wiped the beads of sweat from my upper lip. The CD had started it all, and it was probably Dana's.

Unfortunately, I didn't believe that. Not completely.

I tossed the rest of the collection into the KEEP box for later sorting. I added the picture of Marcus, Dana, and me, too. One of the few pictures of Dana truly smiling. I knew; I'd looked at photo albums over the last few nights. I removed the paintings from the wall and set them next to one of the Goodwill boxes. I felt an urgency now to get this done and go home. It was one thirty.

I left the music off.

I worked for another half hour, in silence, pausing every so often when I heard a tick or creak. I wondered if Dana froze in fear every time she heard those house-settling noises.

I rubbed my eyes, as dry as week-old bread, and sighed. I was done, at least for the most part. I started turning off the lights in the kitchen, dining area, and living area. I narrowed my eyes at the light in Dana's room. Hadn't I turned it off?

I leaned in the doorway to hit the switch—and stopped cold.

The top right drawer was open. The former underwear drawer. I'd closed it. But it was open. Open. The light was on in the closet, too. I couldn't breathe. Light on. Drawer open. Not me. And if not me . . . oh, God. *He was here. In the house.*

CHAPTER THIRTEEN

Adrenaline shot a charge through my body. I tore through the living room, fumbling with the lock as I looked behind me. *Open, open!* My fingers had turned to rubber. I heard grunting noises coming from my throat. Just as I threw the door open I saw someone walking up. A man in the shadows. Coming toward me. I couldn't stop myself. Momentum was propelling me forward. My scream came out as a gargle. All I could do was throw my arms out in front of me.

"Maggie?"

I knew the voice. And then he walked into the lit carport.

"Marcus," I managed, still gasping as I filled the vacuum in my chest with air.

He put his hands on my shoulders. "You all right?"

Seeing him infused such relief, I fell against him. "You scared me."

"You look like you were already scared." He stepped away from me. "What happened?"

I had my own question first. "What are you doing here?"

He looked tired and bedraggled, unlike him. "I kept thinking about you here by yourself." He looked past me. "I figured you wouldn't let Luke help. I called you at home, and then on your cell phone. No answer, so I drove over."

I realized he'd positioned himself so we didn't touch at all. I wanted to reach out, step closer, but I held back. "I turned the phone off so . . ." I wasn't sure I wanted to get into the threatening calls. His puzzled expression induced an answer. I almost always had my cell phone on, the requirement of being a successful real estate agent. "Colin's been calling me, trying to scare me. It's no big deal."

Marcus assessed me in the way he might a witness and not someone he loved: with polite concern. "That's not why you were scared."

I looked behind me. "I think . . . thought . . . Colin was here." I tried to laugh it off, but it sounded ridiculously high-pitched. "I heard a sound and the drawer was open when I know I closed it."

"Let's check it out."

Yes. But I couldn't feel much relief as we walked into Dana's room. The drawer was still open. I'm sure Marcus felt the same way I'd always felt when Dana had pointed at the drawer and said, *Look! Proof!* So what?

"Like I said, I got myself worked up."

He checked the closet, then the window, which was still bolted. "Looks secure."

"It always did," I heard myself say. "When Dana called me over for the same kind of thing. I checked the windows, doors. Everything was locked, no sign of forced entry."

"I suppose he could have locksmith tools."

I blinked in disbelief. "Can anyone get those?"

"Not anyone. But it's in the realm of possibility. He may have taken a course, or stolen them, or even found them at a garage sale."

I wrapped my arms around myself. "I want to go."

"Come on. I'll help you carry these boxes out."

We loaded up my car, and to my surprise he offered to follow me home and make sure everything was secure there. His supposition chilled me. If Colin could get in here, he could get into my house, too. I was even gladder that the trial was only a month away.

Marcus carried the one box I was going to keep into my house. Bonk came in from the backyard and greeted us. After a cursory rub on his head, Marcus checked the house.

I tagged along like the scared little woman of the house. Which is what I was. What had happened at Dana's place still spooked me.

Once we'd made sure no one lurked in any of the closets, Marcus asked, "Where's Luke?"

"At his friend's house. Serena's been a godsend through this." I picked the Enigma CD from the box and pointed to the song title. "This is the song Colin played when he called Dana. She didn't know who did the song, just that it sounded like Enigma. I found this in her collection. It doesn't make sense that she'd have it, not when it had such creepy connotations for her." I chucked it in the bin.

"You think he put it in her house?"

"Maybe he got some kind of sick satisfaction knowing he'd put something in her house. Maybe he hoped she'd find it, like I did."

It felt good to talk about all this, even with the river of doubt that flowed between us. I slipped my arms around him and pressed my cheek against his chest. "Thank you for coming." The ache of need for him to pull me close deepened when he didn't even slide his arms around me. He gave me a pat on the shoulder instead.

"I love you, Maggie. But—"

I stopped the "but" by pulling his face down to mine and kissing him. I didn't want to hear "buts." Our tongues slid against each other, our mouths moving together. We hadn't made love since the assault, and I so badly needed to feel alive, to feel loved. I pushed his overcoat off his shoulders to the floor and started unbuttoning his shirt. I kissed the sparse hairs on his chest as I made my way down toward his stomach. Even more than sating my own needs, I wanted to give Marcus something. I had created this chasm between us and I would do anything to bridge it. Desperation swelled inside me.

"Maggie," he said in a voice that sounded like a protest, but his hands were in my hair, massaging my scalp.

I dipped my tongue into his belly button, unsnapped the top button on his trousers and unzipped them. His penis was firm, but not as hard as I knew it could be. He was tired, of course, so I took matters into my own hands and ran my tongue along that sensitive ridge of skin. That always did the trick, even when he was exhausted. This time it had the opposite effect. I saw an agonized expression on his face, and not the pleasurable kind of agony.

"I'm sorry, Maggie. I just . . . I can't."

I sat down on the floor, unable to stand. "Why?"

He zipped his pants and fumbled with the button, looking everywhere but at me. "I've got too much on my mind right now."

"You're going to blame this case again?" I pushed to my feet, making him look at me. "Or you're blaming me. Because you think I'm lying."

Though Marcus was an attorney who could argue a case eloquently, he had trouble with personal confrontations. That's why it surprised me when he took a deep breath and said, "I know you're lying, Maggie. I understand why. But that lie . . . it's standing between us like an ogre. When I look at you . . ."

I felt my insides crumple. "You see that ogre." He wasn't looking at me. I tugged at his arms. "I'm not an ogre. I'm Maggie. Your girlfriend, who needs you right now." There, I'd said it. "Luke needs you, and I think you need us, too. I don't want to lose you. This will be over soon. If you don't want to see me before the trial"—this time *I* looked away, but only for a second—"okay, fine. Well, it's not fine, but I'll have to live with it. But I don't want this to be over."

He kept his gaze to the floor. "I pursue justice and truth for a living. How can you expect me to be with you when you're going against everything I believe in?" He bent to pick up his coat from the floor. I wrapped my arms around myself as he walked to the door. He bowed his head for a moment, his hand on the door handle. Then he turned to me. "You can say you were mistaken, Maggie. Even now. It does happen; witnesses recant. They rethink things. You can still stop this."

My mouth tightened into a frown. "No, I can't."

He opened the door. I wanted to pull him back inside, but

it hit me then, like a big slap on the face: I didn't deserve to win him back. I didn't deserve him.

Time heals all wounds. The saying bounced around in my brain like a screen saver, but this time I grabbed onto it. I held it tight in my heart as I dropped to the floor and cried. Pitiful wails came out of me. Only seeing the unlocked door broke me out of grief and propelled me to my feet. I locked the door and turned off the light.

"Come on, boy. Let's go to bed." Bonk wasn't much of a watchdog, but I still wanted him with me.

The switches hadn't been wired correctly. After turning off the living room light, I was several yards away from the switch for the hall. That walk in the dark, around the sofa and past the fireplace, had never been more than a nuisance before. Now it felt precarious. I ran my hand along the back of the sofa as I passed it, felt for the step up into the short hallway leading to my bedroom. I left the hall light on and entered my room, closing the door behind me. Locking it. I walked over to the window and closed the drapes tight.

When I turned around, my gaze went right to the open drawer in my dresser. My underwear drawer.

I didn't waste any time. After a sleepless night with a butcher knife on my nightstand, I called a security company and ordered a system to be installed right away. The news of Colin's attack had spurred a rash of orders. This wasn't the type of crime that was well tolerated in this upscale community. They promised to fit me in that day since I was related to the victim.

"Can't believe they let that guy out on bail," the woman I spoke to said.

I couldn't, either, and I couldn't even utter words of agreement.

The guys were installing the system when Luke rode up on his bicycle after school. He watched the men on ladders wiring windows with white shutters on each side. My little Colonial house that looked so safe and cozy.

"What's going on, Mom?"

As much as I wanted to protect him, I felt he should know about any potential threat. "I think Colin Masters has been in the house."

Luke jumped off the bike and let it fall to the ground. "He got in? You really think so?"

"I'm not sure, but I don't want to take any chances. And I want you to be on alert, too. Just until this trial is over."

What if he goes free? a sinister voice whispered.

No, I couldn't even think about that.

"Okay," Luke said, wandering over to watch the men wire the front door.

This is what I should have done for Dana, as soon as she told me about Colin. If we'd had proof, if I'd completely believed her . . . those were the thoughts that I thrashed myself with daily. I was doing something now, though. I was going to send her stalker away for as long as the law allowed.

"Ma'am," the guy who seemed to be in charge said. "I see you have a large dog door. That can be a security risk."

"I know. But he barks if we leave him out. And sometimes we're gone for much of the day."

"The door's big enough for someone to crawl through."

"I know," I said, probably a little too tersely. "Can you wire it so it beeps whenever something goes through it?"

"I can put a sensor similar to the one on the doors that beeps whenever the contact is broken. I'll make it a double beep so you can tell the difference. I'd recommend keeping the panel in place at night and as much as you can. The other problem is with the motion detectors. The dog will set them off. If you don't have them on, you're missing a big piece of your security system."

Damn. I hadn't thought about Bonk triggering the system.

"We can put in a pet allowance so the detectors don't scan below the dog's height. But again, that means someone can crawl on the floor without setting it off, too."

I looked at Bonk, being loved on by Luke. I couldn't send Bonk away, not during this trying time. While Serena didn't mind if Bonk stayed over on occasion, she was too fastidious of a housekeeper to allow it full-time for a month.

"Ma'am?"

I blinked, coming back to our conversation. "Put the pet allowance in. And the sensor. I'll take your advice on the panel."

I walked to the corner of the yard and called Marcus's office. I was relieved when I got his voice mail. "Marcus, it's Maggie. I just wanted to let you know . . . I've installed an alarm system. So . . . well, in case you stop over late some night, like you used to . . . you can't just come in. Okay, that's all I wanted to say. Bye." I hoped he'd call and ask for the code.

A few minutes later the supervisor approached me again, this time an odd expression on his face. "Ma'am," he said, the word grating on me. "I'd like to show you something." I followed him around to the back of the house, to, precisely, my bedroom window. "It's a good thing you're doing this," he said, pointing to the ground.

I saw places where the dirt had been disturbed. A couple of the branches had been broken. I didn't get it, not at first.

"Someone's been standing here. Looking in your window," he said. "There isn't a distinct footprint, because we haven't had any rain in a while. But in my opinion, someone has been here."

I shivered violently, stepping back and nearly tripping myself.

The young man put his hand on my arm. "You all right?"

I nodded with way too much enthusiasm, perhaps trying to convince myself. "You're going to put sensors on those windows, right?" I managed to ask.

"Yes, ma'am."

I walked back to the front yard and collapsed on the front step. Now I knew. There was no point in denying it. He was after me. For sport. And revenge. I had become Colin's target.

CHAPTER FOURTEEN

"Maggie, come in." Stewart took my hand and led me into his office the next day. It wasn't as big as Marcus's office, but he still managed to have a seating area. Framed articles about high-profile cases he'd won covered the walls. He actually highlighted his name in each one in bright yellow. The small coffee table was covered in papers and folders from Dana's case. "Is Marcus in a meeting?"

"I . . . I don't know."

"I can see if he's available. . . ."

"I'm here to see you, actually."

"Oh." He swiped his hand over his balding head. "Sure." He looked puzzled and concerned at once as he sat down next to me. "Maggie, what's going on with you two?"

With the losses compounding, it was hard to talk about it without the threat of tears.

"It's because he doesn't believe you, isn't it?" he asked.

"Do you believe me?"

"Absolutely."

"The case wouldn't go forward without me, would it?"

He lifted one finger. "Well, we have the blinks. Dana blinked yes twice. But people blink. Defense is going to argue coincidence. Reasonable doubt." Two fingers. "Our victim–slash–most valuable witness is gone. You never saw Colin stalking her. One of her co-workers says Colin gave

her, in her words, the heebie-jeebies. He watched Dana continuously whenever he was in the café. It's helpful, but not
conclusive." Three fingers. "Her diary. Shows she was scared
of him, and her fear is compelling. *But* honestly, her diary
makes her sound like a paranoid schizophrenic." I was the
fourth finger. "You. You can put him at the scene. He had no
other reason to be there. He has no alibi. It makes the circumstantial evidence of his stalking real. So, yeah, Maggie,
you're the foundation of our case." He swiped his head again,
and his face sobered. "You aren't lying, right? I mean, you're
not going to break down on the stand when Jerry's at your
throat."

"I won't break down."

He huffed a breath of relief. "No, of course not. You're an
honest gal, and heck, look at you—cherubic face, curls,
someone like you wouldn't lie. Yeah, we need to play up that
cute angle."

"I hate being considered cute."

He wasn't listening. "Do you have a dress with, say, animals on it? Cats! Yes, cute cats. No, kittens!" He was studying me. "Very little makeup. A dab of pink on your cheeks,
make 'em look like apples."

"I don't wear animals on my clothing." On purpose.

He waved that away, missing the growl in my voice. "Buy
a kitten outfit. You need to look like a gal who would never
tell a lie."

I sighed. "All right." Hell, if I could perjure myself, I
could wear cute animals.

"Lose that thing you keep doing." He made a vague gesture at his neck.

"It's completely subconscious, like that thing you do with
your hand." I imitated his nervous gesture.

He looked at the sheen of oil on his palm. "Oh, right.
Well, do your best."

"What if Colin gets acquitted?" I hated to even voice it,
but I had to.

"Maggie, you know what happens. He's free. Can't be

tried again, even if other evidence arises. That's the chance we take when we try a case with shaky evidence. But we're not going to find anything new, so it's worth the risk."

Stewart's phone rang, and he held up his finger and took the call. He sank into his chair and pulled out his notepad. I didn't recognize the names he mentioned, so I found myself looking at the papers. I didn't consider it snooping since it was my sister's case. I tried to look casual, but I was searching for the journal entries they managed to retrieve from Colin's fireplace. I found only two pages, written in a meticulous hand:

January 15
  INFILTRATE: I start slowly, becoming part of her landscape. She is already mine, even though she hardly knows me. It's my delicious secret. I've invested so much in her already, and she doesn't even know I exist. Yet.
  But soon, very soon, I will be in her mind when she eats, when she sleeps, and when she wakes. She will be breathing me, too.

I felt a clammy chill as I flipped to the next page.

April 15
  DEGENERATE: My pet has already begun the disillusionment process, giving me very little feedback anymore. She has scorned my honor. And oddly, I am more excited. Could it be that I'm actually more turned on by the prospect of her disappointing me? Ah, wouldn't a shrink have fun with that, digging into my psyche, asking me how my mother disillusioned me by leaving.
  No, forget her. It makes me angry to think about her, and I don't want to be angry. Must think about my pet.

"His journal," Stewart said from right beside me. "Sick son of a bitch, isn't he?"

I jumped at Stewart's voice and closed the folder. "He calls her his pet. Like something he owns."

Stewart took a seat next to me, his thigh pressed against

mine. "Unfortunately, nothing that obviously ties directly to Dana."

I shifted around to face him, removing contact. "Colin's trying to scare me into backing down." I told him about the phone calls, the disturbance by my window, but not about the open drawers. He'd said Dana's diary sounded paranoid. I couldn't afford to sound the same way.

"Have you reported it to the police?"

"With what proof? Unless we could get his phone records, though I doubt he's making them from a source that tracks back to him."

"That'd be tough. You know how hard it is to get search warrants. We got lucky the first time, but I doubt we'd get phone records based on what you're telling me. You could report him for stalking, get a restraining order."

"But I haven't actually seen him around my house. I've only seen him here."

"And he's got business here."

"If I get something solid, I'll file a report."

He reached out and patted my leg. "Do you have a vicious dog? An alarm?"

"A friendly dog, but I just installed a security system at the house."

He pulled me close in a sideways hug. "Poor Maggie. As if this hasn't been hard enough."

I welcomed his comfort, and yet something held me back. I told myself I was being paranoid in a different way as I became aware of his hand stroking small, intimate circles on my thigh.

In a soft voice I'd never heard him use, he said, "I'm sorry that Marcus is being a schmuck and neglecting you. Let me make it up to you. Let me be a shoulder to cry on."

"Thank you, but—"

"You're not like your sister. A warm, loving woman like you has other needs, too. You need a man who can . . . fill those needs." The way he spoke, along with the circles, made me feel icky all of a sudden. His other hand rubbed my arm, and his knuckles brushed against the edge of my breast. "If you need . . . comfort . . . just to be held . . . or more . . ."

I abruptly stood, and Stewart nearly fell sideways on the sofa. He blinked, as though bringing himself out of a trance. To my horror, I saw that he had an erection pressing against his trousers.

"Stewart, did you just . . . make a *pass* at me?"

He rubbed his hand over his head as he got to his feet. "N-no. I was just"—he tried to adjust his trousers—"offering comfort in a trying time. Being a friend."

I let my gaze drop down to his zipper, letting him know that I knew just what kind of friend he was. "You said I was different than my sister."

His eyes widened. "I meant you're a warm person. She wasn't. That's all."

"You asked her out."

"Yeah, a few times, and she blew me off. She was a freak."

"Because she blew you off?" I asked, trying to quell my anger at his bluntness.

"No, because she acted as though I'd insulted her by asking."

"You said you saw her a few weeks ago at the store. What happened?"

I could smell the perspiration coming off him. "Polite small talk. Nothing more."

"Stewart, can you really prosecute this case feeling that way about her?"

"It's not about her, Maggie. It's about justice, like any other case."

I looked at him, feeling disappointed, disillusioned, and in need of a shower. Another ally was fading away from me. Another person I thought I could count on had let me down, all because of my lie.

"Maggie, don't look at me like that." He dropped down on the sofa with a sigh and rubbed his temples. "I've always been attracted to you. I thought you knew that."

"I wish I didn't know." I walked to the door. "And I wish you hadn't tried to put the moves on me. I'm your friend's girlfriend. Your *boss's* girlfriend."

"Marcus isn't a saint, either. But you're right; I shouldn't have. Can we forget it ever happened?"

I opened the door. "I wish I could."

Had Stewart tried his *smooth* moves with Dana, too? Maybe they'd run into each other that evening and he'd invited himself over. Coerced or manipulated her into giving him oral sex to salve his slighted ego.

I stopped by the secretary's desk on my way out. "I have a totally off-topic question. Are the attorneys in this office fingerprinted?"

"They are now."

I didn't want to make a big deal of it, so I merely nodded and bid her a good day. *They are now.* Which meant they weren't before. Stewart had been with the county attorney's office for years, so it was likely his prints wouldn't be on file.

When I turned to leave, I saw Stewart lingering in his doorway. He'd probably overheard me, though if my question worried him, he gave no indication.

I stepped out into the stark, sunny day. As I reached the bottom of the stairs, I turned and looked up. The vultures were there, watching me. I headed quickly toward the lot.

Every day the temperature crept a little higher. It was now in the midseventies. Acquaintances had a saying: "It must be summer; Maggie's wearing bright colors." That seemed wrong, somehow, in light of recent events. I was in mourning, for Dana, for my crumbling relationship with Marcus, for my peace of mind. And for the moral line I'd crossed.

Midway down the steps I looked out over the parking lot. Like Dana used to do, scanning, looking for him. She'd never seen him when I was with her.

I saw him now. As Stewart said, he had business in the vicinity. Had he chosen Jerry because of his office's proximity to the courthouse? He was locking his car door, or at least he was in that position. But he was watching me. That was his goal, I was sure. To watch, intimidate. Apprehension prickled along my skin, but I wasn't about to let him see that. I shored my shoulders and continued on, taking an out-of-the-way route to my car.

If he approached me, threatened me, I'd have potential witnesses. People came and went. I hoped he *would* threaten me.

He was too smart for that. He looked at me. That look that violated me more than Stewart's hands and words had. Though Colin's expression remained mostly passive, I saw a trace of that smug smile just beneath the surface.

I couldn't help the shiver that shook me and hoped he hadn't seen it. I turned away from him. His voice followed me, low and soft.

"I was watching you that night, Maggie. When you went to Dana's house. I could have reached out and touched you."

I faced him, faced those ice-blue eyes that looked cold and calculating. My words squeezed out of a tight throat: "Why didn't you?"

His mouth formed what would have looked like a pleasant smile if it weren't for his eyes. "I was saving you for later."

I turned away and walked as fast as I could without running. I wouldn't run. I wouldn't give him the satisfaction of knowing just how much that scared me. Because I had wondered, after that night, why he'd run off. That was the thought that haunted me, I realized, the one I wouldn't let myself consider.

Oh yeah, he'd scared her. Scared her good. And she hadn't run back into the courthouse to tell on him. He stood by his car and watched her press the remote unlock device on her black Lexus, get in, and lock the doors. Two Disney figurines hanging from her mirror danced when her head bumped them in her haste. Little dolly with her kid's toys. He wondered what would happen if he tore her head off, as he had that doll.

He pulled the camera from behind his back and switched on the display mode. He'd gotten a couple of pictures before she'd seen him. He'd blow them up, crop them with his software. Put them next to the one of her and Luke he'd taken from her house.

He remained where she could see him in her rearview mirror as she waited at the light. She was looking at him. Even though he couldn't see her, he knew she was looking.

He smiled. It was a different game with Maggie. He didn't just want to possess her; he despised her. She was a strong woman. She would present new challenges. He liked the changes. Yes, they were good.

He meandered toward the building that housed his lawyer's office. Just to cover his bases, he would have a reason for being there. He'd told Jerry how sure he was that Maggie was lying, though not why he was sure. He kept a few things from his lawyer. His guilt, of course. That and something else. But he could assure Jerry of one thing: if he pushed Maggie hard enough on the stand, she'd crack. If she made it there to begin with.

I spent the rest of the day scrubbing my house. I felt the need for control, for a bit of sanity, in my world. The security people had left some dirt on the floors, some grass, and little piles of dust where they'd drilled. I went on from there. My fingers were red, my arms ached, and I was damp with perspiration as I cleaned between the knobs on my stovetop.

Luke sat sideways at the dinette table, the tips of his sneakers on the chair to his right. His brand-new sneakers looked old already; I wondered if he'd done that on purpose. His hair needed a trim, but I wasn't up for the fight that taking him to our hairdresser would be.

Between bites of an apple, he asked, "Mom, what're ya doing?"

"What does it look like? I'm cleaning."

He rolled his eyes. "Yeah, I know that. I mean, you're kinda anal about keeping things neat, but you're never this . . . crazy."

I immediately straightened. "Where'd you get the word 'anal'?"

"That's what Bobby calls his mom. She's worse than you."

"Okay, maybe I'm a little . . . anal." I lifted my eyebrow at the word. "I try not to be, but I can't help it. And I'm not crazy," I said, addressing the second part of that. "I've let the house go lately and I'm catching up." I knew he could see it was more than that.

"It's this trial, isn't it? Would this guy be hanging around if you weren't testifying against him?"

"Yes, I think he would."

"Would Marcus be around if you weren't?"

That took me by surprise. "Why do you ask that?"

"I called him today."

"And?"

"He just said the case has him stressed and, with you being a witness, he needs to put some distance between you and him. He didn't want anything to look bad." Luke obviously didn't quite buy that. "Did you and him have a fight?"

" 'You and he,' " I corrected, buying time. "You're being nosy," I said, unable to answer Luke honestly.

"You're being secretive, Mom. Open Doors and all."

I sagged. Sometimes initiating this honest dialogue backfired. "We had a disagreement about the case. Can we leave it at that?"

"I guess. Can you make up with him, though, so we can see him?"

"I think he's right about not seeing us too much until the trial. Then we can get things back on track." I hoped. I prayed. I'd been so careful with this relationship, not only with my heart but with Luke's as well. Marcus was the first man I'd dated since Wesley's death, but I'd determined that I wouldn't introduce someone into Luke's world—and his heart—until I knew he'd be around for a while. Marcus, having a daughter of his own, understood that and had waited four months before spending time with Luke. After that, they'd hit it off so well, I felt bad for holding back.

"But we'll watch our silly movie, just like always," I said brightly. That was a tradition, one my dad and I had started.

Friday nights we picked a silly movie just to laugh. And I badly needed to laugh with my son. "I got *Uncle Buck.*"

I straightened a framed neon Batman print in the dining room, though what I really wanted to do was take it down. I figured, Luke lived there too, might as well let him add his touches. He'd pushed the limit with this print, though. Before that a talking bass had been our bone of contention. It now resided in a bedroom that looked like a small, war-torn country.

When the phone rang I snatched it out of Luke's hand as he reached for it. God knew what Colin might say to him. Though Luke was annoyed and surprised by my vehemence, when I mouthed the word *Grandma* he was relieved I'd beat him to the phone. He grabbed one of Bonk's tug toys, bopped him in the nose with it, and ran outside. The alarm beeped when the door opened.

After the usual greetings, she said, "Have you changed your mind yet?"

"About what?" I asked, hoping she meant something else, like having her over for dinner the following night. My fingers instantly started twirling the curl below my right ear.

"Lying in front of God and man. Sacrificing your soul to wreak revenge, when revenge is God's. We're taught to forgive and leave things to the Almighty."

My irritation immediately gave way to disbelief. "Are you saying you forgive Colin for what he did to Dana?"

"We must forgive, Maggie."

She hadn't exactly answered me. "There's no way I could forgive that man." Forgive? I wanted to *kill* him.

"How can God forgive your sins when you can't forgive others' sins?"

"Then I guess He can't," I said, hearing anger in my voice. "You can't compare a lie to a brutal rape." I knew I'd sort of admitted my lie, but she didn't call me on it. I watched Luke throwing a saliva-encrusted knot of threads to the corner of the yard, where Bonk bounded after it. "And Mom, don't you dare bring this up in front of Luke."

"Why should I drag your innocent son into your moral

morass? No, he should believe that his mother is a good person."

"I *am* a good person," I growled, though I had my doubts sometimes. I rubbed at a water spot on the granite counter. I noticed I usually cleaned when I was on the phone with Mom.

"I know you are, most of the time. But if you go through with this . . . Maggie, I'm afraid something awful will happen."

The sound penetrated my dream—a dream of a memory, of Dana and me chasing fireflies in our backyard. I groped through the sweet melancholy of the dream to consciousness. What sound hadn't fit into that summer night? I sat straight up as it came to me. A double beep. The dog door opening. I knew Bonk hadn't gone out the dog door; I'd inserted the plate.

I tripped over Bonk, sleeping in the hallway, and hit the wall with a thud. He only grunted. I had at one time liked the split floor plan of this house, master suite on one side, rest of the bedrooms on the other. Now I wanted Luke closer. I wanted to make sure he was safe. First I had to make sure no one else was in the house.

My heart hammered in my chest as I crept through the dark house, my ears tuned to any sound. I saw nothing out of the ordinary, so I turned on the lights. The alarm panel indicated nothing. I checked all the doors: locked tight. Windows, too. Back in the kitchen, I eyed the dog door. I crouched down and checked the plate. It felt loose.

When the phone rang, it startled me into a yelp. Who was calling at three in the morning?

No one but Colin. I couldn't ignore it. I didn't want the phone to wake Luke, for one reason. And I wouldn't hide under a table, not in my own home. I snatched up the handset before the second ring.

"Yes."

"Maggie, you don't think that little old alarm system is going to keep me out, do you?"

"I'm not afraid of you, Colin." Damn shaky voice. "I'm not going to back down. The more you try to scare me, the stronger I'll get."

He chuckled, soft and sinuous. "Tough little Maggie. But you look so sweet when you're asleep."

I hung up. I suddenly felt cold, as though someone had doused me with a bucket of ice water. My gaze darted everywhere along the back of the kitchen: door, window, dog door. I remembered an old horror movie where the calls being made to the babysitter were traced to somewhere inside the house.

"Mom, you all right? Who was that on the phone?"

I jumped, emitting a scream that I quickly muted. "You scared me!" I said too harshly, though it didn't seem to bother him.

"Sorry. I heard some noises, then the phone."

Bonk traipsed in, too, and he walked to the dog door, put his nose against the barrier, and gave me a piteous look. "No, Bonk. You can't go out there, not right now."

"Mom?"

I turned to Luke, who looked sleepy and adorable with his hair in a tangle. I knelt down and hugged him hard. He subjected himself to it for a moment before nudging me away. He'd gotten to the stage where he didn't want his mom's affection. Every night I made to kiss him on the forehead but kissed him on the cheek instead. At least he never ducked.

But now he was looking at me as though I had spinach on my teeth. "Mom."

"I thought I heard a noise. Then the phone rang and startled me. No one was there, just silence." Those lies I did allow, but with no small amount of guilt.

He eyed me suspiciously.

I was still kneeling when I took hold of his shoulders. "Luke, if you hear anything strange in the house, press the panic button and close your door." I'd had panic buttons installed all over the house. "Promise me that, okay?"

"Sure." He was so small, even though he wanted to be big and tough.

I would have suggested he sleep in my room, but he'd never go for that. I ached with the fierce need to keep him safe and with the love I felt for him. I hugged him hard and quick.

"Love you, bud," I said, having been forcefully graduated from "honey" a long time ago.

"You, too, Mom," he said grudgingly. "Just don't get all gooey on me, okay?"

"Okay," I said in a whisper. "Go back to bed."

"You, too," he called out as he headed through the living room.

I'd never get back to sleep. I looked at Bonk, who was still nose-to-panel. "I wish you were a pit bull."

He wagged his tail, though it drooped again. He reluctantly moved away from the door and dragged his feet across the tile.

I looked out the kitchen window, seeing my scared, pale face reflected back at me. Was he out there? More important, had he been inside my home? As I stepped into the motion detector's range, the light flashed on. But he could crawl inside if he suspected there was a pet allowance.

I went in search of a hammer and some nails. I sat in front of the dog door and hammered the panel in place. "Sorry, buddy," I told Bonk, who was watching me solemnly.

I wanted to believe the statement about watching me sleep was a scare tactic, but I heard Dana's voice reciting part of that last poem he'd left for her:

She dreams of me,
When she sleeps,
So fitful through the night,
As though sensing I am there,
Her guardian angel,
Watching over her.
Always.

And I'd heard the all-too-real beep of the alarm.

CHAPTER FIFTEEN

JUNE 19, 2006

I had managed well during my testimony, only inwardly faltering as I promised to tell the truth, the whole truth, so help me God. I didn't have to fake the tears when I'd relayed the events of that night, of finding my sister, of her subsequent suicide. My fingers were twined together in my lap to keep them from straying to my worry curl.

Stewart paced back to me, looking me fully in the eye. "Can you identify the man you saw that night, Mrs. Fletcher? Is he in this courtroom?"

"Yes. It was Colin Masters." I pointed at him. He'd been staring me down from the moment I entered the courtroom.

"Thank you." Stewart took his seat at the prosecutor's table, and Jerry bounced up from his seat as though he had a spring attached to his ass.

It had been hard enough lying when Stewart questioned me. Now I had to face Crawley. "Ms. Fletcher," he started, drawing my name out, ignoring the "Mrs." part of my name. As Stewart had prepared me for, Crawley asked about my sister's mental health and played up my role as her protector. He made me go through the events of that night yet again. He faced me, hands braced on the witness box. "Are you absolutely sure you saw my client that night?"

I looked at my mother, who was seated in the gallery, for the hundredth time since my testimony had begun. She looked disappointed now, though she'd cried during other parts of my testimony. I struggled to keep my eyes from snapping to Colin. It didn't matter; I could feel him looking at me. Hating me. I shifted my gaze to the attorney. "Yes."

"And yet, your initial story was that you'd seen a man stumbling down the sidewalk but couldn't remember his face."

"That's right. I remembered when I saw Colin at the station for the first time."

"That's convenient, isn't it?" Before Stewart could voice his objection, Jerry went on. "Ms. Fletcher, I drove that stretch of road at the exact time you say you did. I couldn't see anyone's face. Do you possess superhuman powers?"

I smiled. "Just twenty-twenty."

I heard someone snicker.

Jerry twitched his nose, something I noticed he did when he was agitated. "It was a dark, cloudy night. How, then, could you see the man's face?"

"He was walking beneath a streetlight. If you drove that road, surely you saw the lights."

Another twitch.

The trial had begun today, and my testimony led things off. I hoped by the end of the week the bench trial would be over. Colin would be on his way to prison, and I could try to put my life back together.

Speaking of Marcus, he was notably absent in court today. Stewart had been appalled by Marcus's lack of support. I tried to tell myself that I understood. The truth was, it hurt. Really hurt.

The last three weeks had been hellish. Trying to get back to work. Feeling so alone. I'd finally stopped taking calls from any unknown number after the last gravelly taunt: *Roses are red; violets are blue; if you tell a lie, you'll die, too.*

I'd taken Colin's power away from him. He couldn't taunt me by phone. I'd stayed away from the courthouse. But, in fact, Colin had taken away my freedom. I spent a lot of time at home, locked away in my prison, listening to the beeps I sometimes heard in the night. I'd lost my son. I'd sent him off to Wesley's parents in Cambridge, Massachusetts, ostensibly to protect him from the trial publicity. But Colin hadn't scared me enough to make me back down.

"In your report you said the man was walking away from Dana's house. This was approximately nine forty-five. Yet the attack probably occurred after that, according to her medical records. And, in fact, your own testimony indicates that the man who actually attacked your sister was still at the house when you got there at nearly midnight. But the man you think was Colin had already left. How do you explain that?"

"When I saw him, he was stumbling. At first I thought he was drunk. Now I think he was walking toward Dana's house. He probably recognized my car and spun around, which threw him off balance."

"If he were hiding from you, wouldn't he have made a special attempt to hide his face?"

Whoa. I wasn't expecting that question. "He did try to hide his face, by burrowing in his coat collar. I saw him as he turned to do so."

"You've got it all worked out, don't you?" Crawley started to move on, but the judge said, "Watch the side comments, Counselor."

"Sorry, Your Honor." He left his contrite tone behind when he looked at me. "Ms. Fletcher, how sure would you say you are that the man you saw that night was Colin Masters? The man who was stumbling or maybe turning away from you. Give me a percentage."

"One hundred percent."

He laughed, looking at the judge as though he were in on the joke. "One hundred percent. Really? Isn't it more likely that when you saw my client at the police station—cooperating with the investigation, by the way—you decided to place him at the scene? After all, he wasn't being charged. And the man who had received oral sex from your sister and probably beat her afterward couldn't be found. You had one chance to make someone pay. So you chose Colin Masters, the poor schmuck who once had a crush on Dana. Isn't that right?"

I couldn't breathe for a moment. Yes, that was exactly right, everything but the poor-schmuck part. I swallowed what felt like a lump of toothpaste in my throat. "No." I looked at my mom, who was pleading with me with her eyes to tell the truth. "That's not right at all."

He asked me the same question in every conceivable way until finally Stewart objected for harassment and the judge thankfully agreed. Jerry had given it his best shot, but I think I had given it a better shot. I was excused. My gaze betrayed me and slid to Colin. His hands were lying palms-down on the table, and his fingers flexed convulsively. His icy glare lanced me.

On shaky legs, I stepped down from the stand and left the courtroom. I'd wanted to stay once my testimony was finished, but I wasn't allowed in case I was recalled. The thought of that tightened my jangly nerves.

I finished Serena's baby blanket and started another one while I waited in the courthouse hallway until the trial recessed for the day. I watched the judge walk out, and finally Stewart emerged with his briefcase, jacket slung over his shoulder. I'd kept my distance from him while we prepared for my testimony, and he had been politely cool. I would need to keep in touch with him during the trial, unfortunately. Marcus and I rarely spoke, and I doubted he would give me any information on what was going on. My mother would be stingy, too, I suspected, as I saw her come out.

She wiped her eyes as she passed me but said nothing. Okay, I'd let her down. I'd let Marcus down, too, and yes, even myself. But I'd stood by Dana.

Stewart put his arm around my shoulder before I could think to position myself so that he couldn't. "You did a bang-up job in there. The best we can hope for is a compelling, sympathetic witness. You could win an Oscar."

I wasn't sure that was a real compliment. Oscars were for actors.

He squeezed my shoulder but didn't remove his hand.

He, in fact, pulled me closer, and I could feel his damp armpits. "Boy, was Jerry pissed that he couldn't break you. I think he's taking it out on the other witnesses. How are you holding up?"

I spotted Marcus standing in the distance watching us. I felt guilty for the way Stewart was touching me, and I hadn't even done anything. I shrugged away, though. "Tired. How did the rest of the day go?"

"The co-worker who said Colin gave her the willies testified. Crawley tried to make her sound like she was jealous of the attention."

"Creep."

"Thurmond testified."

At first, his testimony was deemed positive. Thurmond had studied psychology, though only as a minor. Colin even had submitted to an interview, surprising everyone but me. I knew how arrogant he was. He had a right to be. The assessment came out normal, negating Thurmond's earlier assessment of Colin as a sadistic stalker.

"Crawley sliced and diced him. He—"

Stewart fell silent as Marcus joined us. "How is it going? Sorry I missed the first day. I had something else to take care of."

I hoped my lie wasn't as transparent as his.

Stewart took the opportunity to put his arm around me again, as though we were old buddies. "She held up like a little trouper. You ought to be proud of her."

I decided not to object to the word "little." I wondered, though, if Stewart was toying with Marcus. It worked, making his face flush. He turned to Stewart, ignoring me altogether on the "proud" part, as well as the invitation: "Let's get a cup of coffee so you can give me a recap."

He waited, so Stewart removed his arm after one more squeeze. "Good night, Maggie."

I watched the two walk away. I thought I'd numbed myself over Marcus's distant attitude. Seeing him leave without even a backward glance jabbed at my heart. When I heard Jerry's loud voice announce to someone, "We've got it in the bag," I turned instinctively, finding Colin watching me with that hint of a smug smile. He, in fact, pursed his lips, and when I thought he might say something, I realized he was making a kissing motion. He kept his gaze on me even as Jerry realized he was looking at me and nudged him. Even then, Colin didn't look away. He was enjoying his taunt too much. I straightened and lifted my chin, giving him that same subtle look back.

Colin's torments came in the night, when he called. I never answered, and he never left a message. Just the ring of the phone would send my heart racing. It was his way of letting me know he was still out there. And he was thinking of me.

I was at my office Thursday afternoon, making copies of a flyer for a house I'd listed, when Stewart called. "It's in the judge's hands now."

My breath hitched. "The trial's over?"

"Everything but the verdict. You can be in the courtroom when the verdict is announced. We're hoping it's tomorrow. To be on the safe side, you might want to hang around the courthouse. Then we can have a celebratory drink afterward."

I ignored that part. "Do you think we'll have reason to celebrate?" That was the most terrifying thought, that he'd be acquitted.

"I think we've got a good chance. Because of you, Maggie. If we get a conviction, it'll be because of you."

The defense team had brought in a psychologist "whore," a crude term used for a witness who testified for pay. He'd studied Dana's diary entries and proclaimed her schizophrenic. He'd tried to cast doubt on the whole stalking angle. Crawley had brought in the rest of Dana's co-workers, who testified that they'd never seen Colin act like more than an overeager suitor. The poems were only evidence that someone was stalking her. Someone, but not necessarily Colin. His journal entries didn't mention Dana, but they did prove he had stalking

tendencies. The mystery DNA donor created the biggest
doubt.

I pinched the bridge of my nose. "All right, I'll talk to you
soon."

"Good news?"

I'd forgotten that Serena was standing beside me at the
copier. "We'll probably get a verdict tomorrow."

"Oh, thank God." She gave me a quick hug. "You're so
strong. I can't imagine how you've handled all this."

I'd told her nothing about the threats or, of course, the lie.
I'd tried to keep her out of everything. I knew my friends
would think I'd shut them out, and I suppose they'd be right.
I didn't want to drag them into my darkness. I had nudged
them all away, even Serena.

We were alone in the small room that accommodated the
copying machines. Serena asked in a soft voice, "What will
you do if he's acquitted?"

I couldn't help the shiver that seized my body. "I'll just
die, Serena." Though she took it as an overstatement, I wasn't
so sure. Thinking about that paralyzed me. I couldn't plan for
that, couldn't see anything other than a guilty verdict.

CHAPTER SIXTEEN

Friday morning, when I arrived at the frigid room where Stewart said we could wait for the verdict, I was surprised to see Marcus there, too. I hoped it was a late show of support, maybe a sign that we could patch things up. Stewart took the opportunity to hug me. Marcus, however, didn't stand to greet me in any way, dousing that small flame of hope. I took a seat at the table. Stewart had a briefcase opened on the table, papers set out in neat stacks.

My knitting needles clacked together as I pulled out the blue blanket I was working on.

Stewart chuckled. "I would have never figured you for the knitting type."

I lifted an eyebrow. "And what's that?"

His smile faltered as he sensed the minefield. "You know . . . grandmotherly."

Marcus surprised me by saying, "She makes blankets for the hospital. For stillborns."

"I lost a baby at thirty weeks. The nurse put Jac in my arms, his tiny, lifeless body swaddled in a blanket someone had made so grieving parents wouldn't have to leave the hospital empty-handed. I was able to say good-bye to him and take the blanket home to remember him."

That shut Stewart up.

Marcus stood. "Let me know when we've got a verdict."

He touched my shoulder briefly as he passed, and I had to restrain myself from putting my hand over his. *Stay. Give me hope that you still love me. That you could forgive me.* He moved on, giving me a sad look before closing the door behind him. *I had to do it, Marcus. Why can't you understand?*

My mouth tightened into a frown. We weren't going to survive. I'd destroyed our relationship. I'd also taken Marcus out of Luke's life. I squeezed the blanket with my cold fingers.

Stewart worked; I knitted. I was surprised when he asked, "You hungry?" It was nearly noon.

I was about to say I couldn't think of eating when a man opened the door. "Verdict's in."

Stewart rubbed his hands together. "Showtime."

How could he be so callous when everything hung on the line for me? Even, I knew, my life.

Colin was already seated at his table when we walked in. I sat next to my mother, who had been there through the entire trial. I took her hand and gave it a squeeze. She squeezed back but didn't meet my eyes.

I glanced around and saw Marcus standing near the back of the room. He wasn't looking in my direction. We rose when the judge walked in, then sat again. Colin remained standing, ready to hear his judgment. He looked back at me, and his mouth twitched. Did he think he'd won? Jerry had probably been telling him that. Or maybe Colin thought he was invincible.

I tuned into the judge's words, my fingers rolling that little piece of Dove chocolate tinfoil in my fingers: *Do what feels right.*

"On the charges of aggravated felonious sexual assault and burglary with intent to commit the crime of aggravated felonious sexual assault, I find the defendant guilty."

After waiting with tension coiled in my body, I fell limp. *Guilty. Oh, thank You, God.* I kept replaying the judge's word in my head. *Guilty, guilty, guilty.*

Colin did not seem to have any supporters. No one

gasped or broke down in tears. I couldn't look at him, staring instead at the blanket I'd held in my hands as we'd waited.

The judge continued talking. "The sentencing hearing is tentatively scheduled for August fourth, pending the report from the probation department."

The probation department would investigate Colin's background and the impact his crime had had on our family. Colin would be sentenced based on that.

Crawley argued for bail and, as Stewart had told me would probably happen, was denied. Colin would spend the month before sentencing in the Rockingham County Jail. He was cuffed and led from the courtroom through a side door. He glanced back at me, though, and his look was chilling. Would the years he'd be sentenced to be long enough for him to move on when he was released? Or would he come after me in revenge?

Stewart gave me a thumbs-up from his table as the rest of the people started filing out. I glanced up. *We got him, hon.* Tears burned in my eyes.

My mother stood and blew out a long breath. "This wasn't God's will. I hope He will use it for good anyway."

"He did," I said. "A brutal rapist is behind bars for a long time."

Marcus, I noticed, wasn't anywhere in sight.

I begged off of Stewart's offer of that drink, citing the truth: I was too damned tired. I should have felt triumphant, fired up, happy. To my surprise, I felt empty and ashamed. What gave me a ray of sunshine was knowing Luke would be coming home the next day. I'd missed him so much.

Stewart said, "You'll be able to submit a victim impact statement at the sentencing hearing."

When I walked outside, the last thing I expected was reporters waiting to catch post-trial responses. They were interviewing Jerry, who was proclaiming a miscarriage of justice. When they saw me, they rushed over, hoping, no doubt, for an emotional response.

"Maggie Fletcher, your sister's attacker was convicted. How does that make you feel?"

I hated when reporters asked inane questions on television. *Your father was murdered; how do you feel? Your house has gone up in flames; tells us what you're thinking.*

I wasn't looking into the cameras as I had that night I'd first accused Colin. My voice came out soft when I said, "We got justice for my sister. That's all that matters."

They tried to railroad me into answering more questions, but I gave them a dismissive wave. I walked away, down toward the parking lot. The vultures were still watching, condemning me with their dark stares. When I reached the lot, I spotted Marcus's car, and it looked as though he was sitting in it. I walked over and knocked on the window, startling him out of deep thoughts.

He waved me around to the passenger side, and I got in. All of a sudden I felt angry over his sense of betrayal. Especially now. Especially when he said, "You must be pleased with yourself."

"I'm pleased that we put a sadistic stalker away, yes. I'm pleased that he won't be stalking someone else, at least not in the near future. You should be pleased, too. You won. No tarnish on your reputation." Was that what he'd been so damned worried about? That I'd crack on the stand and cast doubt on his judgment? I couldn't believe he'd pull out the moral issue now.

He shook his head, as though I just didn't get it. His gaze was in the distance. "Maggie, you lied on the stand. You went against everything I believe in. Yeah, maybe we got justice. Maybe we did put a stalker away. But we cheated."

I swallowed what felt like a Ping-Pong ball in my throat. I would never admit my lie, not even now. "What about us?" It was even harder to say those words.

What I hated most was that he wouldn't look at me. "I've lost respect for you, Maggie. I've lost . . . I've lost what I once felt for you."

Tears filled my eyes and I swiped them away. I fought them back, slowly nodding to give me time. "Okay," I said in a throaty whisper. I fumbled for the doorknob behind me, which was infuriatingly hard to find. Finally I turned and grabbed it. I opened the door and stepped outside. He stared at his steering wheel, looking as though he was about to cry, too. "Call me if . . . if you change your mind."

As I walked to my car, I felt in my gut that he wouldn't. I got inside, locked the doors, and sat there as Marcus was doing. I touched the little Mickey and Minnie dangling from my rearview mirror, souvenirs from our last family trip. I spun Mickey in circles. Now I would only have memories of Marcus. No last trip, though. Only the dreams that had died because of my lie.

By ten o'clock I wished I'd asked the Fletchers to bring Luke home that night. I wanted to hold him, his growing-boy pride be damned. I knew it was best that he was coming the next morning, though. I'd already cried out my grief over my lost relationship with Marcus. I'd figured out what I was going to tell Luke about why Marcus wouldn't be coming around anymore. As it turned out, I needed this time to sort my thoughts.

I was going to take Luke to Boston for the weekend, see a play. He loved the theater and, I suspected, loved acting, if the movies he acted out with his friends were any indication. I would put my life back together. Focus on Luke first, restart my career next. I'd been the least productive salesperson in Serena's office for the last month.

Feeling a little more optimistic, I set down the pink blanket I'd been knitting and turned off the light. Bonk got up and meandered down the hall, anticipating my retirement to the bedroom. The phone rang. I didn't have to fear that anymore. Yet I hesitated when I saw *Private* on the screen. Sometimes Marcus's number came through as private, though, so I took the chance and answered.

"Maggie," that low, gravelly voice whispered. "Don't think it's over. We're not finished yet."

I hung up and fumbled with my address book, flipping the little pages until I found myself looking at Marcus's number. I went further, though, and called Stewart.

"Maggie, d'you decide to take me up on that shellabratory drink?"

He'd obviously been doing some "shellabrating" on his own. "No, I need to know something: can Colin make calls from jail?"

"Only collect. Why?"

"Thanks," I said, and hung up. Colin definitely had a friend. A partner in crime. I sank onto the couch and curled up into a ball. And he was after me.

CHAPTER SEVENTEEN

When I opened the door on a sunny Saturday morning, all I saw was Luke. I pulled him into my arms and hugged him tight. He hugged back, making everything feel so much better.

"Oh, I missed you!"

"Me, too," he said, warming my heart.

When I backed away to drink him in with a lonely mother's eyes, I noticed the odd expression on his face. I looked up at Harold and Marion, Wesley's parents. They wore that same questioning expression on their well-bred faces.

I straightened, feeling a pinch of alarm. "What's wrong?"

Harold began to answer, but Luke blurted out, "What's up with the garage door, Mom?"

"What do you mean?" I walked down the concrete path and saw bloodred paint dripping from the word LIAR.

I covered my mouth to contain the sound of fear and surprise.

"You didn't know?" Marion asked.

"No, of course not. I would have painted over it before you got here."

"Who could have done this? And why?" Harold asked, dabbing at the paint with his finger. It was dry.

I started to say, *Colin,* but he couldn't have done this. It had to be his partner.

"It's probably about the trial. Someone trying to make a

point, I guess." I tried hard to look unconcerned. "Let's go inside."

Luke ran in and greeted Bonk, but Harold touched my shoulder as I began to go inside. "Are you sure it's safe for him to be here?" He nodded toward Luke.

Marion said, "He told us you were getting strange calls. Was someone trying to scare you out of testifying?"

"Crank calls. By the time Luke and I return from Boston, this will all be settled down."

They only reluctantly let the issue go. I glanced out toward the street, noticing a neighbor looking at my garage door. I brewed some coffee and asked my in-laws to relax while I took care of the door. Then I ran to the garage, found an old can of paint—never mind that it was blue—and went outside and turned the word into a huge blue flower.

Harold's question haunted me, though: Who could have done this? And why?

Luke and I headed out later that day, after a strained visit with Harold and Marion. Visits with them were never particularly pleasant anyway. I had never been close to them, even when Wesley was alive. I always got the impression that they thought he could have done better, though I later realized they were just overly critical of everything and everyone. Even Wesley had said they were good people but not warm. They'd suggested that Luke stay with them the rest of the summer. If Luke had been in the room, I would have pulled him close at the mere mention of being away from him any longer. I assured them the pranks would end.

Even as Luke and I walked around the Boston Public Garden and laughed at the magician entertaining at a child's birthday party, I kept thinking about Colin's partner, if that's what he was. He'd obviously made the call I'd gotten when I was in the courthouse parking lot. But I'd never seen anyone who appeared to support Colin. A family member would have been at the trial. At the reading of the verdict certainly.

Who thought I'd lied? Colin had been vocal about that. Jerry had believed him. Marcus suspected. Stewart seemed too bloodthirsty to care. I only then heard Luke's voice beside me. "Mom," he said, drawing the one syllable out to three. He was waving his hand in front of me. "Are you in there? Can we get an ice cream?" He pointed to a cart covered with pictures of dancing ice-cream cones.

"Anything you want, sweetie."

He rolled his eyes at the endearment and ran over.

Cone in hand, he licked the drops of ice cream that was already melting a few minutes later. "Too bad Marcus couldn't have come with us. That would've been cool."

I gave a soft agreement, hoping that would end the discussion. I should have known better.

"Mom, when is he going to start coming back around?"

I stopped, turned to him. "He's not going to come around anymore."

"Why not? You said things would be all right once the trial was over."

I felt drops of ice cream drip down over my fingers. "Things have . . . changed between us. Sometimes people grow apart. That's what happened to us."

He absorbed that with a sober expression. "What about me? Isn't he still going to come see me?"

That made me ache. "When adults stop seeing each other, well, it's awkward when they do see each other. It's easier to stay away."

He grew quiet as we made our way back to the parking garage. I had tickets to a small-theater production of *Alice in Wonderland*. When Luke was a child, he loved that story. He was beyond children's stories now, but he was still excited about seeing the play. We were going to a special *Star Wars* exhibit the next day.

"Mom, you forgot to lock the doors!" Luke said as he opened the door and searched for his Game Boy. He'd spent most of the drive playing and the rest fiddling with the radio. "Whew, it's here."

With so much on my mind, forgetting didn't surprise me. I slid into the seat, started the car, and lowered the windows.

The music didn't penetrate my consciousness, not right away. Luke had already started Super Mario on his Game Boy, and its incessant beeps filled the car, along with his own sound effects. I closed the door and put on my belt. Then I heard the song that was playing: "Boum-Boum" by Enigma.

"Luke, change the station," I said, trying to shake the eerie coincidence.

He leaned forward. "It's a CD. Track five."

I slammed on the brakes, sending us both jerking forward. The Game Boy hit the dash and tumbled to the floor. I punched buttons until the disc ejected. The disc. Just as I remembered it from Dana's house. "Did you get this out of our trash can at home?"

He looked at it as though he'd never seen it before. "Nope."

My hand was shaking as I held the disc. "Luke, this is very important. You have never seen this disc?"

He was taking me seriously all right, giving me that same puzzled look I'd seen before. "No, Mom."

"So you didn't put this disc in the stereo? Today? Or at any time?"

"Sheesh, you sound like a lawyer." His expression dampened as he probably thought of Marcus. "No, I haven't touched that disc. Fingerprint it if you don't believe me."

He grunted as he leaned down to retrieve his game. Someone beeped at me, waiting for the spot I'd been about to vacate. I pulled back in, though, and put the car in park. I stared at the disc. I looked for the case. It was nowhere to be found. Just the disc that someone had put in my car. My car that hadn't been locked when it was a habit to lock it.

Even though the car was warm, I felt as cold as the ice cream we'd just eaten. I looked around. But I had no idea who I was even looking for. Not Colin, but an enemy I didn't even know.

◆ ◆ ◆

Colin held a phone grimy from the hands that had held it before. His brief reprieve was making a phone call. His first call. A collect call to the only person whom he would be calling, at least for the time being.

"Get me out of here," he said once the recipient had accepted the call.

"I'm working on it."

"What about Maggie?"

He took a quick breath. "I followed her and her son to Boston."

"And?" Colin prodded, annoyed that he had to.

"I left the CD in her car."

Colin smiled, imagining the look on her face when she heard the song. She'd been spooked about finding that CD at Dana's house. "You know where her weak spot is. It's what you should have focused on last time: her son. You know what you have to do."

"It's already begun."

"I want it to end."

Colin hung up and stood. Soon was not soon enough.

When Luke and I pulled into the driveway Monday afternoon, I searched for any signs of foul play. After finding nothing amiss, I let out a sigh of relief and nudged Luke awake.

"Wake up, sleepyhead. We're home."

Luke was out as soon as I pulled into the garage. "Gonna get Bonk!"

"Wait! Take the bag of tea and tell him thank you." I'd asked our next-door neighbor Mr. Giles to watch Bonk while Luke and I were gone.

I hadn't received a call from the security company. Still, I wanted to make sure no one had been inside before Luke returned. He knocked on Mr. Giles's front door as I unlocked ours. Luke and Bonk were back in seconds. Bonk bounded in, sniffed me, and then checked out the house.

"What'd you do, throw the tea at him?" I asked.

"Naw. But I didn't want to stand there and *talk* to him or anything. I said thanks," Luke said before I could make sure he did. "Here, Mom. Mr. Giles saw them on the porch just a little while ago, said he's sorry he didn't see 'em earlier."

Luke handed me a vase of wilted flowers that had been delivered on Sunday. I squelched the absurd hope that they were from Marcus, in case I was disappointed. I closed the door and took them into the kitchen. Petals rained down on the tile floor behind me. I pulled out the card, puzzled by the "Happy Mother's Day" proclamation on the front. It was a month past.

I turned the card over and my knees went out from under me. I grabbed onto the chair and pulled myself over to it. The inscription, written in green ink, was innocent enough: *Hope to see you soon!* The name beneath that sentence was what had gotten me. *Jac.* My lost baby.

"Who're the flowers from?" Luke asked from somewhere behind me. "Marcus?"

"I . . . don't know."

He was giving me that suspicious look. "Mom. Open Doors, remember?"

He knew about Jac and why I knitted blankets for babies like Jac even if he thought it was a bit "weird." But I couldn't begin to explain the cruelty behind this act. "It's another prank, that's all." Even I could hear the shock in my voice. "Like the word on the garage door."

Luke surprised me by putting his hand on my arm. "You okay, Mom? You don't look so hot."

"I'll be fine. Go on, play with Bonk."

Luke reluctantly accepted my dismissal, going out the back door. I stood by the kitchen window watching them as I dialed the number for the florist. When someone answered, I introduced myself and identified the flower delivery address. I didn't care about the flowers being left on the front porch, but the girl surprised me asking, "Were the flowers in good condition?"

"No, but that's not why I'm calling. I—"

"'Cause instructions were to leave them on the front stoop if no one answered. We thought that was odd, since usually you want to make sure someone's going to be home soon to receive them. But that's what he wanted."

That's when it hit me. He knew I was in Boston. He intended for them to be wilted when I got them. "I need to know who sent the flowers."

"Let me look. . . . It was a cash transaction, a walk-in. Says here 'Jac.' That's all. And it's misspelled, too, without the *k*."

It wasn't misspelled. "What can you tell me about this man?"

"Let me ask Tad. He took the order." She returned a few seconds later. "He said the guy was wearing sunglasses and a cap. He was an older guy, probably in his thirties or forties. But Tad really didn't pay much attention to him."

I made her ask again, but she came back with the same answer. And no, they didn't have video surveillance cameras. "We can replace the flowers—"

"No!" I nearly shouted. "I mean, no, thank you." I hung up, stuffed the flowers into the garbage, tied the bag, and took it out to the can. I picked up the loose petals that led to the kitchen like bread crumbs.

Who knew about Jac? Before I even tried to figure that out, though, I remembered something: the open drawer at my house the night I cleaned out Dana's place. He'd been in here. He'd looked through my things, my personal records. He'd probably looked in my hatbox with the name Jac on the side on my closet shelf and seen the picture of the grave marker and the sonogram.

I felt anger surge at the thought of that personal violation. I always told Luke not to say he hated someone. It's such a strong word. Beyond that, I'd never given it much thought. Sure, I had watched the televised searches for missing girls and seen the men who'd made them dead and felt hatred, anger. I hated what those men did, but I never knew hatred until Colin—and for the person who was doing his dirty work.

‡ ‡ ‡

Tuesday I got back to work. I'd arranged a meeting with Serena to take some of the leads she'd been handling for me. Hers was a small office, with only three agents and herself. I knew my absence, physically and mentally, had been a hardship, and I needed to get back to work for my sanity as well. Luke was in a local summer camp program.

Reese Real Estate was in the quaint downtown section on the Piscataqua River, on Pleasant Street, which became Market Street. Which turned the corner and ran by the coffee shop where Dana had worked. I'd missed the daily grind, the salty air mixed with the scents from the candle shop next door and the Asian restaurant across the street. Our building, tucked side by side in a line of other buildings, looked like a house, with its light blue siding and shuttered windows. We were on the ground floor, easily accessed by beguiled tourists who fancied buying a piece of our paradise.

When I arrived, Serena was scrubbing the front windows. She was dressed impeccably, in linen pants and a silk shirt that camouflaged her belly—nothing suited for cleaning. "Okay, I know you're a neat freak, but I've never seen you quite like this. Don't we have a service that does this?"

Her mouth was set in a grim line. "You're early."

"What does that have to do with—wait, what's going on?" I looked at the window and saw letters at the right side of the smudge of black and soap bubbles: two *R*s.

She didn't look at me. "Just go on inside."

"Not until you tell me what's going on." I made her turn to face me. "Someone wrote something on the window. It was about me, wasn't it?"

I cringed at both the admission on her face and the streak of black on her cream-colored shirt. "I didn't want you to see it. I even got here early, just in case."

"What did it say?" I looked at the letters again and thought of my garage door. "It said: 'Maggie Fletcher is a liar,' didn't it?" The last thing she'd said struck me. "Oh no, this isn't the first time."

She slowly shook her head. "It was here yesterday morning. It's only shoe polish, like the kind the car lots use to write prices on windshields. No harm done."

I took the sponge from her hand and finished the cleaning. "Thank you for trying to protect me. He struck my house, too."

"Oh, Maggie, I'm so sorry. I wanted this to be over for you."

Soap squished between my fingers as I scrubbed. "Someone's harassing me, that's all." I wouldn't tell her about the flowers. "Someone who's allied with Colin apparently. Or he has the ability to astral project or whatever that's called when you can leave your body."

"Maggie, that's crazy—"

"I don't actually believe in that nonsense."

"I mean, *this* is crazy. After everything you've gone through."

I scrubbed off the last of the polish. "I'm not going to let it get to me. I can't. Colin, and probably his friend, tried to scare me away from testifying. This is just retaliation." I dropped the sponge in the bucket. "It'll pass."

Serena hugged me. I didn't need words of comfort, and I was glad she didn't give them. She stepped back. "At least I've got a good lead for you. A couple in Greenland wants to list their house with you. He said they were referred by a friend of the Schillers."

That was the best comfort she could give me: a return to normalcy. I'd recently gotten a card from the Schillers thanking me for selling their home so quickly. I splashed the rest of the soapy water onto the window and started to go inside to fill the bucket with clean water. Something made me turn around. I could feel someone watching me. Probably enjoying this. *Bastard.*

I'd lied to Serena. I wasn't sure if this would pass soon. And more terrifying, I wasn't sure how far it would go.

CHAPTER EIGHTEEN

I was supposed to meet a Mr. and Mrs. Fillmore at their farmhouse at one o'clock that Wednesday. Right after dropping Luke off at summer camp, where they were going to Water Country for a day of frolicking, I drove by the office. My heart sank. Serena was out there again, washing off the lettering and dealing with someone she was trying to ignore.

I found a curbside spot and walked over just as the young man walked away. "Let me." I took the sponge from her. "This is ridiculous. I should call the police."

"No," Serena said, surprising me with her quick response. "Not on my account. I don't want the publicity. That guy"— she nodded toward the man who'd been talking to her—"is a reporter. Seeing me out here three days in a row cleaning the windows got his attention. Tomorrow he'll be out here early, probably, so he can see what it is I'm erasing."

I finished washing away the residue. "I'll come as soon as it starts getting light. I'll take care of it if he does it again."

"And what are you going to do with Luke? Summer camp doesn't start that early. You don't want him seeing this."

She was right. "I'll figure out a way."

When I pulled onto the Fillmore property, my internal property assessor tilted into the way-fixer-upper category. Out in the country. The yard a field of weeds, as was the surrounding property. It had once been a nice family farm. A long time ago.

I assumed the Fillmores were quite old. Not only because of the quiver in his voice; he'd said the kids hadn't taken any interest in the property and neither had the grandchildren, their last hope. He'd sounded like my dad's dad, who had passed on years before: sweet, affable. The Fillmores couldn't find good help and couldn't manage it on their own. They wanted to move closer to town, an apartment with no maintenance. They were already selling off the furniture.

I'd expected a slightly neglected property. This place looked . . . abandoned. It just had that air about it. I didn't see a car, either, though it could be in the garage. Someone had recently trimmed the walkway, at least, and the windows were clean and open to let in the summer breeze. Meager attempts to make the house presentable. The front porch steps creaked as I took them. When I knocked I saw that the door wasn't latched. Since they were expecting me, I took it as an invitation and stepped inside.

"Hello? Mr. and Mrs. Fillmore? It's Maggie Fletcher."

My purse and cell phone were in the car. I would go back and call if no one came out. I certainly wasn't going to hunt them down. I searched for any redeeming features while I waited. *Cozy? Starter farm?* The floorboards creaked, too, which meant the whole flooring system might need to be replaced. *Tear down.* Oddly, I saw nothing of a personal nature. No pictures, decorations, or even fireplace implements.

The place looked empty. Too empty.

Goose bumps prickled my skin. I started to turn around when I saw a note propped up on a box of cheese crackers on the kitchen counter. I felt a modicum of relief and stepped forward. Maybe the Fillmores were out back.

The kitchen was fairly clean, with two bowls and two glasses in the sink. An opened box of bran cereal had been left out. The folded note had my name scrawled across the front. I opened it and read the blocky writing:

DO YOU KNOW WHERE YOUR SON IS?

I blinked in disbelief even as my heart started racing. A setup. This had been a setup. Oh, my God, Luke, on a field trip in a public place with strangers all around! I dropped the note and ran for the door. I had closed it, but I hadn't locked it. So why wasn't it opening? I pushed against it, tried the lock the other way even though I knew I hadn't locked it . . . it still wouldn't open.

He was here.

I couldn't breathe. I sucked in breath after breath as I struggled with the door. My gaze went to the open windows facing the front porch. No screens, and, I now noticed, no glass, either. It had been neatly broken away to make it look clean. I raced toward the front window, threw my leg over the sill, and pulled myself through. I didn't even look at the door to see what had been blocking it. I saw only my car and nearly tripped down the stairs.

Luke, Luke, Luke.

The refrain pounded through my brain as I ran to my car. I amazed myself with the forethought to check the backseat and make sure no one crouched there. I shoved the key into the ignition and nearly cried in relief when the car started. I threw it into gear and backed all the way out of the drive. I saw the faded sign lying in the grass where it was tucked into the bushes near the end of the drive. I saw the words AUC-TION, FORECLOSURE.

With only a glance to check traffic, I backed onto the two-lane highway, threw the car into drive, and tore out. I was panting in panic. *Luke. What had he done to Luke?*

My hands were shaking. I'd been in an abandoned house. Alone. I'd been duped. I could have been killed.

But I was more scared for my son at the moment. I reached for my purse, which I always tucked beneath the front seat when I was showing property. It was small, containing minimal cash, my license, and one credit card. What I wanted was my cell phone. With one hand on the wheel and one hand rummaging through my purse, I screamed in frustration when I couldn't find it. I needed to call the summer camp office.

I finally pulled off the side of the road and gave the search my whole attention. No phone. I'd had it with me; I was sure of that. I'd made a few business calls on the drive out to the farm. I searched beneath the seat, then my seat, then the backseat. No phone. I pulled back out and drove twenty miles over the limit to find the gas station I'd passed on the way out. I hoped a cop would pull me over, but none did.

"Please, Lord, don't let him hurt my son. Please, please, please."

I prayed all the way to the gas station in a voice on the edge of hysteria. I charged into the gravel parking lot fifteen minutes later, fumbling with change as I tore over to the phone booth. I'd looked up the phone number at a traffic light. I dropped a bunch of change into the slot and asked for Marcy, the camp's manager.

Interrupting her pleasant greeting, I said, "Marcy, it's Maggie Fletcher. I need you to find my son."

"What? Maggie, slow down. Luke's with the group at Water Country, remember?"

"I know," I gritted out. "But someone's threatened him. I need you to call George or whoever is with the kids and make sure Luke's all right."

"Threatened? My God, Maggie—"

"Just call him!" I rattled off the number for the phone booth and told her to call me right back.

Two cars' worth of people came and went while I waited. They couldn't help but notice the agitated woman muttering and pacing in front of the phone booth. I thought about what my cell phone's disappearance meant. He'd been there, blocking the door, taking my phone so I'd have to go through this agony. He was cruel. How far would he go?

I jumped when the phone rang and snatched it up. "Yes?"

It wasn't George's voice, nor was it Marcy's. It was *his* voice. "Maggie, I told you this wasn't over." It changed to something that sounded like Jim Carrey. "If I'm lying, I'm dying." He chuckled, the son of a bitch.

"If you touch my son—"

With another laugh, he disconnected.

I slammed the phone on the hook and searched the area. He was watching me. No, he just knew I'd have to come here because he'd swiped my damned phone. Rage and anger bubbled inside me.

When the phone rang again, I grabbed it. "Call your cell number," he said.

I hung up. He was toying with me, tying up the line on purpose. When the phone rang again, I picked it up more slowly. "Yes?"

"Maggie, it's Marcy. Luke's fine."

I nearly collapsed, and the phone fell from my hand. I could hear Marcy talking, and still in a crouch, I grabbed it and heard her say, "He's been with the group the whole time, and according to George, no one's tried to approach him. Should I call the police?"

"I'll do that. Tell George to never let him out of his sight until I get there."

"I will. He's worried about the other kids."

"This guy's playing games with me. He only wants Luke. Tell George I'm coming straight to the park." I wanted to hold Luke, touch him, make sure he was all right.

I started to head out but remembered his last call. I dropped more coins into the slot and dialed my cell number. I followed the muffled ringing toward my car. I popped the trunk. My cell phone was tucked into the corner. Right where he'd put it.

Luke sat in one of the interview rooms immersed in his Game Boy and the new game I'd just bought him. "Grrr . . . boom! Gotcha." I was in an adjacent room with Detective Armstrong and Detective Thurmond. I'd requested that Thurmond be there, too, because he knew Colin best. It amused me how my view of Thurmond had changed since that first meeting when I thought he looked like a member of the Munster family. Now his droopy face looked intelligent and even dignified in a unique way. Once he sat down, I looked at both of them and said, "Colin Masters is stalking me."

Armstrong blinked those bulbous eyes, though he commendably kept his disbelief from showing. "The Masters who's in prison?"

"No. Yes. I mean, obviously it's not him physically. He has someone stalking me." I started with the phone calls I knew Colin hadn't made, then the word painted on my garage door. "He's painted the front window of my broker's office three days in a row."

"Do you have pictures?"

Oh, jeez, I'd never thought about taking pictures. I'd just wanted the words gone. "No. But he'll do it again. And I'll get pictures. Serena Reese, my broker, can tell you. My in-laws can tell you about the garage door. But it's getting worse."

I told them about the CD in Boston and then what had happened today. "He put a lot of work into this. The story about the furniture being sold, hiding the sign, doing a little cleanup. What I can't figure out is how he got the Schillers' name." Then I did. "He was in my house, saw the card they sent me."

Armstrong jotted down something. "But he didn't actually harm you."

I surged to my feet. "He threatened my son's safety!" I sank back down to the chair at his raised eyebrow.

"Do you have the note?"

I twirled my worry curl, feeling some relief from the winding motion. "Gathering evidence wasn't my top priority at the moment. Sorry," I added when I realized how snippy I'd sounded. "I just wanted out of there."

"I understand. We'll ask the sheriff's department to check out the house. Technically, we have a break-in. Maybe the note's still there."

"I doubt it. The guy was there. I'm sure he grabbed it when he left. Maybe the sheriff's office can fingerprint the place." I turned to Thurmond. "Did you find anyone in Colin's life who could be his partner? A brother or friend?"

Thurmond always seemed injected with energy; he had fiddled with a pencil and adjusted his chair and moved constantly as I'd told them what had been happening to me. Now he leaned over the table and drummed his fingers on the surface. "No one. He grew up in a middle-class neighborhood. Everything was pretty normal until he was eight. That's when his father committed suicide. His mother was, according to a couple of the longtime neighbors, a real bitch. Manipulative, controlling. It's what probably sent Daddy packing. They thought she was abusive, but there was never any proof. No marks or bruises. The kid wouldn't say anything. That's pretty normal. They'd rather have the devil they know than the one they don't."

Thurmond propped his ankle on his leg and jiggled it. "When he was ten, Mom dearest met some gambler who swept her off her feet. Promised her a better life but didn't have room for a sullen kid. So she sent him off to his grandmother's apartment, ostensibly for a visit while she and her guy had an extended honeymoon. They never came back for him. He lived with Granny until she died a few years ago. The first restraining order was filed soon after that. Stalking behavior often starts after a major life change or trauma. He went through a series of dead-end jobs. Hasn't had a real job in years, though he reports a nominal income to the IRS as an artist."

Armstrong asked, "What made him the way he is, d'you think?"

"Clearly he felt betrayed and abandoned, first by his father and then his mother. His life felt out of control for a long time. Could be the control factor that drives him, especially with the mother's personality. I found another theory, too, based on Erik Erikson's eight stages of human development. We're born with an innate need for relationships. To form a relationship, we must put ourselves out there and risk rejection or criticism. If a child's trust is constantly trampled, he still needs relationships. But he won't risk the negative aspect of them. So he views the other person as an object, something to possess and control. The possession fills that need inside him, and his object becomes the focus of his life."

Dana had been an object to him. I had become an object, too. A focus for him. My lie probably fueled his hatred as well as his need to possess. Now he was in prison, and *my* focus was on finding out who was helping him.

I took a sip of the bottle of water Armstrong had gotten for me. "He could have half brothers or sisters."

Armstrong said, "We didn't see any family pictures at either of his residences. No letters. So if he has any, he's probably not in touch with them."

"Who visits him in prison?"

"We can check that."

"What's tricky about this," Thurmond said, "is that we don't know what we're dealing with. A minion who might do whatever Colin tells him to? Knowing Colin as we do, that could be as dangerous as Colin stalking you himself. Or is it someone unrelated to Colin altogether?"

"He knows too much about me. He's making this very personal. He sent me flowers from a baby I miscarried ten years ago. Just like he probably saw that card, he must have seen my mementos." I shivered at that, the way I always did when I thought about him in my home. "It's like he's under my skin." The way he'd been with Dana.

Thurmond had written everything down, but his expression showed only frustration. Was he worrying that he'd once again find an answer too late?

Armstrong looked like a man caught in a tight situation.

I said, "I know you can't do anything without proof. Really, I understand that. We don't even have a suspect. I want this on record, that's all." I was struck at how similar this was to Dana's ordeal. Feeling frustrated that nothing could be done, afraid that the officer would think I was imagining things, and feeling so very violated. I stood. "Keep looking into Colin's life. There's got to be a relative or friend, someone important. Who else would do his bidding like this? Risk being caught?"

Armstrong closed his notepad. "I will."

When I went to collect Luke, he was understandably annoyed. His arms were crossed in front of him, his lower lip pushed out as we walked out. "Mom, why couldn't I be in there? I should know what's going on."

"You do know. Someone's playing pranks on me, and I want the police to be aware of it. But I don't want to scare you."

"*You're* scared."

I pressed on to our car. "I'm concerned."

"You weren't just *concerned* when you came to spoil my day at Water Country and make me look like a freak. You were all wigged-out. You hugged me in front of *everyone*."

The way he'd said it, I was surprised *he* hadn't tried to file a report at the station. It made me smile, though, and I was grateful for that. "Sorry, I overreacted." I hadn't told him everything, just that someone had called and asked if I knew where he was. It sounded much less sinister that way. Unfortunately, it made me sound over the edge.

When I reached our car, I stopped cold. Beneath my windshield wiper was a rose. A wilted rose.

CHAPTER NINETEEN

I had warned Luke about the early morning we'd have, but he still groaned when I kissed him on the cheek with a loud raspberry sound and said, "Time to get up."

He lifted his head with a quick jerk and whined, "It's only five in the morning!"

"I know, but this is important. We'll go out to breakfast afterward."

Food was always a great motivator, especially the prospect of greasy stuff like bacon and hash browns, since he was trying to get bigger and grow faster.

I was dragging, too, having slept little the night before. My first dream—nightmare—replayed the abandoned-house scenario, but when I called the camp they didn't know where Luke was. I'd never gotten back to sleep after that.

We drove into downtown as the sun rose. It was eerily quiet—too early for tourists and even most of the people who welcomed them. I was ready for words scrawled across the glass. I hoped he wouldn't use profanity. In fact, as we neared the office I tried to distract Luke by pointing out a family of ducks crossing the road. When I saw the front window, my quick intake of breath brought his attention back.

"Oooooh, my gosh," he said when I couldn't manage words.

The front window had been smashed. I spotted Serena inside, with her husband and Bobby. When I saw what they were doing, my heart slammed through the ground. I pulled to the curb, and we jumped out.

"Serena . . ." It was all I could utter as I watched David Reese, renowned psychologist, picking up pieces of a shattered desk. He was broad-shouldered, with large hands and thick gray hair. He kept a caring and professional eye on his wife.

I recognized the signs of shock: the paleness of her face, the emptiness in her eyes. I had seen that on my own face. I ran to hug her, though she barely returned the gesture.

"I'm so sorry," I said. "I didn't know." I took in the destruction. "I didn't know he'd go this far."

Did I imagine a trace of anger on her face? Only a flash, there and gone? "The alarm went off at two o'clock. We met the police here." She looked around. "This is what we found."

I wanted to hug her again, but that trace—imagined or not—kept my arms at my side. Bobby was excitedly showing Luke the damage in the back offices. It had been a trash-and-slash session, carried out in a matter of minutes while the alarm pealed.

"Was anything taken?"

Serena dumped the elephant figurine she'd been trying to piece together. "No. Someone wanted to tear the place up. Everything . . . everything's been ruined."

David, unhooking the smashed monitor from a dented computer, came over and put his arms around her. She started to cry, which unleashed my own tears. And, I was surprised to find, a pang of envy and longing to have someone hold me when I cried. I felt horrible and callous for the feelings and pushed them away. I also felt guilty, as though I were personally responsible for this, even though I knew that's what he wanted.

I heard bitterness in David's voice. "The police found the sledgehammer they think the guy used. He smashed it through the front door, unlocked it, and went to work."

I noticed black smudges of powder. "No prints?"

"They figure he wore gloves, which would make sense. I doubt he left anything behind. Except for all of this."

Serena, still in David's arms, let out a despairing cry. This successful office had been her dream. She had risked so much to make it work, and she *had* made it work. She'd carefully decorated the place in a soft seaside theme that felt warm and welcoming. Now I, through my stalker, had destroyed it, just as Hurricane Andrew had destroyed everything before.

I started collecting the papers that were strewn everywhere. "Serena, why don't you take the boys for breakfast and then to summer camp? I'll get all the paperwork organized, call the Dumpster company when they open, call the glass company, and start putting everything out back. You come back when you're ready." I turned to David. "I'm sure you have appointments to keep, too."

He nodded. "But I'll work until my first one at ten thirty and then come back between appointments."

The boys, though, emerged from the back area with their arms full of broken desk parts. "Where should we put these?"

Pride and wonderment washed over me at their attitude. "Put them outside in one big pile. We can transfer them to the Dumpster when it comes."

The boys balked at the idea of leaving, so we let them stay. I called Armstrong and let him know about the vandalism, and he promised to check with the officer who'd taken the report. As the employees and owners of the neighboring businesses arrived, they expressed shock and outrage and left with promises to help during their breaks. After David left, I found myself alone with Serena for a few minutes. The boys were out back playing slam dunk with the small pieces into the Dumpster.

I touched her arm. "I quit."

She'd been working quietly, a mixture of expressions crossing her face at times. Now I could see that she wanted me to go but felt bad about it. "No, Maggie—"

"Yes. I can't involve you in my problems anymore.

You've been a wonderful friend through all of this." I took in the room. "But friendship can only stretch so far."

She didn't argue further, just nodded, picked up another box filled with broken things, and walked toward the back door. I didn't hold it against her. I glanced out the front window where cars passed and people gawked. No, I held it against *him*. But how was I supposed to fight him when I didn't know who he was? Or exactly what he wanted?

By the end of the night I felt as though I'd been fed through a shredder. Frustration and guilt clawed at me. My arms and legs ached from hauling debris. I was hot and tired and angry and scared. Jobless. I even felt guilty over feeling sorry for myself, for Pete's sake.

"Mom, have you seen Bonk?" Luke asked, tearing me out of my funk where I was poured into Wesley's green easy chair.

"I let him out . . . well, I guess it was about half an hour ago."

Luke opened the back door and called. Bonk always came right away when called.

"Wait!" I shouted when Luke took a step outside. "I'll go. Stay on the step."

"Mom?" I could hear a tremor of fear in his voice.

"He's fine, I'm sure." But I *wasn't* sure. Anything out of the norm caused alarm. I turned on the backyard lights, passed Luke, and stepped out into the yard. The corners were still in shadow, as was the swing set because of the peach tree. "He's probably just in the middle of doing his business." Around me I could hear the sounds of summer: crickets, distant laughter, even the lingering aroma of a barbecue grill. All of those lovely, normal-life sounds seemed so far from my not-normal life. "Bonk! Come here, boy!"

Our yard was fenced in and buffered by thick, green hedges for privacy. No way could Bonk get out. I walked around the perimeter anyway, ducking down to see if I could spot four legs. I checked the gate in the front and saw that it was latched.

Then I heard a shuffling sound. I stopped. Listened. Followed it to the swing set. The plastic shower curtain we'd put around the bottom of the fort shivered with movement. Whimpering shot my hairs straight up.

Oh no, not the dog. It would tear me up, but it would destroy Luke.

"Mom, didya find him?"

"Stay there!" I ordered, cringing when I realized how harsh it had come out. If something had happened, I didn't want Luke to see. I knew from my research that stalkers sometimes hurt or killed their victims' pets.

I walked closer to the curtain, my heart lodged at the back of my mouth. My feet crunched softly on the grass. The curtain shimmered again. Another whimper. It was darker here, though I could make out the swing set.

I reached for the part in the curtains. I looked back at Luke, at his anxious face and the way his feet were just barely on the step. I held out my hand as another reminder to stay put, not trusting my voice. Another thought occurred to me: what if Colin's partner was using the dog to lure me out? But I couldn't wait for the police to come, not if Bonk was hurt. If *he* was in there, too, Luke could call for help. I'd taught him how to do that. He, at least, would get away.

My fingers trembled as I grabbed the edge of the curtain and gave it a violent shove to the side. I was prepared for almost anything, but I wasn't prepared for what I found: Bonk, in the shadows, straining toward me, in one piece. Bonk, alive. I searched the rest of the tiny space, but only saw the dog—and the cause of his whimpering. He'd been tied to one of the posts with a leash. A leash that wasn't ours. He'd been straining to free himself.

I unsnapped the clip, and he knocked me over in gratitude, licking my face and making happy dog sounds. Luke was calling him, though, and Bonk raced to the back door. Raced, like a dog that was unhurt. I backed away like a crab, in case of a trap. Then I turned and stumbled toward the steps where Bonk was getting loving from a relieved boy.

Except that Luke was studying something on Bonk's rump with a puzzled expression. He looked up at me as I approached. "Mom, that man did this. He put a word on him. 'Lira.' No . . . that's not right."

I looked at the dog's side. The word LIAR had been shaved into his brown fur.

" 'Liar,' " Luke corrected. I'd noticed his dyslexia kicking in since all of this strange stuff had started.

He'd been in my backyard; he'd had my dog. He had sent me a message. But he hadn't hurt the dog. At least he hadn't hurt the dog.

"Mom, when is he going to stop?" Luke asked, his arms protectively around Bonk.

I ushered Luke inside and locked the door. "I'm calling the police."

When Detectives Armstrong and Lanier arrived a short while later, I tried for some lame humor. "We've got to stop meeting like this."

Armstrong only grunted; Lanier at least gave me a ghost of a smile.

I sent Luke to his room so I could talk freely and then led them out to the backyard. They checked the swing set and determined that he'd set no trap for me. They looked over the yard and even walked around the house. When they came around to the front again, I opened the door. They only came in as far as the foyer.

"I think he's playing games with you," Armstrong said.

"Games? He"—I glanced to make sure Luke wasn't lurking—"threatened my son."

"Didn't actually threaten," Armstrong clarified.

Lanier said, "Implied threat."

"Semantics! What about the vandalism?"

"We don't know for sure that it's the same guy."

I tilted my head and made a sound of disbelief.

"What I can say is that so far he hasn't actually attempted to hurt you."

"That's what the cop told Dana when we first reported her stalker."

"But this isn't Colin Masters."

I let out a long, loud breath. I wanted to stamp my feet and throw something. I knew the score, but I didn't have to like it. "Maybe when I'm dead you'll figure out who it is."

Armstrong winced and his expression softened. He lifted the bag holding the leash. "Maybe—"

"Forget that. He's not going to slip up and forget to wear his gloves. Good night, gentlemen. I'm sure I'll be in touch again soon."

As soon as I locked the door and set the alarm system, I walked to Luke's bedroom, but he was sound asleep, fully dressed, with Bonk on the bed beside him. Bonk looked at me but didn't move. Luke's hand was lying on Bonk's back, telling me how scared Luke had been for his safety. The hitch in my chest propelled me to walk over and brush his damp hair from Luke's forehead. I planted a kiss there. I kissed Bonk's head, too. I watched them for a few more minutes, drinking in the sight, and then I left.

I'd been flippant in my send-off to the detectives, but I felt anything but that inside. I was angry and terrified. Right now Colin's partner was trying to scare me. He'd done something every day for nearly a week since the guilty verdict. I had no reason to think he'd stop now. And I had every reason to believe he would stop at nothing to make me pay for my lie.

CHAPTER TWENTY

I was taking Luke to summer camp the following morning when my cell phone rang. I had no clients, no broker, and, until this was resolved, no intention of resuming my career. I was never so aware of a real estate agent's vulnerability until the farmhouse incident. Maybe it was my mother canceling our breakfast date. My heart jumped when I saw the name on the screen: Vasquez. I pulled off the road and took the call.

"This is Maggie Fletcher?" she asked with a slight Spanish accent.

"Yes, I'm Maggie. You're Marisol?"

"Yes." She sounded hesitant. "You left a message on my machine a while back. I . . . I'm sorry I couldn't testify. I hear he could get up to thirty-five years. But . . . he could be paroled, right?"

"It's possible, but he'll have to serve a minimum sentence." Had she called just to verify the sentence? I didn't press her.

"I think we should talk. If you could come here, to Boston. I don't leave the house much."

I remembered her brother and felt my chest tighten. "Sure. Today is good for me." Ever the realtor, I pulled out my notepad and pen, ready to write down directions.

"My apartment is probably the best place to talk." She gave me her address. "Come anytime. I'm always home."

She sounded sad, but I held in any sympathy that might creep into my voice and bid her good-bye.

"Who was that?" Luke asked as I continued on down the road.

I had a fleeting thought to make up something, but I didn't want to cut him out, not when it wasn't to protect him. "That was Marisol Vasquez, one of Colin's victims. She wants to talk to me. In Boston."

It only then occurred to me that maybe it wasn't Marisol. Maybe this was another trap. I would be a long ways from Luke.

"What about?" he was asking as my mind raced.

"I'm not sure. But it sounded important." I wrote out the address she'd given me, then Detective Armstrong's number. "If I'm not there by five, call Armstrong. Tell him where I went."

"Mom, you're scaring me."

"I'm sorry. I'm probably overreacting, but I can't afford to take any chances."

I had wanted to keep Luke home that day, but he'd whined about being bored. There were no field trips planned, so the kids would be inside the building or in the playground. The staff had already been put on alert.

"Mom, he's not . . . He won't hurt you, will he? Like he did Dana?"

"It's not the same guy. He just wants to scare me."

When the phone rang again, I answered without looking at the screen. It was his voice, though; I recognized it instantly, the way he curled my name possessively around his tongue.

"Are we having fun yet?"

I hung up, steeled my expression, and turned to Luke. "Probably a lost signal."

When we arrived at camp, I walked in with Luke (embarrassing him), but I didn't give him a hug. I wanted to so badly my arms ached with it. I'd already done enough damage to his cool reputation. I tucked the piece of paper into his backpack. I waved at Bobby, who was racing to the front, and reminded the staff again about my stalker.

"My stalker." How I hated those words. But not as much as I hated him.

"Maggie, didn't I warn you about this?" My mother's shrill voice drilled into my brain as we had breakfast at a home-style café.

I only picked at my hash browns, hadn't even touched the two fried eggs that reminded me of eyes. "I didn't tell you this so you could go pull an 'I told you so.' I just want you to be aware . . . in case someone approaches you, or something strange happens."

Mom stabbed at her last piece of ham. "Maybe this is the person who really assaulted Dana. Did you think of that? That you put the wrong man away?" She jammed the piece into her mouth and chewed furiously.

"Mom, if you had seen Colin at the police station that day . . . if you'd heard what he'd said about how Dana hadn't fought back . . ." I shook my head. "No way could he know she had no defense wounds unless he was there. Now he's got a friend out there trying to scare me."

I found myself wondering if I should tell my mother about my arrangements, should anything happen to me. I'd stipulated in my trust that Luke live with Serena and David Reese. My son would be miserable with my mother, and she'd probably turn him into an atheist by cramming religion down his throat. I'd decided on the cowardly route by not telling her or Wesley's parents. They could curse me after I was dead, but I had to do what was best for Luke.

Her hands were cool when she grasped my hands. "Take back your lie. Make things right. Then this person will go away. God will restore your life."

"God's not doing this, Mom. A man is doing it. A man taking revenge into his own hands." I pushed my plate away. "I've got to get going. I've got an appointment in Boston." I hadn't mentioned the vandalism at the real estate office. I knew someday that withholding information was going to come back and bite me in the ass if forgot what I hadn't said.

I had more pressing things to worry about, though. I left money on the table for the meal and too much tip, kissed my mother's soft cheek, and said, "I love you, Mom."

She was startled at the statement. We didn't often exchange those kinds of sentiments. She gave me a hug. "I love you, too. I'll pray for you, Maggie."

"Do, Mom."

I would probably need it.

Colin waited for the person on the other end to accept his call, another sign of the powerlessness he suffered here. Asking permission to do every damned thing, waiting his turn, constantly being on alert, and having no privacy.

The man finally accepted the collect call. "It's progressing. I shaved the dog."

"How'd she take that?"

"I couldn't stick around. There were too many people outside as it was. But I'm sure it rattled her."

"I want her more than rattled. I want her terrified. And I want you to stick around and let me know just how scared she is. Since I can't see for myself," Colin ground out. "Pictures?"

"You should get them in the next few days. They're not great, but you'll get the gist. And a couple of her cleaning the office window."

"With a good shot of the expression on her face?"

"When she looked for whoever had done it."

"Fear? Anxiety?" Colin said on a low breath.

"Definitely."

"Beautiful." His fingers twitched at the thought of having new Maggie pictures. Pictures always gave him a feeling of power. As though having them equaled possessing her. Wasn't there some Indian tribe that feared having their pictures taken because they believed the camera would capture their souls? Maybe they were right. "Get them here right away." He realized he sounded like a drug addict desperate for a fix. "What about the other part of the plan?"

"Working on it, but that's going to take time. You'll just have to trust me."

"I trusted you before. You wimped out."

"I won't wimp out this time. Trust me, she's scared. It's only a matter of time."

Colin hung up and smiled. The guard escorted him to his cell, where he settled on his bunk with his sketch pad. He'd been here less than a week and he already had a nickname: Nails. He chewed nails. His fingernails, that was. The tough, nasty guys had been grossed out that he ate the nails. He'd made alliances, though. He knew how to score cigarettes, crack, and meth. He had need for none of them. What he craved was sushi, a six-pack of ice-cold beer, and the pictures.

He reached under his mattress and took out a photo of Maggie he'd taken before the trial. She'd been getting into her car but looking around. Looking for him. He treasured that scared-rabbit look he produced in his pets. He rubbed his thumb over her face. He wasn't going to be in here much longer. "Then we'll meet again, Maggie-the-dolly. We will meet again."

Marisol didn't live in the best neighborhood, but it wasn't the worst, either. The graffiti didn't look threatening and wasn't pervasive. I found a parking spot in the lot and stepped out of my car. As I stretched, I watched for cars that were just driving into the lot. I'd constantly checked the rearview mirror during the drive. I had become Dana, watchful, careful, and, yes, paranoid.

Neither driver of the two cars that pulled into the lot after me looked familiar, though that didn't mean anything. More important, they didn't look in my direction.

Beer cans littered the hallway. I smelled marijuana as I passed one grimy door, searching for the number. Eighteen's door was clean, at least.

I knocked, and a few seconds later the door opened. Above the chain a woman, in shadow, peered out. Her long, dark hair draped over her shoulders.

"Marisol? I'm Maggie Fletcher."

She closed the door, I heard the chain release, and she opened it again. She looked out into the hallway before stepping back. "Please, come in."

I caught my breath when I saw her face. She seemed resigned to the shock, turning to the living room.

"Mama, this is the lady I told you about." She turned to me. "This is my mother; that's my brother, Manuel."

The small apartment was cluttered with furniture, knick-knacks, and laundry in various states of being folded. Mama sat on the couch doing that folding. She hardly looked at me, this Spanish woman with salt-and-pepper hair who reminded me of my mother. Especially with the disparaging look she gave her daughter. Marisol's mother said something I didn't understand, but I got the gist. She didn't want Marisol talking to me.

Her brother, a thin young man, sat in a nearby chair folding and refolding one shirt. His movements were awkward and childlike as he tried to match up the sleeves. He didn't even notice I was there. He spoke in a slur as he gestured to something on the television.

My gaze went to a row of pictures on the fireplace mantel. There I saw what he had looked like in early years, obviously a healthy, robust young man. I saw Marisol, too, beautiful and smiling. Manuel, frustrated by his inability to match the sleeves, threw the shirt on the table and then threw the rest of the laundry all over the living room. His mother calmly picked it up.

"Come, let's sit at the table," Marisol said.

The small table lent a view of the parking lot below, and I knew I'd have to keep my gaze from drifting down. Once Marisol sat on the opposite side, I realized that wouldn't be a problem. She was striking, in more ways than one. Large, brown eyes fringed with thick eyelashes; a lush, curvy mouth; and puffy red lines slashed across her face.

"You're wondering if he did this," she said. "The truth is, I don't know. I may never know."

I nodded, hoping that my expression didn't show how

much I wanted it to be unrelated to Colin, like a car accident or gang violence. "I'm . . . sorry." Such an understatement.

"I wanted you to know . . . I thought I should tell you . . ." She looked up at the ceiling. "You seem like a strong woman."

I was surprised by that assessment. As I am only five-foot-two, most people viewed me as just the opposite. "I don't feel so strong sometimes," I said. My fingers went to my worry curl.

"I'm sorry I didn't testify." She glanced at her mother. "I couldn't take the chance that he would come back. Again."

Maybe Marisol's mother had talked her out of testifying. How odd, that my mother had tried to talk me out of my testimony, too. "Why do you think he'd come back?"

She fiddled with a large bib that was lying on the table. I tried not to think of the implications of that bright blue bib, considering I saw no children's items in the apartment. "This is why I had to return your call. I couldn't do it earlier; I was afraid you would try to talk me into testifying."

"I would have," I admitted. "Maybe it'll make you feel better that we didn't need your testimony after all."

She was staring down at the cracked red polish on her nails. "I don't feel better. I don't think I can ever feel better."

"But he's been put away," I said, though that hadn't helped me any.

"That's what I had to tell you. Colin keeps grudges for a long, long time. I know you feel safe now that he's away."

"I don't," I caught myself saying. Did she know about his partner?

"Good. Because he'll get out. He'll go after you. He'll never let you go."

I twisted my curl so hard I nearly wrenched it out of my scalp.

"The only way," she continued, "might be to run. Hide. Change your name."

"I couldn't do something so drastic." But I knew that was the only way to escape a sadistic stalker. Thurmond had said so. I remembered thinking how terrible it would be to leave your life to escape someone you'd never invited there to begin with. I pushed those thoughts from my mind. "I know he stalked you. Your brother threatened him."

"My brother had his friends beat Colin up. We thought that would be the final answer. I didn't want violence. But, as your sister knew, after he's been stalking you for months, you'll do anything to get rid of him."

My mouth twitched as I fought it from turning down. She obviously didn't know how Dana had escaped him, and I wasn't going to tell her.

"You probably know what Colin did to my brother." She glanced at him for a moment. "I tried to get him put away for that, but there wasn't enough evidence. I don't think the police looked very hard to convict a white man for a Puerto Rican man's injury, especially a known gang member."

She tucked her arms around her waist. "Eight months later, as I left work one night, I was attacked. Raped. And the man who did it, he cut my face. He didn't try to kill me. I thought I was lucky, you know, that he hadn't cut me anywhere that would kill me. But later, I realized he didn't want me to die. He wanted me to live." Her voice had gotten thick, and she gestured toward her face. "With this. With my brother."

Her eyes were wide now. "I thought about Colin right away, you see. But it had been so long since my brother's beating. I hadn't seen him around. I thought it was over. I thought this was just a random attack, as the police did. The police did verify he was living in New Hampshire. They didn't even question him. To be honest, I didn't want trouble anyway. If he attacked me because I accused him of my brother's assault, think what he would do if I accused him of this."

I hadn't realized I'd put my fist to my mouth, the way Marcus did. I had done the same thing and even worse—I had put Colin in prison.

She said, "He comes back. He's never actually spoken to me, but I've seen him a few times, just hanging around. Looking at me. When he looks at you, it's like—"

"You can feel it on your body," I finished, and she jerked her head in a violent nod.

"He gives me this smile, like he's really happy with himself. That's what made me think he'd done it. I wanted to warn you that when he gets out, he's going to come after you. I'm sure of it. Whether it's four years or ten years or even sixteen years. You need to be prepared. I know he'll come back here, too. He is enjoying his handiwork now. Rubbing it in."

I hated that for her, and I hated that I knew exactly what she was talking about. "The assistant county attorney who prosecuted the case said that Colin probably won't get parole considering the offenses he's committed. I don't think he'll ever be able to appeal, either." She didn't look especially hopeful, but maybe she'd lost hope. "Marisol, do you know if he had a friend or associate? Has anyone else approached you on his behalf?"

"No. Why?"

I didn't want to unload my problems on her. "Just curious. I appreciate your warning." I let myself look at her once-beautiful face. I mourned for it as she must mourn every day. I stood. "I know it took a lot for you to go through that again with me."

"I go through it every day," she said in a whisper, looking away for a moment.

I don't know why, but I hugged her. Just quickly and then I walked to the door. Her mother watched me warily. My gaze went to Manuel, who was pulling at his hair and studying the wrenched-out strands.

I walked out and closed the door behind me and made it to my car. I cried for all of them. And I cried for myself, too.

CHAPTER TWENTY-ONE

That evening Luke and I had stuck to our Friday night tradition and rented *Meatballs,* one of my favorite Bill Murray movies. For the first time in what felt like forever, we laughed together. Really, really laughed. Though I couldn't help but notice that Luke kept his hand on Bonk much more often now. I realized I kept my hand close to Luke, too, though I didn't want to become clingy.

We did our good-night kiss routine, and then I just pulled him into my arms and gave him a hug. "I love you," I said, going way over the *I'm too big for that* line.

He didn't complain; he hugged me back, warming my heart.

After I left his room, I scooped up popcorn kernels Bonk had missed and got ready for bed. Even the soft knock on the front door startled me. I was surprised to see Marcus through the peephole. I noticed that I didn't hope he was coming back around now that things were settling. Maybe it was the memory of my humiliation right there in my foyer. Or maybe I'd given up hope. Either way, I felt sad about it.

I opened the door. "Hi, stranger."

He gave me a wan smile, though I saw the same tension I saw in the days leading up to the trial. "Hi yourself."

"Come in."

I thought he'd decline, but he stepped inside. He didn't walk in far, though, before turning to me.

I spoke first. "I wish you'd come when Luke was awake. He's missed you."

"I miss him, too, but . . ."

"I know. I explained the whole when-adults-break-up thing."

"Actually, I waited until after his bedtime on purpose. I need to show you something on the computer."

I felt cold already as I booted up the PC. This wasn't going to be good.

He remained standing while the start-up process began. "Are you . . . are you seeing Stewart?"

I swung my chair around to face him. "God, no. Why?"

"He's given me that impression."

"Slimebag. He made a pass at me. I told him it was inappropriate, considering our . . . well, our former relationship. But I wasn't interested anyway." He looked relieved. "Did he ever talk about Dana? I mean, before the assault?"

"Not that I can remember."

"I just wondered if he belonged to the mystery DNA. I'm not sure it's relevant, but that whole scenario bothers me."

He took a seat. I crossed my arms over my chest, armor for what was coming. My fingers went right to my worry curl. He got a strange look on his face as he watched me. He'd always teased me about it; he had, in fact, been the one who'd christened it my worry curl. After a moment his mouth tightened and he looked away. He must have been remembering that, too. Happy memories that now made us sad.

He started the Internet program and typed in an address that brought up a Web site called Dark Strips. Beautifully rendered faces graced the main page, along with a log-in box.

"We got a tip from one of our snitches in prison. Colin spends all of his free time drawing. Remember we found pictures in his studio? Our guy discovered Colin creates graphic novels for his Web site. That's how he makes his living, through subscriptions. He must have someone on the outside scanning them in for him."

Marcus logged into the site and downloaded several documents. We didn't speak while we watched the download box tick down the remaining time. "I subscribed to see what he's up to. Especially in light of what I heard from Armstrong. He mentioned the harassment to me . . . assuming you'd told me."

"I didn't see any reason to."

With a nod, he opened the document and displayed a page with comic-book-style boxes. I saw a muscular man held in a cage by an evil-looking woman with curly hair. Her name was Malva.

"Is that supposed to be me?"

"I believe so."

I was reading the boxes as Malva was torturing Eroz, the supposed hero. Occasionally he got a jab in at her, slicing off her earlobe in one frame. I grimaced. As I read, though, the undertone became far more ominous. Malva's young son, Callan, had shaggy hair. In one story line she took him to a nearby city, which seemed to be a futuristic version of Boston. They walked in the park. Fed the swans. Ate ice cream. Together they plotted the demise of Eroz.

Marcus had obviously read this, as he was looking at me and not the screen. "What do you think?"

"It's me. And Luke. His partner's been feeding him information about me."

"He has pictures of you, too. In his cell."

"Oh, God." I rubbed my face. "Luke and I went to Boston last weekend. We fed the swans. Ate ice cream. He was there, too. He left a CD in my car."

"Maggie, why didn't you tell me all this?"

I looked at him. "Why do you think?"

He tentatively put his hand on my shoulder, but the move felt awkward. "I'm sorry. And . . . it gets worse."

I read on, dread in my stomach. Malva went to an abandoned factory and nearly got killed by gremlin-looking creatures. When she returned home, tattered and cut, she found her son unconscious, the word EVIL branded on his stomach.

"Now you know why I came over. Why I'm scared for you. Especially since there's someone out there who wants to hurt you. It looks like Colin wants him to hurt Luke, too."

I bent over in my chair, feeling Marcus's ineffectual attempt to comfort me by moving his hand back and forth on my shoulder. "Maybe I should send Luke back to Wesley's parents."

"That's another thing. One of the earlier installments had a section where Malva sends her son away for his safety. He may know where your in-laws live."

He could. "Marcus, what am I supposed to do?" All I could think about was Marisol and her brother. How their lives had been shattered. I couldn't let that happen to Luke.

"There's only one way to really be safe. It's drastic, though."

"What? What is it?" I prodded when he couldn't seem to make himself say it.

"I think . . . you should go into hiding."

I almost laughed. "From the expression on your face, I thought you were going to suggest something horrid . . . like suicide."

He started to touch my hand but hesitated and withdrew before making contact. "I'm not talking about an extended vacation. I'm talking about changing your identity, leaving the area, starting over. Thurmond said that's the only way to get away from sadistic stalkers. And if this guy is doing Colin Masters' bidding, he's just as dangerous." He rubbed his mouth. "There are people who specialize in making people disappear. Not through the government. Not witness protection programs. This is underground."

Marisol had suggested the same thing. "Who does that kind of thing?"

"I don't know. I've heard about people who do this kind of thing, but I can't be involved. It's the only way I can think of to keep you safe. I don't want you to go. But you may have no choice. You can't tell anyone. Not Serena, not your in-laws. Not me. You can't leave anyone vulnerable to this guy. You can't leave any clues that lead to your new identity."

"Marcus, I can't just . . . leave."

He kneaded the bridge of his nose, his face creasing with worry. "That would be a last-ditch move. The only other hope is that we'll catch him at one of his pranks."

"And arrest him on what? Harassment?"

Marcus shrugged. "Unless he does something drastic."

Those words hung like smoke in the air. One of Colin's stalking victims had disappeared. Maybe of her own volition, as I was now thinking of doing. Maybe not. One victim had escaped, too, but in the final kind of escape. The kind where Colin won. And there was Marisol, who could never escape. Her warning echoed in my mind: *He'll never let you go.*

"How would I find one of these people?" I asked, seeing Marcus's expression turn hopeful again.

"Ask around. Maybe look online. Google it."

"Google it," I repeated. As though I were looking up a movie review.

"It's not an easy decision, but I feel better knowing you're at least considering it." He stood. "If you do go, will you let me know? Not where you're going, of course, but that you're safe. Send me a blank card. I'll let people know—Armstrong, Serena—that you've gone into hiding. They'll understand."

I was sad to realize that not many people would care anymore. Not about me, anyway. I could only nod. I'd caused my best friend pain and hardship, disappointed clients, and cut loose my more tangential friends.

He hugged me then, surprising me with the strength of it. Everything else had been so tentative. "Be safe," he said on a fierce whisper.

After he left, I sank to the floor. What was I going to do? And how far would I go to get away from Colin's partner?

◆ ◆ ◆

I spent the rest of the night on Colin's Web site. I read his previous story line with a villain named Luna. I wondered if I was imagining the similarities between her and Dana. Considering the threads connecting me to Malva, I doubted it. Those threads made it hard to read the clash between Eroz and Luna and especially the gruesome end of Luna's life.

The story lines were violent, raw, and at times blatantly sexual. I forced myself to read because this was my only peek into Colin's mind. I wanted to learn how he thought, how he saw the world. Apparently, if Eroz was supposed to represent Colin, he thought a lot of himself. It was ironic, though, that Eroz was often dominated by the villain and, according to the dates, during the very time that Colin was dominating Dana. I downloaded the story published the year that he'd stalked Marisol and found those same threads of similarity. In the story the villain's boyfriend was killed, but I figured he was supposed to represent Manuel. I wondered if this would be enough to involve the police but answered the question before it had even fully formed. Colin was smart; he played along the edges without incriminating himself. Yes, one could see the similarities if one was looking. I doubted it would be enough to bring charges.

It was nearly four in the morning when I focused my bleary eyes on the clock. I turned off the computer and dragged myself from the chair. The room went dark as the computer breathed its last breath and shut down. I could see the faint glow of the streetlight shining through the closed curtains.

I could also see, I realized with a start, the silhouette of a man. I sucked in a breath and felt the now familiar charge of adrenaline. Just as I chided myself for imagining things, it shifted and evaporated. I rushed to the window and snapped open the curtains. A figure darted around the bushes and disappeared from view. I heard the soft thump of footsteps. Not my imagination.

"Come back here, you coward!" I screamed. I stood at the window for a long time, my arm pressed to my chest, hand at my throat. I wasn't sure why I remained; maybe I couldn't move. Maybe I hoped he'd come back so I could see his face. He never did.

Not that night. But I knew he'd be back later. Again and again. Until he got what he wanted. Not knowing what that was chilled my very soul.

CHAPTER TWENTY-TWO

I leaned like a drunk against the kitchen counter and watched Luke play in the backyard with Bonk. Even Luke had commented on my fatigue at breakfast that morning. At least he hadn't complained about the lack of our usual Saturday morning pancakes. Doing more than pouring milk into a bowl was too much to contemplate on no sleep. I was afraid to fall asleep during the day, to not be able to watch Luke every minute. I downed another gulp of coffee and picked up the phone.

I couldn't keep living this way.

When Marisol answered, I could hear Manuel screaming in the background. It made my heart hurt for her. I scanned the yard for any signs of danger.

"Marisol, it's Maggie Fletcher. Have I called at a bad time?"

Her voice sounded so sad when she said, "It's always a bad time. What can I do for you?"

Colin had sentenced her to a life of guilt and pain. That he enjoyed gloating occasionally by showing up made me angry and terrified at once.

I had to swallow before I could speak. "I have a question, and I don't want you to take it the wrong way. I was wondering . . . with your brother's past connections . . . do you know someone who can make people disappear?"

"You mean murder them?"

"No, I mean change someone's identity. So they could go into hiding." When she was hesitant, and probably confused as to why I was asking, I felt compelled to explain. "There is something I didn't tell you yesterday. Your warning about Colin is graver than you realized. I don't even have the time that he's in prison to feel safe. That's why I asked if you knew of anyone associated with him. He's got someone stalking me. Threatening me and my son."

I heard her intake of breath and the fear in her voice. "Oh, Maggie, I'm sorry. I . . . I do know someone who could help you. At least he used to do that kind of thing. A friend of a friend of a friend, you could say. People use him when they need to get away from the law. Or creditors. I can have him contact you, if you want."

"I want. I'm not sure that's what I'm going to do. There's so much to consider." Luke would hate leaving. Changing my identity, losing my last name, that was hard to think about, too. "But I want a backup plan."

"Okay, I'll give him a call. He is called Doctor. Just Doctor. No one knows his real name. Which, I guess, shows he's good at what he does."

"Thank you, Marisol." After a moment, I asked, "Why didn't you ever use his services? Especially after Manuel's beating?"

"I thought about it, but we need the state funds for his medical care. I couldn't leave my mother behind because Colin might use her to get to me. And taking them both would have been hard, too hard."

My mother. Would Colin's partner hurt her as a way to spite me when he discovered I'd fled? Very possibly.

"I'm sorry, too," I said, though she hardly needed my sympathy.

"Just get away from him. While you're in one piece."

I was already shattered. I wanted only to save my son.

As Luke and I navigated through the crowd that evening, he was dissecting the elements of the play we'd just seen in Prescott Park.

"Then it was really cool when the frog told the boy about the forest, thinking he'd die there, and . . ."

I usually listened to everything Luke said, no matter how trivial, but particularly when he was excited about something. Tonight I was searching the crowd for the face whose expression gave away cruel intent. Most of those faces were in shadow, though, making detection hard.

"But the boy *knew* the frog was sending him into danger, and he played it really cool. . . ."

I made the appropriate noises as we approached the crosswalk. Luke loved stories, but reading was still a chore. He was especially interested because this play had been based on a local actor's screenplay. I hated that I couldn't concentrate—and enjoy—Luke's enthusiasm.

"And the way the actor could freeze himself . . ."

"Yeah, that was pretty amazing," I said, genuinely impressed that a boy could hold one position for several minutes.

But my eyes continued to scan as we crossed traffic and headed to the parking lot. Stay with the crowd and we'd be safe. I'd had to park at the far end of the second row, so people weren't as plentiful here.

All around us I heard people laughing and talking. The evening was cool, even for July, and smelled of evergreens and the aromatic smoke from a nearby restaurant. It was a beautiful summer night, the kind I relished. I couldn't wait to get back to my secured and wired home.

I was so busy concentrating on people that I hadn't been paying attention to vehicles. I heard people exclaiming, and someone yelled, "Watch out!"

I turned to see a truck heading right at us. No headlights. No one at the wheel. I shoved Luke out of the way, barely scrambling to the side before the truck rammed into the back of the car next to ours. I heard a man shouting, "That's my truck!" He ran over and helped me to my feet while taking in the sight of his truck smacked into a Mercedes-Benz.

Luke jumped up. "Mom, you all right?"

I hugged him to me after taking him in and making sure he was unhurt, too. "I'm fine."

"What happened?" somebody asked.

"I don't know," the truck's owner said. "Maybe I didn't put it in park."

The truck had been parked across from the Mercedes. "That's probably what happened," a man said. "With the slant of the asphalt, it could have rolled over."

"Yeah, but why now?" the owner said. "It's been here for an hour and a half."

Why now? The question struck me. My first panicked thought had been that Colin's partner was driving, before I'd seen that no one was behind the wheel. Had he, in fact, been waiting for Luke and me to walk in front of the truck before giving it a push? I was unable to take my gaze from where the two vehicles had collided. The truck was relatively unscathed, though the Mercedes's bumper was crunched in and the taillights smashed. Not a long distance, not enough to produce lethal momentum. But if my child had been between them . . . I couldn't think of it.

"The truck's in neutral," the owner said after he'd leaned in the driver's side. "I never do that."

"Was your truck locked?" I asked.

"I'm not always good at locking it. But why would someone put it in neutral?"

I only shrugged, silencing Luke with a look. I didn't want to get into my troubles, and I knew Colin's partner would leave no evidence to prove this was intentional. I searched the gathering crowd, feeling his gaze on me. I wanted to get out of there.

"You're sure you're okay, lady?" the owner asked as I headed to my car.

I nodded. Yet another lie to pile onto the others.

Once Luke and I got inside and locked the doors and I started the car—after checking the backseat—Luke asked, "Mom, do you think—"

"I don't know what to think," I said, not wanting to hear

that kind of speculation coming from my young, innocent son.

Something else had been distracting me during our evening. Another installment of the story would be posted that night.

"Yes, you do," Luke accused. "You're scared."

I backed out of the spot and waited behind the row of cars in line to exit. I didn't mind admitting a lot of things to Luke. That was part of our honesty pact. Sad. Frustrated. Mad. Scared was the hardest to admit. "Yes, I'm scared."

That only made him look more afraid. I guess I should have downplayed the truth. I added, "I don't know whether Colin had anything to do with it. Maybe it was only an accident, bad timing, whatever. But right now I'm scared enough to suspect anything out of the ordinary." I looked over at Luke. "How would you feel about leaving town? Starting over. Completely over. New names, new town, new life." I was testing him. Maybe preparing him.

"I don't want to leave Portsmouth. I've got my friends here. Bobby."

"I know. It wouldn't be easy. We'd have to leave everyone behind. No letters or phone calls. No visits."

"No, I don't like that. New names, too?"

"Last name only. I wouldn't make you change your first name. We'd be like spies, going undercover." Yeah, make it sound exciting. "Incognito. We wouldn't have to worry about this guy anymore. He and Colin wouldn't find us."

"We'd leave Grandma behind, too?" Luke asked, a little too optimistically.

"We'd have to ask her to come along. I know she isn't the most fun person, but she loves you very much. If Grandma goes with us, we'll set some ground rules."

"What about Nana and Papa?"

"I'll have to explain everything to them, I suppose." They would want Luke to stay with them, but I couldn't be sure he'd be safe there. No way could I live apart from my son. I wouldn't let Colin take that away from me, too.

Luke and I let Bonk out as soon as we got home. I

checked the phone log and saw three calls from private numbers on the screen. Calls to gloat? I was sad to see Luke watching Bonk, the dog's protector should anyone try to hurt him. Luke's shoulders were stiff, his fists balled at his sides. He looked tough and vulnerable at the same time. It was the same way I watched Luke, I realized. I wiped my eyes before he could see the tears beginning to form. I'd done this to him. By testifying, I'd changed our lives. I'd put him in danger. And I couldn't take it back.

As soon as Luke was in bed, I slipped into my office and checked Colin's Web site, still logged in from the night before. The new installment was ready. I read it online.

Malva takes her injured son to a doctor who fixes the painful brand without asking questions. As they're leaving, a car swerves around the corner—and heads right at them. Their surprised eyes are highlighted in the headlights. Malva jumps to the side barely in time. The injured Callan doesn't. In the final box she holds him as he dies in her arms.

My stomach twisted in anger and fear. I checked the window—no silhouette. I clicked on the forum link and found an appropriate topic: feedback. People couldn't effuse enough about the artist's techniques, his busty women, and his exciting story lines. I posted my own critique:

> You got it all wrong, Colin. Obviously you've never loved someone fiercely. You've never been a father. Malva wouldn't let her son die like that. She would have pushed him out of the way and taken the impact herself.

I logged out, my mouth in a firm line. I hadn't even given it a thought, pushing Luke out of the way first. It was a mother's instinct. Maybe Colin's mother wouldn't have done something so selfless. I suspected that he'd never loved anyone enough to put them first. He'd probably never loved anyone, period.

The phone rang. A private number. I jabbed the ON button and said, "You missed."

"Pardon?" a Hispanic voice said. "I'm looking for Maggie Fletcher."

"Oh. This is Maggie." I tamped down my anger. "Sorry, I thought you were someone else."

"I guess so. Marisol gave me your number. I'm Doctor."

I felt relieved and apprehensive at the same time. "Thank you for calling."

"She told me you were trustworthy, a single mother, and that you're in danger."

I looked at the screen, now showing my posted jibe. "Yes, we're in danger. A man I helped put in prison has someone stalking me."

"You're willing to give up everything?"

"Yes." I wasn't so sure, but I was becoming more so with every minute. "I've got a few things to settle first."

"Of course. Money will be one of them. It's not cheap to change identities."

"I understand that."

"You know that you can't tell anyone where you're going, who you're becoming?"

"Or who I'm seeing to get it done."

I heard a soft chuckle. "Very good. If you leave any clues, any threads, the stalker will find them if he's determined enough."

"He is." I thought of everything he'd done to me and what he had done before the trial.

"Marisol said the guy in prison, he's the motherfu—he's the guy who cut her face, who beat Manuel."

"Yes, he is."

"You had the guts to testify, put him away."

"I did what I had to do. He raped my sister. She committed suicide. I'm determined, too."

"You've got *cojones*. I like that. It means you'll do well through the process. And for you, I give you a discount."

I didn't care about the money at that point, but I thanked him. "How do I find you?"

"Marisol knows how to find me. It's better to deal through her. No numbers that can be traced from your phone records. Everything is done in cash. No paper trails. And when you come here for the pictures and other paperwork, make sure he's not following you."

I thought of the way he'd followed Luke and me to Boston. "I will."

"Get your affairs settled. When you're ready, call Marisol. I'll be in touch soon after."

We hung up, and I pulled my knees up to my chest and hugged them tight. I had started another ball rolling. Maybe, just maybe, we'd feel safe again.

I wondered, when we left, who would be considered the winner. I had escaped Colin and his partner. But he had taken away my life.

"Man, you're one sick puppy." Heraldo, Colin's cellmate, peered over his shoulder at the storyboard he was working on. "Is that why you're locked up, doing that to some woman?"

Heraldo was skinny, with tight black hair and tattoos that were nearly lost on his dark skin. He was a mix of Hispanic and black, and as far as temporary cellmates went, he was a good pick.

Except when he was nosy.

"It's just fiction," Colin said, as he always said when Heraldo teased him. He knew about prison snitches and about prisoners who testified against their cellmates.

"You are good, though. Gotta give you that. It's nice to be entertained, know what I mean? And I got the prettiest digs in the place, for sure." He nodded to the artwork on the walls.

Colin merely grunted, focusing again on his story. It was coming to its violent conclusion. Except that there wouldn't be a conclusion in the real story, not until he got out. He wanted Maggie to suffer. His partner was seeing to that for now, but Colin wanted the pleasure of finishing her off. The prospect kept him going, day after day, hour after hour, and minute after minute. All dragging endlessly on except for the time he worked on his stories. Those, and being able to vicariously stalk Maggie, kept him alive inside.

Obsession had been a driving force for a long time. This time, it wasn't about simple obsession. It was more than a game. It was about revenge. Maggie Fletcher was going to pay the highest price for her treachery. And he was going to enjoy every minute of it.

CHAPTER TWENTY-THREE

I had worked furiously all week to get everything in order, keeping Luke with me nearly every minute, except when I went to Boston twice to meet with Doctor. I didn't want Luke involved in that. I'd had his and my mother's passport pictures taken in a nearby town instead of having them done at Doctor's apartment.

Doctor was younger than I'd imagined. Nicer than I'd imagined, too. He led me gently through the process and even gave me a sympathetic smile when he saw my bereft expression as he explained what would happen.

I had only told Serena of our plans to leave town but hadn't said anything about changing our identities. I'd made arrangements to sell Dana's house and rent ours, with the funds going into an overseas account. Serena hadn't asked any questions. I absolutely wouldn't involve her.

Luke and I had spent the last few days packing the items we wanted to take. The night before our departure, we would turn out the lights at ten o'clock and leave them off for three hours. If Colin's partner was lurking around, he would have given up on spying for the night. Everything Luke and I left behind would be stored in a unit under Serena's name. I was holding out slim hope that we could return to our home and our lives someday.

At one o'clock, I woke Luke. "Time to go."

In a way, it was like waking early to go on vacation. There was excitement, yes, but more sadness than anything. Luke felt it, too. I could tell, especially when he took one last look around the room before walking out.

Our first stop would be Marion and Harold's. I would tell them about our plans and promise to visit periodically. They wouldn't like it, but, as I'd told Doctor, I was determined. My mother was going with us. She had no one else. We would meet at her house, and she would drive tandem. We would sell our cars in Concord and buy replacements under our new identities.

Luke and I stuffed the Lexus as full as we could. I left some of my stuff behind so he wouldn't have to leave so much of his. I had learned that the most important things were those you couldn't replace. People, of course. Bonk, who was sitting in the backseat. Memories, like my memory boxes. A few mementos. Dana's diary, which Marcus had managed to get released for me. Nothing else was all that important in comparison.

I tucked an envelope between the seat and console, to be mailed from a postal box on the way out. A blank card for Marcus.

Like a family who run out on their debts in the middle of the night, Luke and I pulled out of the garage and quietly left our lives behind.

PART TWO

THREE YEARS LATER

CHAPTER TWENTY-FOUR

When the phone rang, I answered in my cheery voice, "Ashbury Homes and Land, Maggie Donahue speaking."

Silence.

"Hello?"

After another second I hung up.

"No one there?" Burt, the broker, said as he came to collect his messages. A skinny man in his fifties, he reminded me of a quintessential nerd with his black-rimmed glasses and short-sleeve shirts, even in the fall. His movements were quick and jerky, as though he were always in a rush.

"Third time this week."

"Hope you're getting some heavy breathing out of it," he said with a chuckle as he headed back to his office.

"Har har," I muttered under my breath. Spoken by someone who had never received harassing phone calls.

This wasn't harassment. Probably a dropped cell call, which happened out here occasionally. The reception was better now that the Lutheran church had rented out their steeple for a cell phone tower (amid much controversy).

I found myself looking across the street at the strip of shops and cafés, the cobbler sweeping leaves onto his neighbor's section of brick sidewalk, the kids' boutique owner pasting pumpkins in her window. To the right was the town common, a square of grass and trees and a bandstand. A large yellow dog was lifting his leg on the corner of the Civil War statue, and his owner was trying to get the dog to stop. Life in a small town. For some reason I felt a shiver. "Someone stepped on my grave," the old saying went.

I was no longer an active real estate agent, though I had gotten my license under my new name. My focus was on Luke, on making up to him everything I'd inadvertently taken away. Now I had a nine-to-five job as the office manager. I missed the selling, the thrill of signing a deal, of finding just the right home or lot for a client. I didn't miss the disappointments, the long hours, and phone calls at all times. Even though Luke was drifting away—or maybe because he was—I was glad to be home more.

The door opened and my heart gave a little jump when Aidan Trew walked in. When he'd rented a lakeside cottage two months earlier, he'd noticed my Irish last name, taken from my father's ancestors, and we'd chatted about our genealogy. He was tall, with black, wavy hair and gorgeous blue eyes that reminded me of sky reflected on the lake. I'd enjoyed the harmless flirtation that had inspired giddy, girly feelings I hadn't felt since I met Marcus.

"Hi there," I said, hearing the smile permeate my voice. "Didn't think I'd see you again."

He sat down and planted his elbows on the front of my desk. "Hello, Miss Maggie of the Donahues. Good to see you again." His smile, and the way he looked at me with complete focus, made me feel funny inside. He reached out his hand and I took it. It was more than a handshake, though, more like a touching of palms and fingers, lingering a bit too long before he withdrew. "I liked the area so much I decided to come back for another visit."

"Be careful; that's how I ended up here." That much was true. Wesley and I had stayed here for a few days many years ago, after my miscarriage. We'd needed time to grieve and heal. When I'd looked at the map for a place to run, I remembered this lovely town with the lake. It was as far to the west of New Hampshire as I could go without leaving the state, which I didn't want to do. "So you're looking for a place to rent?"

"Same one if it's available."

"We're at the end of leaf-changing season, so things are beginning to open up again. And quiet down. Once it starts dipping into the forties most of the tourists and seasonal folks head out." In the summer and through leaf-changing season the town was alive with activity, events and traffic. Small boats, canoes, and children launching off floating docks rippled the lake's surface. Now a sense of somber solitude descended that I related to all too well. I pulled up the rental listings on the computer. "You're in luck. The tenants left yesterday and it hasn't been winterized yet."

He filled out the rental form—left-handed—and wrote a check for four weeks' rent. I remembered little things about him. He chewed Black Jack gum that smelled like licorice. He read Harry Potter. He had an Underdog figurine hanging from his truck's rearview mirror. Oh, and he'd made me think of skinny-dipping in the lake on a hot summer day.

He deftly manipulated the key I gave him between his fingers as he said, "Want to have lunch sometime?"

He took me off guard. I enjoyed our flirtation, but carrying it a step further made me nervous. So it surprised me when, "Maybe," came out of my mouth.

He gave me an incredible white-teethed smile and stood. "How about tomorrow?"

No, I'm busy, I'm celibate, I'm— "Uh . . . sure."

"Great. See you then." He backed the door open, gave me a wave, and headed out.

Anxiety fluttered in my stomach. I'd forgotten how to connect to people. Restless, I walked to the door and told myself I wasn't watching him walk away. I even looked in the other direction, but inevitably my gaze drifted to the right, where he was backing his truck into the street. Despite my ambivalence, I caught myself smiling.

It had been a while since I'd had reason to smile. At least I wasn't afraid anymore. It had taken me until just recently to feel a warm contentment. To feel safe. I was letting Luke participate in after-school programs. Last spring he'd acted in a school play and his glow of pleasure made me realize how insulated we were. I wasn't ready to begin dating, or at least I hadn't thought I was. I wouldn't be ready to give someone my heart again, not for a long time. But lunch . . . well, it was just lunch.

Burt walked into the lobby for a coffee refill. "Did I hear you accept a lunch date?"

"Nope, not a date, just lunch. Gotta eat anyway."

"Told you he liked you," Burt said with a lift of his eyebrow. He had teased me when Aidan popped in from time to time during his last visit to ask questions when he could have easily called. And there *was* the way he smiled at me. As far as anyone in Ashbury knew, I'd moved here because I needed a change after a recent tragedy. The most socializing I did was take Luke to the farmers' market on Saturdays.

I'd been fooling myself about why I'd chosen Ashbury. Not because it seemed safe and warm, with memories of my trip here with Wesley. After all, it had been a time of mourning and healing. I chose this town because I knew I would not get attached. It was lovely but gave off an air of standoffishness. Buildings were pristine "don't touch" white. Residents were polite but not warm. Even the sign on the outskirts of town wished visitors a happy return home. As in, *Glad you're going.* I'd never felt like an intruder, but I'd never felt at home, either. That's what I liked about Ashbury. No one had reached out to us, and we hadn't reached out to anyone else, either.

The teasing light left Burt's expression when he saw the stack of printed listings in my in-bin. "Haven't you called these yet? They're coming up for renewal next week."

I didn't mind calling listings to renew them . . . when they were our listings. "Isn't it time you and your brother called a truce? I don't feel comfortable trying to steal his listings." I could hardly ignore the irony that a woman who'd committed perjury had a moral dilemma with this.

"It's your job, Maggie. Besides, just yesterday he knocked down one of my signs. Now call those people, sweet-talk them into moving their listing to us, and smile when you're doing it."

I forced myself through the calls, bid Burt good-bye, and walked out. The short summer was already over; it was barely seventy, though it felt nice in the sun. As I headed to the lot where I had parked, I looked around, a habit that would be hard to kick. The tourists compounded the problem: strangers, strangers, everywhere, and I didn't know what the enemy looked like.

Outside the downtown district, streets splintered off to embrace sprawling Lake Laurel. Older homes with lawns now covered in leaves sat one next to the other. I pulled into the driveway of a bright blue house with white trim, wondering whose red Jeep Cherokee was parked to the side. Mrs. Caldwell, owner of the house, was outside in her work boots and too-large gloves planting small bushes. Her scant frosty hair was piled up on her head and tucked beneath a cap.

"Hello, Maggie," she greeted, putting her hand on the small of her back to help her straighten. I'd asked her to call me by my first name, though she hadn't extended the invitation likewise. "Luke's around back raking leaves for me. Told him I'd pay him a dollar an hour." Her expression soured. "If my kids were around, I wouldn't have to pay someone."

I always wanted to say, *If you were this crabby and demanding, I don't blame them for moving.* I headed around the back, fully expecting the sullen frown I saw on Luke's face as he raked with lackadaisical movements. At twelve, Luke was still small for his age, something that bothered him greatly. Probably not as much as doing labor for next to nothing. I'd give him extra if he didn't complain too much.

He, like me, kept his curls trimmed now. I didn't miss mine so much, except for my worry curl. I missed his curls, but he wasn't about to listen to my beauty advice. I'd once told him that girls loved boys with curls, and he'd given me a horrified look.

"Hey, kiddo," I said, jerking him out of obviously grim thoughts. "It's nice of you to help Mrs. Caldwell."

He dropped the rake, crossed his arms in front of him, and walked over. I got the usual mumbled, "Don't know why

I have to come here after school . . . ," as he passed me on his way to the car.

Speaking of crabby. I'd already gone over and over it, so I didn't answer. We lived too far from town for him to be at home by himself, especially now that the nearest neighbors would be leaving for the winter. I was probably being over-protective, but I didn't care. Mrs. Caldwell had provided the perfect situation. She needed the money, so I paid her to watch Luke, who walked to her house from school.

He was already sitting in the car, head down and body sunk into the seat, when I walked around to the front. My heart felt heavy at the sight of him. Not just a sullen preteen. Something else was bothering him and he wouldn't tell me. I'd begun to realize Luke and I lived in our safe, insulated worlds, bumping into each other, but not really connecting.

"How's Mr. Caldwell doing?" I asked as I passed the kneeling Mrs. Caldwell. He had Parkinson's, one of those diseases that strike so randomly and cruelly.

She tipped her gloved hand in a so-so sign. "Has his good days and his bad days, but mostly they're bad anymore."

"He's lucky to have you."

She grunted. "But who am I lucky to have? Kids never call or visit. Betcha they'll swoop right in when I go." She stabbed at the ground with her spade.

As I turned to leave I noticed that the ROOM FOR LET sign that had been in her front yard for the last six months was gone. I glanced at the Jeep.

"You rented the room?" I asked.

"Yep. To a nice feller, name of Sweeney. About your age." She gave me a smile that smacked of matchmaking. "Decent looking, very muscular. *Somebody* ought to be happy 'round here."

"Not interested," I said, waving off the idea and thinking of Aidan. Just lunch.

"Shame, a pretty young thing like yourself all alone."

"I'm not alone. I have Luke." I gave her a smile and backed toward the car. That's when I looked up at the dormer windows of the second floor and saw someone watching from behind the white curtains. Since I knew the Caldwells' bedroom was on the main floor, I figured the person must be Sweeney.

I waved, out of obligation, but he didn't wave back. He only stood there, his hulking frame behind the incongruous lacy curtains. I dropped my hand and got into the car. As I backed up, I looked once again at the window. He was still there.

"Did you meet the new tenant?" I asked.

Luke only shrugged, a movement that had taken the place of words in recent months.

"Is that a yes or no?"

"No."

I started to reach out to brush a strand of hair into place but ended up brushing a white speck off the seat instead. I backed out into the street and asked the futile question, "How was school?" I got a shrug for an answer.

Lake Laurel Road followed the edge of the lake, with asphalt roads splintering off every now and then toward the water. At the northern tip I turned onto Oak Leaf Lane, past the cottage where our closest neighbors, the Weavers, were packing up for the season. We exchanged pleasantries, and I wished them well during their winter stay in Florida. Then Luke and I continued to the house we now called home. It was built in the eighteen hundreds, complete with an outhouse that I'd had all kinds of ideas for when we first moved in. Two pots of wilted geraniums sat near it, a reminder of my procrastination.

I loved the smell of old homes, that mixture of aging wood and perhaps the essence of life that still hung in the air. That's what made me love the idea of renovating one, the idea of renewing the old. I had walked in with the realtor and envisioned a new kitchen and windows while Ty Pennington's voice pointed out before and after. The previous owners had turned one of the upstairs bedrooms into a walk-in closet and large bathroom for the master suite. I'd had so many ideas, and yet I'd done nothing since we moved in. Worst of all, I wasn't sure why. I'd bought paint, leafed through hardware catalogs . . . but hadn't gone further than that.

I parked my bright red Kia SUV in the old barn a few hundred yards from the house. The barn always smelled musty and a bit oily. I used it as a garage, as the previous owners had done, even though it had no door. "Run with me," I said instead of asking.

"Nah." He pulled himself from the car and plodded to the front door.

I paused, watching him. He looked . . . defeated. He *was* gaining weight, just not the good kind. He was starting to get flabby around the belly. I grabbed my purse and caught up to him. I ached to put my arms around him, but I couldn't push past the invisible barrier between us.

"Tell me what's going on in that head of yours."

He wouldn't my gaze, and that scared me. "Nothing. I just want to go inside."

I took hold of his arm, hoping that would force him to look at me. "Run with me. I miss you coming along."

Running had started out as a way for me to feel in control of my life, at least a small portion of it. If *he* found us, I wanted to be in the best shape I could. Luke had started running with me, and a tenuous, silent bond had formed between us. Because I chose to testify, he'd lost his home, his friends, and the father figure that Marcus had become. It still hurt to think about that. I'd put justice for my sister over my relationships and, worse, over my son. At least Colin had gotten a sentence of seventeen and a half to thirty-five years and wouldn't be eligible for parole until the minimum sentence was served. I was sure he was being the role-model prisoner, counting down the days . . . the days before he could try to find me. Colin's partner hadn't found us in three years. I'd started to relax, and running had become fun.

Then, soon after school had started three weeks earlier, Luke stopped coming with me. He ate junk food, sat around, and the worst part was that he'd shut me out.

"I want Open Doors again."

"Mom, can we just go in?"

"Are you having trouble with one of your teachers? A student?"

He shook his head without uttering a sound.

He was in the same community school as last year and was now in the sixth grade. He'd been working with his drama teacher on and off through the summer. A former Broadway actor, Walter Hempstead praised Luke's acting skills and was dedicated to mentoring him. Hempstead had chosen his most promising students from last year's class to work on a corny skit he'd written called *A New Year,* chronicling one boy's first days at a new school. Luke, who'd been working hard on his reading skills, had the lead.

"Is this about a girl?"

He spit out the word, "No!"

"Do you feel depressed? Aunt Dana used to feel down, even when she had no reason to."

"I'm not depressed," he said, my first real answer.

With a strangled sigh I unlocked the door and disabled the alarm. I doubted my mother's sudden heart attack and death had anything to do with it; he'd never been close to her. She and I, though, had grown closer in the last three years. She had stopped pushing her interpretation of the Bible as the only one when I'd finally told her that forcing people sometimes pushed them away from God, not toward Him. We went to church, not because of my mother's urging but my own. I think she knew it, though she never mentioned it. Or the lie.

I saw the others in church eye us, as though trying to discern our sins by what we wore or maybe how enthusiastically we sang the hymns. Maybe they could sense sin inside me. Not only the sin of my lie but also the sin of nonforgiveness. I could never forgive Colin. And I could not forgive myself, either.

Bonk greeted us at the door but promptly ran outside. I hadn't installed a dog door. When he got his freedom, he tore through the woods chasing squirrels.

I changed into sweats and sneakers and stretched in the living room where Luke had planted himself on the couch and turned on his Xbox. He still built roller coasters, but he'd expanded into other simulated games, too. Working the

controls was the most exercise he got lately. I was in the best
shape of my life now that I was working out and eating better. I was leaner, with muscle definition, and my face had
sharpened as I neared my thirty-second birthday.

"Be back in a few," I said, giving up hope that he'd join
me. His attitude scared me, especially since he wouldn't
communicate. We hadn't had Open Doors in months.

Bonk ran inside when I opened the door, his desire to run
apparently sated.

I ran out my frustrations and fears, feeling sweat trickle
down the back of my neck and between my breasts even as
cool air burned my lungs. In the deep winter months I used
a treadmill, but I preferred breathing in the fresh air and
beauty. The land between my house and the one on the next
street was vacant. I'd worn a path along the edge of the lake
and back through the woods.

Blood pulsed through my veins. Adrenaline vibrated
through my body. My daily runs filled me with a sense of
power, energy, and even something that felt oddly sexual. Of
course, I wasn't sure how accurate that was; it had been way
over three years since I'd felt the caress of a man's hand, the
sweet invasion of his maleness. Three years since I'd experienced anything sexual, unless you, uh, counted when I sat a
certain way in my Jacuzzi tub and the jets hit me just right.

Fog crept from the recesses of the forest around me, re-
minding me of some ghostly monster in a horror movie.
Shafts of fading sunlight filtered through the nearly naked
trees. I loved the fall, especially the sweet smell of pine needles and the pungent tang of dying leaves. The smell of
things that once were so alive and were now gone.

I heard the chorus of crickets, the chatter of birds settling
in for the night, and the crunch of leaves beneath my feet on
the trail I had forged. I never plugged my ears—and distracted my attention—with music. For a long time I scanned
these woods looking for movement that was out of place, a
shadow that didn't belong to a tree.

I stopped at the halfway point where a felled tree made
the perfect bench. I caught my breath and watched the sun

disappear behind the terrain on the opposite shore. The county owned the land on the other side of the lake, leaving it undeveloped. To the distant far right and left I could see the twinkle of lights through the trees. I saw a canoe out on the lake, floating perfectly still, not even making a ripple. Something about it bothered me in a spiritual way. Before I could figure out what it was, I heard a rush of sound behind me. I jumped to my feet and turned, my heartbeat accelerating again. I saw birds scatter in the way they do when they're startled.

Through the thicket of tree trunks, bare branches, and fog I saw nothing but shadows in the waning light. I listened, at least tried to listen, over my own breathing. After a minute I heard the slightest shuffling sound. I narrowed my eyes but saw nothing moving. It was probably a deer; that's what I told myself. I looked at the path that looped back through the woods. I would take the lake path back tonight. Just in case.

He watched her drop down on the tree trunk and catch her breath. So pretty, with her hair short and her body firm. So alone. Very, very alone.

When he moved forward, a twig broke beneath his boot. Suddenly the birds shot out of their night roosts with a clatter of sound. She stood and searched the woods, her expression alert and suspicious. So she hadn't forgotten to be afraid. Good.

Very, very good.

CHAPTER TWENTY-FIVE

"So, tell me about yourself," Aidan asked at lunch the next day. "Who is Maggie Donahue?"

The question threw me off. So did the answer my mind gave: *I am a mother, nobody's wife or girlfriend or even friend. Admittedly I have created those last two deficits. In my quest to survive, to protect Luke and me, I have lost a part of myself. I have hidden away, hoping—and failing—to recapture a better time. Now, sitting here with you, I can see I'm afraid to move forward.*

I toyed with a package of crackers. "There's not much to tell." I thought of that canoe on the lake. Not even creating a ripple. Like me.

"Okay, let's try another one," he said with a grin. "What brought you to Ashbury?"

A simple question, one I'd been asked several times. "I lost my sister a few years ago as a result of a violent crime. I needed a change of pace and I wanted to live somewhere I felt safe. I'd been here before, liked the place." I shrugged the way Luke did, as though that would suffice for everything I'd left out.

Usually when I gave people that line, I could tell they wanted to know more but were polite enough not to ask. Aidan seemed to take it at face value. We sat at the window table at the sandwich shop across from my office. We'd finished lunch and now lingered over our hot teas, making small talk meant to dig deeper. His fingers stroked the contoured edge of the table, a subconscious gesture that was somehow erotic. Probably because his hands were strong, fingers long . . . hands I could easily envision running over my body.

He was from Boston and worked as a contractor for an investigative agency that looked into child-care providers. He made sure people's kids were safe. It made him all the more attractive, which made me wish he'd been a lawyer.

"What brought you back here?" I asked.

"You."

I blinked. Wow. There was honesty for you. In my wildest ego dreams I had wondered if he'd returned because of me but had dismissed it. Now I was both flattered and scared.

"From that first time I saw you, I couldn't stop thinking about you," he went on. "I want to get to know you better."

I fiddled with my spoon, spinning it round and round. Finally I looked up at him. "Why?" I think that surprised him, too. I smiled to soften my bluntness. "I mean, we live in different states. You know nothing about me, about what I want. So I'm curious as to your intentions."

I was sure someone who looked like Aidan wouldn't have to travel far to find a woman who could accommodate his physical needs. In his midtwenties I guessed, perhaps he was looking to settle down. If that was his goal, I wasn't the right prospect.

"Fair enough." He leaned back in his chair, a man completely comfortable in his skin. "I'm not thinking that far ahead, to be honest. I'm simply enjoying being here . . . with you."

I couldn't help but smile, even though he hadn't answered my question. But he seemed sincere, so I returned the sentiment. "I enjoy being with you, too. But you should know, I have a twelve-year-old son who's going through serious preteen angst. And . . . well, I'm not really in a place to think about a long-term relationship."

"Consider me forewarned," he said with a slight lift of the corner of his mouth.

I swallowed hard. I'd heard the expression "bedroom eyes" before and didn't know exactly what it meant. Now I thought I had an idea. When I looked into his eyes, I thought of fluffy pillows and sweat and heavy breathing. Imagining his hands on me, his body inside me . . . gawd, the thought of a fling was tempting. While my blood tingled, I just wasn't sure I could separate my physical and emotional selves.

He let his gaze linger on me just long enough to make my insides quiver before he looked out the window. Two boys ran past laughing so hard they could hardly stay on their feet.

"Ashbury seems like a safe haven," Aidan said.

" 'Safe' is a relative term."

I'd considered moving to a big city like Boston, someplace closer to Marion and Harold, though now I was glad we weren't close to them. I'd thought about getting lost in crowds, but I didn't want to raise Luke in a city. So I'd gone in the opposite direction, a town one-fourth the size of Portsmouth.

"Do you feel safe here?" Aidan asked, looking at me with curious intent.

I supposed I'd opened myself for the question, though I still found it a bit strange. "Sure." Except for the eerie feeling in the woods last night. I glanced at my watch. "I'd better get going."

Aidan grabbed the bill the waitress had left. "My treat."

"Thanks. I'll get the tip." When he opened his wallet I saw a picture of a boy and girl. The boy looked like a young version of Aidan, sitting next to a younger blond girl. The picture looked too old for the child to be Aidan's.

Though he caught me snooping, he didn't explain what the picture was about. He walked me back to my office, bussed my cheek by way of good-bye, and headed off. I watched him walk away, watched his easy gait with his hands jammed in his front pockets and gaze to the ground. Thinking. *About what?* I wondered.

I gave myself one more second to admire the way his

jeans fit his derrière before I went inside. When the phone rang, I answered it more cheerfully than I ever had.

No one was there.

Through his upstairs window, he watched the boy trudge up the driveway after school. His shoulders drooped; his feet dragged. He looked bullied. As though he was feeling the double shame of being picked on and then not standing up for himself.

He'd watched the boy yesterday. Something was definitely on his mind. Maybe he could help. He put on his sweatpants and laced up his sneakers. It amazed him how perfectly things worked out sometimes. "Serendipity." A fluffy word for something profound.

A knock on the door interrupted his thoughts. The old lady's voice called, "Mr. Sweeney?"

She'd tried to get to know him in a nosy way. He'd politely dodged her questions. He didn't want to contradict anything he'd told her when he'd inquired about renting the room. He put on his headphones, turned on his radio, and let the music fill his mind for a few minutes.

When he opened the door, she said, "Oh, you are in there," from the end of the hall where she was placing linens in the closet. "I wanted to give you some extra towels." When she handed him a stack, she said, "Didn't you hear me knock?"

"Sorry, must have had my headphones on. Thank you, ma'am."

He tossed the towels onto his bed and went downstairs and outside. Where the boy was sitting on a bench swing reading some papers. Where he looked up and smiled as Sweeney approached.

Just before Luke had seen my car pull in, he'd kicked his leg out in some karate-type move. Then he'd lanced an imaginary foe with the rake handle. When he saw me he abruptly started raking.

"Hey, tiger, who's the enemy?"

His face turned red as he pulled the last of the leaves into a pile. "Sweeney taught me some moves."

"Sweeney? The new tenant?"

"Yeah. He's cool. He said he'd teach me Tae Kwon Do."

I looked around but didn't see him. "Where is he?"

Luke's expression soured. "Mrs. Caldwell was going on how you and Sweeney should meet. I think she scared him off."

"Oh, brother."

"Hello, Maggie," Mrs. Caldwell said, stepping out on the front porch. "I knocked on Sweeney's door, but he must have those headphones on again."

"I'd like to meet him, since he's going to be around Luke. But I'm not looking for anything romantic."

"Woman shouldn't be alone," Mrs. Caldwell said. "Especially with a young son. He needs a father. You shoulda seen Luke and Sweeney out here kicking and punching."

"Luke gets along well with Walter Hempstead, too, at school. He's teaching Luke to act." Did I sound as defensive as I felt? I wasn't depriving Luke of male companionship, honest.

I bid Mrs. Caldwell good-bye and Luke and I headed to the car. I glanced up at the window. It was too dark to see if anyone was there.

Luke was watching me. "I told him you had bad breath and never took baths. That you were always in a bad mood."

"Okay," I said, drawing out the word. "And *why* would you tell him that?"

"I know women . . . well, they need to be with a man sometimes. They get lonely." He was looking away now. "I don't want you to start seeing Sweeney or something."

I knew what Luke meant, and it stabbed me in the heart. If I dated the man, Luke might lose his friend. "You were trying to scare him away from me?" I clarified, finding it both annoying and funny. "Don't worry; I have no intention of trying to hook up with him." I thought of Aidan, though, and that lightened me a little. "And where did you hear about women needing, er, something?"

"Guys at school." He made a face. "They like to talk about sex and stuff."

"Oh, brother." I'd started noticing that Luke froze whenever a Victoria's Secret commercial came on. We'd had talks over the last year, but they were incredibly awkward for both of us.

As I got into the car, I had to wonder: was I imagining the feeling of being watched?

By the end of the week, Aidan and I had had lunch four times. I felt myself being drawn inexorably toward him and it terrified me. It also made me feel alive for the first time in years.

On Saturday, I invited him to meet Luke and me at the park, where we'd started taking Bonk so he could socialize with other dogs. I wanted Luke to meet Aidan, but I didn't want them to get too chummy. I needn't have worried. Luke acted sullen and quiet.

Ashbury Park was big, bordering the lake on one end and baseball diamonds at the other end. The crisp breeze kept most folks inside, apparently, as only a handful of people were out strolling or walking their dogs. The air was tinged with the scent of burning leaves and Aidan's licorice gum. I breathed deeply and tried to loosen the knots in my stomach.

Aidan asked Luke, "So, I hear you're into acting?"

"Yeah." At my prodding look he said, "Walter says I'm pretty good, that maybe he can get me some connections in the business."

"*Walter*, is it?" I asked.

"That's what he wants me to call him." Luke jammed his hands into his baggy jean pockets and hunched his shoulders. "He says I'm his protégé."

"Sounds like a dedicated teacher," Aidan said casually, though he seemed to be studying Luke.

Luke didn't look up at the question, just shrugged noncommittally. Before Aidan could ask anything else, Luke picked up the Frisbee and tossed it past Bonk, who gave chase. Luke clearly didn't want to talk anymore; he was off and running . . . away.

Aidan asked, "Is he like this with all your guy friends?"

"I don't have any guy friends," I said, not sure where Aidan fell in. I suspected he was fishing, though. I didn't have anything to hide. Well, not in that department.

Instead of pursuing that line of thought, though, Aidan surprised me by asking, "How long has he been acting like this?"

"Sullen, cranky, withdrawn? It started about a month ago. About the time school started. I ask if there's a problem at school, but all I get is that damned shrug." I toned down the frustration in my voice. "It's probably just normal preteen stuff."

"Maybe," Aidan said, still studying Luke. "He talk to you much?"

"Only about little things. Luke was excited about the play, talking about getting into character and the soul of an actor, but now . . . I don't know. He doesn't seem interested in anything but video games."

"And that worries you," Aidan said. "How's his appetite?"

"Strange. His small size bothers him, so he's always eaten well. Lately, though, I've caught him with bags of chips and candy bars. He's started gaining weight around the middle. That's probably the good thing about this Sweeney guy; he's teaching Luke Tae Kwon Do."

"Sweeney?" Aidan asked with interest.

"A guy who's renting a room from the lady who watches Luke after school. He has nothing to do with the odd behavior; that started before Sweeney came to town."

"What's he like?"

"I haven't met him yet, but not for lack of trying."

"Is he avoiding you?"

"Maybe. Mrs. Caldwell, the woman who watches Luke,

wanted to matchmake us, and then Luke told him I was an ogre, so he wouldn't be interested. I think it scared him off. I promised Luke I wouldn't seduce him." I grinned. "Besides, I'm otherwise occupied."

"Good." Aidan looked at me, really looked at me. *Bedrooms. Pillows. Sex. Hmm.* He looked good in faded jeans and a black T-shirt that molded to the contours of his chest.

We paused by the fence that surrounded the kiddie area. A woman and her young daughter were at the other side.

I leaned against the thick fence post and watched Luke in the distance. Even playing with Bonk didn't light up Luke's face like it used to. I loved watching the two of them play with the tug toy or chase each other. Luke had a shadow in his expressions that reminded me alarmingly of Dana. He wandered over to a large tree, hoisted himself up to the first limb, and kept climbing higher and higher.

"Hey! Too high!" I called.

He dangled from a branch and dropped to the ground. I expected him to get to his feet with a limp, but he launched up and grabbed the Frisbee again.

Aidan was leaning opposite me, studying me with a concern I found powerfully comforting. "Tell me more about him, about the changes," he said.

"He's gotten overly modest, won't let me see him in his underwear. Not that I did a lot, but when I walk past his room when he's changing, he slams the door shut. I figured that was normal teen boy stuff. I used to have to wrangle him into the shower. Now he takes them all the time and spends a long time in there."

The glint of sun on Aidan's hair contrasted with the dark look on his face. "Does he jump out of trees often?"

"I usually have to yell at him for climbing one of the trees here. I caught him on top of the barn last week, nearly gave me a heart attack. He tells me it's just guy stuff. To be honest, I don't know what's normal at this age."

"Of course, some roughhousing is normal. Risky behavior, though, may mean something else."

"Like what?" I asked.

Aidan rubbed his chin. "From what you've described . . . well, Maggie, I hate to say it, but it sounds like someone is abusing him."

"You mean bullying him? I'd considered that, that some kid was giving him a hard time."

"No, I mean abusing him. Sexually."

My eyes widened. I hadn't expected that. "No. I can't believe that, can't believe he wouldn't tell me."

"Kids feel ashamed because they feel guilty. Sometimes their abuser blames them or threatens them if they tell anyone."

Aidan was serious. By his shadowed expression and knowledge of the subject, I had a feeling he knew about this kind of abuse. Maybe because of his job and maybe . . . maybe personally.

"I've met all of his teachers. None really seem like the type."

"They never do," Aidan said softly, staring at the ground for a moment before looking at me. "It's important that you find out what's bothering him."

I nodded, feeling the knots in my stomach return full force.

"What do you know about this Hempstead? He seems to spend a lot of time with Luke."

I waved that away. "He's a milquetoast kind of guy. Soft-spoken, balding, probably in his early forties, has a girl-friend. I can't imagine him doing something so . . . awful."

"You'd be surprised how many male offenders who molest boys consider themselves hetero."

I hated even thinking about it. "I'd wondered if Luke was into drugs. There's so much out there now. But I haven't found any evidence, and he's never acted high or foggy. Aside from some break-ins that have happened in nearby towns, this area is relatively crime free. That's why I liked the idea of a small town."

"It's not safe anywhere. Small towns harbor criminals of every sort, sometimes lurking behind the façades of kind people."

That made me shiver. "I'll remember that."

"Could be that he's just got heavy stuff on his mind." Aidan looked at me intently. "I think you've got heavy stuff on your mind, too."

I pushed away from the fence and meandered toward a white gazebo where people got married and had their prom pictures taken. Someone had left some silk ivy that wound through the triangular slats.

Aidan's suspicions weighed heavily on my heart. Could it be as bad as that or just preteen drama? I would talk to Luke that night and try to find out.

Aidan walked beside me, letting me sink into my thoughts for a few minutes. I could see Luke in the distance, sitting on the ground petting Bonk. Luke hated that I never let him out of my sight when we were here. Or anywhere. It was a habit I'd gotten into three years ago; it had never left me. I leaned against the gazebo column, turning at an angle that gave him some visual freedom for a moment.

Aidan stepped up beside me, touched my arm. "Did I overstep my bounds?"

I nodded toward Luke. "No, I'm glad you said something."

"I mean about you." The soft, slow strokes of his finger on my arm made it hard to put words together.

"I don't like people getting too close," I said in all honesty.

"Why? What are you afraid of, Maggie?"

I lifted my gaze to his on those words filled with heartfelt concern. "Everything."

His hand moved to my cheek, his thumb caressing my jawline, and then he lifted my chin. He moved slowly closer, maybe giving me a chance to object. Part of me *was* objecting, but it was only a voice deep in my subconscious. The rest of me wanted to feel his mouth on mine, welcomed the rush of bubbles to my blood. The kiss started gently, a brush of his lips to mine, and then another, and then it intensified quickly. I'd never particularly liked black licorice, but on his tongue it tasted exquisite.

His hand wrapped around the back of my neck as he pulled me closer and deepened the kiss. My ardor surprised me as I moved my tongue against his. I heard and felt his quick exhale and then felt his consummate control as he softened the kiss and pulled back.

I had never felt light-headed or dazed after a kiss. I actually had to blink to bring myself back to reality.

I saw the same daze in his eyes as he drew his hand from my neck and let it linger against my face. It was such a tender gesture I wanted to cry out when he let his hand drop. No one had reached out to me in so long, and now this beautiful stranger was, and it made me want him and want to run away at the same time.

"Don't be afraid, Maggie," he said in a soft voice. "I won't hurt you."

He took my hand and led me from the gazebo. I wanted to ask how he could assure me of that. No, I couldn't depend on his promises. It was up to me to keep from getting hurt.

"I saw you kissing him," Luke accused as soon as we got into the car. "Gross."

I was going to point out that technically Aidan had kissed me, but that wasn't true. I'd been an equal participant. "Yes, we kissed." Bonk was panting in the backseat, his head between me and Luke as I waved good-bye to Aidan. I pushed Bonk and his dog breath back.

"I don't like him."

I looked at Luke. "Why not?"

He gave me that frustrating shrug.

"Not good enough."

"It was like he was probing me. Studying me."

Yes, but there was a reason for that. "Luke, you would tell me if someone was . . . hurting you. Wouldn't you?"

He blinked in surprise at my question, but he didn't answer.

I couldn't believe I was even pursuing this kind of conversation with my son. "If someone was touching you, coming on to you in an inappropriate way, you would tell me."

"Yeah, sure." He gave me a look as though I were the one who'd been acting strangely. He crossed his arms, faced the windshield, and huddled down in his seat. "Can we go home now?"

I knew pushing him wasn't going to get me anywhere. I would try one last tactic. "The way you're so distant lately scares me. I don't like being scared. I want you to tell me what's going on. I don't care what it is, or how bad. If it's drugs, or someone's bullying you at school, or even if it's a girl—"

"Mom, nothing's bothering me but you." He hadn't even looked at me. That was probably a good thing, since I'm sure I looked as though he'd just poked me with a fork. Maybe he had seen my expression, though, because he said, "I'm just tired of you bugging me all the time. There are a couple of guys who're jerks, sure. And it's tough being new in town when everyone else has lived here for-freakin'-ever. The play is the one way I belong. I've got a lot on my mind, with the play and all."

"Are you mad at me for moving us here?"

"I was, at first. But it's okay now."

He'd made a few friends, and I knew they teased him about his overprotective mother. I had only just started letting him hang out. He was even going on an overnight camping trip with Chuck Levinson's family the following Friday.

Just as I put the car into gear and headed out of the lot, he asked, "Mom, are we on the run? Like outlaws or something?"

"Why do you ask that?"

The shrug. "Sweeney says everyone has something to hide. Even people you think are the most innocent."

"Is that so? What else does Sweeney say?"

"We talk about deep stuff like good versus evil. Guy stuff."

"About whether we're on the run?"

"It does sound kinda weird, you know. Not talking about what happened with Dana and the trial, changing our last names."

"You haven't mentioned any of that to Sweeney, have you?"

"Nah. But the stuff you don't say can say . . . well, stuff. Sweeney says what you don't say tells more about a person than what you do talk about."

"So what's his story?"

"He was an accountant, and his wife died, and he needed to get his life back together. Rethink what's important. He's writing a book about love and life. Forgiveness."

"You and this guy have become pretty good friends, huh?" I was trying to phrase it casually.

"Yeah, I guess."

Fast. I'd left out that part. "I want to meet him. Keep him from disappearing into his room before I get there next time." At Luke's suspicious look I added, "Not because I'm lonely and need something."

"Yeah, you're seeing someone else." He stared out the window at those mumbled words, fogging up the glass.

"I'm not *seeing* him. I'm just . . . seeing him. There's a difference."

We were going out the night Luke went camping, an honest-to-goodness date. I hadn't mentioned that to Luke, and I wondered what that said about me, according to Sweeney.

As we passed our neighbors' house a few minutes later, I saw that it was all closed up. It was sad, somehow, even though I didn't know the Weavers beyond a wave and a bit of casual conversation. I'd once promised to keep an eye on the place for them.

Luke and I got out and went inside. I was going to change and get my run in. When I walked into my closet, I stopped at the sight of a book lying on the floor. Black, simulated-leather cover, gold-edged pages. Dana's diary.

I still hadn't had the guts to read it. I opened it once and read a random line—*I feel like I'm being raped every day*— and closed it. Dana had started the diary when Colin first began to feel threatening. I'd told myself that it was private and put it in her memory box. That box, up on the top shelf, was skewed.

"Luke!"

He'd come upstairs to his room, which was catty-corner to mine. He leaned in the doorway. "Yeah?"

"Have you been in my closet?"

"Why would I do that?"

"Being nosy?" I lifted the diary. "Were you looking at this?"

He crinkled his eyebrows convincingly. "What is it?"

"Dana's diary."

"Nope." He ducked out and went into the room where we kept the computer. Could one of those games he liked to play be causing his strange behavior? I didn't like snooping, but it'd be justified in this case.

I held the diary in my hand; it felt warm. Was Luke lying? As odd as he'd been acting lately, I had to believe he was. Last week he'd left the milk on the counter. The ajar passenger door of my car had run the battery down. He'd denied those, too. I put the book on the shelf and changed. I looked at it once more before I headed out for my run.

CHAPTER TWENTY-SIX

Wednesday I dashed home at lunch instead of meeting Aidan. I wanted to find some reason for Luke's change of behavior, but I was scared of finding something, too.

I looked around his room, finding books on method acting and even *Breaking Into Acting for Dummies*. Some had Walter Hempstead's name inscribed in them. He was probably one of the most caring people I'd met in Ashbury.

I found a *Playboy* magazine beneath Luke's mattress. That was probably normal for a kid his age, and in a way, it relieved me. He had, at the end of last school year, expressed some embarrassed interest in one girl, but he hadn't mentioned her recently. He was a boy, though, growing into a man. Curious in the way adolescent boys are. I tucked it back where it had been. On the computer I found nothing worrisome in his in-box and Internet history. He'd obviously borrowed games from friends. They were worrisome, but only in the stealing-cars-and-shoot-'em-up way.

I felt like a heel for snooping, but it had been worth finding nothing more than a girlie magazine. It still left the question: what was going on? He'd mentioned a couple of jerks at school. He was embracing Tae Kwon Do. Was he too ashamed of being bullied to admit it? Was he afraid I'd intervene?

When I left the house, the storm clouds that had been

threatening all morning smothered the sky. As I passed the Weavers' house, I did a double take. I thought I'd seen movement in the big glass window. I slowed and tried to look past the reflection. Was the light on? They probably had a timer set to turn lights on at night, but it was daytime. If it hadn't been overcast, I wouldn't have even noticed.

But I had. I saw no vehicles in the vicinity. Surely if someone was there to rob the place, they would have parked out front for ease of loading. Still, I pulled into the driveway and got out. I heard nothing out of the ordinary. I could see, though, that the light in the living room was on. Maybe they'd just set the timer for the wrong time. I peered through the window, cupping my eyes for a better view.

The television was still on the stand, as was the stereo. The rest of the interior was dark, so I couldn't tell if anything was disturbed. I walked around the house, checking the doors and windows. Everything looked intact.

I walked back to my car, but I felt that odd sense of . . . what? I couldn't tell exactly, but it was the kind of feeling that prickled all my hairs to attention. I spun around, seeing the shadow of movement inside the window again. Was it my imagination? I was getting out of there.

I reached Luke's school, where the cell reception was better, and called the police station. "I'd like to report suspicious activity. I think." I described the situation to an Officer George Pederson who promised to check it out. The Weavers were part of a program where seasonal residents left keys with the police. Then I headed into school.

I felt even worse about my snooping after my meetings with some of Luke's teachers gleaned the opposite information from what I'd been fearing: Luke was excelling in his classes, doing better than he'd done last year.

Mr. Hempstead, in particular, effused over Luke's talent as we sat on gym bleachers. "He's got the gift, Mrs. Donahue." He patted my hand. I felt a ripple of distaste go through me at the soft, almost mushy feel of his skin. "I'm so glad you respect your son's talent, and that you trust me with him." He only left his hand on mine as long as the brief pat, though. Maybe I was thinking about how Stewart Cooper had begun touching me inappropriately.

"He sees you as a father figure, I think. He reads the books you loan him, quotes you, and he appreciates what you're doing for him."

"I do hope I can help him grow into his full potential. It's very exciting to watch. Now that the school auditorium is finished, we'll have a much better venue for our plays." He indicated the gym with a grimace. "I won't have to schedule around sports. Eventually this school will have a first-class acting program." He rubbed his hands together in his excitement.

"You haven't noticed anything different about Luke's behavior in the last few weeks?"

"He's been studying for a rather intense role. He's probably just getting into character."

"This is for the winter play?"

"We're getting ready for that, too. But this is another play that I wrote. It's about a young man who gets drawn into a cult, and how he ultimately escapes." He hunched closer and lowered his voice. "This is just between you, me, and Luke, but I'm hoping to pitch it to the playhouse for a summer production. I'm fine-tuning it now, with Luke's help. And I'm going to cast him as lead."

"That's great. Luke must be so excited." But he hadn't been acting excited. "Has he mentioned anyone by the name of Sweeney?"

"Nope, doesn't sound familiar."

Odd. Mr. Hempstead was probably the man Luke was closest to. "Thank you for your time."

"For Luke, anytime. Did he mention that we're getting together on Sunday? He hasn't been wanting to stay after school much, and we need to get in some rehearsal time."

"No, he didn't, but I'm sure we can work it out." I knew why Luke didn't want to stay after school—Sweeney.

I left, feeling a little better about Luke. Could he be that much into a role, particularly one so grim? Should he even be playing such a role? Maybe learning the dangers of cults would teach him to steer clear.

When I followed up with the police department on the way to Mrs. Caldwell's house, Pederson said, "We didn't find anything."

"Maybe the light was mistimed."

"The light wasn't on a timer."

"Oh. Well, did you turn it off at least?"

"It wasn't on. Probably just a reflection."

Those words left me cold. I was going to protest, but he closed the call and hung up. The light had been on. I was sure of it. Wasn't I?

When I pulled into Mrs. Caldwell's driveway, I noticed the absence of the Jeep Cherokee. Sweeney was gone once again. I'd tried knocking on his door Monday, but apparently he was wearing his headphones. Yesterday he hadn't been there, either.

Luke was raking leaves when he looked up at my approach. I felt the shame across my cheeks, as though he'd see me and know I'd been looking through his things. "Did you and Sweeney work on your moves?" I asked, trying to sound nonchalant.

"Yep, and then he had to go to the store."

I wanted to ask which store but held my tongue. Luke clearly thought I was too invested in meeting Sweeney, which was why I'd stopped mentioning how he was never around when I arrived. My son saw nothing strange about the fact that for a week and a half I still hadn't met the man who had captured his interest.

Maybe I was overreacting. After all, Sweeney seemed to be a good influence on Luke, and Mrs. Caldwell kept an eye on them. Maybe I was overreacting to Luke's change of behavior, too. But I just couldn't convince myself of either.

Burt always hovered over me when I opened the mail. I was at my desk slicing open envelopes the next day, and he was reading over my shoulder. I had politely suggested that if he wanted, he could sort through the mail first, but he obviously preferred this method.

One blank envelope, addressed to the office in general, caught my eye. I pulled out a plain white sheet of paper and held it up:

> *REPENT!*
>   *Reach for the son, as I have, and know true satisfaction. Only God can forgive your sins, but by reaching for the son, one can learn to get down on her knees and beg forgiveness. You are not alone.*

"Must be for you," Burt quipped, laughing at his "joke."

I answered the ringing phone and a moment later put the caller on hold. "It's Jim Martinson." Our latest conquest in the Bill–Burt war.

When I saw Aidan crossing the street I bid Burt good-bye and headed out. I was looking forward to our lunches a little too much. I needed to back away, but I was enjoying the lighthearted feeling of enjoying life, and the rush of infatuation. Even the anxiety was a nice change. At least I felt *something*. I wasn't giving it any more weight than that. I couldn't. Aidan was only visiting, and I needed to focus on Luke.

I didn't want to make too much of the fact that I kept a stash of black licorice in my desk drawer these days.

When I stepped out into the crisp, sunny day, I heard Aidan's voice saying, "No. I don't believe it."

I paused when I saw him on his cell phone. He met my gaze and held up a finger. *Give him a minute, but don't leave.*

"How? They said it was appeal-proof. What kind of technicality? . . . Shi—" He caught himself on my account, perhaps, but was totally focused on his call. He pressed his hand against the brick wall beside him, flexing his fingers in frustration. "When? . . . All right. Keep me apprised. . . . Yeah, I'm sorry to hear it, too. Damn." He disconnected, pressed his forehead against the bricks for long enough to take a breath, and then looked up. It amused me that he could muster a genuine smile for me after hearing such disturbing news. He casually pulled me against him, a subtle public display of affection. When he held me there for a moment, though, I wondered if he just needed human contact.

Once he loosened his hold, I looked up at him. "What's going on?" Asking probing questions seemed unfair, since I couldn't offer honest answers of my own.

He leaned against the wall and pulled me in front of him. "A friend of mine . . . his daughter was raped four years ago. Her testimony helped put her rapist away. The guy's case was just overturned on a technicality. He's free, pending a new trial. It means he has another chance to go after her, make sure she doesn't testify again. It means he could actually go free."

I could see the tension and worry in Aidan's face. I felt it, too, but not only for his friend. I'd asked Marcus if Colin could ever appeal his case. He could appeal it to the moon, Marcus had said, but unless someone came out of the woodwork to give Colin an alibi for that night, it would never happen. Even if he did, the witness would likely be discredited. After all, Colin had been there that night.

When Aidan touched my chin, lifting my face toward his, I realized that I'd been lost in my thoughts.

"Sorry, didn't mean to bring you down," he said.

"What are friends for?" I asked with a half smile, though I wasn't exactly sure what we were.

"It makes me crazy to think of these criminals walking the streets, looking for their next victim. He's free because someone screwed up." Aidan's gaze was on his fingers twining with mine. His blue eyes burned with passion when he looked at me. "One study estimates between one and five percent of our population are child molesters."

It was definitely a personal issue. I sensed that what he did for a living tied into something that had happened to him. His fire touched something in me, too. It was oddly arousing, though not in a sexual way. I hadn't felt passion for anything in a long time.

I focused instead on what he'd just said. "My God, are you serious about that number? It's terrifying."

"The worst part is that they're often people the child

trusts. In this case it was a neighbor." He shook his head in disgust. "Your sister . . . did they catch whoever hurt her?"

I hadn't told him anything about Dana, other than she'd died as a result of a violent crime. I nodded.

He stroked my face, and I closed my eyes at the touch, at the compassion of it. I wanted a normal life. I wanted love, romance. I wanted Aidan. And I hated the wanting, hated the chink of vulnerability that wanting created.

"Let's eat," he said.

"I can at least tell you some good news," I said as he took my hand and led me across the street. "I think Luke's okay."

When Luke and I reached the Weaver place on the way home, I slowed down. The light wasn't on.

"What's wrong?" he asked, following my gaze.

"Just checking. I thought I saw the light on yesterday. I even had the police check it out. I feel kinda silly about it now." Still I remained for a few seconds, watching that window.

Finally I pulled away, and only then did I think I saw movement. Probably my imagination.

"Hey, why don't you run with me tonight?" I said when we pulled into the barn. It was getting darker earlier, and I didn't want to run alone.

"Nah, too cold." To demonstrate, he blew out little puffs of foggy air when he got out of the car.

"You don't feel it once you get warmed up." But I knew it was a lost cause.

We let Bonk out and I quickly dressed in sweats and sneakers. I stretched and headed out, meeting Bonk on the way back in. "Come on, boy! You can run with me!"

He did, for a few minutes. Then he picked up the scent of something and darted into the darkening night. "Lousy dog," I muttered between huffs of breath. Not that he was much of a protector, but he would have made me feel a little better.

Since that odd feeling the week before, I'd been more cautious, watching the woods, listening for anything out of the ordinary. Now I could hear a distant barking and, farther away, a sound that always made me feel alone: a coyote howling. I ran the loop, though, chiding myself for being spooked about nothing. I searched for Bonk but saw nothing in the sea of brown leaves, shadows, and thick sea of trunks. Half a mile away there was another old house like mine. I didn't know if anyone was there.

My house was warmly lit, and through the window I saw Luke sprawled on the couch watching television. I continued on, ignoring the cold spike in my lungs and the ache in my legs. Only a hint of dying light led the way.

I saw the light even before I'd neared the Weavers' house. The light, warmly inviting in any other circumstances. Not now. I slowed, calming my breath as I approached. I stopped several yards away, looking into the living room. The bitter wind that had made my run harder blew leaves into a frenzy all around me. I was poised in a tense state when I heard a sound behind me. Before I could turn, something hit me from behind.

I pitched forward, throwing my hands out to break my fall. I heard myself scream. My heart was pounding so hard I thought my ribs would break. Or was that footsteps? When I hit the ground, I scrambled onto my back. I expected to see a man or beast hovering over me.

I saw nothing. Heard nothing over the sound of the leaves as they resettled. I got to my feet and ran, even though every muscle in my body screamed. I couldn't hear a thing above my pounding feet on the leaves and my wild heartbeat. I imagined someone only inches behind me, reaching out to grab my shirt and pull me off my feet. My lungs burned by the time I reached the house, where Bonk was waiting.

Reaching the glow of the front porch light filled me with relief. I hit the front step and spun around. No one. I searched the woods and the street but saw only the movement of branches and leaves as another wave of wind charged through.

When I turned to Bonk, who was sitting at my feet now, I blinked. And screamed.

He was gripping a skull in his mouth.

Luke opened the door. "Mom, what happened?"

I could only point. His eyebrows kinked as he knelt down in front of Bonk. "Come on, boy. Let's see it."

Bonk dropped it and sauntered inside. Casual as could be. Worthless dog.

"Don't touch it," I said as Luke did, indeed, touch it.

In fact, he held it up for my inspection. "It's a rabbit skull, I think. Been dead awhile."

The bones were clean and weathered. The mouth was gaping open, teeth still intact. The empty eye sockets were just as eerie. He tossed it into the yard. "Is that what you were screaming about?"

I followed him in, then closed the curtains and peered out at the darkness beyond. "I was at the Weavers' house. The light was on again and I was trying to see inside. Something hit me from behind." I lifted my sweatshirt. "Is there a mark?" My damp skin felt chilled, even in the warmth of the house.

I felt his finger trace an outline on my tender skin. "Yeah, you've got a red mark."

I walked to the bathroom, flipped on the light, and twisted around. A red blotch marred the middle of my back where it throbbed in pain.

"What do you mean, something hit you? Like a deer? Or a bear?" He obviously thought that prospect was exciting and ran to the front window to look.

I opened my mouth to say how I thought it was a someone but only said, "I don't know. It was hard. It didn't feel furry."

"Antlers, maybe? That'd be cool if it was a moose or something."

"Real cool," I muttered.

He peered into the doorway. "Maybe we should go out and take a look."

"No!"

He jumped. "Jeez, Mom, it's only an animal."

I lowered my shirt. "I don't know what it was, and wild animals can be dangerous."

Fortunately, he didn't argue. He looked out the window once more and then settled onto the couch. I limped into the kitchen, more aches announcing themselves. I'd landed on my hands, but one knee had hit the ground. I washed the dirt off my hands and nearly walked into the pantry door as I headed to the towel bar.

"Luke, what did I tell you about closing doors?"

"What door?" his voice sailed in from the family room.

"The pantry door. I almost walked right into it."

"I didn't open it."

I leaned into the family room. He didn't look the least bit mischievous or guilty. "You're sure?"

"Yeah. I took a juice and ham from the fridge." He held up the package of lunch meat.

I knew it was closed when we'd come in that evening. I looked at the open door. Fear clawed at my throat. I could hear Dana's voice as clearly as if she were standing next to me: *The closet door was open. I know it was closed when I left, Mags. These are the games he plays with me. Little things to let me know he's been here.* The front door had been locked when we'd arrived. Dana's door had been, too. The alarm hadn't shown any intruders, but it was hardly state of the art.

Luke broke into my harrowing thoughts. "Mom, what's the big deal?"

I couldn't take my eyes from the door. Maybe I was paranoid.

And maybe I wasn't.

"I need to use the computer," I said.

I was sweaty and cold and desperately needed a shower, but I more desperately needed to do a search, just to make sure. Aidan's phone call echoed in my mind. I logged in and Googled Colin's name. I misspelled it three times before my stiff, trembling fingers could get it right.

Seven hundred and thirty-six thousand entries were found. "Quotes," I muttered, adding them and doing another search.

I stared at the first entry, underlined and in blue:

Stratham man found not guilty in new trial.
    Colin Masters is once again a free man thanks to twelve
jurors who found him not guilty of all charges . . .

I couldn't breathe. Skimming down the list of entries, I saw a few more about a new trial and then others about different Colin Masterses. I clicked on the link, which led to an article on the *Seacoast Times* Web site.

> *After gaining a new trial due to a technicality, Colin Masters was acquitted by a jury today. Masters was originally convicted of aggravated felonious sexual assault and burglary with intent to commit the crime of aggravated felonious sexual assault in connection with the rape of a Portsmouth woman on May 16, 2006. He was sentenced to seventeen and a half to thirty-five years in prison. Rockingham County Prosecutor Alice Brookson blamed the absence of their key witness, Maggie Fletcher, for the acquittal. "Apparently Mrs. Fletcher changed her identity. We were unable to find her," Brookson said.*
> *Some say it's a travesty of justice. Others say it was an innocent man's last chance for justice. One juror confided, "I figured the guy probably did it, but I wasn't convinced one hundred percent so I had to vote for acquittal."*

"Ohmygod, ohmygod," I whispered, feeling everything inside me crumble under a great weight. I looked at the date of the report: *he'd been out for six weeks.*

I ran to my bedroom and dug through my Maggie Fletcher memory box. I flipped through my little black book, as I'd called it. I probably could have recalled the number under ordinary circumstances; now I could hardly recall my name. I dialed a number and waited. I could have screamed when the answering machine picked up. Marcus's voice instructed me to leave a message. Did I want to leave my number? Any message at all? My mind scrambled as the machine beeped.

"Marcus, it's Maggie. I just found out . . . he's out."

I heard a click and then Marcus's voice. "I'm here." I heard soft music in the background and then a woman's voice. He said something to her I couldn't hear and then, "Maggie."

My belief in the justice system was crumbling, and he was on a date! "Marcus, *how*? How, how, how?"

"You just found out?"

"Yes. I Googled his name."

I heard Marcus exhale. "We messed up. I'm afraid it's just that simple. When Masters waived his right to a jury trial, we should have filed a motion. The motion was never filed. His attorney found out, and the case was overturned. We scheduled another trial, but I couldn't find you." He laughed softly. "When I suggested you hide, well, you did a damn good job of it. We tried to find you for months. You and Luke were just gone. And without you, there was no case."

I felt anger, disgust, and disbelief rise in my throat. "He can't be retried."

"Unfortunately, no. Double jeopardy. We can only hope there will be another woman, another case. More evidence."

"How can you hope there will be another victim?" I nearly shouted, then took a breath. "I'm sorry. I know what you meant." I scrubbed my fingers through my hair, yearning for my worry curl. "Because we both know there will be another victim. And it might be me."

"I assume you changed your name. You moved away. If we couldn't find you, how could he?"

I thought of the open pantry door, my car door, the milk being left out. I couldn't be sure, though. I wasn't even positive he'd done those things at Dana's house. "I hope," I said, though I didn't feel it. "Whose fault was it? That the motion wasn't filed?"

"I think it was Stewart's, but he wouldn't admit it. He's no longer working with us."

"Because of this?"

"A woman involved in a case accused him of fondling her. A couple of other women came forward. We let him go."

Stewart had screwed up. That loomed larger than anything else he'd done.

Marcus said, "If Masters is smart, he'll leave you alone."

"He's smart, Marcus. That's the problem. He's smart *and* he's vengeful. I've got to go."

I hung up and held the phone to my chest. It hurt to talk to Marcus, and I sure didn't want to hear his patronizing assurances.

"Mom, you okay?" Luke's voice seemed to come from a great distance.

I turned, trying to calm myself. "Colin Masters is out of prison. He was retried and found not guilty."

Luke's shoulders sagged. "Now you're worried he's going to come after us again."

"Worried? More like scared to death."

"Mom, if he could find us, he would have sent his partner here already."

"True," I said, grabbing onto that realization. His partner had to be nearly as resourceful as Colin. Then again, maybe his partner *had* found us and Colin wanted to be the one to finish me up. What had he been doing all this time?

My phone beeped where my tightening fingers had pressed the button. I set it down.

"You're not going to keep me home all the time again, are you?" Luke asked.

"No. But I want you to be watchful. Especially around the house." I gripped his arm as he started to leave. "Do you swear you didn't open that pantry door?"

"Maybe I did," he said. "Probably just didn't realize it."

I let him go, wondering if he'd only told me what I wanted to hear.

CHAPTER TWENTY-SEVEN

I almost canceled Luke's camping trip Friday night. Almost. But he'd been looking forward to it and it was the last one the Levinsons would take this year. I almost canceled my date with Aidan, too. I wouldn't be much fun. And I knew a night without child would be the likely time to fall into bed with Aidan. I wasn't sure how I felt about that. My body crackled at the prospect. My heart, however, was protesting. *Protect yourself,* it screamed. *Every time you've given me away, I got broken!*

But no, I assured myself. This wasn't about love. I wasn't sure I could love again. What I was feeling was lust. I suspected, though, that my heart was indeed opening to Aidan, and that scared me.

We ate dinner at a cozy restaurant in the town just north of Ashbury and returned to Aidan's cottage for wine. I'd met him there, since I'd been visiting with the Levinsons prior to our date. Aidan had probably figured out that I just wanted my car handy, a measure of control.

We sat out on the sleeping porch, overlooking the black void that was the lake. A massive storm system hovered to the west, and every few minutes the sky—and the lake— would light up as lightning arced across. Aidan had suggested storm watching as an enjoyable pastime. I thought he was a little strange, but now I could see the attraction. We were on a couch, snuggled under a scratchy blanket. I sipped the merlot in my glass, swirling the liquid around to savor the taste. I'd tried valiantly to pretend that things were normal, but he'd asked me several times where I'd drifted off to.

"I told you I wasn't going to be much fun tonight," I said. "I'm probably bringing you down."

He squeezed me closer. "What are friends for?"

I laughed softly. "Touché."

"I wish you'd tell me what's going on. Even if you could narrow it down a bit. Does it have to do with Luke? Or is it just a mood?" At least he hadn't suggested PMS.

I looked at him, his face defined by the flickering candlelight. "Bad news from home," I said. I interlocked our hands, scissoring our fingers back and forth. "I'd rather not talk about it, if you don't mind."

He did; I could see a trace of frustration even in the soft light. I felt it in the way his fingers tightened. He had never probed much, and neither had I. I got the sense that we were both holding back on our pasts. Maybe he was because I was. Right then I didn't want the past to come between us, so I leaned forward and kissed him.

What started as unspoken communication quickly fired into passion. Our mouths mashed together, tongues slipping and sliding against each other. As we kissed I unbuttoned his shirt and slid my hands around his waist and his back. He was hard and muscular, and he made the sexiest sound when my hands made contact with his soft skin, as though he'd been dying for my touch, too. I loved the way he cradled my face as we kissed, that sweet sense of possession. I hadn't realized how much I missed being possessed. How much I missed being touched. Now I'd opened that door and I was going to pay big for it.

Don't think, Maggie. The blanket had fallen away, and we didn't even notice the cool air. He murmured my name as he slid his hands beneath my blouse, along the edges of my lacy bra, and up to my shoulders. He tracked across my breasts on the way down, touching just enough to tantalize.

He pulled me close, my chest pressed against his, and kissed me deeper than I'd ever been kissed before. I tasted the wine and a trace of the Black Jack gum he'd been chewing earlier. He ran his hands over my back, long, graceful strokes. His fingers drank me in as they rubbed across my flesh. He brought my body back to life.

I felt his desire, pressed against me and in his rapid breathing, and yet he was amazingly chaste in his touch. I could, in fact, feel a tremor going through him in his restraint. I had decided to give in to my desire. Even if it was this one time and he returned to his world and I stayed in mine, I wanted him. He made me feel, and I so badly wanted to feel again.

"Aidan," I whispered against his mouth. "You don't have to hold back."

I heard a groan deep in his chest, of desire and, I thought, regret. He kissed me again, pulling me hard against him. I could hear his heartbeat hammering inside that beautiful chest.

He kissed me again and murmured, "It's not time yet."

I pulled back and looked at him, seeing the agony of his words.

"Are you having your period?" I whispered dramatically through my hoarse throat.

He laughed, or more like barked a laugh, and dropped back on the couch, pulling me with him. "Oh, Maggie." He scrubbed his hand over his face, shook his head, so obviously trying to get a handle on his ardor. But why?

I had to lean up to look at him. "No protection?"

"No, it's not that."

I couldn't believe that he didn't want me. All the signs were there. I sat up, straddling his hips, and leaned into his face. "Then why are you stopping?"

He framed my face with his hands, big hands that felt good wherever they were on my body. "It's not the right time yet."

With a loud exhale of breath I leaned back. "What makes it the wrong time?"

I was making him uncomfortable, not only with my prodding questions, but also because I knew damn well where I was sitting. I could see the strain in his expression as I shifted.

"You do. You've been somewhere else—somewhere dark—all night. I think . . . we need to be at the right place before we . . . go farther."

My darkness, and his respect for it, touched me even as it annoyed me. That it obviously wasn't easy for him helped. I eased off him, leaning against the back of the couch. I'd wanted to escape, and maybe I would have been using Aidan to do that. I didn't think he'd mind, though. Maybe I was being too much like a guy.

He took my hand. "Maggie, I don't want to mess this up. You'll understand . . . soon."

"You're married!"

He laughed again. That was a good thing, I thought. I was that far off the mark. "I've never been married."

"How old are you?"

"Twenty-seven."

I smiled. "And polite enough not to ask my age back. I like that." He was younger, as I'd suspected. He looked even younger with his waves in disarray and a sensual sleepiness in his bedroom eyes. Did he know what he wanted? He seemed mature. He'd seen darkness, too. Impulsively I pulled his hand to my mouth and kissed the back of it. "I'd better go. I've got to let Bonk out."

I tried to move away, but Aidan's hand tightened on mine. "I could go with you. Sleep over."

"And make me crazy all night? No way." I tugged free and got to my feet. The thought of having him hold me through the night squeezed my chest so painfully I knew it'd be a bad idea.

"Maggie . . ."

"It's okay. You're right; it's not the time." Looking at him lying there with his shirt open, I ached at the question: would it ever be right? The more time I spent with him, the harder it would be to pull away. The ache told me it was already going to hurt. My fear told me how much it scared me to think about opening myself up.

"You're all alone out there," he said, following me inside.

I shivered unexpectedly at that statement. "I've got Bonk."

"Yeah, he's probably a hell of a watchdog."

"He'll bark." And wag his tail. "Besides, I've got—" I was about to say *a knife in my car,* but that would invite questions I didn't want to answer. What could I say, really? The pantry door was open? The neighbors' light was on? Something had knocked me down last night while I was out in the woods at night?

Oh, God, I'd sound like Dana. Her paranoid rantings, her neediness. No, I could never be like Dana.

"Maggie?"

I blinked, realizing I'd broken off in the middle of a sentence and was probably standing there with my mouth open. "Sorry, just thinking." To bring up my concerns would mean telling him the whole story. "I was going to say, I've got the lights on and I can run fast."

He hesitated. "Why don't I at least follow you home, make sure everything's all right?"

"Why are you worried?" Had I somehow let out that I was afraid of the dark?

He shrugged. "The break-ins in the area. And you look a little worried."

I forced a smile I wasn't anywhere near feeling. "I'll be fine." I suddenly wished he lived closer. I wished I could ask him home. I wished I were strong enough to do that. "Really. We haven't had any break-ins here in Ashbury. The police patrol the area, especially on the weekend nights when the robberies tend to happen."

He reluctantly nodded. "Call if you need me."

I slung my purse over my shoulder and tapped it. "I've got my cell phone."

He walked me to the car, standing beside me wearing regret on his face. "Good night, Maggie."

He kissed me tenderly, but I recognized that restraint. I

finished the kiss and opened my door. I wanted him way too much. I'd never known a man to hold back like that. Marcus had pushed for more than a kiss on our second date, though he'd reluctantly given me time. Wesley had been shy, and I'd had to be the aggressor. Aidan was something else altogether. Not shy. He'd been a perfect gentleman. Too much so.

I waved as I started the car and backed up. Going home alone was the sane thing to do but it wasn't what I wanted to do. Not by a long shot.

Aidan felt his whole body vibrate with wanting Maggie as she pulled away and disappeared into the night. That had been the hardest thing he'd ever had to do. Some rules, at least, couldn't be broken.

He sat on the front porch, letting the night air cool him down. She'd been quiet. Somber. She'd glanced around the restaurant during dinner, as though looking for someone. Her beautiful light brown eyes had, at times, filled with apprehension. For a while he'd wondered if she suspected there was more to his return than what he'd told her. But she'd been with him, after all, trying to smile past whatever was bothering her.

Dammit, if she'd only open up to him. Then he could tell her everything. As he watched the fog forming over the lake, he tried to imagine her reaction when he did.

CHAPTER TWENTY-EIGHT

He kept the flashlight beam low, just in case. Maggie probably wouldn't be home tonight, though. He'd watched her and
Aidan having dinner. The touch of their hands across the
table, smiles filled with the glint of lust or love or whatever
they wanted to call it. She would probably sleep at his house
tonight. Or they might return here. Just as Dana had done,
Maggie was spoiling his plans by falling for Aidan. Aidan
was spoiling his plans, too, but he would get his chance. He
was a patient man. After all, he'd already waited this long.

He heard the crunch of tires on gravel and doused his
light. Her little red SUV pulled up to the house. The headlights went off. And she stepped out . . . alone.

It was past eleven thirty when I drove down my road.
I couldn't tell if the storm was moving in or passing by. The
lightning flashes were brighter now and the rumble of thunder a little louder. But still no rain. To my relief, I saw no
light in the Weavers' house.

My house, however, was pitch-dark. Hadn't I left the light
on? That I couldn't be sure was completely disconcerting.

I knew Dana must have felt the same way, wondering if
she were imagining things. Once the possibility that it

wasn't your imagination crept in, it was hard to shut it out. I didn't pull into the barn but parked in front of the house. I stepped out, closed my car door, and waited for my eyes to adjust to the darkness. The half-moon was high above me, but the canopy of branches overhead dimmed its brightness. I clicked on the flashlight that I kept in the car. In my other hand was the kitchen knife I'd tucked between the console and my seat.

I maneuvered the flashlight, knife, and key, looking behind me every other second. After fumbling in the dark trying to jab the key into the lock, I managed to get it open. The alarm was armed but beeping intermittently. What did that mean? As I was trying to figure it out, something nearly knocked me over as it jumped on me. Fur and a wet tongue. Bonk! He whined, acting antsy. I punched in the alarm code and petted the dog. "Go ahead, boy."

He ran out into the darkness but didn't take off as he usually did. I heard his footsteps on the leaves not far from the house. I remained in the open doorway, reaching in to flick on the foyer light. Nothing happened. My insides clenched. I flashed the light inside and saw nothing out of the ordinary. I also noticed that the oven clock wasn't on and neither were the lights for the satellite dish receiver. The house felt cool.

Oh, crap. The power was off. I shivered, blaming it on the cold. I locked the door and searched the house again with the flashlight. The air inside felt as dead as air in a sealed crypt. I made my way upstairs to the room my mother had occupied. Luke and I had moved the desk there just a week ago so I could pay bills without the distraction of the television.

The stairs creaked beneath my feet as I reached the top step. The bedroom faced the front of the house. With the flashlight I searched every corner of the room, even the closet and under the bed. I couldn't ignore the thrum of danger in my veins, the way it pulled at my temples. I glanced out the window just as lightning flashed in the sky. I saw my car briefly before it went dark again. I felt my way to the desk in the corner, set the flashlight on the chair, and found the utilities bills file. Using my cell phone, I called the emergency service number. As I dived through layers of voice mail, I wondered, *Was this why the Weavers' light hadn't been on?*

Dammit, pick up! I was stuck on hold. Between snatches of classical music a polite voice piped in assuring me that my call was very important and they'd be with me shortly. They listed three areas where electrical shortages had taken place because of the storm. Ashbury wasn't one of them. But I already suspected that, since Aidan had power when I'd left.

I aimed my flashlight at the highboy dresser. The surface was covered with picture frames. Mom kept a small dish for her few pieces of jewelry. I touched the cross on the gold chain, the one she'd been wearing when she'd died. Sadness descended unexpectedly upon me. We'd had our differences, but she had been my mother. One of my few close living relatives. I needed to create a memory box for her, too, to join the other three.

Even Harold and Marion Fletcher had become enemies of a sort. During mine and Lukc's last few visits with them, I had sensed a coolness and even distrust. They didn't like not having my address or home phone number. I'd created a Hotmail account where they could e-mail me, but that wasn't enough. I'd explained that I couldn't take the chance of Colin's partner searching their files. The safer I felt, the more fiercely I wanted to protect that feeling. They took it personally that I'd rented a car to visit them. When Harold followed us as we left Cambridge, though, I had to hide my fury from Luke. We headed into Boston, our plan anyway, and lost Harold. I wasn't sure that I wanted to see them anytime soon.

My heart felt heavy as I set the phone down on the corner and looked at the pictures. Most were old, and only one included my father. One was of Mom with her parents when she was a girl. I selected three for the memory box and set them on the bed. I opened the top drawer to put the rest in and found stacks of letters. I felt vaguely as though I were snooping, but I would have to look through everything anyway to sort what needed to be kept.

I held a sentimental hope that the letters were from my dad, though that was unlikely. I wanted to think there was some deep love there, but I suspected they'd stayed together because of Dana and me.

Lightning flashed, giving the room a ghostly, two-dimensional look. I flipped through a couple of the old envelopes, from my mother's sister. When I got to the plain white envelopes, my heart skidded to a stop. They were addressed from the New Hampshire State Prison. They were addressed to my home. Here.

I tore the envelope trying to get the letter out. One plain page covered in neat handwriting. I flipped it to the back and my gaze shot to the signature at the bottom: *Colin.*

"Oh, God." The words tore thickly from my throat. I turned the letter over and held it in the flashlight's beam. My fingers shook, making the letters wiggle.

Dear Angelista,

They'd been on a first-name basis. I flipped through the rest of the envelopes. They were all from Colin. He and my mother had been corresponding. How? Why? She must have intercepted the letters at the mailbox. Since I had most of our mail go to the post office box in town, I rarely checked the box here.

The cheerful wait music drifting from my cell phone sounded in odd contrast to the clammy fear overtaking me. I read the letter:

I am beginning to feel the joy you have often described in your letters. The joy of knowing God. It fills me with a lightness, a wonderment, even here in this place with little joy. I find myself praying now, in the quiet times after lights-out, in the morning before we are let out of our cells. I feel peace. I want to touch others as you have touched me. I know God will bless you for reaching out to me, the man accused of raping your daughter. Such a huge gesture, Angelista. Such a big heart. Perhaps you can teach me how

to forgive like that. Perhaps someday I can forgive Maggie
for lying to put me here. I hope to make things right with
her someday.

"Is anyone there?" a small voice asked, startling me from
my reading. I grabbed for the phone.

"Thank goodness. My power is out." I gave her my account number and name and waited while she checked to see
if service was out in my area.

Her voice sounded puzzled and cautious when she returned a minute later. "Mrs. Donahue?"

I could barely hear her over the thunder. "Yes?"

"Um . . . you canceled service, effective today."

I couldn't speak. Finally I uttered, "My service was canceled?"

"Yes, ma'am. Mr. Donahue made the request. He said
you were vacating the premises. He gave the Social Security
number on the account as verification."

I felt that familiar dread tightening my insides. "There is
no Mr. Donahue." I wasn't counting my son, of course, who
would have no reason to turn off our power.

Now it was her turn to become silent. "Um, well, we
checked account number and Social Security number. That's
how we verify—"

"Okay, I got that. Now turn the power back on. And put a
lock on the account so that only someone who goes to your
office with picture ID can change the account."

"We can do that. And if this was our mistake, we'll credit
you for the time you were out of service."

I wanted to laugh. This wasn't exactly an inconvenience.
"I don't care about that as long as you get my power turned
on immediately."

"Of course." I heard her pecking at a keyboard as I recited
my Social Security number. "I've got you all set for reactiva-
tion. It'll be sometime Monday—"

"No. Uh-uh, that's not going to work. It needs to be
turned on *now*."

"This is an account issue, ma'am. Our offices won't be

open until Monday morning. I can put a rush on this, being it was a mistake and all. But that's all I can do right now."

I squeezed my eyes shut. It wasn't a mistake. Someone had done this. Someone. I glanced at the letters. I wasn't even sure what I said, but I disconnected. I put the cell phone in my pocket, grabbed up the knife and flashlight, and scanned the room again.

My heart slammed into my ribs when the top step creaked. I ran to the door and aimed the flashlight. Nothing. I spun the light everywhere, keeping the knife gripped in my other hand. I stood still, listening to the house. Lightning flashed into the room behind me, followed closely by thunder so loud it rattled the windows.

Dana, I know your fear. I'm so sorry I couldn't stop it.

Dana. Her power had been turned off, too. *Accidentally.* She'd come to stay with me that night, and she'd been so afraid. She hadn't told me about Colin yet, so I thought she was overreacting. Had he done it?

I didn't know where to go. I wasn't sure the house was safe, but going outside didn't seem wise, either. I went back into my mother's old bedroom and locked the door. Stared at it. Then I sat on the bed and stared at the door. I listened between the rumblings of thunder.

I heard another creak. The house was settling, as I'd told myself numerous times before. A slight scratching sound. What was that? I scooted back against the headboard and wrapped my arms around myself. Kept the knife at my side.

I couldn't hide here all night, though. My heart would give out, wondering if every noise was him coming for me. I doubted the door would hold up if he tried to bust through. I had to let Bonk in. I could take Aidan up on his offer to stay the night. I wrapped my coat around me and rubbed my arms. Could I camouflage my fear enough to sound rational? It was logical, wasn't it, to stay with someone on a cold, stormy night because your power was off? *Yes, yes, yes!* I dialed the cottage, but the answering machine picked up. Where was he?

The rain began then, not gently but pounding against the

windows like the spray of gunfire. I pushed myself off the bed and listened at the door. The rain obliterated any subtle noises I might hear. I gripped the doorknob, quietly unlocked it, and yanked it open.

Nothing. I aimed the flashlight into the dark hallway. The other two doors gaped into darkness. The thought of him standing there waiting for me to descend the stairs iced my blood. I flashed the light into each room and then closed the doors. I sidled down the stairs, watching above me and below, my back to the railing.

The rain was loud, louder than it should have been. As I reached the last step, I listened again. Then I turned the corner to face the front door—that was wide open. With a yelp I ran. Not to close it. If he was inside, I wasn't about to shut myself in with him. Not like last time. I ran outside into the blinding rain.

"Bonk!" I screamed as I ran to the car. "Bonk!"

I felt arms grab me. A hooded figure. My flashlight dropped to the ground. I screamed, kicked, and pushed, but he wouldn't let go. Where was my knife? Had I dropped it? "No!"

"Maggie!"

The voice was familiar. Aidan. Oh, God, Aidan. I blinked through the rain. Wanting to see him, to be sure. Yes, Aidan wearing a hooded coat, only I'd knocked the hood off. Rain streamed down his face.

"Maggie, what's wrong?" he asked, and I heard the fear in his voice, too. He held me by my shoulders. "Talk to me."

I probably looked as though I'd gone mad. Especially when I gripped him, buried my face against his wet coat, and sucked in deep breaths. I needed a moment to get myself together. Yes, I'd sound mad if I told him what I was afraid of. I'd sound as needy and desperately afraid as Dana had. Though Dana had had reason, I had doubted her. Aidan might doubt me, too.

I finally gathered my senses and looked at him. "I can't find Bonk. My power's off." And then, "What are you doing here?"

"I called to make sure you'd gotten home all right. The

phone kept ringing. I was worried." He glanced at the house and then back at me. "With reason, apparently."

I looked back, too, seeing the front door flung open, imagining myself tearing out into the night. "I just got spooked, with the power being off and the storm. And"—I searched the yard—"Bonk's not back."

Lightning scored the sky above us, and I cringed reflexively before the thunder even cracked.

"You'll stay with me."

It wasn't a request, but I wasn't about to protest. My head, unprotected as well, was frigid. He led me to the front door, and I looked inside to make sure Bonk wasn't there. Aidan, I noticed, was looking around, surveying the house.

"He's-s s-still outs-side," I said through chattering teeth.

"We'll find him." Aidan took my keys from my numb, wet fingers and locked the door. He continued to look around, though not for Bonk. He was checking the outside of the house, the upstairs windows.

"Maybe he's in the barn," he said. "Get in my truck. I'll check."

But I went with him, that dark space too frightening to let him go alone. We both called Bonk, but he didn't appear.

I ran around back to the outhouse. The door, with its ubiquitous half-moon cutout, was propped open. I'd planted geraniums in the former toilet, but they'd dried up with the cold weather. I peered in, but still no Bonk.

"Maybe he found shelter somewhere else," Aidan said. "We can check the house up the road, make sure he's not ducked under the porch awning." He put his arm around me and led me back to the truck as another wave of thunder vibrated the earth. I saw the faint glint of my knife on the ground. I'd dropped it without even realizing it. How was I going to protect myself—and Luke—if I couldn't even hold on to a damned knife?

I also had a darker thought. What if I had held on to it? What if I'd stabbed Aidan? That was why I never wanted a gun in the house.

"Maggie? You all right?"

I blinked, bringing myself back to the moment, to Aidan, watching me with concern at the expression on my face. I nodded.

Even in the drenching rain he opened my door for me, helped me inside, and closed it before running to the driver's side. I stared at my house through the blurry windshield, the windshield wipers not clearing it for even a second. I had no clothes or toiletries but I wasn't going back in that house tonight.

He reached into the backseat area of his cab and pulled out a blanket, which he tenderly wrapped around me. "You're shivering," he said, making a hood over my head.

I started to look in the back. "Do you have another one? For yourself? I probably knocked your hood off when I . . ." When I freaked and fought him.

"There's nothing but a couple of old towels. I'll manage."

He drove slowly, the headlights lighting up the rain and not much else. He pulled up to the porch and hit the brights but found no dog huddled on the porch. We called again, but the rain obliterated our voices, so Aidan honked his horn several times.

"Dogs sometimes come when they hear a horn blasting." He tried again. "We'll give him a couple of minutes." He turned to me. "Maggie, you looked terrified. Still do. What happened?"

I was shivering, even though the heater was up full blast. I couldn't look at him, not without giving away my fear. "I just got spooked. You know, woman-all-alone thing. My power was off. I heard creaking sounds. The power company said someone had accidentally canceled my account. Bonk was gone. And I freaked." I finally turned to Aidan now that the lie was over. "I wasn't expecting someone to be outside. And you grabbed me."

He almost looked . . . disappointed. As though he knew I was lying. Too bad. I wasn't bringing him into my nightmare. Especially not now.

He pushed a stray lock of hair from my upper cheek. "If something's going on, tell me. Let me help you."

"I'm fine." I was tired of lying. I hoped it didn't show in my voice. I searched for Bonk, avoiding Aidan's piercing gaze. "Hopefully he'll go into the barn when he returns."

"I'll put towels on the floor for him."

I love you, I thought, startling myself with the thought. I loved his kindness to Bonk, and to me, too. We pulled into the barn and he made a small pile of towels in the corner.

We had to give up on Bonk. The truck inched along the road that we couldn't see. I wasn't sure how he knew where to turn, but he did. It felt like years had passed since I'd left his cottage.

When we pulled up, he expelled a breath. "Damn. The lights are out here, too."

We ran inside, stripping off our wet coats in the mudroom before entering the cottage. Aidan disappeared into the darkness and returned with towels for both of us. He lit a kerosene lamp and set it on the kitchen counter.

"Come sit here," he said, indicating a chair at the table. I obeyed the curious command. He stepped behind me, and then I felt the thick towel gently rubbing my head. Something inside me melted like hot candle wax. He was drying my hair.

"Why do you cut your hair so short?" he asked, his fingers massaging my scalp through the towel. "Hiding from your curls?"

"I . . ." I could hardly think with the ripples of pleasure coursing through me. "I just wanted a new look."

He stopped, tilted my chin so that I had to look into his serious blue eyes. "Are you ever going to tell me the truth?"

"What do you mean?"

"I know you're hiding something. I can see it in your eyes."

Damn. I'd always had easy-to-read eyes. I took the towel from him and walked into the living room. "I can sleep on the couch." At his silence I turned to him. Even in the dim light I could see his frustration. I wanted to trust him, but I didn't trust myself not to fall in love. To take the comfort and everything else he offered. Not when I desperately needed to connect to life again. It was easier—and better, especially now—to keep him at a distance.

I could tell by the way his shoulders relaxed that he'd given up on the conversation. Maybe even given up on me. It was better that way.

He walked into the one bedroom and came out with clothing that he handed to me. "Here. One of my shirts and some drawstring pants. They'll be big on you, but they should work in a pinch."

I took them with a grateful smile.

"If you don't feel too threatened, we can share the bed. With our clothes on. It's going to get cold until the heat kicks on again."

A few minutes later we arranged ourselves on his queen-size bed. The pillow smelled like him, earthy and manly and everything I missed about sharing a bed with a man. I caught myself groaning, my face buried in the pillow. Our bodies touched, connected at leg and hip and arm. As the temperature began to dip, he pulled me so that I was lying on his chest, my leg over his. We didn't speak or kiss or even say good night.

My hand rested on his stomach, and I relished the feel of his body beneath my fingers. I inhaled the scent of him through the thick shirt he wore. I drifted, but never fell, into sleep.

I felt the power return in the wee hours, the heater kicking on and stirring the air, warming the room. I remained where I was, though. I relished feeling safe.

It didn't last long. As the chill left my body I had a disturbing thought that brought it back: how had Aidan known where I lived?

CHAPTER TWENTY-NINE

The next morning I drank the coffee Aidan had started while I was in the shower. He was now taking his shower while I spoke with someone at the electrical co-op who actually had some authority.

The woman said, "I'm not sure how this happened. Obviously your account was confused with another Donahue account."

"According to your recorded message I heard a thousand times, you tape your customer service calls. Could you pull up that call?"

"We just changed our phone system and haven't gotten that part back online. But I assure you we'll look into this and find out what happened. And make sure it doesn't happen again."

Was it a mistake? I wished I could believe that. Otherwise, Colin had come into my home, taken the information from my bills, and found my Social Security number as well.

I could hear keys tapping in the background. "I apologize for the inconvenience, Mrs. Donahue. You should have power by this afternoon."

"Thank you," and, *Thank God,* I thought as I hung up.

The cottage had a sunny feel to it with its soft yellow walls and white cabinets. The owners had painted a mural of sunflowers all around the windows of the dining nook. I could see why it was so popular.

Aidan's cell phone rang, vibrating on the countertop where I was flipping through the pages of one of the early Harry Potter books. Too bad the phone wasn't one of those models where you could see the number without having to open it. It rang four times and stopped. I had no right to be curious about Aidan when I wasn't being forthcoming with him. That detail didn't stop me, though. I knew some things about him. He liked kids' books, including ones that had spiritual meaning, like *The Chronicles of Narnia*. We'd talked about subjects as diverse as terrorism and the history of coffee. He had copies of *Psychology Today* and *Rolling Stone* magazines with his name on the label. He watched little television but indulged in *Monk* sometimes.

I suspected there were many more things I didn't know about Aidan.

I opened the small pantry door to see if he had anything to eat. There wasn't much in the fridge, unless I wanted to whip up some fresh pasta and sauce. He had French bread, garlic, and olive oil. The pantry was pretty bare, too. Aidan lived sparsely, at least when he was traveling. He'd only had the essentials in the bathroom: deodorant, shampoo, soap, and hair gel. I found a box of Cocoa Puffs in the pantry. Well, it would do.

I was about to close the door when I saw the white box on the floor. I recognized his handwriting on the lid: *Research*. I wondered what kind of research went into searching caregivers' backgrounds. I was about to take a peek when I heard him say, "Hey."

I wasn't sure if it was an admonition or greeting. I forced a smile. "I'm foraging for food."

Lies. I was sick of lies, of hiding, of being afraid and suspicious.

"No food in there. That's my work."

I held up the box of Cocoa Puffs. "Is this your cereal?"

"Yep. Hungry?"

I nodded.

"Hope this is okay. Obviously I wasn't expecting company in the morning."

Obviously. Man, woman, chemistry, night without child. The question was, why not? One of several questions that haunted me. I gave the box a shake. "This is fine. I sometimes have Luke's cereal. Makes me feel like a kid again." Aidan's grin stirred my heart. "Oh, your cell phone rang."

He dialed in as he took down two bowls, phone scrunched between his ear and shoulder. As I took out the milk I heard a female voice say, "Aidan, you'd better get your ass back here soon! This bloke is driving me crazy."

Aidan chuckled and I pretended I hadn't heard. I guess he could tell I had.

"My sister, Jessica," he offered graciously when he didn't have to. "She works with me. A friend of mine is handling my end of things while I'm on leave. I'm guessing they don't get along too well."

"Is that the girl in your wallet?"

"Yeah."

He opened his wallet. My gaze first went to his driver's license. Aidan Trew. Age jibed with what he'd told me. Then I looked at the picture. Two kids with haunted faces standing so close together they seemed fused.

"Not long after that picture was taken my father killed my mother and we went to live with her parents. They raised us."

"I'm sorry," I said, knowing too well how inadequate that phrase was. I wondered why he kept this sad picture with him. I asked, "What happened to your father?"

"He skipped bail. No one's seen him since."

So Aidan knew the unremitting ache of unpaid justice, too. He grabbed two spoons out of the drawer.

I was still standing near the counter as he headed to the small table that overlooked the lake. "You took a leave of absence from your business. To come here?"

He realized that I might have pinned him in a corner this time. "Yeah," he said slowly.

"To see about a woman you only knew casually. You often do things like this?"

He took the jug of milk from me, looking me in the eye. "Never."

I didn't know what to say. Why would he leave his job to pursue something with me? It made me nervous in ways I couldn't begin to explore.

He kissed me long and sweet and afterward kept his fingers on my chin. "I don't want to scare you away, Maggie. Right now I think that could easily happen. Later, we can talk about why I'm here. Why you're here. We've got to place trust in the universe that it will reveal its secrets when the time is right. And we have to stick around long enough to try to understand them."

I took the milk back and set it on the table. Stared at it. I wasn't sure what to make of his words. Was he hinting at my secrets? I suppose I'd been vague enough to warrant questions. If he dug deep enough, would he find out that Maggie Donahue had no history? What would I find out about him?

"I'll keep that in mind." Afraid to dig deeper, I said, "They're going to turn my power on today. I went to someone in a higher position. They say if you can't get a turkey to help, find an eagle."

He didn't smile. "Are you going to tell me why you were so afraid last night?"

"The boogeyman." Only my boogeyman had a face. A name. "I'm glad you came over." And now the question that had been buzzing inside my brain all morning. "But how did you know where I lived? I'm not listed in the phone book."

I searched his expression for any sign of discomfort but saw nothing. "I did a reverse lookup of your number on the Internet."

Okay, that worked. We poured our cereal and milk in exactly the opposite order; I poured milk first and then the cereal.

"If your electricity doesn't return, you and Luke will stay here." Finally I saw a spark of a smile. "Under vastly different sleeping conditions."

Not that anything had happened. Aidan had been a perfect gentleman, despite the temptation of waking up in close proximity. Despite the physical evidence that he obviously wasn't 100 percent choirboy.

I finished my cereal and washed my dishes in the sink. "I should get going. Luke will be back from his camping trip. I'm anxious to see how it went. I mean, excited." After last night, I wanted to know he was okay.

Aidan came up behind me, standing close but not quite touching me. "You've got time before Luke comes back."

"I want to check the house, see if Bonk's back." I gave him a smile. "Things don't look so scary in the daylight."

He turned me around to face him, leaving his hands on my shoulders. "Promise you'll call if you need help. I'll give you my cell number. Call me, anytime." He lowered his voice. "Even if it's just the boogeyman."

"Okay," I whispered. Wishing I could. Knowing how easily I could hold on to him like a bit of flotsam in a turbulent ocean.

No, no, no. Just like a drowning person, I could pull him under with me.

I expected Bonk to be waiting at the door or at least in the barn. He wasn't anywhere. Aidan and I both called as we circled the house and expanded out into the woods. I heard no paws pounding on damp leaves. No barking. Where was he? My throat tightened in fear.

"It was a heck of a storm last night," Aidan said. "Maybe he's hiding somewhere."

"No, he'd be back by now." The sun was out, though the air was cold and damp. Tree branches littered the ground from the battering winds. Fog slowly burned away like the Wicked Witch of the West after meeting water.

"Maybe someone took him in."

I knew Aidan was trying to be optimistic. I couldn't say why I was scared. "He'd still be back by now." I tucked my arms around my waist as I expanded the circle we'd already searched.

"If he's not back soon we'll put up flyers."

I could only nod as we headed to the house.

Aidan insisted on checking the rooms, and honestly, I didn't protest all that much. "Nice place," he said. "Homey." He'd said that last word wistfully.

He prowled the family room first, pausing at the pictures on the wall. "Luke's father," he said, looking at a family portrait. "I can see the resemblance."

"Wesley's been gone for over six years. It's hard to believe." My voice had gone soft, as I realized how much time had passed. "He was my first love."

Aidan gave me a look that stirred my soul, especially when he said, "But not your last." He picked up one of my knitting needles from the basket and poked his palm with it. "Good weapon, on the fly." *Ooh, excellent idea.* He picked up the tiny pink blanket in progress. "Is there something you haven't told me?"

That was such an understatement I could have laughed if what he was holding weren't so dear to my heart. "I knit blankets for stillborns and send them to the area hospitals."

His expression softened, but he didn't ask any more. Maybe he knew.

Upstairs my bedroom was neat, as it always was. A stack of remodeling books sat on my nightstand. All my plans in stasis, just as I was. I still watched Ty and HGTV, for inspiration, I told myself.

Aidan checked under beds and in closets, even in the cabinet beneath the sink. Good God, I wouldn't have thought about that.

When he saw my expression, he said, "I read about a case where a stalker made himself a hidey-hole in the woman's bathroom cabinet."

"Good to know," I said, not letting on how good it was to know.

He checked the windows, rubbed the alarm contacts. It felt strange having him in my home, even stranger watching him touch everything. Other than the light that managed to come in through the windows, it was fairly dark inside. I'd picked out larger, energy-efficient windows but hadn't ordered them yet.

Luke's room was the usual mess. Posters of the plays we'd seen were plastered like bills all over the wall. Some of the nicer ones were framed, my gift to him.

Aidan eyed the scattered envelopes in the bedroom that used to be my mother's.

"I did that," I said but didn't explain further. Those envelopes sank my stomach again.

"Do you have a gun?" he asked as he looked in the closet.

"No way. Absolutely not. Guns scare me as much as any bad guy."

"They're also your ultimate protection."

"I know." I'd thought about it. "I also know if you're not prepared to use it, it can be used against you. And then there's the possibility of Luke finding it. When I was a kid, a neighbor boy found the gun his dad hid in a locked box and blew his face off."

Aidan grimaced. "Point made."

At the front door, he pulled me close and kissed the top of my head. There was something protective and regretful about the gesture. He tipped up my chin. "Call me." I watched him leave and wished I could open up to him. I felt the sense of loss shadow me, and yet I didn't really have Aidan.

I pushed those thoughts from my mind and raced upstairs. I only had an hour before I could pick up Luke. I sat on the floor amid those envelopes and read all twelve of them.

From what I gathered, my mother had initiated contact with Colin in the months after he was incarcerated. Her goal: to save his soul. She knew he was guilty, but she offered her forgiveness. Not once did he admit to the assault or even the stalking, but he accepted her forgiveness anyway and her offer of salvation. I suspected my mother was also trying to save my soul in the bargain. It was hard to be angry with her, but I still screamed in frustration at her naïveté. And at what she'd inadvertently done.

Colin, I saw, played her like a pro. He asked her to lead

him to the light, accepted God, the whole shebang. He even forgave me for my lie. His words were downright tender. My mother must have been so proud of herself. He'd probably been using her to get information about me. I knew he hadn't forgiven me. Because he never once mentioned that his case had been overturned. After his release he'd given her a new address, a post office box, to send letters to, citing a transfer. The box was in Stratham. I wondered if he'd come here during his new trial preparations. Probably not. He wouldn't want to risk me seeing him. He'd no doubt been banking on the fact that I'd gone to ground.

I bundled the envelopes and stuffed them in the metal trash can next to the desk. When I stood, I caught sight of a small, pink envelope with my name on the front. I picked it up, the last envelope in the drawer. Because it blended into the wood interior, I hadn't seen it last night. I gently slid my nail beneath the flap and pulled out a delicate, scalloped piece of stationery.

> Dear Maggie,
>
> If you are reading this, then you have discovered my correspondence with Colin Masters. Undoubtedly, you are confused, and probably angry. I am sorry for this. But I felt I must make this situation right with God. I reached out to Colin, and he took my hand and let me lead him to the Lord. I forgave him, Maggie. I know you have a hard time with this concept, but I'm asking you to please consider it. Let Him punish Colin in His way.
>
> I forgave you, too, Maggie. I love you.
>
> Mom

As I folded the note and slid it back into the envelope, the power came back on. I heard a couple of beeps and the heat kick on. I was caught in an odd state between relief and grief. My hands trembled as I put the envelope back in the drawer and closed it. My mother had always done what she thought was right. She was never aware of how much it hurt those she professed to love.

With my lie, I had done something bad for a good reason. Like, I realized, my mother had done. I felt an odd stirring in my chest at her final words. She'd warned me that something terrible would happen if I lied on the stand. How right she'd been.

I knew she'd only done what she thought was right. Necessary even. But she'd led a sadistic stalker to my door. And he had no intention of letting God right his wrongs.

Colin watched Maggie slow down in front of the house, as she always did, from his comfortable spot on the Weavers' plaid couch. Or so the plaque by the front door had said: *Welcome to the Weavers' place.* He had indeed made himself welcome.

The course he'd taken to become a locksmith all those years ago had come in handy many a time. He knew alarm systems, too. If people realized how easy it was to bypass them, they'd freak. The one Maggie had had in Portsmouth was harder to get past. Hers here was a snap. He'd rewired it so it only looked as though it were armed.

The dog whined, and Colin leaned over and rubbed his head. "I know you want to go home, fella, but I have another message I want you to take to your mistress."

Colin had heard her scream when the skull had reached her. Bacon grease had made the old bones savory again.

He'd been about to have a grand time torturing Maggie last night. The weather had cooperated, as had the power company. Even Maggie, by coming home alone. Then Aidan had shown up. Colin had watched from the upstairs window as Aidan had gone through the motions of checking the exterior of the house and looking for the dog. Protective, valiant—pain in his ass.

He would have other opportunities. He opened his knife and felt the blade's edge. Nice and sharp. He still had plenty of fun in store for Maggie Donahue. She was going to pay for every one of those hours he'd spent in prison.

"Stay here." He gave the dog an ear rub before walking

over to Maggie's pretty little house by the lake. He unlocked the front door and inhaled the clean, flowery scent.

"Oh, Colin," he mimicked in a high-pitched voice. "Make yourself at home."

"Why, Maggie, I think I will."

He went upstairs to her room, bouncing on the top step that creaked. He stretched out on her perfectly made bed. Should he take her there? Violate her in her own bed? It depended on whether the kid was there. Colin didn't want any distractions.

No, because when he had his final encounter with Maggie-the-dolly, he wanted to focus completely on her. Wanted to revel in his power of possession. Her humiliation. His utter control. Her complete submission. Her begging, pleading, crying.

His revenge.

CHAPTER THIRTY

Ghosts, goblins, and gap-toothed pumpkins were springing up all around town. One yard had a sheet ghost hanging from a tree, a nylon rope tied around its neck to secure the ball that was its head. It seemed a bit morbid, but it was probably my mood. The day had turned gray, cold, and overcast. It seemed much of the town was staying indoors today by evidence of the lack of people out and about. One family was decorating their yard, bundled in their coats and gloves.

Luke had announced he was too old to go trick-or-treating the Halloween after we moved here. I suspected he'd stopped because he had no one to do it with here. Another loss I'd caused.

"Are you going out with Chuck on Halloween?" I asked.

"The Levinsons are giving a party for the kids."

"Wonderful," I said in a falsely cheery voice. "What kind of costume should we make?" When Luke was eight, he'd dressed as Shakespeare. None of the kids got it.

"I'll figure something out." As in, *I don't need your help.*

"You should go dressed as a sullen, moody kid." I snapped my fingers. "Oh yeah, that's what you are."

He gave me the evil eye even as I smiled to temper the words. It wasn't fair that kids grew up. He was in that awkward stage between boy and man, wrestling with hormones, desperate for a growth spurt. *Was it more than that?* I still wondered.

"What are you looking for?" Luke asked as we drove home.

I realized I was in full paranoia mode now. I would recognize Colin's eyes no matter what else he'd changed over the years. Those ice blue eyes, full of smug hatred, still haunted my dreams. I was also looking for a brown dog wandering the streets trying to find his way home.

I used Luke's shrug as my answer. I had to tell Luke about the possibility of Colin being in town. Luke needed to be careful.

I was hoping Bonk would be waiting for us before I had to explain that he was missing. Unfortunately, as we pulled up to the house, I saw no sign of him. Luke, of course, asked, "Where's Bonk?" as soon as we got inside.

"I . . . I don't know. We had a storm last night. He ran out and hasn't come back."

"Let's drive around, see if we can find him."

I didn't mention I'd already done that before I'd picked him up. I'd called Animal Control, too.

Luke and I spent the next hour taking all of the little roads that led to the lake, getting out at each one and calling Bonk. Even after the sky had darkened, we continued looking. I tried to hide how concerned I was. Luke was worried enough on his own. Adding my worries that Colin was in the area wasn't going to help.

"We'll look again tomorrow," I promised. "Why don't we eat at the pizza parlor since we're out?"

An hour before we finished, asked the employees at Antonio's to be on the lookout for our dog, and headed home.

My chest tightened when I saw the Weavers' light on. Did the curtains shift as Luke and I passed? I'd been staring so hard I couldn't discount a trick of the eye.

As soon as I parked in the barn Luke jumped out of the car and started calling Bonk again. I checked the pile of towels but saw no sign that he had ever used them. Tomorrow we'd canvass the woods and make sure he hadn't fallen into a hole.

As we walked toward the front door, I said, "Luke, we need to talk."

"Mom," he whined, suspecting that I was going to try to probe his psyche again.

"It's not about why you're so quiet lately."

He eyed me dubiously. "I've got to take a shower."

His recent habit of taking frequent showers had been one of those things that worried me. But boys his age did smell more pungent.

"Come back down when you're done."

I heated water for tea, hoping to eradicate the chill in my bones. The pipes groaned and creaked when the upstairs shower turned on. One of the many projects on my list. Three boxes of tiles sat in the kitchen corner, mocking my procrastination. I'd once been a reluctant perfectionist. Now I just couldn't engage.

I stiffened when I heard a scratching sound. I took the kettle off the stove to listen. More scratching. I followed the sound, my body on full alert. I tracked it to the front door. Something was outside. I looked out the front window but saw nothing. I pressed my ear to the door and thought I heard a whining sound. Bonk! Maybe.

I grabbed a knitting needle and approached the door. I turned the dead bolt, gripped the knob, and opened the door.

Bonk came bolting in, his whole rear end wagging in his happiness to be home. I felt just as relieved and happy, setting the needle down and hugging him after relocking the door.

"Where have you been?" I asked, inspecting him for any cuts. Then I saw his rump. A spasm clenched my stomach. I fell back onto the floor. Bonk seemed oblivious, as he had the last time. I finally grabbed hold of him so I could see what had been shaved into his fur. No letters. No warnings. Just a smiley face.

A smiley face?

Cheerful. Innocuous. Oh, but the message was clear. Colin was back in my life and he wanted me to know—I was in his sights. *He'll never let you go.* Marisol's voice in my head, her urgent whisper of warning. I couldn't deny it now. He was going to make me pay for what I'd done.

I pushed to my feet and took my cell phone out of my purse. My hand trembled, but somehow I dialed Aidan's number. When I heard his voice, I leaned against the counter.

"Hi," I said in a voice that didn't even sound like me.

"Hey," he said, and I could hear him smiling. "Bonk's back."

"Great! Is he all right?"

I stared at the design on his rump as I ran my hand through his fur. "Perfectly fine."

"You sound funny. Everything okay?"

"I'm just tired. Good night."

I slid down to the floor, feeling deflated and very small and vulnerable. Bonk, thrilled to have me at his level, licked my face. I didn't know how long I sat there petting Bonk, but Luke's voice broke me out of my thoughts.

"Bonk's back! Where'd you find him?"

"He just . . . came home." *Or someone brought him home.* That thought shot my gaze to the front window, but all I could see through the part in the curtains was black.

"Hey, dude, where've you been? We were worried about you."

I waited, soaking in Luke's happy voice until it changed in tone. "Uh, Mom?"

I nodded, and for a moment I couldn't stop the jerky motion. "I know." I cleared my throat. "That's what I wanted to talk to you about. Colin Masters is here. In Ashbury."

Luke knelt down beside me. "How did he find us?"

"He did; that's all that matters. He's letting me know by doing this." I pushed away the shock and tried to gather my thoughts. When had the odd things started to happen? Almost three weeks ago the milk had been left out. My car door had been open a few days after that. Colin's way of playing with me? Or just coincidences? I tried to picture the people in town, tried to pinpoint those who had come in the last few weeks.

Fear clutched my heart as I thought of one in particular. I looked at Luke. "What does Sweeney look like?"

He flinched at the fierceness in my tone. "Why?"

"Luke, tell me."

"He's big, over six feet tall. And he told me he was small for his age, too, Mom. He told me stories about how kids used to pick on him, just like they pick on me, for being scrawny. And then over one summer he shot up and no one picked on him again."

"I don't care about that; just tell me about him. What color are his eyes?"

"You think Sweeney is Colin?"

I wanted to scream at his evasiveness. "That's what I'm trying to find out." No, I didn't want it to be. Not the man who'd had access to my son. Not the man who'd won my son's admiration. Colin's rage was with me, not Luke. I didn't want to believe Colin would try to get to me through him. "What does he look like?"

"Jeez, you're making it hard to think. Let me see. I guess they're brown."

"Not light blue?"

"No. I would remember that. He's got blond hair—"

"Dark blond?"

"No, light. And he's got a cool goatee." Luke traced his finger down the center of his chin.

Hair and eyes could be altered. Mostly, though, it was the way Sweeney had avoided me for nearly two weeks that worried me most. "Let's go pay him a visit."

"What?"

Filled with determination, I got to my feet and looked for my purse. "We're going to drop in. You've said such nice things about him, and he's teaching you to defend yourself. Seems like I should say thanks—in person." I could hear the jaggedness in my words; apparently Luke could, too.

"Mom, what are you doing? Sweeney isn't Colin."

I grabbed my keys and headed to the door. "I'm sure he's not, but let's visit anyway."

He didn't immediately come. "Don't spoil us being friends, Mom."

To see how much this friendship meant, in such a short time, really bothered me. And it hurt that I was again threatening something Luke valued. In truth, Sweeney had been good for Luke. He seemed more alive when he'd been around Sweeney. Like I was with Aidan. "We'll make it casual, okay? Like we were in the neighborhood and we thought we'd stop by." The hysteria, though, was building inside me. The more I thought about it, the more scared I became.

Luke reluctantly joined me in the car. I was so focused on the mysterious Sweeney that I forgot to check the light at the Weavers' house. A few minutes later we pulled up to the bright blue house. All the outside lights were off. Sweeney's light was on, but his Jeep wasn't in the driveway.

"He's not here, Mom. Let's go."

"Uh-uh." I got out and walked to the front door. I wasn't going to leave without finding out about Sweeney. I couldn't. Luke dragged himself from the car just as the front porch light came on.

Mrs. Caldwell opened the door. "Maggie? What can I do for you?"

"I hope we're not intruding. We stopped by to invite Sweeney out for ice cream." *Very casual,* I commended myself, hoping she couldn't see my hands curled into fists.

"I'm afraid he's out right now. He goes out in the evenings quite a bit."

Another notch of fear. "Where does he go?"

Her eyebrows knitted together. "I don't know, and it's really none of my business."

"Can we come in? I'd like to wait for him." I glanced at my watch, though I didn't take note of the time. "He's got to be back soon, right? Not much is open this time of night." I nudged my way inside, hearing Luke mutter behind me.

The older woman said, "Well, I'm . . . I'm feeding my husband right now. We'll be going to bed soon."

I saw the man in a wheelchair at the table, his body sagged and hands trembling. "I'm so sorry. We are intruding."

"Well, yes—"

"We'll just sit in the living room. You go on. Don't worry about us." I pulled Luke inside, where he appeared to be looking for a chance to escape. Mrs. Caldwell hesitated, not sure what to say. I felt terrible pushing her like this. Before she could come up with a way to politely oust us, I asked, "What do you know about Sweeney? I assume you did a background check."

"I, uh . . . well, nothing official. I called someone at his former employer's and asked about him. The man had nothing but good things to say. I also called a former landlord and got the same response. Besides, he was so nice, I was glad to have him stay with us." She smiled. "I remind him of his grandmother, who raised him."

I had started to feel a grain of relief at the employer and landlord calls until she'd said that. Colin's grandmother had raised him. His partner could have easily given Colin references.

"Is his name really Sweeney?"

She was starting to get annoyed by my questioning, evident by the deepening lines on her face. "It said so on his driver's license. I did check that, and I made a copy." This she said in a defensive manner, as though I were questioning her thoroughness.

"I'm sure you were careful before letting someone into your home. Could I see that copy?"

At that her shoulders stiffened. "Of course not. Maggie, really, I need to get back to my husband. I find this conversation entirely inappropriate."

Luke made another noise of embarrassment, but I ignored him. "Mrs. Caldwell, it may seem so, but Sweeney has become an important person in my son's life and I've yet to meet the man. Don't you find it odd that every time I come to pick up Luke, Sweeney is nowhere around? He's either gone or hiding in his room. But he's always around when Luke is here."

"Trust me, if I thought there was a problem, I'd tell you. They're always outside, or in the living room, never up in his room. I sometimes watch them. Not because I'm suspicious," she added tersely. "I enjoy seeing them interact. They laugh, they talk, and they do those fancy karate moves."

It hurt that Luke was talking and laughing with a stranger and not me.

Mrs. Caldwell continued, "I can assure you that nothing untoward is going on."

Saying that I suspected he could be a psychopathic stalker—and possible murderer—wasn't going to fly; I could see that. "A mother can't be too careful."

Mrs. Caldwell nodded toward Luke. "He's a big boy. Surely he'd tell you if something was going on."

I couldn't be sure, but I held that in, too. How could I explain that it might not be obvious? That Sweeney could be manipulating Luke?

"I'm afraid you're going to have to leave. I must get back to my husband."

"Do you need any help?" I asked, knowing that it sounded as though I was using any excuse to stay. Really, I did want to help. This was only the second time I'd seen her husband, and I'd wondered how this small woman managed.

"I've been handling this by myself for a year. I don't need help now."

I detected bitterness in her voice, though I knew it was aimed at her family and not me.

"*Mom,* let's go," Luke said through gritted teeth.

When I turned, in defeat, I saw headlights through the front window. The car that was stopped in the road sped forward.

Sweeney. Even though I hadn't seen the vehicle, I knew it was him. He'd seen me and continued on but not before trying to figure out what I was doing there.

I even caught myself eyeing the stairwell, imagining a dash up to his room. Mrs. Caldwell wouldn't be able to stop me, not at first. Then again, she could call the police. I backed toward the door. "Sorry to bother you."

Her head wobbled, not an acknowledgment of my apology.

"See you tomorrow," Luke said hopefully.

She did nod at him as she followed us to the door and locked it behind us.

"I thought you didn't like coming here," I said as we walked to the car.

"I do now, Mom. And you almost spoiled it."

I looked in the direction the vehicle had gone. Was I just imagining my fears about Sweeney in light of my revelations? I hoped so, but I couldn't take a chance. I needed to find out who he was before Luke saw him again. The next time Sweeney's car was here, I was going to write down the license-plate number and ask Aidan to look it up. If he investigated nannies, surely he'd know how to look up plates.

Once we got home, I sat on the front porch step and dialed the number I'd retrieved from my old black book. I had to be prepared to take drastic measures. Marisol's voice was soft and wary when she answered.

"Hi, it's Maggie . . . Fletcher."

"Maggie. You're all right?"

"For now." The way she'd asked . . . "I have some bad news to report."

"Colin Masters is out of prison. I know."

"I just found out, and he's found me. I want to get in touch with Doctor, arrange for his services again."

I heard a soft catch in her voice. "He's dead. AIDS."

I felt that same catch in my throat. For him. For my chance at escape. "I'm so sorry. He was a good man."

"He'd turned his life around after he got off heroin years ago. But it was too late."

"Do you know anyone else who might be able to help?"

"I'm sorry, Maggie, but I try to stay away from that element. And . . . we're moving. My aunt down in Florida broke her hip, so we're going to move in and take care of her."

I was sure Colin had something to do with that decision. "Good for you." I meant it.

"I wish I could help." She meant it, too.

"Be safe and happy," I said, and hung up.

Next I dialed Aidan.

His surprise that I'd called again was clear in his voice. "Change your mind about needing a strong, virile man to chase away the boogeyman?"

I tried to laugh at his attempt at humor. "Can we talk tomorrow? Luke's got a rehearsal session with Mr. Hempstead at school after church. I'd like to talk to you alone."

I had to admit I was taken aback, and slightly hurt, that he hesitated. "I'm sorry, Maggie. I've got to go out of town. It's . . . business. Can we meet in the evening?"

Business on a Sunday? "Luke will be with me then."

"Are you all right?"

Other than being scared out of my mind . . . "I'm fine. Mostly."

"Damn, Maggie. I'm sorry. I can't get out of it." His regret was clear. "Can we talk tonight?"

"I need to get some information first." I'd been hoping that Sweeney's car would be at Mrs. Caldwell's before I met with Aidan. "Maybe tomorrow night. After Luke goes to bed."

"I'm there."

It was a comfort, and yet I couldn't allow myself to enjoy it. I still had to figure out just how much I wanted to tell Aidan. How much to involve him.

"Thanks."

My throat was so tight I couldn't swallow. Then I'd know for sure if the man who had captured my son's affection was the sadistic stalker who had caused my sister's death. I shivered. And who wanted to cause mine, too.

CHAPTER THIRTY-ONE

"Mom, don't," Luke said as I drove past Mrs. Caldwell's house Sunday after church and lunch.

"I'm just passing by." I memorized the license plate on the Cherokee.

"You know, you're so worried about Sweeney, who's a really nice guy, but what about Aidan? Maybe he's Colin in disguise."

"He's not," I said.

"Well, neither is Sweeney."

We slowed to let a woman and her dog cross the road. Luke leaned toward me. "What if Aidan is Colin's partner?" I caught myself rolling my eyes at Luke's desperation to divert suspicion from Sweeney, but he continued. "Mom, think about it. Aidan comes back to town supposedly to get to know you. Don't get me wrong; you are . . . well, Chuck says you're an MILF."

"An MILF?"

Luke blushed. "A Mom I'd Like to . . . well, you know." He blushed. "Anyway, in acting class we talk about character motives. Doesn't it seem strange that Aidan would come all this way on a chance?"

Yes, I'd thought that, too. Despite Luke's motives, he had touched on my doubts. "Maybe." Aidan had never stated his intentions, though I'd made it clear I wasn't interested in anything serious. That should have sent him back to Boston if he wanted a relationship. He wasn't just after sex. In fact, he was curiously adamant about not crossing that line.

As we approached the school, Luke said, "He's the one who appeared out of the blue trying to get to know you. Sweeney doesn't even ask about you. If I were you, I'd be worried about Aidan."

We got out and walked to the entrance. The door was unlocked, as Mr. Hempstead had told Luke it would be. I walked him to the classroom, surprised to see only the teacher. "Where's everyone else?"

"You know how it is on Sundays. Only the dedicated students come."

I ruffled Luke's hair. "Well, he's definitely that. Have fun." To Hempstead I said, "Thanks for being so dedicated yourself."

"My pleasure."

As I walked out of the school, I spotted a piece of paper skittering across the parking lot. Hating litter, I walked over to pick it up. A breeze took it a few more feet away. Finally, near the far edge of the parking lot, I got the jump on it. It was a waterlogged report belonging to some student. I glanced at the classroom window where Luke and his teacher were going over something. Instead of bothering them, I would send it to school with Luke on Monday.

As I turned, I saw part of a blue vehicle in the park across the street. Dark blue, like Aidan's truck. The line of evergreens bordering the edge of the parking lot blocked most of the vehicle. When I walked a few steps to the right to get a better look, I heard an engine start and saw the back end of a truck bed as it backed up and drove into the park.

Suspicion thrummed through me. Whoever it was hadn't wanted me to see him; that was evident. Sweeney, or at least his vehicle, was at the Caldwells' house. But Colin did have a partner. I thought about following the truck, but the park roads exited to two different highways. The driver could take either one and be long gone.

Aidan's words came back to me: *Later, we can talk about*

why I'm here. Why you're here. We've got to place trust in the universe that it will reveal its secrets when the time is right. And we have to stick around long enough to try to understand them.

I thought he was talking about my secrets. After all, he had been kissing me crazy, so I wasn't thinking clearly. Now I was. I ran back to my car and locked myself inside. "No. I can't believe I'd fall in love with—be infatuated with the person who sent me flowers from my dead son." Wouldn't I recognize that kind of evil? Colin felt evil to me, though he'd fooled most of Dana's co-workers with his false charm as he pretended to woo her.

"Pretended to woo." Those words sickened me. Aidan had first come to town sometime before Colin's retrial. Could he have sent Aidan? Had he tried to charm me in order to find out more about my life? I'd always felt he was holding back. Because of his suspicions about Luke's behavior—and his concern for him—I thought Aidan probably had a rough past. There were times I got the impression he was going to tell me something I wouldn't like. I thought maybe it was about that past. Now I wasn't so sure.

I started the car as a chill worked its way down to my bones. I pulled out of the parking lot, though I was hardly aware of the drive. Now that the thought had burrowed into my mind it wouldn't let go. Aidan was from Boston. Colin had lived in Boston while terrorizing Marisol. A coincidence? I had to find out. I couldn't let myself get any closer to Aidan until I did.

I checked my rearview mirror as I drove. Instead of going home, I turned left and parked in front of the real estate office. I unlocked the cabinet that held all of the rental property keys and pulled one down.

Aidan watched Maggie leave the parking lot and head into town. Damn. She'd seen him. That could be troublesome. He'd watched her pull into the parking lot and walk Luke into the school like a good mother. Then she'd chased a piece of paper like a good citizen. Then she'd looked right at his truck. Time would tell if she suspected that it was him. Now he had to focus on the task ahead.

He parked behind the school building and walked around to the front. On a Sunday, the only other car in the parking lot likely belonged to Walter Hempstead. Aidan quietly opened the door that Maggie had only recently come out of and eased it shut. Paper orange pumpkins smiled at him from the walls. He followed the sound of soft voices.

"The scene is at night," he heard Hempstead say. "So I'm going to close the door and the drapes to create the right mood."

Aidan heard a door down the hall close. The hallway was dim. Only filtered sunlight crept in at angles, casting odd designs on the carpeted floor. He stood at the door he'd heard close. Music began playing, something slow and lethargic. He could hear voices murmuring inside. He peered through the spaces between papers that were taped to the door window, seeing a wall opposite. The room was to the left. Hempstead and Luke were around the bend.

Aidan turned the knob in increments, listening for any telltale break in the conversation. The music helped to cover any noise he might make. He opened the door only wide enough to slip through and sidled to the corner. He'd already started the video camera function and angled the camera around the corner. It could take photographs and record video in dim light conditions without a flash. It could record things the naked eye couldn't see.

"At this point Lewis is in touch with his deepest secret," the teacher was saying. "He is no longer ashamed. He welcomes it. And Miles is his teacher, his mentor. He reaches out to Miles in this scene. You know your lines. Be Lewis."

Luke's voice was uncertain as he recited, "Miles, I don't know how to begin. Show me. Teach me."

"Touch me. First here. Then lower. It gets easier after the first time."

"I don't . . . like doing this."

A pause. "Luke, you've got to get into the character. An

actor plays people that he's not. It's good when you don't feel comfortable with the role. It teaches you to stretch yourself."

"But can't I just pretend to touch you? I'm not actually going to do . . . that onstage, am I?"

"It depends on what venue I can sell this to. But it pays to be prepared. The discomfort you're feeling . . . embrace it. Study it. That's what makes you a great actor. The more you do it, the more comfortable you'll be. But you want to remember how it felt the first few times. That's what you're going to portray, Lewis's discomfort, every time you perform this scene. And then the beauty of awakening."

Luke was obviously dubious, given his silence. In a terser voice, Hempstead said, "I can get someone else to play the role. Todd, Malcolm, any of them would jump at the chance."

Aidan slid out, unable to take it anymore. He didn't want Luke to see him. Only that kept him from storming in and squeezing Hempstead's throat. Aidan slammed the front door and ducked into an empty classroom. From an angle through the interior glass window, he could see Hempstead peer out into the hallway.

"What was that?" Luke asked from behind him, anxiety in his voice.

"I . . . I don't know. Someone must have come into the building. All right, let's take a breather on this, pick it up another day. But remember, I'm the key to your success, Luke. You need me to make it."

Son of a bitch. Using the kid's dreams to sate his sick desires.

Luke passed by, his shoulders hunched and his arms tight around the notebook pressed to his chest. He walked outside and paused, as though to take a breath. His agony and shame were palpable. He continued toward the sidewalk.

Aidan stepped into the classroom as Walter Hempstead was gathering his books. When he saw Aidan closing the door behind him, he hunched like a frightened mouse. "Who are you?"

Walter must have sensed the rage and hatred in Aidan. As Aidan approached, Walter dropped the books and reached for his pocket. He fumbled with a wallet with white, trembling fingers. Girlish fingers. He yanked out several bills and stretched his arm toward Aidan. "Here. This is all I have. Take it."

"I don't want your money, Hempstead. I have a lesson to teach *you*."

I felt many things as I slid the key into the door lock and turned the knob. Colin had forced me to do things I never dreamed I would do. Perjure myself on the stand, for instance. And now breaking and entering. I hoped that I would look around, find nothing incriminating, and leave without Aidan ever knowing. He was, after all, supposed to be out of town that day, which meant that couldn't be his truck I saw in the park.

My heartbeat slowed as I walked inside. I closed the door behind me and took a deep breath. I had crossed the line. I couldn't turn back, I thought, with familiar self-derision. Where to start? I headed to the bedroom first and looked in places I wouldn't have had any business looking during my stay there. I opened dresser drawers but found only clothing. A few things in the closet. Nothing beneath the bed.

That's when I remembered the box in the pantry. I sat on the floor and lifted the lid. Inside folders were stacked upright, all neatly labeled. My fingers trembled as I flipped through the tabs. Most were names I hadn't heard of. But the last one, that one I knew. I felt as though I were going to be sick.

It read: *Maggie Fletcher/Donahue.*

Me.

He knew. He'd known all along who I was, who I'd been. I pulled out the folder and opened it. A few pictures fell out because my hands were shaking so badly. I set the folder on the floor and picked up the pictures. They were of Luke and me. Some were only of me. They were taken in the summertime, during Aidan's first visit. The trees were lush and green then, and Luke had been happy. All were in public places, like the park or the grocery store.

The noise didn't register at first. I was so lost in those pictures and what they must mean. Then it did register and I jerked my head up to look at the door—that was open. Aidan stood there, staring at me in disbelief. My gaze dropped to his rumpled shirt. To the streak of blood going down the front.

CHAPTER THIRTY-TWO

Sweeney was surprised to find Luke at his door on Sunday. "Hey, dude, what's up?"

"I got done with my rehearsal early. Figured I'd come over for a bit, if it's okay with you. Mom isn't coming for another hour."

Sweeney patted Luke's shoulder. "I've always got time for my bud. Got a surprise for you." He led Luke to the old punching bag he'd picked up at a flea market yesterday. He'd gotten permission from Mrs. C. to hang it from a tree limb. "Figured we could work on your kicks, strengthen your legs."

Luke's face lit up. "Kewl!"

Sweeney knew the kid wanted to bulk up. It had been a great way to—what was the word? Oh yeah—bond with him. "You ever going to tell me who's picking on you?" Sweeney asked as Luke inspected the bag with his hands. "Got to be someone at school, right? Student."

Luke had never said he'd been bullied, but Sweeney figured that's why he'd warmed to the idea of learning self-defense moves. Sweeney had once been the small kid; then he'd taken his turn at being a bully when he shot up four inches and fifteen pounds over the summer. He remembered the fear in the smaller kids' faces. He'd recognized that fear and shame in Luke's eyes. So Sweeney had started working on his Tae Kwon Do moves nearby. It wasn't long before Luke became interested.

Luke picked at a crack in the vinyl trim, his expression grave. "What if I told you it wasn't a student?"

"Who is it then?"

"A teacher," Luke whispered.

"A teacher's bullying you?"

He hesitated before nodding. "Something like that."

"Son of a bitch. Want me to take care of him?"

"Like how?" Luke said in alarm.

"Lots of ways to take care of bullies."

Luke shook his head. "Forget it. It's no big deal." He gave the bag a wimpy punch and pulled his hand back with a yelp of pain.

Sweeney walked up to the bag, trying not to roll his eyes in disgust. "Let me show you how to use it. Pretend it's your teacher."

As they worked on the bag, Sweeney said, "Heard you and your mother came by last night."

Luke averted his eyes. "Oh . . . uh, yeah. She wants to meet you." He rolled his eyes. "You know . . . moms. Not in a romantic way or anything. She's just all 'I have to meet the guy who's hanging around my son.' Maybe you could, you know, stay around tomorrow when she comes to get me."

He quelled a smile. Yeah, he bet Maggie wanted to meet him. "I'll try and do that. I can't wait to meet your mom."

He wasn't quite ready to meet her yet. Soon, though. Very soon.

I'd never seen that particular look on Aidan's face before. He looked wired and bewildered all at once as he took in the folder on the floor and, in particular, the pictures I'd dropped.

"Maggie," he said in a hoarse voice. "Let me explain."

"Stay away from me!" I sprang to my feet and backed toward the rear door, my gaze on the front of his shirt and the blood in the creases of his fingernails. I didn't think it was his blood. Then whose? *The truck. At the school.* I couldn't let myself think of Luke just then, not if I wanted to keep my sanity. "I know who you are." I looked frantically around and found an old butcher block of knives. I grabbed one and held it out.

He hadn't moved, though. "Maggie, I'm not sure you do."

"You followed me here. Tracked me down." I pointed the knife toward the floor. "Took our pictures!"

"I was hired to find you."

"By who?"

"I can't say. Put the knife down and let me explain. It's going to take a few minutes."

I reached behind me and opened the door. "I don't care what you have to say. I won't believe a word of it anyway. Just let me leave and I won't hurt you."

I ran across the sleeping porch where we'd snuggled, down the steps, and around to the front, ready for him to try to intercept me. This time I wouldn't drop the knife. I was gripping it so hard I wasn't sure I *could* let it go.

Thankfully, he remained on the porch as I reached my car. "I was investigating you," he said in a calm voice. "When I was here in the summer. But I came back because—"

I slammed the door shut, started my car, and threw it into reverse. Gravel spit out from beneath my tires. I rammed it into drive and sped forward. Aidan was talking, but I couldn't hear him. I just wanted to pick up my son and make sure he was all right. It was nearly two anyway. Knowing that Aidan had been near the school—and I was now sure it was Aidan—gave me the willies. Had he been spying on me? Waiting for Luke? I sped through town, thankful that traffic was nonexistent. I slowed down only when I spotted Luke sitting on the school steps. He looked unharmed, unbloody. I had to stop myself from running out and pulling him into a bear hug. I needed to calm down, bury my shock and fear. He already thought I was nutty.

He looked as morose as I'd ever seen him as he dragged himself to his feet and trudged over. Neither Mr. Hempstead nor his car were anywhere in sight.

"Where's your teacher? He just left you here?"

"I'm not a baby anymore, Mom. We . . . finished early, so he left."

I held my tongue. I'd have a word with Luke's teacher about that. "And you've been sitting here by yourself?" I wondered if I should alert the school officials to my situation so they'd be on the lookout for any strangers lurking around. I'd never forget the feeling when I'd been lured to that old farmhouse and seen that note. Yes, I would tell them.

"I wasn't here. I went over to Mrs. Caldwell's. Figured you'd rather have me over there than here by myself."

I noticed he hadn't mentioned Sweeney, though I was sure that's why he'd gone there. Just the thought of Sweeney tightened my stomach. If his car was there, I was going to stop. "Did you see Aidan around?"

He furrowed his eyebrows. "No."

Luke had buckled himself in but was slouched in the seat. He was staring into space, his face tense. I recognized the redness around his eyes as his precursor to tears, though it had been some time since I'd seen those.

"Are you in character?" I asked, trying to pull out whatever was bothering him. Instead he looked at me as though I'd called him fish scum. "What's wrong?"

He shook his head, his mouth in a firm line, and looked out the window. His pain, and that he wouldn't share it with me, made me want to cry, too.

"Luke, please talk to me. Don't shut me out."

He turned to me, maybe hearing the tears in my voice. Sometimes he seemed so small and young, especially the way he was looking at me right now. "Mom, you said I should go the distance to follow my dreams. You've always been really supportive of my acting."

I was relieved that it had nothing to do with Sweeney or Aidan. "Of course I am. I want you to follow your heart."

He seemed to be looking for the right words. "What . . . what if I didn't want to act anymore? Would that be all right?"

"Of course, sweetheart. People change, and so do their

dreams." I smiled. "You wanted to be a duck farmer when you were seven." He didn't smile back, though. "You don't want to act anymore?"

He shrugged. "I do, but . . ."

"But what?" I asked after waiting a few seconds.

"I dunno. I just don't know what I want to do."

"I'll love you no matter what you decide." I reached out to ruffle his hair, something I did all the time when we lived in Portsmouth. I hesitated as I usually did lately. Then I continued the motion. Was his angst about my approval? I hoped not. I'd always been careful about not putting pressure on him, just as my dad hadn't put pressure on me.

When I sensed Luke wasn't going to say any more, I put the car into drive. A minute later I turned onto Mrs. Caldwell's street.

"Mom, not again."

"It's on the way."

Sort of. The street did lead back to the one that went around the north end of the lake. I figured Sweeney would make himself scarce knowing I'd be picking up Luke. I wasn't surprised to find the Cherokee absent, but I was to see a police cruiser parked in the driveway. I pulled in without giving it a second thought.

"What's going on?" Luke asked.

"I don't know. Stay in the car."

I ran toward the open door and approached the distinguished-looking man with the rigid stance in the living room. "If something's happened, talk to the tenant. Sweeney. He's staying in a room upstairs, and I don't think he's who he says he is." It all spilled out as I jabbed my finger toward the stairway.

"Maggie, what are you doing?" Mrs. Caldwell said, coming out from the back bedroom.

I took her in, searching for signs of distress. "I saw the police car and thought—"

"Your wild imaginings about Sweeney?" She turned to the man standing between us. "This is Maggie Donahue. Her son comes over after school, and she's been paranoid about my tenant." She turned to me. "This is Munroe Wilson, chief of police and friend. My husband passed away today. Munroe is here to help me make arrangements."

"Oh." I gathered my thoughts. "I'm so sorry. How . . . did it happen?"

"He was trying to get out of bed, fell, and hit his head on the corner of the dresser."

Munroe turned his hound-dog eyes at me. "Want to tell me why you think the tenant's not who he says he is?"

Because I feel it wasn't going to cut it. "The man who was stalking my sister three years ago, and who assaulted her, just got out of prison. I testified against him. And now he's found me. He's been in my house, turned my electricity off, and took my dog. Just like he did before the trial, when he was trying to scare me into not testifying."

The white-haired man's eyes widened. "He hurt your dog?"

"No. But he shaved . . . well, he shaved a happy face into his fur." I waved away Munroe's skeptical expression. "He didn't hurt the dog. That wasn't his point, thank God. He was sending me a message. He wants me to know he's here. He's just toying with me now. His partner is in town, too. Aidan Trew, who's renting a cottage from the real estate company I work for."

Munroe held up his finger. "Ah, you're the woman who reported the Weavers' light being on."

"Yes! That's part of his game. I suspect that the man who goes by 'Sweeney' is actually Colin Masters. If I could take a look at his room, I'm sure I'll find something that proves what I'm saying."

Mrs. Caldwell said, "I can't let you into his room." She turned to the police chief. "She's been trying to meet this guy for two weeks."

"He's befriending my son, but he's always unavailable by the time I arrive to pick him up. Don't you find that strange? All I want is to meet the guy who's spending time with my son. I don't think that's asking too much. Which is why I think he's Colin." I realized I couldn't ask Aidan to run Sweeney's plates for me now.

Munroe looked at me, patronization written all over his face. "Mrs. Donahue, you can come to the station and file a report if you'd like."

I heard the unsaid *but*. "But I sound like a lunatic," I finished for him.

He only tilted his head, in a *you said it, not me* way. "It doesn't sound like you have proof of anything." He looked at Mrs. Caldwell. "You haven't had any problems?"

"None at all," she was quick to say. "He's a pleasant young man, other than that goatee thing. To think I'd once considered matching him up with Maggie."

Munroe tuned me out altogether by turning toward the older woman. "Elaine, I've got Phil coming to pick up Ed later today."

As I turned away to give them privacy my eyes caught sight of a pink flyer on the coffee table.

REPENT!

> *Reach for the Son of God, and he will pull you close. Accept his grace and his forgiveness, and he will accept you as one of his children. We, at the Lutheran Church of Ashbury, invite you to join our family. We, too, will embrace you, and accept you as one of our own. You are not alone.*

At the bottom was the church's address.

"Where did you get this?" I asked, without thinking that I was interrupting them.

Mrs. Caldwell looked at the flyer. "It was left beneath my windshield wiper a few days ago." She turned back to Munroe, but I kept staring at the flyer. What had the one we'd received at the office said? Something about reaching for the son, but it didn't say "Son of God." It wasn't even capitalized. That flyer hadn't identified any church, either.

Reach for the son. I felt a cold chill. It had been in there twice, something about reaching for the son. Was Colin hinting that he was reaching for *my* son? Had he gotten the idea from this flyer?

I dimly heard Mrs. Caldwell bid Munroe good-bye. The

warm expression left her face when she looked at me. Before she could say anything, like ask me to leave, I tried again. "Please, Mrs. Caldwell. I'm not comfortable letting Luke come here after school until I can make sure Sweeney isn't the man who attacked my sister."

She let out a sound of pure exasperation, spun around, and hiked up the steps. I followed quickly, before she changed her mind. I hadn't wanted to use the money angle, but it had worked.

She kept glancing toward the front window. "If he catches me in his room . . ."

"What? Do you think he'd hurt you?"

She looked at me with disdain. "I would be utterly embarrassed. Now, be quick. I shouldn't even be doing this." She slid her key into the doorknob and turned it. The knob didn't move. She tried again. "Hm. He's not supposed to change the lock."

I tried it, to make sure she wasn't faking it. She wasn't. "Makes you wonder what he's hiding, doesn't it?"

"He's a private person. And how am I supposed to call him on changing it when I shouldn't be trying the lock in the first place?" She was asking herself, not me.

"Let me look at the copy of his driver's license."

"You just don't give up, do you?"

"I can't, Mrs. Caldwell. It's too important."

She went back down the stairs and dug through the filing cabinet. When she uttered another, "Hm," I had to stop myself from pushing her out of the way to see for myself.

"Missing, I presume?"

"Misfiled, probably. It's a lot of work when . . . when I was taking care of Ed, the whole house, all by myself."

I didn't have the patience to partake in her pity party. "I can't let Luke come until I know that Sweeney isn't who I suspect him to be." I had made that decision earlier, and nothing had changed my mind.

I walked out of the small room and was face-to-face with Luke. He was staring at me—no, glaring. "How long have you been standing there?"

"Long enough to see you bully Mrs. Caldwell into letting you into Sweeney's room."

I herded Luke to the car. "So you know about my ultimatum: you're not to see Sweeny until I meet him. Sorry, but that's the way it is. Until then, you come to my office after school."

He stormed to the other side of the car and threw himself in the backseat, then slammed the door shut.

I took my time, inhaling deeply before getting in. "Tomorrow we'll stop by and see if Sweeney is here."

We drove in silence. Finally I said, "You were right about Aidan. I think he may be Colin's partner."

"So you won't be seeing him anymore?"

"No. I probably don't have to tell you this, but if you see him, stay clear. And be careful."

I pulled down our road, glancing at the Weavers' house. Dark. Our house wasn't, at least not completely. I had left the inside lights on for Bonk. But sitting on the front porch was a pumpkin with a flickering candle inside.

"Kewl," Luke said, jumping out.

"Stay back!"

He looked at me as though I were crazy. "Someone left us a gift."

"It may have been Colin." I approached the pumpkin as though it were a bomb. I looked inside but found only a candle. The face wasn't a typical Halloween one. I stepped back and studied it. "Oh . . . my . . ."

"What?"

I wouldn't say it. I wouldn't tell my son that the pumpkin's face had Colin's likeness. I wouldn't say it because he'd think I was even more paranoid. I simply walked up to it, blew out the candle, and hoisted it into the woods. It shattered when it hit the ground.

"Mom! Why'd you do that?"

"Only two people would have left that for us. Aidan or Colin. Either way, I don't want it anywhere near our house."

Somewhere in the distance, perhaps in the dark barn, I thought I heard the sound of soft laughter. I faced the barn, my shoulders stiff. I reined in my urge to run inside the house like a coward. Yes, I was afraid, but I wasn't going to give him the satisfaction of seeing it anymore.

Luke was shut in his room by the time I walked inside. I wished I could shut myself away, too. Bonk was whining, eager to go out. It relieved me that he wasn't traumatized by his time with Colin. I snapped a leash on Bonk. "Get used to this, my friend. No more running free for you."

I walked down the steps and tugged him back. As he sniffed around, I kept an eye on the woods around us. Luke was upstairs, but I could hear his music roaring through the window. If Colin was out there chuckling I wouldn't hear it.

I looked in the direction of my running loop. There wouldn't be any more running for me, either, not with Colin here. Colin and his partner. I was outnumbered, alone, and scared.

After Bonk finished his business, I pulled him inside and locked and armed the system. The light on the answering machine was blinking. I pressed the button and heard Aidan's voice.

"I know you don't want to talk to me, but I need to explain everything. You're in danger, Maggie. I think you already know that. You need an ally, and you might not believe it, but I'm a good bet. Call me."

I erased it, walked up the stairs, and knocked on Luke's door. He didn't hear or didn't want to hear. I called, "Good night," anyway. Let him steam for a bit. I hoped he'd come to understand why I was so afraid. I'd never told him about the Web site. And so much that had happened was only threatening to me. I didn't want him terrified, but he needed to understand the danger.

I wandered into my room and closed the door. I stripped out of my clothes and slid into warm pajamas. I felt worn-out, both physically and emotionally. Still, when I saw Dana's diary, where I had left it on the closet shelf, I pulled it down. I'd been afraid to read it. I wasn't afraid anymore. Indeed, I had to read it, to try to understand Colin's behavior.

*He came in again today. I feel so stupid, being uncomfortable
about him when the other girls think it's so sweet how he's attached himself to me. I think I'd know infatuation—Lord knows
I've never really seen it in anyone's eyes, though I see how Marcus looks at Maggie. What I see in Colin's eyes is something calculating. He brought me a fern today. How did he know I liked
ferns? I only keep them inside my house. He handed it to me, expecting me to take it. As much as I love ferns, this one gave me
the creeps. I gave it to one of the other girls on my shift. I threw
the teddy bear out that he gave me last month. There's something
about his gifts. Like he knows what I like. Like he's crawled inside me.*

And I keep asking myself, how do I get him out?

CHAPTER THIRTY-THREE

When I arrived at work on Monday, I made sure to close my car door soundly. Had that been Colin, too, opening my door to make me think I was crazy?

"Maggie."

The voice spun me around. Aidan. Looking so genuinely racked I could almost believe he hadn't intended to cause me harm. Almost. "Stay away from me, or I'll call the police." I started backing toward the sidewalk.

"I know you're upset—"

"*Upset?* Oh, you have no idea. It's not like you were hiding a wife or something."

"It was a job, at least to begin with."

"A *job*?" I kept backing away. He slowly followed. "You were stalking me! You tried to have us run over, for God's sake!"

He stopped. *"Have you run over?"*

"Don't play dumb. I'm on to you now. I know who you are; I know what you did for Colin. I don't care if he hired you to do it; you're still guilty. Yes, I am in danger. From you and Colin!"

A man across the street heard my shrill voice and called, "You all right, ma'am?"

I turned and strode into the office. Aidan didn't follow. As soon as I got inside, I checked, seeing his perplexed expression—a charade, no doubt, just like the one he'd been pulling as he'd kissed me.

"You're kidding. That slimy son of a—" Burt, on the phone, censored himself as I arrived. "My office manager does. . . . Yeah, of course. . . . All right, good to know. Thanks for the call."

When he signed off, I was pretending to not have listened. I stored my purse and was about to sit down when Burt said, "Maggie, one of the community schoolteachers turned himself in for child molestation yesterday."

I felt my stomach turn. "Who?"

"Walter Hempstead. He's the acting teacher—"

"I know who he is," I said, too abruptly. "Luke's in his class." Luke spent time with him alone. And Luke had mentioned giving up acting. "I'd better go to school—"

"I'd wait until after school, if I were you. You go storming over there and pull him out of class and he'll be mortified. Luckily no one will have to testify, since Hempstead confessed. He said there were three boys, but he won't give names. My wife's cousin's best friend works at the police station. Apparently Hempstead was beat to heck when he walked in. Won't say a word about how he got that way. I'm hoping one of the kids he was abusing set him straight, but I guess it was pretty bad for a kid to have done."

I pictured Luke when I'd picked him up. He hadn't looked as though he'd inflicted pain on anyone, though he'd been so down. No, Luke couldn't have done it.

My thoughts jumped to Aidan, walking into the cottage with blood on his shirt. He had speculated about Luke's behavior being tied to abuse. I thought I'd seen Aidan near the school yesterday. Had Aidan beaten the man up, forced him to turn himself in? It seemed preposterous, especially in light of what I now suspected. No, what I knew.

"You think he was molesting Luke?" Burt asked, obviously having watched my ruminations.

"I don't know."

"Talk to him tonight. Sounds like the school board is going to take this opportunity to educate the students about sexual abuse. They're going to offer counseling, too. He'll be okay."

If he'd talk to me. It made sense. It also made me sick to my stomach to think about it. And angry. "I've got to leave early, though. I want to pick him up right after school." Rather than have him walk here. I wanted to get him as soon as I could.

"Sure, of course."

When I went across the street to the diner at lunch to pick up a sandwich, I could hear people talking about Hempstead. It reminded me that even small towns had their horrors. Then I remembered something Aidan had said when he'd first returned to Ashbury. We'd been talking about small towns being safe havens. He'd asked if I felt safe here. It wasn't just a casual question.

Why?

Probably playing with me. *Like Colin did,* I thought with a tremor. All this going on, and now Luke needed me. Even if he didn't know he needed me.

I took a deep breath. For now I would concentrate on my son.

When school let out, I was already parked out front, along with all the other parents. I saw the grim faces on kids who'd learned the news about one of their teachers. I spotted Luke, who, unfortunately, looked as though he was heading toward Mrs. Caldwell's house. I called him over, and he plodded my way instead.

"Hey, kiddo."

He barely acknowledged me. I wasn't going to make idle chitchat as we drove home. It would be too hard. When we pulled up to the house, I said, "Let's go out to the lake and talk."

He seemed resigned, even though I'd tried to sound as light as I could. Guess I'd failed.

The lake's surface was ice smooth and probably nearly as cold. We walked along the shoreline, and he picked up flat, dark stones and tried to make them skip across the water.

"I heard about Mr. Hempstead," I said, finally able to bring out the words.

Luke only nodded.

"He confessed to molesting three boys." No response from Luke, who was looking at the ground. "He touched you, too, didn't he?"

He paused. "Are you going to be mad?"

I sucked in a deep breath to keep myself from crying. "No. Of course not. You didn't do anything wrong. He did."

"But I let him. He said he was going to help get me on Broadway. I believed him." He finally looked at me, and I saw that same expression he'd had the day before: near tears. "We were working on a secret screenplay, and the boy . . . he was in love with his teacher. . . . I wanted him to help me, and he kept saying I had to play parts that I didn't relate to, and I did things . . . I didn't want to do."

I pulled him hard against me, breaking through that barrier that had been between us for so long. My heart shattered when I felt his chest heaving softly. We cried together. "It's okay," I said over and over. "You didn't do anything wrong. He was preying on your dreams." I'd heard through Burt's grapevine that Hempstead had made up his acting credentials. He'd only done set work on a Broadway play.

I looked at Luke. "He didn't . . . didn't . . ." I couldn't even say it.

He stepped back and wiped his eyes. "No, he didn't put it in me." At my surprised look at Luke's phrasing, he added, "The kids were talking about it. I didn't say anything, not to anyone. I don't want them to think I'm a freak."

"There's nothing to be ashamed of, but I can understand you wanting to keep it private. Just promise me you'll talk to the school counselors. They can help you to deal with this." I rubbed my fingers against the center of his chest. "Inside here."

"Mom, if I tell you something, will you promise not to get freaky about it?"

"Uh . . . okay." God, what now?

"I think Sweeney did it. I mean, making Mr. Hempstead confess."

"You do? Why? Did you tell him what was going on?"

"Not totally. But he maybe figured it out."

I nodded, grappling with the fact that Luke had confided in Sweeney and not me. "Is that why you were learning Tae Kwon Do?"

"Sort of. I wanted to feel strong. In control."

"I can understand that." But not the confiding part. "I doubt Sweeney did it."

"Why? 'Cause you don't like him?"

"Because I think Aidan did it."

"Aidan? Isn't he a bad guy? Why would he do that?"

This time I shrugged. That was what I wanted to know, too.

Monday evening Elaine Caldwell sat in her easy chair in the living room and looked up to the top of the stairs. At Sweeney's door. He hadn't come home the night before and hadn't been home all day. At first she'd been sad that he wasn't around. It was so quiet now. Even the boy hadn't come today. Making the funeral arrangements had taken up the morning, but the rest of the day had dragged interminably by.

Maybe Sweeney wasn't coming back. He'd never made any time commitments, and she hadn't pressed for one. She assumed he would let her know if he was leaving, but with young people today, who knew?

She was annoyed that he'd changed the lock. She didn't like not being able to inspect the room. What if he'd damaged it? Or put up pornographic pictures? Those were also against her rules. It was her home, after all, and he'd broken her rule by changing the lock. He'd been sneaky about having it done as well. It was that justification that had propelled her to have a locksmith come out and make a key to the new lock. Now she felt the weight of the key in her hand. It was her duty to inspect the room, right?

She looked out the window before taking the steps one at a time. Not a one step creaked, she thought with pride. Honestly, she didn't like having someone else in the house. Yes, the money was nice. Sweeney, too, was pleasant enough. In the night, when she heard him come or go, she woke and lay there for hours. Thinking of the stranger in her house.

She slid the key into the lock and turned it. *Who's the sneaky one now, Sweeney?*

The room appeared to be neat. The bed was made. On the other side of the bed she found a pile of clothing she guessed was clean. So he hadn't moved on without notice. Now she could take a look in his things and be able to assure Maggie that Sweeney was all right. Assure herself, too. She was pretty sure she hadn't misfiled the driver's license copy.

She opened the dresser drawers, finding nothing unusual. In the bottom drawer, though, she saw a stuffed dog's head; it had been pinned in the drawer. Inside she found sheets of paper with sketches on them. These were close to being pornographic. The violence depicted in the drawings made her squirm. The woman, that poor woman, was being eviscerated in one. In another, she was tied spread-eagle to a surgeon's table and the man was taunting her with a knife.

The woman, Elaine noticed, looked a bit like Maggie. Elaine closed the drawer and turned to the long dresser. A vinyl tablecloth covered the mahogany surface and was littered with pots of paint and paintbrushes. An easel had been set up nearby. He was coloring in another of those horrid scenes. A suitcase peeked out from beneath the foot of the bed. She pulled it out and opened it. Two sharp knives lay in a makeshift foam pad, and an indent in the foam indicated another one was gone. Lethal knives. Another violated rule: no weapons. Why would a nice young man like Sweeney have them?

She took in the painting again. Maybe because he wasn't so nice.

She slammed the case closed, pulled upright using the bedposts, and came face-to-face with Sweeney, watching her from the doorway.

CHAPTER THIRTY-FOUR

I feel like I'm going crazy. I know how it sounds when I tell Maggie what's going on. She must think I'm nuts. Maybe I am. But I can feel Colin everywhere I go. I feel him in my house when I come home. And then I see the open door, the made-up bed, and I know he's been here. I almost wish he'd trash the place so I'd have proof. How's it going to sound, reporting an open door to the police? "Yeah, right, lady. Let's fit you into this nice white jacket."

Crazy would be a good place to be. It would be better than what I'm going through right now.

Dana's words, from her diary, resonated through my mind as I waited for Luke to emerge from the school counselor's office. We'd all talked for a while, and then the counselor asked to speak with Luke alone.

On the way there, he had suggested that maybe I see a counselor, too. For my problem.

I closed my eyes, rocking on the bench, and thought, *I'm so sorry, Dana, for doubting you. I wish I'd known.*

"Mom?" Seeing the expression on Luke's face, I gathered that I had actually spoken my thoughts. He looked around. "Who are you talking to?"

"No one." If I'd said, *Dana,* he would probably haul me into the counselor's office. I stood, clasped my hands together.

I wanted to touch Luke, but I didn't know how to anymore. A hug in the moment was easier than a supportive touch. I resolved then that we would both relearn how. I touched his sleeve. "How'd it go?"

That damned shrug.

"Do you at least feel a little better?"

"I guess. She said they're going ahead with the play we were working on. I'm still the lead. If I want to."

"Do you?"

He looked at me, and I saw the corner of his mouth turn up in a slight smile. "Yeah, I think so."

"Good." I gave him one quick hug then. "I'll see you after school. At my office." I was sorry that I'd made that ghost of a smile disappear. "I'm serious, Luke. Until I meet Sweeney, he's off-limits."

I kept thinking about that religious flyer. As always, the things that bothered me sounded trivial if I put them into words. Just as Dana had said in her diary, how could I report that someone had left a jack-o'-lantern on my front porch or left the milk out? I was sure that Aidan had probably ditched all the pictures of Luke and me by now.

As I walked to my car, I searched the parking lot. Colin was here, somewhere. I had to be ready for him when he decided to show his face. I needed to walk the treadmill every night.

I stopped when I saw the note tucked into my car window. With great hesitation, I flipped it open, ready for just about anything.

> *Maggie, we have to talk. I'm across the street at the park. It's a public place. There are people around. I'll stay ten feet away from you at all times. Please come. Aidan.*

I saw him leaning against the front of his truck. He gave me a contrite wave. I felt a hitch in my breath at the sight of him. A left-over feeling. Meant nothing. All right. I would talk to him but only because I wanted to know if he'd forced

Hempstead to turn himself in to the police. Only because of that.

I parked two spots away from Aidan's truck and remained near my car. The morning was cold, and puffs of my breath hung suspended in the air. A woman and her two children played in the near distance. A man jogged around the perimeter. Cars drove by. Aidan was right; it was quite public.

He had walked around when I'd pulled in but remained a few yards away. "Thanks for coming."

I thought it was foolishness on my part, especially when I felt something deep and intrinsic inside at being near him again. And, unfortunately, it wasn't fear.

"Tell me about the blood on your shirt."

He'd been standing outside this whole time, or so his pink cheeks said. He wore no hat on his dark waves and only a thick cable sweater. Something about his eyes spoke of quiet desperation, of agony and even a trace of fear.

"It was Hempstead's."

"Why?"

Aidan glanced around and then came closer, still keeping a distance between us. I didn't want to invite him to sit in my car, and I wouldn't sit in his truck with him. He didn't suggest either, though I could see he was cold. He leaned against my car, facing me, his hands jammed into his jeans pockets. I could smell his black licorice gum.

"I had a feeling someone was abusing Luke. I could see it in his eyes. It's hard, as a parent, to see it. Parents don't want to see it. But I know that look, Maggie. The pain and the shame and the weight of holding in a terrible secret. It's all there, if you know what you're looking for."

He knew. I saw the shadow in his eyes. He knew that pain—and shame—personally. I thought of that picture in his wallet—those haunted eyes. His jaw muscles moved furiously as he chewed his gum. "From what you said, Hempstead was the likely choice. Luke had rehearsal on Sunday, a perfect day to take advantage of an empty school."

"That *was* your truck I saw."

He nodded, looking chagrined. "I thought I was in a good spot, but then you suddenly appeared and looked right at me. I couldn't talk to you, not then. I get in a dark place, and I don't want to talk to anyone. Besides, how could I explain what I was doing there when I'd told you I was going out of town? But I had to find out if Luke was all right. And I knew you wanted to talk." He closed his eyes and tilted his head back. "You *needed* to talk to me, but I couldn't lose that opportunity." He looked at me, and I saw the agony that decision had caused him.

"No, I'm glad you made that choice. What happened?"

"I went into the school, and . . . I could tell what was going on. I banged the front door to interrupt them. Luke took off like a cat, and I went in and had a chat with Hempstead. Suggested that he turn himself in and get help for his perversion."

I tried not to think about what Aidan had seen, tried not to ask him. "Suggested? It sounds like you beat the hell out of him. Not that I object, mind you."

He placed his hands on the roof of my car and stared at the ground. "There's one thing that makes me crazy. I can't control my rage when they try to justify their actions. They try to convince *me* that it's not such a bad thing, that the kid is enjoying it; sometimes they even blame the kid for seducing them." He looked up, and the fire and rage in his eyes burned even now. "Hempstead tried to tell me he was only expanding the boys' acting abilities. Maybe he'd convinced himself." Aidan's fingers tightened against the frame. "I changed his mind."

I shivered, even in my wool coat with my arms wrapped tightly around my waist. I had talked to Hempstead about Luke's change of behavior. I had trusted him. It twisted my stomach into knots. "I can't even come up with words harsh enough for how I feel about him."

"Don't worry. I called him every one of them and a couple you probably haven't heard."

I hadn't realized that I'd moved closer as he'd talked. Now I stood a few inches from him. "What if he recants?"

"He won't. I brought my video camera with me. And don't ask to see it. I keep it for backup, in cases like this, or for court evidence when necessary. I never let parents see the video. I'll never watch it. And I'll never forget those moments when it was all I could do not to bust in and tear out his throat right there in front of Luke."

"He never saw you, did he?"

Aidan shook his head. "I didn't want him to. I wanted it between me and Hempstead." His voice lowered. "I didn't want Luke to be ashamed that I'd caught him. That's how he would have seen it, you know."

"Thank you," I said, confused by how I felt about Aidan, about who he really was. "You said you don't let *parents* see the tapes."

"I only fudged the truth a little. I'm a partner in a private investigation firm called Trackerz, Inc. On the surface we look for deadbeat dads and help with missing-children cases. What we really do is the kind of stuff that law enforcement can't do, either legally or due to lack of resources. If parents suspect their kid is being molested, I investigate. Get evidence. Coerce a confession. If a noncustodial parent takes off with the kid, I track them down. And if someone indicted for molestation skips, I find him. Or her, on occasion."

Aidan pulled out his wallet and, in a separate compartment, showed me his driver's license and private investigator's license. Both were in the name of Aidan Taggart. "Trew's my working identity."

I stared at both identification cards, unable to speak for a moment. I needed to absorb all of this. I'd gone from falling in love with him, to thinking he was an evil co-conspirator, to discovering he'd turned in the man who had been molesting my son, and now . . . this. It made me dizzy. "So you beat up child molesters?"

"When it's necessary. I make no apologies."

"And the thing about looking into nannies?"

"We have people who do that on the prevention side. But we concentrate on the bigger issues."

"We? You and Jessica?"

"Yeah."

There was still so much he wasn't saying, but I could see the truth of what he had told me in his eyes. I was so taken in by that, I'd almost forgotten the reason I'd distrusted him. "Where do I fit into this? Someone hired you to find me." My eyes widened. *"Because they thought I was abusing my son?"*

"No, not exactly." He ducked his head again. "I can't tell you who hired me, Maggie. It's unethical. Someone wanted to make sure Luke was all right. They were concerned, that's all."

"My in-laws, the Fletchers. Has to be." I didn't ask, because I knew he couldn't answer. "So you came here, rented the cottage, pretended to flirt with me—"

"I never pretended anything. I watched you and Luke and Bonk in the park, I sat near you in restaurants, and I took pictures and notes, as I always do. Then I did something I never do. Something that's against my rules. The more I watched you, and looked at your pictures, and saw this beautiful light in your face and the way you laughed"—he reached out to touch my cheek but hesitated—"I started to feel something I'd never felt before. I fell in love with you. I mean, I've *really* never felt anything like this. It started out so simple, but this was the hardest case I've ever taken. And I've had some hard cases. But I've never had a moral conflict before. I kept telling myself to keep my distance, to do my job and walk away. Two things kept me from doing that."

I realized I hadn't been breathing as he'd talked. "What?" I huffed.

He did touch my cheek now, but only lightly. "My feelings for you. I knew how difficult it would be to make anything work when our friendship had started out under lies. I knew we'd have one of these talks. But I didn't care. I wanted you, Maggie. It was as simple as that."

I blinked, unable to respond to that.

He said, "When I returned, I gave my reports to my client, refunded their money, and told them the truth. I assured them that you were doing a great job, but if they wanted to hire someone more objective, I'd understand. I don't know if they ever did."

I felt my chest fill with his words and, more important, the passion I heard in them. But I still had so much to think about. "What was the other reason you came back?"

"I found out Colin was getting another trial. Even my client didn't know about that. When I came the first time, I knew about your husband, your sister, the first trial, everything. Then I had to go on another assignment. When I returned, my assistant told me about the retrial. It was kept pretty hushed, and once I started looking into it, I understood why. The attorney's office didn't want it known that they'd screwed up. And the defense, obviously, didn't want you to catch wind and return to testify.

"By then, the trial was over. He was free. I started digging into who he was. I talked to Detective Thurmond, who told me what he was. So I came back, unsure if you knew what was going on. When I doubted that you did, I had to figure out how to let you know. I didn't want to tell you who I was yet, and why I'd been here the first time. I wanted you to tell me who you were first. I didn't want to scare you, which is what I ended up doing anyway."

I moved away from Aidan, feeling overwhelmed. He'd been looking out for me. Trying to tell me about Colin. Then I remembered something. "Last Thursday, that call from your friend about his daughter. There was no call, was there?"

He shook his head. "I just wanted to get you thinking about it. I started getting desperate when I realized you were scared and wouldn't tell me why."

"It worked." I looked around even now, wondering if Colin was watching us. "I thought you were his partner, the one who was terrorizing me before and after the trial."

"I'm sorry, Maggie. Maybe I should have gone about it another way. I wanted you to trust me before I dropped everything on you." He ducked his head. "And I see you don't know whether to trust me now."

I pinched the bridge of my nose, feeling a monstrous headache forming. "I don't know what to think right now." I didn't like lies. Look at where my lie had landed us, after all.

He moved closer, gently cupping my face in his hands. "You can trust me with your life. But you don't know that yet. I understand. What I want *you* to understand is that I want to protect you and Luke. I'd even like to try to talk to him about what happened, maybe help him through it. But I can only do that if you trust me." When I hesitated, he said, "At least tell me where Colin could be. You know this town better than I do."

"There are a lot of closed-up homes this time of year. Even . . . well, even my neighbors' house. There's someone, though, that I'm suspicious of." I told him about Sweeney, and I even mentioned the flyer. "That's probably my paranoia—"

His hands, now on my shoulders, tightened. "Don't censor yourself. Trust your instincts."

"I . . . I don't know what to trust anymore. Or who." I backed away from him. "I have to get to work. I'm already late."

"Have lunch with me."

"I can't." I got into my car and started it. As I backed out of the spot, Aidan stood there watching me. He had me so mixed up, so upside-down. I realized a warped irony: Aidan's phony name was Trew. Could I believe anything he was saying now?

Colin sat in the living room reading a bio of Hitler. Sure, the guy had his faults, but he was a genius. Nobody ever gave him credit for that. There was nothing wrong with world domination. He'd simply gone about it the wrong way.

Not that Colin was into world domination. One person at a time suited him just fine.

He trimmed his fingernails with his teeth, chewing on the jagged bits of nail. It was a habit he'd started as a kid, watching the way his mother dominated and manipulated his father. Habits born out of nervousness or anxiety were the hardest to break. Colin had decided long ago that the action comforted him, so he stopped trying years ago.

The religious flyer he was using as a bookmark had been his inspiration for something better than repenting. He'd used Mrs. C.'s old computer to write out a new version of the flyer. His poems could have gotten him stalking charges, if they'd been linked to him. He didn't want Maggie to have anything tangible. He wanted to keep it all in her mind so she'd sound adorably crazy when she told anyone. If she told anyone.

The only problem with that plan was whether she would get it at all. What if it was too subtle? Yesterday, when he'd gone to Keene for his sushi fix, he'd mailed another letter to her. This one would be a little more to the point.

He fingered the flyer. " 'REPENT!' " he said, reading the large block letters. Yeah, right. An old memory surfaced, though, that quelled his smile. Once he'd gone to live with his grandma, he'd had to go to church with her every Sunday. She'd always give him two quarters to put into the collection plate, as though maybe she thought that would help get him into Heaven. He had long ago crossed the line, and now all those quarters wouldn't help his soul.

He looked up. "Sorry, Grandma." But hadn't God made him the way he was? Maybe he was meant to weed out the weak and sinful. Maybe he should try harder.

Mrs. C. always had those insipid shopping channels blaring, but now it was blissfully quiet. Except for the sound of a truck engine idling outside. He went to the window and looked out through the sheer, amber curtains. Damn. It was the nuisance boyfriend, Aidan something-or-another. Luke had told him about Aidan, and Colin had had to squelch his annoyance at the intruder. At first he hadn't even wanted the kid in the picture, but Luke had become part of his plan.

The plan: revel in being home, revamp his Web site, and gorge on sushi, beer, and the other carnal pleasures he'd been denied. With those desires sated, he'd had only one left: make Maggie pay. He'd gone to Ashbury and taken note of her schedule and habits. When she picked up Luke from Mrs. C's, Colin had seen the ROOM FOR LET sign. The sun had even been reflecting off it in golden, eye-blinding rays, making it seem ordained.

Aidan wasn't. It was then that Colin realized Aidan wasn't in the truck; he was next to his Cherokee. Just as Colin started toward the door, Aidan returned to his truck and sped away. Who the hell was this guy? Colin was going to find out.

Maggie would eventually find out who Sweeney was. He hadn't planned to hide forever. Fortunately, he'd taken precautions so he'd beat Maggie to the punch.

It was time to move in for the kill. He'd enjoyed watching Maggie crumble a little every day, just as most of his pets did. Even strong Maggie wasn't immune to being alone in the dark, to getting knocked down by a mysterious being, and being reduced to looking around like a scared mouse. Now he was going to have some real fun.

CHAPTER THIRTY-FIVE

When I walked into the office, Burt had a somber look on his face. "How's the boy?"

For being a bit of a jerk, he had his nice side.

"I think he'll be all right. Thanks for asking." I didn't want to divulge too much.

Dora, Burt's nineteen-year-old daughter, pulled open the door and flounced in. She always wore pastel colors that accented her peaches-and-cream complexion and cornflower blue eyes. This morning, though, her eyes were dim and serious. "Guess who died last night?"

"Who?" Burt and I asked simultaneously.

Dora twisted her straight blond hair into one long rope. "Judy called. She works at the police department, so we get all the juicy news first," she told me. "Mrs. Caldwell committed suicide."

I sucked in a breath. "No."

"That's a damned shame," Burt said. "Nice lady. Guess she'd been living for taking care of her husband. With him gone . . ." He shrugged.

I had to sit down. "How?" I finally managed to ask.

Dora grimaced as she slashed her fingernail across her wrist. "In her bathtub. Her tenant found her."

Those words froze me. "Sweeney?"

"Whatever his name is. He'd been out of town most of the

day—drove to Keene just to get some sushi, I hear, whoever heard of that?—and returned to find her in the tub. Sad, really. She gave up so much to take care of Ed. Probably felt she had no purpose in life anymore."

Burt patted my desk. "I'll talk to Munroe, see if there's anything I can do. You all right, Maggie? You look a little shell-shocked. That's right, your son goes to her house after school. Was he close to her?"

I only shook my head.

"I can stay, Daddy," Dora offered, nodding toward me.

"That's sweet, but I'm fine. Really."

Dora seemed to have none of her father's sour attitude. I hoped she stayed that way.

I sat there for several minutes after they left, feeling oddly disconnected. Even when the phone rang, I couldn't bring myself to answer it.

"Sushi." The word knocked at my mind. Colin loved sushi. They'd found take-out containers in his studio. Chopsticks.

I was going to meet Luke after school again, just in case he went to see Sweeney.

"Morning," a voice said, startling me. The mailman set a stack of mail on my desk and headed on his way.

I don't know how long I stared at it. I'm sure if anyone happened to look in, they would have thought I was waiting for it to do something. Finally I pulled off the large rubber band and started sorting it. A plain white envelope with my name typed on it caught my eye. I slid the blade beneath the top edge and shook out a plain white paper, also typed.

It read:

> *Thank you for offering to judge in our annual poetry contest! Your time and effort are appreciated by our many applicants hoping to win the Poetry Institute Fellowship. Here is the entry you are to judge. Scoring is as follows:*

I skipped over that section, confused as to why I was getting an entry and why there was no contact information

to send my score to. Then I read the poem . . . and understood.

I'm a little spider, hiding in your closet.
Watching, waiting, for you to come home,
To see you kick off your shoes in the foyer,
And breathe that breathy sigh,
As though you've shed the world's problems,
When you walk into your safe harbor.
But now I'm dead, and can watch you no more.

"Maggie?"

I jumped this time, and the page went flying out of my
hand. I hadn't even heard Aidan open the door, much less
walk in. I couldn't afford to be so lax.

"Sorry. Didn't mean to startle you."

"It's okay. I . . ." I might have told him about the poem,
but his expression looked far graver. "What is it?"

"The Jeep Cherokee . . . it's registered to Colin Masters."

I crumpled, overwhelmed by everything, burying my face
in my arms and taking in big breaths. I sensed Aidan coming
around the desk, perhaps to comfort me. I couldn't have that.
I sat up, and he backed off. I couldn't let myself need Aidan,
whom I still wasn't sure I could trust.

"I just . . . I need to absorb."

He picked up the paper that I'd thrown in my surprise and
set it on the desk without looking at it. Colin had sent poems
to Dana, but he'd never couched them in the form of other
things. So I couldn't be sure. But I knew one way I'd be able
to tell. Until then I laid the paper in my in-bin.

"Maggie, let me handle Colin."

"I can't do that. He's my problem. He's here because I
chose to testify against him." I pushed to my feet, feeling my
legs wobble. "Now that I know, I'm going to talk to the police chief. I'm going to file a report on everything."

"And then?" he asked, hovering close to me, obviously
noticing my wobbly state.

"I need to figure that part out."

"He's not just here to play games. You know that."

"I'll go into hiding again. The only reason he found me was because my mother wrote to him in prison. She wanted to save his soul."

Aidan stood between the door and me. His voice was soft and low when he said, "*I* found you."

"That's what you do for a living." But he had a point, dammit.

I moved around him and opened the door. He paused when he made to pass by me on the way out. "Let me come with you to the police station."

"And tell them what? How you tracked me down because someone thought I was an unfit mother? How you probably illegally obtained information that confirmed Colin's identity? No, I need to do this by myself."

"You don't trust me, Maggie. I understand that. But now you know why I'm here. How I feel. I don't want to lose you. Even if you can't get past why I came into your life, I still don't want anything to happen to you and Luke. Remember that."

I nodded, locking the door and scanning the street for a familiar face. I had the awful feeling I'd be doing that for the rest of my life. It was Colin's terrifying voice that added, *However long that is.*

Colin was surprised to see Luke walking up the driveway. He knew Maggie was getting antsy about not having met him yet, and that was before she suspected who Sweeney might be. He glanced at his watch, though, and got his answer. Luke was supposed to be in school. He'd cut class to see Sweeney. Colin smiled. *What a great kid.*

He let Luke walk up to the door and press the ringer. Colin answered and invited him inside. The house was dark, the curtains drawn. It smelled musty.

Luke walked in slowly, his eyes searching. "Where's Mrs. Caldwell?"

"Dead."

He blinked, perhaps thinking Colin was kidding.

"She offed herself," he said, gesturing for Luke to take a seat on the couch. Colin settled into Mrs. C.'s easy chair, the one she'd told him not to sit in. "She was all broken up about her husband dying, I guess. I found her."

Now Luke's eyes widened with the morbid curiosity of any average kid. "Really? What . . . what was it like?"

"She cut her wrists in the bathtub. There was so much blood in the water it looked dark red. Her hands had floated to the surface, but her face was underwater, everything but her nose, which peeked out of the water."

"Ew." Luke sat back and erased the avid interest showing on his face. The kid was obviously conflicted. Fascination versus respect. "She must have been pretty sad."

"Yeah, I guess. It happens when people get old. I found my grandma dead, too. She died in her sleep."

"Mine died of a heart attack. I never saw her, though. Mom wouldn't let me." His eyebrows knitted together. "So many people are dying lately. First Grandma, and then Mr. Caldwell, and now Mrs. Caldwell."

Colin chewed on what little thumbnail had grown out. "I found my dad dead, too."

"No way. How'd he die?"

"He took the coward's way out. He was weak. He let my mother rule him. Control him. There wasn't anything I could do about my mom, being a kid. But he was a grown-up, and he still cowed under her. I hated him for it. When I was eight, he hung himself in the garage, where my mother would find him when she came home from work. Only I found him first. I cut school and found him dangling there with his piss all over the floor. Then I waited on the steps until my mother came home." Colin lowered his voice, for effect. Sharing a secret. "I liked seeing the look on her face. She lost her footing on the brake and nearly ran into him. Then she got all mad at me for not calling the police, for not saving her from seeing that. But that's what he wanted. And she deserved it."

"Wow." Luke had sucked in his lower lip as he'd listened. "My dad died from cancer. My mom was really sad, too. I'm glad she didn't kill herself."

Colin felt just a hint of regret that he'd have to take Maggie away from Luke. Normally, she would have been off-limits. If only she hadn't lied. If only she hadn't wrecked his life for three years. He looked at the boy, wondering what it would be like to have a son. The kid had no one but some uptight grandparents in Massachusetts. Maybe he'd stay a part of Luke's life. Teach the boy, as Colin's grandma had taught him, how to be persistent when you wanted something. To go after it no matter what.

"We have a lot in common," Colin said.

Luke's expression darkened. "Mom won't let me see you until she meets you. She's all wiggy about you. She thinks you're . . . well, someone she doesn't like."

"You mean Colin Masters?"

Luke tilted his head. "Yeah, how'd you know?"

"Because I am Colin Masters."

"Yeah, right." Luke's laugh faded. "You're kidding, right?" But the kid was smart enough to put it together. How would Sweeney know about Colin Masters? Colin made a point to remain relaxed. He didn't want the kid to run. To his credit, Luke remained on the couch, though his body had stiffened. "You are?"

"Yeah. Does your mom really think I'm going to hurt her?"

Luke nodded. "She said you were in town."

"Did she tell you how I knew you were here?" When Luke shook his head, Colin said, "Your grandmother wrote to me in prison. She and I became friends. You see, she knew what your mother had done. She wanted to try to make things right."

"What did Mom do?"

"You don't know, do you? No, of course not. She would have lied to you, too." Colin took a deep breath, as though imparting this truth was painful. "Maybe I shouldn't tell you."

Luke leaned forward, hands kneading the loose denim on his jeans. "No, tell me."

Colin pretended to consider it. "Ah, I guess you're pretty grown-up. You should know. She lied. During the trial, she lied about seeing me near your aunt's house. She broke the law when she did that. I kinda understand why. She so badly wanted someone to pay for her sister's assault. Just because I liked your aunt, she thought I did it, even though there was never any evidence. Her boyfriend, Marcus, wanted someone to pay for the crime so he'd look good. I went to prison for almost three years because of your mom's lie."

Luke was raptly listening, but those expressive eyebrows of his furrowed again. "Are you going to hurt her because she sent you to prison?"

"No. I became a Christian while I was in prison, thanks to your grandmother. What your mother did, that's all behind me. I came to Ashbury because I want to talk to her. I want closure so I can move on. And then, by divine fate"—he lifted his hands heavenward—"I rented a room in the very house that you come to after school. I met this wonderful kid I came to think of as a sort of son. That's why I haven't approached your mother yet. I knew as soon as she knew who I was, she'd make us stop hanging out. That thought made us sad, so I put it off. And I thought, maybe God put us together for a reason."

Luke was digesting everything. The part about him feeling like a son to Colin, that had gone over well. He'd seen the kid's eyes soften, his mouth tighten. "You think God brought us together?"

"Yes, I do. I mean, what are the odds?"

Luke mulled that over. "You did help with . . . well, you helped by teaching me Tae Kwon Do." His expression hardened. "But you tried to scare Mom. And you tried to run us over."

"What? No way. When?"

"After the trial. Someone shaved the word 'LIAR' into our dog's fur. And painted it on our garage door. And someone took a truck out of gear in the parking lot so it would run us over. That's why Mom changed our names and we had to move here."

"Think about it. I was in jail after the trial. How could I have done all those terrible things?"

"She said you had a partner."

Colin chuckled. "A partner. Right. I don't know anyone well enough to ask them to do something like that. You want to know what was really going on? See, your mom knew she'd done a bad thing, lying on the stand. She was afraid that someone would find out and *she* would go to prison. So she fabricated—made up—all that stuff, just to make it look like someone was trying to hurt her. She wanted a good reason for going into hiding. That truck, maybe it slipped out of gear by accident and she tried to make that part of her conspiracy. I'm sorry to tell you all this, Luke, but you should know the truth."

He absorbed that in a surprisingly mature way. "How do I know you're not making this up? You told me your name was Sweeney. You lied, too, said you were an accountant."

"Sweeney's my nickname from when I was a kid. So technically it wasn't a lie. But yeah, I did fudge the truth a bit. I told you why. And as far as whether I'm making it up about your mom lying, just ask her. Study her face. You'll be able to tell if she's lying 'cause she won't be expecting the question."

"Mom really wigged out when someone shaved that smiley face into my dog's fur." Luke was looking at Colin, maybe wondering if he had done it.

"Like I said, it was probably just a Halloween prank. The dog's okay, isn't he?"

"He seems fine. He wasn't hurt either time."

That was another rule: never hurt animals. They had pure souls. Like kids.

Luke pushed to his feet, his shoulders slumped. "I guess you won't be meeting Mom anytime soon then?"

"I'll talk to her, but I doubt she'll let us hang out anymore, even if we make peace." He stood. "I'm going to miss you, kid."

Luke looked as though he was about to cry, but he bucked up well. "Me, too."

"Hey, I forgot to ask . . . how'd you like the gift I left on your front porch? The carved pumpkin. Pretty cool, huh? I worked on that thing for *days*."

The kid's face fell. He could hardly push out the words, "M-Mom threw it out into the yard. She didn't know who it was from."

Yeah, Colin knew that. Still, he managed to look surprised and hurt. "I figured you'd know it was from me. The pumpkin was sitting around here for a while. Should have put a note on it, huh? Or . . . maybe that wouldn't have mattered."

Luke shook his head, and Colin had to fight not to smile. "Thanks, anyway. It *was* pretty cool." Luke walked toward the door, every step looking as though his feet weighed as much as a concrete block. He opened the door but turned around. "Are you still going to come to the school play Thursday?"

Colin was surprised by the warm feeling those words evoked. "No one could stop me from being there."

No one could stop him. He couldn't wait to see Maggie's face when she saw him there. But he'd been dreaming about another expression for a long time: Maggie-the-dolly realizing she was about to die.

CHAPTER THIRTY-SIX

After I told Police Chief Wilson everything, I ended with, "And now I know that the man who calls himself Sweeney is, in fact, Colin Masters. There's only one reason he would be here in this town—to punish me for testifying against him."

Wilson, who had listened to my story with an expression as stony as New Hampshire's Old Man of the Mountain, said, "Maybe there's another reason he's here. Look, I know who Sweeney really is."

My mouth dropped open. "What?"

"He told me last night, when we responded to his call about Mrs. Caldwell. We had a chat while we waited for the coroner to come 'round."

My heart now felt as stony as the granite mountaintop that had once looked like a man's face—and had become the state's emblem. "Did you check into Mrs. Caldwell's death?"

He actually chuckled and shook his head. "He said you'd probably accuse him of having something to do with her death. It looked exactly like what it was, an old woman who'd lost her purpose in life. Mrs. Donahue, or whatever your *real* name is, I admit that his coming here might look suspicious to you. After all, you may have lied to send an innocent man to prison."

"He wasn't innocent!"

"Now, that's not what the jury said."

"That's because I didn't testify."

"That's neither here nor there, ma'am. Fact is, Colin Masters was exonerated of that crime. He never was charged with stalking your sister. I think your guilty conscience is jump-starting your imagination. You really want me to write up a report about someone leaving a pumpkin on your front porch? Or shaving a happy face into your dog's fur? Those sound like Halloween pranks, or, in the case of the pumpkin, a gift. As far as something knocking you down, we do have wild animals in these parts. Seems if the man was after revenge, he would have done a lot more than just knock you down, you think?"

My fingers curled into fists in my lap. "He likes to play with his victims before he moves in. Now he's trying to use my son, to befriend him for reasons I don't even want to contemplate." I took a quick breath. "During your little chat, did he say why he'd come to the very town I'm in?"

"He admitted that it looked like he was here to cause trouble. I certainly considered that, and I won't dismiss the possibility. Then he showed me the letters your mother sent to him in prison. He was so touched that this woman could find it in her heart to forgive him that he knew he had to forgive you. He said he needed closure so he could move on, and to get that closure, he needs to talk to you about what happened."

I couldn't stop the huff of frustration that escaped me, not only at Colin's story but also that the man sitting in authority in this town had bought it. "Then why hasn't he approached me? Why is he using a fake name?"

"He didn't want to scare you. He wanted to settle in, work on his book—a fictional story about a man wrongly imprisoned—and find some peace first. He wanted to make sure he had no anger toward you. I believe he's telling the truth. He certainly seems sincere." Wilson learned forward, his elbows on the desktop, his fingers steepled together. "It's you I'm worried about. You seem awfully close to the edge."

I surged to my feet. "You have *got* to be kidding me. You

think Colin, who stalked and assaulted my sister, is a nice guy, but you think I'm crazy?"

"There's no proof that Colin did anything, ma'am. I *have* seen evidence that you're on the verge of being hysterical."

I quelled my first instinct, which was to, well, get hysterical. "I was right about Sweeney, though. He wasn't who he said he was."

"And neither are you."

I hadn't thought about that. "I went into hiding because he had someone stalking me."

"And if he is stalking you, I'll take action. But unless he poses a threat to you or your son, there's nothing I can do. Now, if your son has something else to add, I'm glad to listen. Especially in light of what happened at the school. Colin does have a great affection for your son, but not in the Hempstead way."

Luke would have nothing but good things to say about Sweeney. This was what Colin had in mind, I realized. Keeping everything subtle so I'd sound nuts if I reported him. I closed my mouth, keeping that suspicion to myself.

"If it makes you feel any better, he's going to have to vacate the house tomorrow. The Caldwell children are coming in to arrange a memorial service and take care of the house. If you can make peace with Colin, he'll probably be on his way."

Colin and I make peace? That almost made me laugh. He hated me as much as I hated him. Neither one of us was going to back down now. "I am afraid for the residents of Ashbury when their chief of police is either blind or gullible," I managed through a scratchy throat, and left his office.

As I walked toward the exit, I saw two officers escorting a man in handcuffs. My stomach turned. Walter Hempstead only briefly met my gaze before looking down. I gulped down a breath and walked over to him. Because he was tall and I was short, he couldn't avoid me.

"You are a good actor, Hempstead. You made me think you were a human being." I spit in his face, spun on my heel, and stalked out. I wanted to scratch his eyes out. I wanted to castrate him. That was all I was going to get away with, though, in police headquarters.

The officers had stiffened when I'd started walking over. Once they saw that I wasn't going to cause a scene, they allowed themselves smiles that I saw when I glanced back before exiting.

Aidan was waiting by my car, as I knew he would be. "Well?"

"I spit on Hempstead," I said, even now stunned that I'd actually done it.

"You *what*?"

I relayed my statement and how my little bit of spit had landed on his cheek. "At least something good came of the visit. Wilson didn't believe me." Aidan listened intently as I gave him a summary.

"What are you going to do now?"

"Start sleeping with a knife. And when he comes in, I'll stab him to death."

I had said it blithely, as I got into my car and went through the motions of starting it, but I wasn't at all sure I could stab someone. Even someone as evil as Colin Masters.

"Run with me . . . please?" I asked Luke after we'd gotten home. "I don't want to run by myself." There. I admitted it.

I had to stop myself from blurting out the truth about Sweeney the moment I'd picked up Luke at school. I needed to sound sane and calm, to gather my thoughts.

"I guess," he said, and we went inside to change.

He paused as we passed the remnants of the pumpkin. His expression grew hard. I pictured myself hurling it off the porch and wondered if that's what he was remembering, too.

Winter was definitely here. No more running or the sound of crickets. The thought of it left me cold inside, too. What would be happening when spring came around?

Bonk whined, now tethered to me by a long lead. I tried not to notice the smiley face.

"He hates that leash," Luke said. "But I guess we don't want him running off again."

Sun slanted across the lake as we ran along the waterside part of the path. It felt good even if it didn't chase away the chill. Soon it would slide behind the trees and the temperature would plunge.

I tried Open Doors. "Was Hempstead the reason you stopped running? Were you hoping if you got flabby he wouldn't be interested in you that way?"

At least Luke couldn't shrug when he was running. "I dunno. Maybe."

"I spit on him today." That got his attention.

"Really?"

I smiled. "Yep. Right on his face."

"Where'd you see him?"

Uh-oh. Hadn't thought about that. "At the police station."

"What were you doing there?"

"Asking about Mrs. Caldwell," I said, not entirely a lie.

Luke and I were both out of breath by the time I reached my favorite breath-catching spot. I sat on the log and stretched my legs. Luke, too cool to admit he was out of shape, bent his body in half and braced his hands on his knees. Bonk, nowhere near ready to stop yet, tested the limits of the lead.

I squinted in the sunlight that put Luke's face into shadow. "Luke, we need to talk."

"Oh, man. I knew this running thing was a ruse."

"It wasn't a ruse." Wherever he'd gotten that word from. "The truth is, I'm afraid to run alone right now."

I was surprised by the skeptical look on his face when he said, "Because of Colin."

"Why do you say it like that? Like I have no reason to be afraid of him?"

Luke straightened. "He won't hurt you."

Those words got me to my feet. "How do you know that?"

Even in shadow, I could see him brace for an argument.

"You know, don't you?" I said. "You know Sweeney is Colin."

"He told me today."

"Today?" I wanted to scream, to shake him. "You saw him *today*?"

"Yeah. I was going to ask him to come over and meet you. He told me everything."

I had to catch my breath for different reasons now, mostly because my chest felt so tight I could hardly suck in enough air. "Everything. His version of everything."

"Mom, he just wants closure. He didn't hurt Aunt Dana."

He'd no doubt given Luke the same story he'd given Wilson. Luke believed it, too. His trust terrified me more than anything else. "You didn't see how he looked at me that day at the police station. He told me that Dana didn't fight him. That was true; she had no defensive wounds. There is only one way he could know that; he was there." I walked closer. "If you'd seen what he did, you wouldn't even think of talking to him."

"Mom, he was acquitted. Heck, even Grandma liked him. She wrote to him, forgave him. If you heard what he said to me, and saw how he is with me, *you'd* know he couldn't do something so awful. I don't want you bad-mouthing him. He's my friend. My best friend." Luke narrowed his eyes. "That's why you were at the police station. You were telling them about Colin. You always have to ruin everything!"

He turned and headed back to the house, leaving me stunned, bewildered, and feeling betrayed. Fear paralyzed me, and Bonk tugged free and ran after Luke. I knew how Colin could manipulate people, though. He was good. A twelve-year-old fatherless boy was an easy mark for a master.

I felt as though the air around me weighed hundreds of pounds, and it pressed down on me until I could easily picture myself sinking into the ground.

No, I had to think this through. I pulled myself up and walked back toward the house. What were my options? Kill Colin. That one appealed on a purely base level, though it was the least likely to succeed. Throw myself on his mercy. I doubted he had any. Run and hide again. Colin would probably find us, especially since he still had an ally in my family.

Ally. I remembered Aidan's desperate phone message. Oh, how I wanted someone on my side. Reaching out had become incredibly hard for me, though. I wasn't sure I could completely trust Aidan even though my instincts—and heart—seemed to think I could.

As I walked, an idea hit that would touch on two of those issues. I needed to show Luke what Colin really was and to do so, I'd need Aidan's help.

I went inside and listened for the sounds of Luke in the house. I heard Bonk's nails tapping on the floor above, and music. Then I called Aidan's cell phone. "Hi."

"Maggie," he said, as though breathing it as a sigh of relief. "Are you all right?"

"I need your help."

"Anything."

I had to admit liking the sound of his devotion, even before he knew what I was asking. "I need your credit card number and address." As a test of the tenuous trust between us, I added, "You'll have to trust me on what it's for."

After only a slight hesitation, I heard him moving. "Ready?" He recited the information.

It touched me that he trusted me so implicitly. Would I ever be able to trust him the same way? I wasn't sure. "Thanks. I'll reimburse you."

"You know I don't care about that. Maggie, I want you to think about something: Let me move in with you and Luke. On the couch or guest room, of course. I'd feel a lot better being there, making sure everything's okay. Sitting here worrying is driving me nuts."

"I'll call you later." I hung up.

One part of me wanted to pull him close. The other wanted to push him away. As I neared the top of the stairs, hard rock music pounded through Luke's closed door. I went into my mother's old room and booted up the computer. Then I logged onto Colin's Web site. The front page had been updated. Apparently the site was still thriving. I clicked on the link to subscribe, entered Aidan's information, and waited for the automated confirmation to appear in my mailbox. I could have used my card, but I didn't want to give Colin the satisfaction of knowing I was subscribed.

I navigated to the current story and pulled it up. Eroz's latest nemesis was new; Malva was probably long gone. Tortured and killed, no doubt. Now Eroz was dealing with a curvy woman named Petra, whose only resemblance to me was her short hair. She didn't have a son; this time her male sidekick was her boyfriend, Dolph. In the latest installment Dolph was considering joining up with Eroz after realizing that Petra was working for the dark side. It felt all too real, all the scarier because I suspected Dolph was Luke.

Going back three years, I downloaded the stories about Malva and her son, Callan. I didn't read them.

I knocked on Luke's door. "I want you to see something."

He reluctantly came, though his posture belied his suspicions about my request.

"Has Colin ever told you what he does for a living?"

"No. It never came up. What is it, whacking little girls?"

I winced at his snide remark but kept my cool. Colin had inserted himself between my son and me, and I hated him for that. "He creates graphic novels and sells subscriptions on his Web site. Marcus found out about the site before we left Portsmouth. He came over late one night and showed it to me. This was the story line at the time." I waited until Luke read through the last ten pages of the story. His eyes were wide as he took it in. I cringed at the violence and nudity I was exposing my son to, but it couldn't be helped. "I knew, as Marcus did, that Colin was basing Malva on me, and Callan on you. See where they get hit by a car? Just like we almost got run down by that truck."

"Yeah, but Colin was in jail. He couldn't have done that."

"No, but I'm sure he had his partner set it up."

I hated the skepticism I saw in Luke's expression, but I had to keep going. "This is what he's working on now. I think I'm

Petra and you're Dolph. See how Eroz, who's probably based on Colin, is manipulating Dolph, turning him against Petra? That's what Colin is trying to do now, with you and me."

Luke scrolled to the next page and then the next, absorbing everything on the screen. Finally I clicked off the monitor and leaned against the desk. "Are you listening to me?"

"Are you serious about Colin being the artist? I can't believe he didn't tell me."

"There's a lot he's not telling you."

"But he's good. I mean, really good. He creates the stories *and* he gets to act out all the parts by drawing them. That's too cool."

I couldn't believe it! He was actually impressed. "Okay, I'll give him the talent part, but Luke, don't you see what he's doing? He's basing his stories on his stalking activities. Before the Malva story line, a woman named Luna looked a bit like Dana. This is how he lives out his fantasies, using real women as models for his cartoons."

"Mom, I'm sorry, but I didn't see the resemblance. Petra looks like"—he held his hands way out in front of his chest—"this. I mean, you may be an MILF, but you aren't Petra."

"He's smart enough to keep the resemblance slight. He's being very careful so I have no real evidence against him."

Luke stood and completely shocked me by tapping me on the cheek. "That's because there isn't any evidence." Before I could say a word, he sauntered back to his room.

I wanted to scream, cry, and throw up, and not necessarily in that order. I kicked at the CPU, for all the good that did. Then I went into my bathroom and took a hot shower to wash away all the ugliness I'd just seen. It wasn't until I got out that I realized I'd left the Web site logged in. I peeked into the hallway and saw that Luke's door was open, his stereo off. I saw movement in the third bedroom and heard him softly tapping the keys. I tiptoed down the hall and stepped into the open doorway.

He jumped. "Mom, you scared me."

"That's because I caught you doing something you

shouldn't be." I nudged him off the chair and flipped to the Dark Strips Web site where he'd been reading the current story line. "See anything interesting?"

He shrugged, but obviously he hadn't seen what I wanted him to see. I canceled the account, went downstairs, and brewed some tea. I needed evidence. I got out the digital camera.

"Bonk, come here, boy."

He got up from where he'd been sprawled in the walkway and ambled over. I took out one of his dog treats and gave it to him. Then I showed him another one. "Stay." I snapped a couple of pictures of the happy face, for what it was worth. I ventured outside, just as the last of the sunlight was leached from the sky, and took a couple pictures of the smashed pumpkin.

I looked around as I walked back in, seeing shadows move in the dark barn where I no longer parked. Hearing the leaves flutter and scrape in the breeze. The air froze my damp hair, and I quickly ran inside, as though I needed another reason.

Tomorrow I would call the power company and see if they'd found out how my power had been disconnected. I wished I'd kept the religious flyer. I'd looked in the garbage can, but it had already gone out. Colin had been dangling his triumph in my face. Reaching for the son. *My* son. What had Colin been saying with the poem I was supposed to judge? I pulled it out of my purse.

> *I'm a little spider, hiding in your closet.*
> *Watching, waiting, for you to come home,*
> *To see you kick off your shoes in the foyer,*
> *And breathe that breathy sigh,*
> *As though you've shed the world's problems,*
> *When you walk into your safe harbor.*
> *But now I'm dead, and can watch you no more.*

I did that! I would kick off my shoes and let out a breath of relief to be home. That was before I'd known about Colin, when I'd felt safe. I looked at the closet in the foyer. Colin had watched Dana from her foyer closet. He'd watched me that terrible night. I grabbed a knife from the butcher block and advanced on the closet. It didn't have slats, though the bifold door was slightly bent, leaving a crack between the two panels.

My heart thudded as I approached. *I won't let the knife go,* I mentally chanted over and over. My fingers ached, I was holding it so tight. I pushed the door open and searched the dark confines of the closet. The closet was deep and had no light.

"Mom, what are you doing?"

I spun around, yelping at the sudden sound, then I turned right back to the closet. The older coats I'd been meaning to donate to Goodwill took up the rear section. I rummaged through, finding no skulking figure in the back. Then I faced Luke, who was watching me as though I'd lost my mind. Especially since I was holding a knife.

How could I explain about the spider poem? Or even the religious flyer? My interpretation of them *would* make me sound mentally out-of-whack. I don't know why, but I straightened the robe I wore over my pajamas. "I was . . . just checking."

"For Colin." He shook his head and continued on into the kitchen, where he poured a glass of milk. Before he ascended the stairs again, he said, "You really should get some help, Mom. Maybe you could talk to the counselor at school."

I watched him disappear around the corner, heard his footsteps on the stairs and then his door close. Only then did I dare to look at myself through his eyes. Kitty-cat pajamas that he'd given me for Christmas, thick socks jammed into boat shoes, fuzzy robe, and . . . knife. Probably a crazy look in my eyes. No, not the way I wanted my son to see me.

I started to close the door, but a thought stopped me. I pulled out the old coats and laid them on the floor. They'd be donated tomorrow. I pushed the remaining coats to the rear of the closet and saw something that sparked fear in my heart. I retrieved the flashlight. I wanted to be absolutely sure. I aimed the light at the smudge on the wall.

The squashed spider.

CHAPTER THIRTY-SEVEN

I used to worry about everything. That the pain in my leg was a cancerous tumor. That forgetting things meant I was developing Alzheimer's. Now I know what worry is really about. I worry about being raped. I worry about being killed. I worry about being crazy. I don't even know which is worse anymore.

I tucked the diary underneath the couch cushion next to the knife. I'd hidden kitchen knives and knitting needles everywhere in the house. The tricky part had been putting them within my easy reach but not Luke's. For the moment I had one beneath the cushion of the couch, the handle sticking out. I removed it and struggled to my feet. It was just after five in the morning following a night of fitful dozing punctuated by disturbing dreams.

Like Dana, I needed proof of sinister intent. I looked out the window, seeing the first traces of light in the sky. I could barely make out the road leading out. Colin had been here, probably several times. He'd been inside my house. That was a realization that clamped over my heart like the jaws of a cold, sea-drenched monster. Somehow, through the dead bolts and the alarm system, he'd slithered in. I thought of the light at the Weavers' house that went on and off even though it had no timer. While I'd stood in front of their window something—or someone—had knocked me down. Had it been Colin, fearing I would find his hideout? If he'd broken in, he could park his vehicle in the garage, hidden from view.

I knew the police would never check it again. I'd already exhausted their patience and my credibility. I was going to have to check it out first. Which meant, *I* was going to have to break in.

A liar and a trespasser, now twice. All for good reasons, but the sins were still just that—sins. I went upstairs to change, avoiding the top step that creaked. After bundling myself in warm clothing, I cracked Luke's door and peered in to make sure he was still asleep. His soft snoring confirmed it, but I walked closer anyway. He was nearly lost in the pile of sheets and blankets. Our intrepid watchdog was out like a hibernating bear at the foot of the bed. I shifted my gaze back to the bed. Luke looked so much like my little boy, sweet and innocent. It made my heart ache that he'd changed so much.

I'd changed, too. I could never go back to the Maggie I'd been before Dana's assault. I could only move on as a person who had broken the law and her own moral code. Who would break it again.

I crept back downstairs, grabbed my camera, and walked outside. Fog hovered above the lake's surface and filled the air with gauzy texture. I walked on the damp mat of leaves rather than the noisier gravel. The moist air clung to my face and dotted my eyelashes by the time I reached the Weavers' house.

I looked in the front window but saw nothing out of the ordinary. At first. Then I saw a beer bottle sitting on the end table. I thought it unlikely that the Weavers would have missed that in their final cleaning. The garage, unfortunately, didn't have windows. Since I hadn't noticed anything out of the ordinary last night, I was fairly certain Colin wasn't here. I wanted to look for signs that Bonk had been kept here and that someone had been here recently.

I walked around to the back where the rear kitchen door had glass panes. I wrapped the towel I'd brought around my gloved hand and punched the glass. It took four tries, each one harder than the last, to finally break it in. Pieces of glass fell to the floor inside. I carefully reached through the opening and unlocked the door.

I felt guilty for my intrusion as I stepped inside. I would arrange to have the glass fixed that morning, of course. Even though they might never know I'd been here, I still felt bad. I walked into the kitchen, but before I'd even begun my search, I realized something: The house was warm. Not toasty, but too warm for a house that was sitting empty for the winter.

I walked over to the temperature gauge and took a picture of the seventy-degree setting. Then I went into the kitchen and touched the bottom of the sink. It was damp. He had been here recently. I listened for any sound in the house. I would have alerted him if he'd been sleeping here, though I didn't think he'd go that far. He would stay here as long as it took to harass me or watch me and then leave. Tomorrow, though, he'd need a place to stay. I took a picture of the sink that I doubted would come out. I took one of the beer bottle, too. If I could get the police to check, the Weavers could probably verify that they hadn't left the temperature at that setting and maybe didn't even drink this brand of beer.

If Colin had parked his vehicle in the garage, perhaps there would be evidence of that, too. A puddle of fluid, tire marks. I walked across the wood floor to the door I guessed would lead to the garage. I unlocked the interior door and opened it. I got a vague impression of something red and large, but before my brain could register it, something hard slammed into the back of my head.

I tried to turn. Pain and fear gripped me. So did darkness. The last thing I remembered was hitting the floor—and being sure I was going to die.

Colin stood over Maggie's body. So she'd finally gotten brave enough to investigate this place. Too bad she hadn't come earlier, when he would have had all night with her. It was tempting to finish her off now, but he wasn't ready. He wanted to drive her a little closer to mad. Besides, the kid would wake up soon and wonder where his mother was.

Colin grabbed the camera that had skidded across the floor and deleted the pictures she'd taken. He'd been watching her since the sound of shattering glass had woken him. So much for his new place to stay.

He worked fast, turning down the temperature, opening the doors to let in the cold air, and wiping out the sink. He kept checking on Maggie, who showed no signs of waking. A small trickle of blood: good, not a lethal blow. He took a glass of water and tossed it up at the ceiling, causing it to drip down on the floor. He set the heavy metal doorstopper he'd hit Maggie with next to the couch and then laid her head near it.

He grabbed the beer bottle and cleared his sheets and pillow from the bed. He then stepped into the garage, started his car, and left. Only then did he make a call.

I heard voices. I'd died, and maybe Mom and Dad and Dana were coming to greet me. My head felt as though it were cracked in pieces, so maybe I hadn't. What had happened? My mind slogged through recent events. The couch was damned hard. No, I'd woken up. Gotten dressed. Broken into the Weavers' house. Beer bottle. Water in the sink. And . . . what I thought was Colin's car in the garage.

I tried to open my eyes, but they felt taped shut. He was here. He and someone else. Two voices. His partner.

I felt someone touch my wrist. "She's got a pulse."

"What the hell is she doing in here?"

I knew one of the voices. I finally managed to open my eyes and looked up into the face of George Pederson, the officer I'd first spoken with in Ashbury. Relief surged through me. "He was here," I croaked. "Colin Masters."

Pederson looked at the other officer with chagrin. "She's been obsessed with someone being in this house." He looked back at me. "Are you all right?"

"I don't know." I was on the floor. Something was burrowing into my head.

As I tried to move, both men knelt down to help. I felt woozy, nauseated, and very cold. I looked at the thing I'd been lying on: a smiling dog forged in iron.

"You're bleeding." The officer I didn't know got up and walked into the kitchen.

"No, don't run the water. There's already water in the sink. Someone was in here running the water," I tried again. "Proof that someone was here."

"There's water on the floor, too," Pederson said. "You must have slipped, fallen, and hit your head on the doorstop. There's water on the ceiling. Must have a leak."

No. That couldn't be. "Colin was here. I saw his car in the garage, and then he came up from behind and hit me."

The officer whose tag read: PAUL CRUTCHFIELD opened the door and looked out into the empty garage.

"He's gone, of course," I said. "I've got pictures." I reached for my camera, which was also on the floor, and flipped through the digital display. "He erased them." Of course. I used the arm of the couch to help me to my feet and looked at the end table. "He took the beer bottle, too."

"The sink is dry," Crutchfield said, holding up a finger. He grabbed a paper towel and ran it beneath the faucet.

It was cold in here now. Colin had thought of everything. "He must have been sleeping in the bedroom when I came in." I stumbled down the hall. The bed was stripped of linens, leaving no trace of someone having slept here. I slumped, holding on to the wall when the house spun. "What time is it?"

"A little after six."

"I've got to get my son up for school."

Pederson grimaced. "Mrs. Donahue, we're going to have to take you into the station." He nodded toward the very clear evidence that *I'd* been in here. "Trespassing's against the law."

I felt my stomach churn. "You're going to arrest me?"

"Afraid we have to."

"Wait a minute. How did you know I was here?"

"A neighbor out walking his dog saw you breaking in."

Oh, perfect. Colin had reported me. Bastard.

"We can take you to the clinic when it opens. You should have that looked at."

"My twelve-year-old son is home alone. I need to get him up and ready for school."

The two men looked at each other, weighing what to do. I was pretty sure they'd never had such a situation.

"Look, you know who I am. I own a home here. I'm not violent and obviously had no intent to rob the place. I suspected—and was right—that Colin Masters was here. So I broke in, yes, to check it out. The Weavers know me. I said I'd keep an eye on the place, and that's what I was doing. Let me get my son to school and then I'll come in."

Pederson let out a long breath. "All right. But I want you at the station promptly."

"I'll be there. I'll contact a glass repair company and get this fixed."

"I'll call Nick. He'll take care of it. And bill you."

I nodded.

They watched me walk home, and I tried not to weave or stumble. I felt dizzy and in pain, holding the damp wad of paper towels to my head. I ducked into my house and went to work cleaning the blood from my hair before Luke saw it.

With my head in the sink, I wondered: why hadn't Colin just killed me there? An answer pulsed through my mind the same way the pain was doing: *He's saving you for something else.*

CHAPTER THIRTY-EIGHT

By the time I arrived at the police station—promptly—Wilson was in. I was taken to his office, where he looked at me as though I were a naughty kid and he the principal. Substantiating that impression, he said, "Mrs. Donahue, what am I going to do with you?"

At least they hadn't cuffed me when I arrived. "Arrest Colin Masters for assault. On me."

Wilson tilted his head, looking at my scalp. "I heard you slipped and hit your head."

"No, Colin bashed me in the head and then made it look as though I'd slipped. I'll guarantee you won't find a leak in that ceiling."

He let out a long sigh. "Just be happy I'm not arresting you."

"You're not?"

"I spoke with the Weavers, who vouched that you had said you'd keep an eye on the place. One more incident like this, though, and we're going to have to take action. Get you some help. You're free to go."

I stood. "One more incident and maybe I'll have proof. And then you'll have to take action." I walked out on shaky legs and headed to my car.

I'd only told Burt that I'd be late for personal reasons, not sure whether I would have to amend that by telling him I was going to jail. Especially since I'd told off the chief of police the other day. Burt was on my phone, taking a rental call, when I walked in. I gave him an *I'm sorry* look; handling rentals was my job. After he'd hung up, he said, "Maggie, is everything all right? You've been distracted lately, gone a lot. Is it Luke?"

I could have said yes, but that wasn't fair to either Burt or my son. "It's more than that. I'm sorry about being out again. I hope . . . well, I hope it will be settled soon."

Burt stood at my desk going through the mail. "Me, too. Oh, the mail already came. There's something for you."

I saw the envelope on my blotter. Plain white. No return address. Postmarked from Keene. I approached it slowly. Flipped it over with the tip of my fingernail. I thought about throwing it away but figured I should see what Colin was up to now. I sliced it open and shook out its contents: one photograph fell facedown on my desk. Dread filled me as I flipped it over. Then . . . surprise. Nothing gruesome. A dark-haired toddler girl at a park. Nothing written on the back. The picture itself was a message. But what?

The door opened behind me, and I heard a man say, "I'd like to talk to someone about rentals."

Burt said, "Maggie's the one you should talk to."

He vacated my desk as I turned to face the man who belonged to the pleasant voice. My stomach lurched. I felt dizzy all over again.

Colin smiled at me before taking a seat in front of my desk. He'd grown his hair back in; it was dark blond and short. As Luke had described, Colin had a goatee that formed an arrow from his bottom lip to his chin. I hadn't seen him since the trial. He looked different; he was wearing colored contacts to camouflage those cold, blue eyes.

"I'm losing my rented room today, so I need another place to stay," he said as though we had no history.

I glanced toward the short hallway, but Burt had already closed his door. I walked around the desk, using the edges to balance myself. I took deep breaths before saying, "There is no way I'm helping you stay in this town. You probably killed poor Mrs. Caldwell."

As though I hadn't just accused him of murder, he said, "Maybe you have a room in your house I could rent. That one upstairs toward the front is nice. The bed is soft. Not as soft as yours, but it'll do."

"You son of a bitch," I growled just as Burt walked back out again.

He stopped, taking in my snarling face and Colin's pleasant one. "Maggie, what's going on?"

"This man raped my sister and now he's stalking me."

Colin stood and shook Burt's hand. "Sorry to cause trouble. I didn't rape her sister, or at least that's what twelve members of a jury said. And I came here to make peace with the woman who lied on the stand to try to convict me." He nodded toward me. "But I've come to like Ashbury very much. I may be looking to purchase something."

"I will not deal with this man. He's playing games. That's the only reason he's here."

Burt looked uncomfortable, unsure what to believe. I wasn't going to try to convince him of the truth. I'd done that and failed many times.

Colin said, "You can talk to the chief of police. He'll vouch for me." He flashed me a slight smile. "Maybe I should work with you, sir. So I don't upset little Maggie here."

"Uh . . . okay." Burt looked at me. But what could he do? Turn a customer away based on the anger and fear in my eyes? "Give me the rental book, please."

I handed him the hefty binder that included pictures of our properties. Burt indicated that Colin should follow him into his office. As soon as the door closed, I slumped down into my chair, nearly missing it altogether. I sucked in breath after breath, trying to steady my heartbeat.

Dora burst through the door. "I need to talk to Daddy. My car just conked out in the middle of Main Street."

"He's with someone," I warned her as she opened the door.

"Daddy—oh, hi," she said. I heard that same soft smile in her voice that I'd heard in mine when Aidan first returned to town. "Sorry to bust in, but my car broke down."

Since Dora was their only child, I suspected her parents coddled her. She'd also been sheltered, so to see Colin pause as he slid by her in the open doorway scared the hell out of me.

"Go ahead and take care of it," Colin told Burt. "I'll get some coffee and wait."

Colin still had that same way of looking at me as though he were touching me, even with his fake brown eyes. He walked to the coffeemaker and took his time preparing a cup. I heard Burt ordering a tow truck.

As Colin walked past my desk, he tossed something at me. "Use the key next time. Much easier."

Instinctively I caught it. A brass key gleamed from the palm of my hand. He'd thrown the key from his left hand, where it had been held in a folded napkin. No fingerprints.

Dora came out and gave Colin a contrite smile. "Sorry to oust you."

He emanated genuine warmth. "No problem. So you're Burt's daughter. I'm Colin Masters."

She shook his hand, her blue-eyed gaze glued to his. "Dora."

"A pleasure." And he meant it.

She giggled and flounced out, giving him a backward look. He watched her with such interest it made my jaw tighten.

"Keep your eyes off her. She's only nineteen."

He winked. "Nineteen's legal."

"Come on back," Burt said, and Colin sauntered into his office.

No, not Dora. She was sweet and innocent. She'd never survive Colin.

I stared at the key in my hand. Then I knew. It was the key to the Weavers' house. Colin was rubbing it in, that he'd called the police on me. That he had a key. And if I took it to the police? What would it prove? It would be Colin's word against mine that he'd tossed it to me. I knew who Wilson would believe.

I stared at that door, listening to them talking, laughing.

My life was falling apart again. This time, though, it was even worse.

The two men emerged at last. I was going to pretend not to notice, but Burt made that impossible. "Maggie, draw up a rental agreement with this information." He handed me a piece of paper with Colin's personal data on it. "He's going to write a check for one month in advance." He paused. "All right?"

I knew he was concerned, and I wasn't going to crumble in front of either of them. I turned to the computer, fully aware that Colin was watching me from where he sat on the couch. I focused on the screen, inputting the information, typing the name of the man I hated. Colin had chosen the Hallowell place. It was past my street, around the bend, and, unsurprisingly, across the lake from my house. It would be very private. With binoculars, he could watch me from across the large cove.

Burt had left the door open, but he couldn't see in, nor could I see him. He was on the phone again.

In a low voice Colin said, "Dana tried to ignore me, too."

He was baiting me. Hoping I'd snap, maybe even try to scratch his eyes out or kick him. I wanted to do both and more, but I'd probably only get in one little scratch before he subdued me. Then the police would cart me away and this time they'd put me in the slammer. I stared hard at the screen, concentrating on what I needed to put in the different fields.

"She never fought me. Didn't scream or try to get away. She knew she deserved it."

Those last words stopped me. She had thought she deserved it, but why had he thought so, too? I couldn't ask him, couldn't speak.

"You'll fight me to the end. I'm looking forward to it," he said in an eerie whisper.

The front door opened, and I nearly drooped in relief at the sight of Aidan. Though he wasn't as bulky as Colin, Aidan was strong and as valiant as a white knight. He was looking at Colin with a cold intensity. Then Aidan looked at me, sitting at my computer as though this were a normal transaction on a most normal day.

"What are you doing here?" Aidan asked Colin.

"I imagine the same thing you did when you arrived in town. I'm setting up a rental. Nice little place, very remote. Quiet."

I wondered how much Colin knew about Aidan. Had Colin slipped into his cottage and searched his things? Probably.

Aidan vibrated with anger. His shoulders were wide, body stiff. "What are you really doing here, Masters?"

Colin looked infuriatingly relaxed as he leaned back against the sofa. "Well, I didn't come here to spy on Maggie and report back to her in-laws. Nope, I didn't do that at all." He looked over at me, probably hoping I didn't know the spying part. On that, at least, I could give him no satisfaction by reacting in shock.

Thankfully, neither did Aidan. "No, you came to harass Maggie, to play games, and to use her son as a pawn."

Colin shook his head and chuckled. "What an imagination you two have. I have just as much a right to be here as you do."

I stood. "If you want to make peace with me, then do it. Right here, right now. Then you can move on."

"Sure. All you have to do is admit you lied, Maggie. Not only to me, but to everyone back in Portsmouth. On television, the way you accused me. That's what I need you to do."

I hated the way he said my name. I hated that he'd mentioned the lie, too, in front of Aidan. "Right after you admit you raped and assaulted my sister."

Burt walked out then and, if he noticed Aidan's rigid stance, didn't indicate it. "Everything all right at the cottage?"

"I need to talk to Maggie," he said.

Colin said, "And I'm still waiting for Maggie to process my paperwork and give me a key so I can be on my way."

I sat back down and finished the last few fields. Printed it out. Slapped it down on my desk. "Sign there."

He did and then counted out the rent in cash. I handed him the key; he thanked Burt and me and sauntered out of the office.

Burt motioned me into his office. "Maggie, I can see something's got you upset. Why don't you take the day off? Take the rest of the week. It's slow. We're going to be cutting our hours soon anyway."

I remembered Serena's office and how Colin had punished her to get to me. "Actually, it's probably better if I give you my resignation."

"Wha—? But why?"

"Partly because I hate making those slimy calls to steal away your brother's listings. Mostly, though, I don't want you dragged into my problem. That would be Colin." At the door I turned back to Burt. "Don't let him near Dora." Not that he could stop Colin if Dora was as charmed as she seemed to be; if he was determined to make her his next pet.

I gathered my purse and walked out with Aidan, who asked, "Are you all right? What's he up to now?"

I kept walking, wanting to focus on action and not my thoughts. "He wants to stay in town. Maybe even buy a place here." I knew Aidan was probably wondering about Colin's accusation. I had to consider what I'd tell him. Maybe he'd think I deserved all this. "He broke into your place, too. That's how he knew about you spying on me. He gathers information to use later. He went through my files and got the account number and my Social Security number so he could turn my electricity off."

"I thought it was a mistake."

"I doubt it. The girl said Mr. Donahue gave them my numbers for verification." I glanced over at him. "So it *was* my in-laws who hired you."

He let out a sigh. "They only wanted to make sure Luke was all right. And you. They care about you, too."

"Of all the violations I've suffered lately, that's the least of my worries." But it still stung.

As we reached the parking lot, we saw Colin leaning against the side of his Cherokee. He appeared to be soaking in the sun, a peaceful expression on a face turned skyward.

Aidan walked over to him. His voice remained cool and calm when he said, "You hurt Maggie, her son, or her dog, and I will kill you."

I believed him, all the way down to my toes. Those words both fortified and scared me.

Colin's smug smile remained in place. "You'd kill me? For her?" He tipped his chin toward me.

Aidan nodded. "You're going to have to go through me to get her. Be a lot smarter to move on, let it go."

"Maggie should have thought the same thing three years ago." Colin got into his vehicle and slammed the door shut.

I walked to my car, needing to sit down before my legs wobbled out from under me. I didn't want Colin to see he'd had that effect on me. I unlocked the door and slumped into the seat. Aidan knelt down beside me. "What does he mean by that? About you lying?"

"I did lie." I was surprised at how easy it was to admit to Aidan. "I'd never uttered the words before. "I knew he raped my sister. He as much as told me at the police station when he came in for questioning. He said she'd never fought him, and he enjoyed telling me that."

"Son of a bitch," he said through a mouth tight with rage.

"When I saw him walking out of the station, and found out he probably wouldn't be charged due to lack of evidence, I committed one of the Ten biggies, broke the law, and lied. And now he's here to punish me for it."

The headache that had been dull all morning sprang to vivid life. I'd forgotten about seeing a doctor. That was way down on my priority list. I lowered my head and kneaded my forehead.

"Maggie? What happened to the back of your head?"

I mumbled, "Colin hit me."

"What?"

I lifted my head at the rage and disbelief in his voice. "This morning"—it felt as though it had happened days ago—"I broke into my neighbors' home. I kept seeing a light on inside, yet it wasn't hooked up to a timer. I suspected that Colin was in there. I was right."

"And you haven't reported this to the police?"

I laughed, which took him off guard. "They arrested me. Well, not technically. There weren't any handcuffs involved." I told him the whole story.

"I'm taking you home," he said, pulling on my hands until I came to my feet. He held me close. "Let me take care of you. Protect you. You only have to trust me."

I nodded, too caught up in the fierceness I saw in his dark blue eyes and in the gentle way he held me.

He locked my car and walked me to his truck, letting out a sigh of relief that filled me as well. I could trust him. He could protect me.

"Should you see a doctor?" he said as he helped me inside.

"I don't want to have to explain how it happened. I don't want to lie about it, either."

He walked around to the driver's side and got in. Gave my hand a squeeze. "I'll take you to your place. You probably have a better supply of first-aid stuff."

"Part of being a mom," I said wearily. That and the terror that a psychopath had turned my son against me.

"Luke seems like a good kid."

"He is." I closed my eyes. "But he needs a father. Colin played him perfectly, just like he played my mother. He preys on people's needs. And their fears." I pressed my cheek against the leather seat. "I'm so tired of being afraid. I'm tired of being strong, too."

I felt Aidan's fingers graze my cheek. "You don't have to be anymore."

I fell into that sense of security as much as I did the feel of his hand. I amazed myself by falling asleep for the rest of the drive. When we pulled up to my house, I woke. My home, once my sanctuary, was now tainted. "Colin sent me a poem about a spider watching me from the closet and being squashed. I found a squashed spider in the foyer closet."

He helped me down from the truck. "I've seen a lot of sick sons of bitches in my life. Child molesters. Wife beaters. But I've never seen anyone like Colin." I heard a trace of apprehension in his voice. "I'm not sure we have many options as far as dealing with him."

Aidan led me to the kitchen, where I took out the first-aid supplies from the pantry. He sat me down at the kitchen table and cleaned the wound. I remembered how he'd dried my hair, how wonderful that had felt. This didn't feel quite so nice.

"I've tried talking to the police, but they think he's a nice guy and I'm the nut."

"I don't doubt that," he said, and when I narrowed my eyes he added, "because that's what Colin wants."

"What he wants is to break me. Then he'll move in for the kill—ouch!"

"Sorry. What the hell did he use on you?"

"A doorstop. Is there an imprint of a dog on my head?"

Aidan shook his head. "Maggie, you're something else."

"Desperation makes me do crazy things."

He gently washed the gash. "I think you'll live, but it's going to hurt for a while. Have you been dizzy?"

"When I move fast. I've had a heck of a headache."

"I'll bet."

He walked over to the sink and wrung bloody water out of the washcloth. "How's Luke doing?"

I knew he meant after the Hempstead thing. "With this Colin thing, we haven't had much of a chance to talk about it. He said Hempstead never . . . penetrated him. Thank God for that."

"That's good, but any kind of molestation can leave a mark on a kid's soul."

"I know." I looked at him as he turned toward me. "It happened to you, didn't it?"

He leaned against the counter, twisting the washcloth in his hands. "Yes. My father."

"Gawd. I never understood how someone could molest any child, but especially his own flesh and blood."

"I was nothing more than a play toy to him. It didn't matter whether I was related or not."

"I'm sorry." I couldn't think of much else to say, but I wanted to know more.

"In some ways I wish it never happened. But then again, it made me what I am today. It drove me to do what I do."

"The picture you keep in your wallet. That was taken during the time when . . . when you were being molested, wasn't it?"

He nodded.

"Why do you keep it?"

"To remind me what to look for. When I see that hollow look in a kid's eyes, I know."

I stood and walked over to him, rubbing my fingers against his chest. "You keep the darkness so close to you."

"I don't know any other way to be," he said in a soft voice. "He didn't penetrate me, either. But the scars are still there."

I liked that he wasn't ashamed. He looked right into my eyes and shared his soul. I took his hands in mine. "It's all part of who you are. And that's okay."

He gave me a slight smile and kissed me, but the darkness was still there in his eyes. "He killed my mother because she caught him with me. She came home early. Her reaction . . . I knew that my feelings about this being wrong were right. She freaked, took Jessica and me to the car. Then she went back inside. I don't even know why, but she never came back out. She disappeared. When the police came the next day, because her co-workers reported her missing, I told them everything. He was arrested for molestation, but they couldn't do anything about my mom until they found a body. They never did. Then he got bail and ran."

"And you're looking for him, aren't you?"

"All the time. I'm worried that he's doing it to some other kid." I heard a fierceness in Aidan's voice. "I catch all these creeps, put them in prison, but I can't find my own father."

I leaned against him, pressing my face against his chest. "You will. Someday you will."

He tilted my face and kissed me. I felt so much in that kiss: gratitude, desire, maybe even love. I slid my hands around his neck and deepened the kiss. I could once again feel his restraint. Maybe he was concerned that I was injured. I ran my hands down his sides and across his back. Down the firm curves of his derrière over faded jeans.

"Maggie," he whispered, but I kissed away the rest of his words.

"I'm not that hurt," I managed.

His hands came up to brace my face in the way that I'd come to love in such a short time. "Maggie, I kept my distance from you because you didn't know who I was."

"You don't have to anymore."

I pulled him over to the living room and down onto the couch. I wanted to feel him all over me, inside me. I wanted to relive those words he'd said to Colin, to soak in the way he was looking at me now. I'd never had a man look so intensely into my eyes before, letting me see everything inside him as he touched me everywhere. In those dark blue eyes what I saw was deeper than desire. It stirred me to my very soul.

He kept looking at me that way as we tore each other's clothes off, and later as we moved together, skin-to-skin and face-to-face. On the couch where I'd hidden a butcher knife, we made love. He brought light to the place of my fear. Only when he came did he close his eyes and so obviously savor the feeling. He kept moving, bringing me along moments later.

After we caught our breath, he slid to the side but didn't move away. His arm was slung across my bare stomach where he lovingly traced circles on my damp skin. I followed the contours of his face, eyebrows, a nose that had once been broken, and his mouth. I'd never had such a sensual lover before. I couldn't even begin to put into words how I felt about him. How he made me feel. That was frightening, too, but it wouldn't scare me away.

He must have read that on my face, because he said, "I don't want you to be afraid of me. I might lose my temper with the scumbags I track down, but I'd never lay a hand on you or Luke."

"I'm not afraid of that."

"Good." He ran his thumb across my mouth. "I meant what I told Colin. I'd kill him to protect you."

I shivered, but not out of fear. Those words touched me in ways no other words of love ever had.

He traced the edge of my chin. "You haven't known me all that long, but I've known you a long time. I've watched you, looked at your pictures, and thought about you every day since I first tracked you down." He gave me a lopsided smile. "I guess that sounds like something a stalker would say, but it's true. I fell in love with you, Maggie. I've never wanted a woman the way I want you. I fudged the truth when I said I'd come back without a plan. You were my plan. I wanted to win your heart before telling you the truth about how I'd come into your life. I knew you'd be angry, and I was willing to let you have time to sort that out."

I kissed him hard. I felt the same way about him, that never-before feeling, the rush of intensity and something very close to love. But I couldn't say it. I lost everyone I loved, and I couldn't stand the thought of losing Aidan. He'd become that important to me. That scared me most of all.

Almost as much as Colin did.

Almost.

Colin had walked through the woods toward Maggie's house. He'd followed them to her road and then parked one road down. He couldn't take the chance that Aidan would check the house next door. Normally boyfriends or brothers didn't bother Colin too much. Aidan did. He had a fierceness that backed up his threat.

Colin walked to the back of her house and peered around the side. She and Aidan were walking to the truck looking flushed and satisfied. He pulled her into his arms and kissed her before helping her into his truck.

Not good.

Colin heard Aidan say, "I'll go to the cottage and pack while you pick up Luke. I'll meet you back here. We can go out for pizza."

They pulled away a minute later, and Colin let himself into the house. He turned on the computer upstairs and went to the history. Just as he figured, Maggie had logged onto his Web site using Aidan's information. He hoped she enjoyed the story line. Obviously not, since she canceled her subscription a short time later. At least she hadn't posted on his bulletin board as she had years earlier. Bitch, taking him to task for his portrayal of a mother's protectiveness. Like he'd know anything about that.

He found one of her kitchen knives next to her nightstand in her bedroom. He tucked it where it would be handier. "Just being helpful."

Then he headed back to his truck, where he had another task to do. Something just for Maggie.

CHAPTER THIRTY-NINE

Aidan hauled the box of files out to the truck and set them in the backseat. He wondered what Colin had thought as he'd dug through the folders. The thought of his invasion irritated Aidan, but he had more important things to think about.

He needed a plan. Colin wasn't the type to be intimidated or threatened into leaving. Maggie had told Aidan about Marisol's brother. Unfortunately, there were two possible outcomes: either Colin would win and hurt Maggie—Aidan couldn't dwell on that one—or he'd do something that would land him in jail. Or maybe there was a third outcome: Colin could die.

At least Maggie trusted him now. That was a big step in keeping her safe. He couldn't let himself think further than that until Colin was out of the picture. Yet how could he not think about holding her, making love to her? He'd told her everything, and she hadn't flinched. Most important, she hadn't offered him pity.

He walked to the front door, which he'd left open, and reached in to close it. Something struck him in the head. He dropped to his knees. What had happened?

Colin stepped out from behind the door, holding a brass lamp he'd taken from the end table. As Aidan tried to get to his feet, Colin struck him again.

No, you've got to get up. You can't leave Maggie alone. Can't . . . The room was fading in and out. *Stay with it.*

Colin stood above him, leaning against the couch. "So, you're willing to kill for her? Are you willing to die for her, too?"

The next blow sent him flat on the floor. Frustration and anger swamped him, even overriding the pain. He'd been ambushed, unable to even defend himself. The next blow sent an explosion of pain through his head, and then a numbing darkness settled over him.

When Luke saw me, his expression fell. I suspected that he'd planned to go to Mrs. Caldwell's house to talk to Colin. I'd foiled his plans.

"I thought I was supposed to come to your office," he said when he got in, forgetting any other greeting.

"Hi, how was your day?" I chirped in a false-cheery voice.

He either ignored or didn't get my sarcasm. "Okay."

"Did you see the counselor today?"

"Yeah."

The distance that Colin was creating between Luke and me made the abuse situation so much harder to handle. So much more frustrating.

"Are you still trying to meet Sweeney?" Luke asked when I took the road leading to Mrs. Caldwell's house.

"His name isn't Sweeney; it's Colin."

"I'm still gonna call him Sweeney. It's his nickname."

I held my tongue, knowing I needed to play this carefully. "He came into the real estate office today. When I ignored him he told me that Dana tried to ignore him, too. And look what that got her."

"Mom, if you knew him the way I did, you wouldn't be saying those awful things about him."

"He's only pretending to be nice to you."

"Why? Why would he pretend?"

I looked over at him. "To get to me."

He rolled his eyes.

I saw two cars and a moving van parked outside the Caldwell house. Their children were probably packing things up. I felt for them. I hoped they wouldn't find any nasty surprises, as I had done.

"Sweeney must have already moved out," Luke said. "He said he wasn't going to leave town, though."

He sounded worried about that prospect.

"He won't leave until he punishes me for testifying against him."

Luke gave me an odd look but turned to stare out the side window. I headed home, filling him in on our new roommate.

"Is he sleeping in your room?" he asked, giving me a look that reminded me of my mother.

"No, he'll stay in Grandma's old room."

I was hoping Aidan would be there by the time we returned. He wasn't. When almost an hour had passed, I called the cottage and the cell phone. No answer. I ran our conversation through my mind but remembered nothing about his going elsewhere before coming here.

I walked down to the lake and lifted my face to the setting sun. The combination of cold air and warm sun felt good, but that only lasted a few minutes. Where was Aidan? I kept turning around and looking at the road, listening for the crunch of tires against gravel. I heard birds settling in for the night, the occasional twig falling to the ground, but no truck.

Finally I walked back to the house, tried calling him again to no avail, and called Luke. "Let's see what's keeping Aidan. We can take Bonk to the park and then bring pizza home."

We headed to Aidan's cottage. He didn't have much to pack up. Maybe he'd taken a call from his business partner.

His truck was in the driveway, the door open. The front door was open, too. A few papers were lying on the ground. I beeped the horn and then got out. Luke stayed in the car.

"Aidan?" I called as I ascended the steps. I felt my chest tighten at the absolute silence inside. I pushed the door open and was about to call again when I saw him.

I dropped to my knees and crawled to him, stifling the scream that wanted to escape my throat. "Aidan. Oh, my God." He'd been beaten badly, his head getting the worst of it. "Aidan, please talk to me."

He was breathing, but he didn't respond to my voice at all. I lurched up and ran for the phone. The house had been trashed, too; I saw that the television was missing. I ran back to Aidan as I waited for the emergency operator to pick up. I rattled off the information and listened as he gave me directions. And I prayed in that same rapid-fire whisper my mother used to use.

Hours later, I stood next to Aidan's hospital bed in the ICU. He was unconscious and wired up to several machines. His face was swollen and bloodied, his eyes puffy and closed. *Like Dana.* Luke remained near the door, tired and defensive. He didn't believe that Colin had done this. The Ashbury police didn't, either. There had been burglaries in the area, and one person had been assaulted when he'd walked in on a theft. They were investigating, of course, but I knew how that would turn out.

I had called Aidan's sister after pounding my memory cells for the name of his business: Trackerz. Jessica, in tears the moment I'd told her what happened, said she would find a way there that night.

I stepped closer and touched his arm. My shaky voice whispered, "Aidan, I'm here for you. No matter what."

It felt as though a giant fist were clenching my heart and lungs. He was here because of me. And ultimately because of my lie.

I heard footsteps running down the hall, and then a young

woman with short blond hair burst into the room. Her green eyes went immediately to Aidan, and she came to a halt so sudden, it was as though she'd hit a glass wall. She dropped her coat to the floor. Her hand went to her mouth, muffling a wounded cry. "Aidan."

"He's still unconscious, but they say it's not a coma." When she turned to me, I said, "You must be Jessica."

She nodded, looking at Aidan again. "You're Maggie." I wasn't sure how to interpret the way she'd said those words, but it wasn't friendly.

"I am."

I held out my hand, but she turned and walked over to Aidan. I could see her struggling with whether to touch him or not. That she wanted to was plain. She was probably in her early twenties, with a slim but muscular build. It was also clear that she loved Aidan by the pain that racked her face. It made me ache that I'd threatened that in some way. She saw me as an intruder . . . and worse, someone who had endangered Aidan.

"The doctor said his brain sustained some swelling, but it's under control now. They won't know the extent of the injury until he wakes up." I felt tears track down my face. I was trying to hold in the anger that raged inside me. The memory of Marisol's brother came to mind. Would Aidan be brain damaged? Colin had inflicted both injuries. Both times he'd focused on the head. "He said it could have been worse. Like that's supposed to make us feel any better."

"It *will* be worse if he doesn't come out of this. Or if he comes out . . . different." She stared at him with the same intensity I'd seen in his eyes. "I was more afraid for him here than ever before."

"Why? It sounds like he deals with some pretty bad people on a regular basis."

She turned to me then. "Because of you. He never gets emotionally involved with a case, and that's what keeps him focused. His feelings for you are a distraction."

I could only agree, feeling more guilt swamp me.

She stood there for a few minutes, swiping tears from her

cheeks as though they burned her skin. Then she turned to me. "Who did this to him? Was it the guy who's stalking you?"

I wondered how much he had told Jessica about my situation. I saw such fire in her eyes and in the set of her shoulders. She reminded me of a terrier, out to grab onto an intruder's pant leg with her teeth and try to bring him down. Oh no. I wasn't going to drag her into this. Aidan would never forgive me. *I* would never forgive me if she were hurt. "They don't know. There have been some burglaries in the area over the last few months. Aidan's watch, wallet, and some items from the house are missing."

She weighed my words like someone very good at seeing lies. But I had become good at telling them, and I held my bland expression. Finally she turned back to Aidan. "Granddad's coming, Aidan. He's cutting his visit to Aunt Karen short and catching the first flight out of Salem in the morning. She sends her love and prayers."

I remembered that Aidan's grandparents had raised them. His grandmother had passed away a few years ago. He and his granddad were close, just as my dad and I were. Both men were Irish, too. Just hearing Aidan talk about the Irish celebrations at the pub his granddad owned in Boston had made me acutely miss my dad.

A nurse came in and asked us to leave Aidan alone for a while. Luke hung back as we walked to the lobby that was as smartly decorated as a cruise ship's sitting areas. I gave Jessica the name of Aidan's doctor. "You'll probably get more information out of him than I will, since you're family."

I'd told them he was my boyfriend, which had gained me loose credibility. "I've got to get my son home. He's got school in the morning." And mandatory rehearsal if he was going to participate in the play on Thursday. "But I'll be back tomorrow morning after I take him to school. Here's my business card." I wrote my cell number on the back. "I'm in Ashbury, about twenty minutes from here. You're welcome to stay with us while you're here."

She shook her head. "I want to be close by."

I nodded, understanding why she wouldn't want to stay with me. "I'm sure I'll see you tomorrow then." I looked at Aidan, whom I'd so recently made love with. My throat tightened and I couldn't say anything else.

When I pulled into our driveway, Luke asleep in the backseat, I felt an ache of loneliness . . . no, of being *alone*. I'd only had an ally for a short time, and I felt his absence to the core of my bones.

I nudged Luke awake and followed him into the house. As he trudged up the stairs, I searched for signs that Colin had been there. They wouldn't be obvious. Squashed spiders. Dana's diary being left out, I realized. I found nothing.

Later, as I settled into bed for a fitful few hours of sleep, something bit into my fingers. Blood droplets oozed from a straight cut across my fingertips and fell onto my white sheets as I yanked my hand from beneath my pillow. I pressed my fingers against my mouth and pulled up the pillow to find one of my kitchen knives. I bent over the side of the bed and looked for the knife I knew I'd hidden between the mattress and bedspring. It wasn't there.

Colin had moved it.

The next morning I sat in the hospital waiting room carefully turning the pages of Dana's diary with my sore fingers.

> *I told Mags today. I know she was disappointed that I'd waited so long. She believed me, though, and that was such a relief. She wants me to go to the police and make a report. The problem is, I have no real proof. The poems, yes. But they're not threatening. Everything else sounds paranoid. Even I think so.*
>
> *I'm afraid all the time now. Even in my dreams. I wake up sometimes in the night, my heart pounding, and think I feel him in the room. His presence. His evil. I feel it more and more lately. As though he's moving in for the kill. He looks so smug, as though he has it all planned out. What it is I don't know. That's what scares me most.*

Two days later:

> *He came in for coffee to go this morning. He played it cool, too, not sitting down, not asking for me. When he walked past me, though, he whispered something. I swear he said, "There's only one way out." I couldn't be sure. But I kept thinking about it. One way? Death. I know that's what he meant.*
>
> *And in my car another poem:*

> *Such a playful pet,*
> *Skipping over my heart,*
> *Playing games with my soul,*
> *Toying with me.*
> *Unaware that I possess her already,*
> *That she cannot get away.*

I couldn't read any more. I closed the journal and tucked it into my purse. I could feel her fear, her hopelessness. I now dreaded every day, feared the unknown.

Jessica and her father, Charley, emerged from the critical care area. I was no longer allowed in because I wasn't immediate family. They'd let me in yesterday because I was the only person with Aidan.

I stood, studying Jessica's and Charley's faces for an indication of Aidan's condition. Thank God they weren't crying. Charley, whom I'd met briefly before they'd gone in to see Aidan, looked like a rotund version of my father. His strawberry blond hair was still thick, and I imagined that in better times, his green eyes, like Aidan's, held a sparkle.

"It's looking better," Charley said, lowering himself into a chair. "The nurse said he woke during the night and tried to say something, but she couldn't understand him. Then he lapsed back into sleep."

In a flat voice Jessica said, "It sounded like your name." She remained standing, her arms wrapped around her waist. "They had to restrain his arms. He was trying to pull out the IVs."

Charley shook his head, a smile on his face. "That's my boy. He's still got fight in him. It's a good sign."

"He's got brain activity," Jessica said. "We can be hopeful at least. Whoever did this . . . really wanted to hurt him. All the damage was to his head. The guy has to pay. One way or the other." I recognized the hunger for justice in her eyes. Jessica, I knew, would lie on the stand to convict the man who had done this to her brother.

"We need him to tell us what happened," I said. I remembered that from Dana's ordeal. The police needed a positive ID. That was my only hope, that Aidan would be able to identify Colin as his attacker. I was skeptical of the justice system, though. Would Colin get only a few years, if it even went that far? Had Aidan seen his attacker? So many ifs.

Charley was studying me much the same way Aidan did. "You care a great deal about my grandson, don't you?"

I could only nod, the words thickening in my throat, tears filling my eyes.

"I told the nurse to let you see him."

"He charmed her into it," Jessica said, her mouth in a tight frown. She obviously didn't approve.

"She said only for a minute," Charley continued. "Go on then."

I didn't hesitate. I walked on shaky legs to Aidan's room, loving him more with each step. Hating Colin more with each step, too.

CHAPTER FORTY

I reached Ashbury in time to fill up my car and get to the school in time for the play. I bundled up in the overcast, dreary weather and shoved the nozzle into the tank. I had to switch hands, since pressing the lever hurt my bandaged fingers.

A minute later I heard someone singing—and badly—from the other side of the pump. I recognized the song that had come out in the eighties. When the singer sang the chorus over and over, though, I realized the significance of it: Bryan Adams's "Cuts Like a Knife." I looked down at my hand, held at my side. Then I looked around the pump.

Colin was pretending to ignore me, but the lift at the corner of his mouth indicated he knew I was there. Had, in fact, been waiting for me to look over.

Doing a terrible job of acting, he gave me a surprised look. "Maggie, fancy meeting you here."

That he *sounded* so sincere was unnerving.

I wanted to take out my nozzle and spray him with gasoline. I wanted to throw a match on him. Anger flared as hot as that fire would be.

"How *is* Aidan, by the way?" Colin asked, seeing my anger for exactly what it was.

I thought of Jessica's words earlier. "You'll pay for that. You may have found a loophole in the system for Dana's assault, but you will pay for what you did to Aidan. He has nothing to do with this . . . vendetta you have against me."

"Oh, but he does. Anyone you go to for help, Maggie, has something to do with us. Remember that before you try to involve his family. That little sister of his is sure feisty, isn't she?"

I had to hold on to the car for support. I knew Colin had seen my shock, dammit. He enjoyed it, enjoyed my fear at what he was saying. How much had he heard? Did he know that Aidan might recover, or was he hoping he'd end up like Marisol's brother? Would Colin hurt Jessica and Charley?

I removed the nozzle and slammed it onto the hook. I couldn't stand to be in Colin's presence for another second.

"But I really like Dora. She's something. I might even delay my next target for her. Just for a while."

"Next target?" I couldn't help asking, though I hated myself for doing so.

"You got the picture I sent?"

"You're targeting little girls now?" I said, infusing my voice with disgust.

"Nah. Her mommy."

Her mommy. Dark-haired girl. About two years old. Serena's daughter. Serena.

I struggled to keep my expression bland as I snatched my receipt from the machine and got into my car. *What have I done?* He watched me drive away. I saw his pleasant smile in my rearview mirror. I fought not to gun the engine and burn rubber. I knew that's what he wanted. What he thrived on. I wouldn't let him spoil my one pleasure that day: watching Luke in his play. I drove to school and found a place in the parking lot. I couldn't help looking over at the park, even though Aidan's truck wouldn't be there. He'd be here now if Colin hadn't done that terrible thing only because Aidan was helping me.

Because I cared about him.

I made one call before going inside. When Jessica picked up, I said, "It's me, Maggie. I need to tell you something.

The man who may have done this to Aidan, he was at the hospital today."

"What?" I heard her relay what I'd said to Charley.

"Tell the hospital staff to beef up their security." They were already keeping an eye on Aidan's room.

"Did he threaten Aidan?"

"No, but . . . he mentioned you."

"Me?"

"Just mentioned you. I think he was trying to taunt me. But we can never be too sure. Be on the alert for a guy about your age, with . . . well, he could have dark blond hair and light blue eyes, or eyes any color. Maybe a goatee that kind of looks like a horn. He could even be bald. He's big, muscular. With a mean face." That he couldn't change.

"Is this the guy who's stalking you?"

"I've got to go, but be careful. All of you."

I'd warn Serena, too. She was going to hate me for bringing this on her.

I slipped inside and found an empty seat near the back of the auditorium. I knew so few of the people there. I'd recently planned to get involved in school activities, maybe even the PTA. That was before Colin had come back into our lives.

The lights dimmed, and the principal welcomed everyone to the first event of the school year held in the new auditorium. I'd heard Luke reciting his lines in his room last night. I'd offered to read the other parts, but he'd politely declined. So I'd stood on the other side of his door and listened. He stumbled a bit, his dyslexia always worse when he was stressed. I'd pressed my cheek against the door and remembered better days, when he reached out to me and asked for help with his reading. When he and Marcus had laughed about their dyslexic goofs.

I tuned in when the play began. Luke was the new kid in school, encountering his share of stereotypical classmates on his first day: the bully, the besotted girl, and the potential best friend who was an outcast. It was corny, sweet, and simple.

I couldn't have been prouder of the way Luke handled his lines and embraced the role. I tried not to think about how close he'd come to giving up his dream because of one perverted teacher.

When the girl came onstage, her hands pressed together at her chest, batting her false eyelashes, I laughed—and stopped when I heard the song: Enigma's "Boum-Boum." The people on either side of me glanced in my direction when I gasped. Everyone else chuckled when the girl tripped over her feet in her romantic exuberance. I couldn't laugh. Couldn't breathe. How had this song become part of the play?

Luke. I knew Luke had suggested it, and Colin had no doubt suggested it to him as they'd discussed the play. Colin was right now imagining my reaction. Bastard. He had managed to spoil the play anyway.

The play wrapped up, and then the children from the music class gathered onstage to sing. I felt as though I were floating above everything, there but not really there.

Finally the principal thanked everyone, the lights came up, and we were dismissed. The audience clapped as they began to stand. The kids poured out from behind the curtain and jumped off the stage to be praised by their proud parents. I saw Luke emerge and search the audience. I waved, but I doubted he saw me. He seemed purposeful as he clambered down and tried to maneuver through the crowd toward the opposite side of the room. Toward—my heart dropped—Colin Masters.

Colin patted his shoulders and Luke beamed at whatever he'd said.

"Excuse me," someone said behind me.

I'd come to a standstill. I stepped out of his way. Colin was also searching the crowd. Looking for me, no doubt. Wanting to see the expression on my face. I made my way toward them, my mouth set in a firm line. They stood off to the side, probably where Colin had been during the play.

What scared me most was the genuine affection I saw on Luke's face, the way he lapped up whatever Colin was saying about his performance. Luke finally looked up as I neared him, and his face sobered. I didn't get a smile. He, of course, knew I'd be angry that Colin was there. I didn't want to give Colin that satisfaction, but it was hard to hide it.

"Hey, Mom," Luke said, obviously ready for my reaction. Colin said, "Our boy did good, didn't he?"

I felt my stomach turn, but I ignored him and hugged Luke. "You did great. Let's go celebrate with an ice cream."

"Can Sweeney come?" he asked hesitantly. "We were going to invite him out before."

"No." I kept it simple, despite the fact that I wanted to scream, *Can a psychopathic stalker who assaulted your aunt and your mom's friend join us for ice cream? Hell, no!*

I took his hand and pulled him through the dwindling crowd without even looking at Colin. I was proud of that accomplishment.

The ice-cream parlor was packed, so we opted to get a half gallon of Luke's favorite, rocky road, at the store. I kept my thoughts to myself for the time being. He must have sensed them, though, because he chattered about this one's performance and how the "walls" fell down right before the curtain opened. All in an effort to keep me from saying anything, I was sure.

We sat down at the table in front of heaping bowls of ice cream. Bonk sat at Luke's side, waiting patiently to lick the bowls.

"That was an interesting song they played during the girl's scene."

"That was my idea," Luke said, licking ice cream from where his hand had dipped into the bowl.

"It was Colin's suggestion, wasn't it?"

He shrugged. "Maybe. So what?"

"Remember the song that was playing in our car stereo in Boston? I got freaked out because it was the song he played when he called Dana. Because the CD hadn't been in the car when we got out. Same song, Luke. Colin suggested that song to get to me."

He set down his spoon and looked at me. "Mom, go

ahead and say it. You're not happy about Sweeney being there."

"His name is Colin Masters. He made up the name Sweeney to fool us. And being unhappy about it is an understatement. I'm terrified. Furious. Hurt. He's using you to get to me. He injured Aidan badly. He wants to hurt me, too." I held up my bandaged fingers. "This is only a start."

I'd told Luke about the knife being moved that morning when he had asked what had happened to my fingers, but that Colin didn't coincide with the man he knew as Sweeney. Luke simply couldn't make the connection.

"You said you hid the knife," Luke said. "Couldn't you have forgotten about putting it under your pillow? Or maybe you did it in your sleep the night before."

"Luke, I'm going to say this once: You are never to see him again. If I catch you even talking to him on the phone, I will ground you forever. Do you understand?"

His nostrils flared. "Colin said you lied on the stand to convict him. He said you made up the partner story so we'd have a reason to move. Because you didn't want to be caught in your lie. Mom, is it true? Did you lie about seeing him that night?"

The question nearly knocked me over. I should have known Colin would pull this. I focused on the easy part. "I didn't make up the story about the partner. You think I tied up Bonk and shaved the word 'LIAR' into his fur? That I painted it on our garage door?"

Luke had no answer for that. "But you were acting kinda strange."

"Because I was scared. Just like I'm scared now. Colin is manipulating you. He's pretending to be a nice guy because he knows you want a father figure in your life."

He licked at his spoon. "He didn't have a father, either. His dad hung himself in the garage. He told me lots of stuff about his life."

"All to win you over. He wants to punish me for testifying against him."

"Did you lie, Mom?"

I looked into my son's eyes and realized that I couldn't lie to him. "Yes, I did. Because I knew he assaulted Dana and he was going to get away with it. He was going to stalk and rape more women. I couldn't let him do that."

Luke pushed away from the table and got to his feet. "You're a . . . a . . . hypocrite! And you don't even know for sure if he hurt Dana. I don't think he did. I think he's the good guy and you're the bad guy!"

With that he tromped upstairs and slammed his door shut. I laid my head on the table and closed my eyes. Bonk whined beside me. I let myself think he was consoling me. He probably only wanted the ice cream.

I was alone. Scared. Angry.

There's only one way out.

That's what Colin had told Dana and she'd taken his suggested route in the end. Maybe that's what he'd said on the phone that terrible day. At the moment, I felt her despair, but I couldn't let it overtake me. I had Luke to protect. I wasn't as weak as Dana. I knew things about Colin that she didn't. I knew that he would do everything possible to keep himself out of the police radar. That going into hiding would only incite him. That escaping would be nearly impossible.

I needed to get the police on my side. That was the first step. Maybe getting a call from the Rockingham County attorney would help Police Chief Wilson understand what Colin was. If Wilson would then overcome his ego and realize that Colin had played him, maybe he would look harder into Aidan's attack. Maybe he would offer us some protection.

I called Marcus at the office this time. When he answered, he said, "Maggie, what's going on?" He knew, of course, that I wouldn't be calling him if something weren't wrong.

"I'm sorry to bother you—"

"It's Masters, isn't it?"

I let out a ragged breath. "He's here. He befriended Luke. He attacked my . . . my friend. Put him in the hospital. And he's coming after me next. Right now he's toying with me, but he'll step up his actions, just as he did with Dana. I need you to talk to the police chief here. Colin's even won him over. Because he got acquitted, the charges mean nothing. The man needs to know how Colin plays the police, what he is."

"Yes, of course. Give me his information."

It relieved me that Marcus was taking me seriously and not trying to placate me with senseless reassurances. I gave him Wilson's number.

"I'll talk to Thurmond first, get some data together. Hang tight, Maggie."

"Thank you," I whispered.

"I'm so sorry," he said, and hung up.

I wondered what he was sorry about. Screwing up the first trial? Not finding me? None of that was his fault.

I called Jessica to check on Aidan.

"He's trying to talk again," she said. "His words are slurred."

Slurred. I remembered the way Marisol's brother spoke, and my heart fell. "But he's trying to talk. That's a good sign."

"The doctors say it is."

I heard Charley in the background. "Tell her what it sounds like he's saying."

After a reluctant hesitation, Jessica said, "We can't be sure."

"What?" I said, hoping it was Colin's name.

"It sounds like he's saying . . . 'Save Maggie.' "

I let out a whimper. Even now he was trying to rescue me.

"Does that make sense?" she asked.

"It's a good sign. It means he's still in there. I've got to go, but call if he says anything else. Or if he wakes up. Oh, and Jessica? Be careful."

I sat there for a long time, thinking about Aidan. I smiled. I wiped away tears. I even managed a halfhearted laugh. He was going to be all right. Everything else we could deal with.

We.

No way was I going to lose him now.

I set the bowls of melted ice cream on the floor for Bonk

and leaned against the counter. The empty butcher block sat in front of me. What if Marcus couldn't sway the police chief's opinion of Colin? It was painful to remember how Aidan had vowed to kill for me. Could I kill to protect my family? Could I take a life? I'd had a hard enough time living with my lie. Taking a life, no matter what the reason, would be far worse to live with. I hoped, though, that if it came down to it, I could. I feared that it *would* come down to that. Soon.

Then I realized something: I'd left one knife in the butcher block, the one I'd tucked beneath the couch cushion when I slept there the other night. I looked beneath the cutting board next to the refrigerator—that knife was gone, too. I carefully felt above the television set and then raced upstairs to my room to look beneath the mattress. All the knives were gone.

Taking a breath, I lifted my pillow—and felt that breath leave me in a gasp. Every knife was beneath my pillow, each pointed in a different direction.

Like a deadly star.

CHAPTER FORTY-ONE

As I drove back into town the next day, after visiting with Aidan, I looked for Colin's Cherokee. I was pretty sure he hadn't followed me to Keene again. While I waited in my car outside the school, I called Wilson.

His "Yes" reeked of impatience.

"Have you heard from Marcus Antonelli yet? He's the Rockingham County attorney."

"No, he hasn't called."

"He's going to tell you what we learned about Colin Masters. If you won't listen to me, maybe you'll listen to him."

"Well . . . all right. I'll see what he has to say. Good-bye, Ms. Donahue."

Well, what did I expect? I'd told him off. I'd spit on Hempstead. I was no longer living in a state of stasis. I was no longer numb. Colin had injected the fight into my blood. Aidan had injected passion. If I was going to survive, I would need to embrace both.

The kids begin to emerge from school. When the crowd turned to a trickle with no sign of Luke, I curled my fingers around the steering wheel. I'd give him one more minute. Fifty seconds. Thirty-five. Twenty. Two. I got out of the car and headed into the building, where I found one of his teachers.

"Is Luke feeling better?" she asked as she tacked up a list of test scores.

"Better?"

"He was out sick today, or at least that's what the secretary told me."

My stomach churned. "I dropped him off here this morning."

"Oh." She cleared her throat.

I turned and ran. I could think of only one place he would go, but it was a hell of a hike for a kid. Had he smuggled out his skateboard that morning? No, I would have seen it. I drove by the Caldwell house just in case. No vehicle in sight.

Anger and fear swamped me as I drove to the cabin Colin was renting. The other houses on his street were closed for the winter, some with boards over the windows. I saw in the near distance a vehicle out front, but it wasn't the Cherokee. Maybe he'd bought a new car to throw me off. As I pulled up to the house, I saw movement in the woods to my left. I felt a jump in the pulse at my throat. Someone was hiding behind the tree. I pulled ahead, and the person stayed with my movements, the same way a praying mantis did when you tried to spy on it.

I threw the car into reverse and spun gravel and in that instant I saw my son shift out of view again.

I rolled down the window. "Luke! Get your butt over here!"

He peered around the tree, his face pulled into the expression of one about to be executed. He looked cold, even bundled in his coat. With his backpack slung over one shoulder, he limped slowly around to the passenger side.

As soon as he opened the door, I screamed, "What do you think you're doing? And what happened to your leg?"

He paused. "I tripped. I was hoping Colin would finally get back so he could take me to school—"

"Before I caught you. Dammit, Luke!" I rarely cussed in front of him, at least without a quick self-reprisal. He flinched.

"Get in," I said. "You don't know how dangerous this is."

He finally got in and closed the door. "I just wanted to

talk to Sweeney. Since you won't let me hang out with him anymore."

As though this were my fault. I looked at the black Lexus in the driveway. "If Colin's not here, whose car is that?"

"Marcus's."

I couldn't have been more stunned. "Our Marcus?"

"Yeah. He came to talk to Colin and told me to go home. He said not to tell anyone I saw him here."

What was he up to? I couldn't imagine that a "talk" with Colin would come to any good. "Stay here," I said, and got out.

As I neared the car, the door opened and Marcus stepped out. I was surprised at the shabby way he was dressed and at how he'd grown pudgy around the face and waist. He wasn't happy to see me, either.

"What are you doing here?" I asked.

"I didn't want you to know. Or anyone. I'm going to have a talk with Colin. Persuade him to move on."

On to someone else, I couldn't help thinking. But I was still perplexed as to why Marcus would come all the way here and, in fact, track Colin down. "How did you even know he was here?"

"I found out what he drove before I came to town. I happened to see him pulling out of this street. It wasn't hard to figure out which house he was in. Look, I don't want you and Luke here when he returns. I want to handle this quietly and leave."

"Why?" I couldn't imagine Marcus Antonelli using brute force. It was not only out of character; it was also plain foolishness.

"Maggie, just leave. Trust me. And don't mention that I was here to anyone."

"But why are you here? Doing this for me?"

His expression softened. "I care about you. I feel somewhat responsible for this happening, and I want to make it right. Now go."

"Why don't you talk to the police chief? You can convince him—"

"Go, Maggie."

I did as he asked, walking back to my car.

"He's going to make Colin go away, isn't he?" Luke asked as I backed up.

"Marcus knows how dangerous he is. He's going to ask him to leave us alone, yes."

Luke said nothing more as we drove home. Once there, I grabbed my binoculars and stepped outside. I couldn't see the house, only the roof through the bare trees.

The thought of a confrontation worried me. I knew what Colin was capable of. Marcus might think Colin only picked on girls. After what he'd done to Aidan and Marisol's brother, I knew differently. Marcus had had a dark, determined expression on his face. I wasn't sure he would be deterred. That he was doing this for me made me responsible once again. I couldn't shoulder any more guilt.

As I pulled on my coat, I called up the stairs, where Luke was hiding in his room. "Luke, I've got to run out for a while. I want you to stay here."

"All right," he said from the top of the stairs.

I would be Marcus's insurance policy. If Colin touched him, I'd call the police. This time I'd have good reason, at least in their estimation. Not to mention that the Rockingham County attorney would back me up.

I took the road before Colin's and parked at a winterized house. Thanks to the recent rain, the leaves were damp and quiet. I walked through the woods and adjusted my track so I came out just behind the house Colin rented.

I heard the crunch of tires on gravel and ducked to a crouch. Colin's red Cherokee pulled up next to Marcus's Lexus. I thought I saw Colin glance in my direction as he got out, but he shoved his hands into his pockets and walked toward where Marcus was standing. Once Colin was out of sight, I darted from the tree line to the back corner of the house.

"I suppose this is the 'out of town by sunset' speech I'm about to hear? Marcus, after all we've been through, I'm disappointed."

I crept to the side of the house, but bushes kept me from being able to press against the exterior and move closer.

"Leave Maggie and her son alone. It's over."

"Oh, but it's not over. Not until Maggie pays. You must love her still." Colin smiled. "No, that's not it at all, is it? You don't want your own dirty secret coming out if I'm caught. You've already lost Maggie, but you'd still lose your credibility. Maybe your career. You might even end up in prison. Wouldn't that be poetic justice?"

I froze at those words. What was he talking about?

"Why? I didn't beat and rape a woman."

"No, you just helped the man who did beat and rape a woman get out of jail. The man who raped your girlfriend's sister. Who's the bigger scum?"

"You son of a—"

Colin's tone changed suddenly. "Let's talk about this inside. It's freezing out here. Maybe we can come to an agreement, eh?"

I heard the door open and close. The heater kicked on a moment later. I couldn't breathe. What were they talking about? An agreement? I inched toward the living room window, damning the sound of the heater for covering anything I might be able to hear.

Then something pushed me hard against the wall, and my head hit in the same spot where Colin had conked me at the Weavers' house. I fell to the ground in a heap.

When I woke, I had no idea how long I'd been out. I groggily opened my eyes and tried to orient myself. I wasn't lying down. I couldn't move. My eyes snapped open. I was sitting on a hard chair in the kitchen. No, I was *tied* to a chair. Across from me I saw Marcus . . . also tied to a chair. Facing me.

Colin stood beside him, his head tilted as he looked at me. "Welcome back, Maggie. You missed all the excitement. After I knocked you out, Marcus here decides to pull a gun on me. But I got the better of him and, here's the best part, made him carry you into the house and tie you up." He nodded toward the gun lying on the kitchen table. "I think my old buddy here, my *partner,* was going to off me."

After all we've been through . . .

I tried to remember what I'd overheard. Marcus had let Colin get away with Dana's rape? He was Colin's partner?

"I'm not your partner," Marcus snarled.

"But you were." Colin's smile was genuine as he took the two of us in. "Tell her what happened, Marcus. Or should I?"

His expression softened when he looked at me. "Maggie, I'm sorry." He said it the same way he'd said it the other night on the phone. But this time it had different meaning.

"Do you want to know why I beat Dana so badly?" Colin asked me. "Because she screwed everything up. That night, I was watching her. I'd planned to approach her. But a man stopped by. I'd never seen him before, so I knew he wasn't someone in her life. And I knew *everyone* in her life. I watched the man go inside, watched how she tried to console him—he was agitated about something. She started with wine and talk and then tender caresses. Except her hand went from his arm to his leg and then to his crotch. She unzipped his pants and took him into his mouth." The angry expression transformed to a smile. "Guess who that man was." As if I hadn't already sensed the truth, he nodded toward Marcus.

"I never meant for it to happen," Marcus said. "I was upset about Celine trying to take Tawny out of the state. I *needed* you. And you weren't there for me."

I felt as though he'd slapped me in the face twice. Once for betraying me with my own sister and then for blaming me.

Marcus said, "It would never have happened again. I'd had too much to drink, that's all. I was vulnerable."

"*I was vulnerable,*" Colin mimicked, leaning against the table, his arms crossed in front of him. "What a crock. You were weak. A coward."

From the shame on Marcus's face, I could see it was true. Even though I knew how much Colin was enjoying our little interplay, I couldn't help but let the pain at his betrayal show. "With my own sister?"

"She seduced me. Ask Colin; he was there . . . watching."

"I give him that," Colin said. "But it does take two to tango."

Marcus looked at me. "I screwed up. And I paid for it a thousand times over."

It was hard to find any sympathy for him. I turned to Marcus. "So you must have been shocked when I told you Dana had been assaulted." As we talked, I wiggled my ankles, trying to loosen the bonds. I tried not to look at the gun on the table.

Colin said, "I'll bet he figured I'd be arrested and no one would know any better. Except they found his DNA at the scene."

"I still would have been all right, if you hadn't made that damned appeal on the news that night," Marcus said to me.

Colin shifted, blocking my view of the gun. "I saw him pulling you away from the cameras and recognized him as the man with your sister. When I saw you at the hospital I realized you two were involved. Then I realized I had an ace in the hole. By then, it would look pretty bad that Marcus hadn't admitted the DNA was his. Which also meant he wanted to hide the fact. Of course, he didn't want to lose you or his dignity."

"I didn't want to hurt you, Maggie. And I didn't want my ex-wife using my slip for her case."

Colin chuckled. "Yeah, a real swell guy you are."

I asked Colin, "Why didn't you just turn Marcus in?"

"Because I knew, even if they did confirm the DNA was his, they'd still be looking for me to protect their CA. So I simply used it as leverage to get information on the case. And my partner, Marcus here, assured me I wouldn't be prosecuted because they didn't have enough evidence. Everything would have been fine . . ."

"And then you lied," Marcus spit out. "That was me you saw walking away from Dana's house that night. I knew you were lying. You ruined it."

Now I knew why he'd pushed me away, why he'd tried to get me to recant. "Marcus, you hypocrite," I said, using Luke's earlier accusation. "You told me you couldn't face me because of what *I'd* done." Then something else occurred to me. "Oh, my God. You were the one making the threatening calls, weren't you?" I looked at Colin. "Because he was your partner. That's what you said."

"I didn't want to be his partner," Marcus said. "I had to. You forced me into it. He forced me into it. So I tried to scare you into backing off. But you wouldn't."

I was seeing everything—including Marcus—in a whole new light. An ugly, glaring one. "And after the trial, when Colin was in jail . . . you still tried to scare me. Why? Oh, I know. You wanted me out of town. You wanted me on the run, under another name. That's why you suggested it. So you could maneuver another trial, after leaving a loophole, and not have me as your witness. You didn't even try to find me, did you?"

Colin actually giggled, taking us in. "This is so much fun." He turned to Marcus. "Cathartic, even, don't you think?"

I was only focused on Marcus, though. "You . . ." I could hardly catch my breath. "You sent me flowers from my dead son! You despicable . . ."

"Maggie, I never hurt you."

"No, but you almost had me and my son run down!"

"I knew you'd get out of the way. I had to scare you. I was getting desperate. I'm sorry about that."

"Yes, Marcus, you are sorry. And I'm just sorry I never saw it."

Colin added, "Marcus didn't want to use your son. In fact, that's why he failed. So when I was convicted, and threatening to expose him again if he didn't do something, I told him to use the secret weapon."

"And you showed me the Web site to seal the deal."

Marcus hung his head. He'd already said he was sorry. There was nothing more to say.

I felt the rope around my left ankle give a little. I couldn't try to free my arms, since they were in plain view in my lap.

Marcus looked at me. "It hurt to lose you, Maggie. I loved you. And I hoped you were doing well. Then when you called, I knew I had to do something."

"Oh, come on," Colin said. "You were saving your own ass."

Marcus hadn't wanted me to tell anyone he'd been here. He'd sent me away. "You were going to kill Colin?"

Marcus didn't answer, but I could see that had been his intent.

Colin sighed dramatically. "Yes, that's the sobering end to our partnership." He walked into the living room and opened a black briefcase. The knife he pulled out was long and lethal. He cradled it lovingly as he returned.

That's when reality hit me. I was going to die. What would happen to Luke?

"You're thinking of your son, aren't you?" Colin asked, leaning into my face. "Well, you don't have to worry. See, you're going to leave town suddenly. With the way you've been acting, no one will be surprised. I'll stay in touch with the boy. Be his mentor. Teach him the ways of the world."

I struggled and screamed at that, and he watched with satisfaction. It terrified me to realize he could pull that off. Maybe I had brought this on because of my lie, but Luke was an innocent.

Colin had settled against the table again, watching me as though he were enjoying a play. I kept thrashing, but only because I was trying to loosen my ankles and arms.

Finally he stood. "Okay, Maggie, give it up. You won't get them loose." He took us both in, turning his head from me to Marcus and back again. "One of you is going to die. I'm going to let you both decide who gets it. The liar or the cheat. Who will pay for their sins?"

"Maggie, this is your fault," Marcus said. "Yes, I made a mistake, but you made this happen by lying."

He was trying to make a case for me being the one to die. I couldn't believe it. Didn't he know Colin wasn't about to let either of us live?

"Kill me first," I said.

Marcus was shocked. Maybe he realized that meant he'd have to witness it.

Colin shook his head in disappointment. "Marcus, Marcus, Marcus. Her new boyfriend puts you to shame. He'd *kill* for her. I bet he'd die for her, too. In fact, he just might." He turned to me. "Brave Maggie. In some ways I've admired you. As afraid as you were, you never wavered."

That wasn't true. I'd wavered plenty of times. I couldn't keep my eyes off the blade hovering above me. I had to force my gaze to Marcus. I saw pain and regret. And I saw him for what he was: a coward.

I heard Colin's subtle intake of air as he lifted his arm. I braced for the impact. The blade arced down. Slicing through the air. Plunging into Marcus's chest. He let out a guttural sound as he pitched sideways in his chair, landing on the floor.

I heard another gasp, too, from behind me. I turned as much as I could and saw something that terrified me more than anything Colin had done—my son, looking in the window. He ducked, and I heard his footsteps on the ground as he raced into the woods.

Colin grabbed the gun and tore out of the house. "No!" I screamed. Luke had a limp. And Colin was much stronger and faster.

I had to go after them. I struggled again, but it was no use. I couldn't free myself. I forced myself to look at Marcus. He was breathing shallowly.

The knife. It was still in his chest.

"Maggie . . . ," he said breathlessly. "I'm so sorry."

"Shut up." I didn't want to think about him or what he'd done. I had to keep my mind on what I needed to do. "I'm going to take out the knife and cut my ropes." And then what? Call the police? Or run after Luke first? Colin had a gun.

I tipped my chair over, too, crashing to the floor next to Marcus. The impact on my knees made me cry out in pain. My cheek smacked the linoleum floor, sending jagged pain through my jaw. I twisted to the side and maneuvered myself so that my hands touched the knife blade. When my fingers wrapped around the textured handle, I felt . . .

"Oh, God, it's in your heart!" My voice was a near shriek. "I can feel your heartbeat through the knife."

"Take . . . it out," he whispered.

"You'll bleed out. You'll be dead in seconds, maybe minutes." That was why he wasn't bleeding much.

"It's your only . . . hope."

Leaving it in was *his* only hope. I saw agony in his face, but not only the physical kind. I saw, at last, regret. Shame. He'd been willing to sacrifice me. Not only just a minute ago but also when he'd let a deranged stalker go free. I now had to do what I could to save my son.

"Take it," Marcus said on a quick breath.

"I'm sorry, too."

I tugged on the handle with my tethered hands until it pulled free. Marcus's gasp shuddered through my body. Blood gushed out, and I watched it as one hypnotized. The red river flowed closer to me, and I pushed away with the foot that touched the floor, which was a little flexible thanks to my maneuvering. I pushed too hard, though, and the chair hit the table leg with a jarring thud. The knife fell out of my sweaty hands and slid across the floor.

"Luke, Luke, Luke," I kept chanting as I scooted across the floor toward it. I reached out, stretching my fingers as far as they would go, until I felt the steel. I flicked my finger and finally brought the knife back to my grasp.

I listened for any sounds outside but heard none. I hoped Luke had sprinted through the woods to the road. Maybe someone would happen to drive by, but it was unlikely this time of year.

Turning the knife toward me, I moved one hand against the other and sawed at the rope. The blood turned the white rope pink as the cotton fibers soaked in the liquid. I sawed back and forth, expecting the rope to break away each time. It took five tries. I cut the ropes at my ankles and got to my feet. I looked at Marcus, still breathing shallowly, groaning softly. I tilted him so that he lay faceup, grabbed a towel from the kitchen, and laid a heavy pot over it to stop the bleeding as best as I could.

I felt as though I had a hole in my heart, too. I whispered, "Good-bye," and ran to the door.

It was too late. I saw Colin walking toward the house with a struggling Luke. If I tried an ambush, I might stab Luke instead of Colin.

I looked at Marcus. Colin would know I'd gotten free. I ran over, removed the pot and towel. He was heavy as I tilted the chair over again, but adrenaline shot strength into me that I'd never known. His eyes were blank. I knew he was gone now.

I sat in my chair, wound the ropes around my ankles, and laid the rest over my lap. Then I saw the blood on my clothing and hands. I heard footsteps outside and Luke screaming, "You're supposed to be my friend! What are you doing?"

If Colin saw the blood, he'd investigate. I grabbed the coat that he'd taken off me while I was unconscious and slid into it as I threw myself back onto the chair. I was just wrapping my wrists when Colin burst through the door.

"Mom," Luke said, and I heard the regret and agony in his voice, saw it in his face.

"Don't you touch him," I said, knowing my threat was useless. So I tried pleading. "Let him go." I'd try anything.

"I didn't want to hurt you," Colin said to Luke. "But you had to go and get nosy."

"I was only making sure Marcus wasn't trying to bully you into leaving."

"Those are the breaks, kid."

That just killed me. He'd put himself in danger by trying to protect Colin.

Luke shifted his body and kicked out his leg in a move that Colin had undoubtedly taught him. Colin was far quicker. He grabbed hold of Luke's leg to twist him around and then shove him to the floor. I heard his body land with a hard thud, heard his *oof*. Colin's hands were around Luke's neck.

I launched out of the chair and plunged the knife into Colin's back. He collapsed on top of Luke, who scrambled, with my help, to get out from under him. Colin tried to push himself up, but his hand kept slipping on Marcus's blood. I'd backed up, Luke's hand in mine. The knife was still protruding from Colin's back. He reached behind and grabbed it. Pulled. It came out with the same flow of blood I'd seen on Marcus. I heard the hiss of Colin's lungs as air oozed out of the puncture wound. He was gasping. Blood bubbled out.

He had the knife now. He struggled to get up. He looked at me again. His eyes narrowed; his mouth moved. I saw his fingers relax, and then his body collapsed.

Luke pulled me to him, burying his face against my chest and sobbing. "Mom, I'm sorry. I trusted him. You kept telling me . . . but I didn't listen . . . and now . . ." He looked over at Marcus and broke down again.

"Shh," I said, still watching Colin to make sure he wasn't faking his death. I'd seen far too many horror movies to turn my back on him.

What I wanted most was to close my eyes and make it all disappear. But I couldn't look away from all the blood.

I thought I was imagining things when I heard sirens. Luke and I backed toward the door. I opened it just as three cruisers, probably the entire Ashbury police force, screeched to a stop in the driveway.

We stepped outside onto the small front porch. Wilson was the first to approach, his gun drawn. He was flanked by the others.

I lifted my hands, not sure what was going on.

"Where is he?" Wilson asked.

"Who?"

"Masters."

Pederson motioned for me to lower my arms.

"He's inside. Dead. So is the Rockingham County attorney." My words seemed to come from a great distance.

The men went into the house in full defensive stance. Wilson emerged a few minutes later as I held a shaking Luke tightly against me.

"Why . . . why are you here?" I asked. "How did you know?"

"We got a call from Keene. Aidan Taggart woke up and fingered Colin for the attack. He said to find you immediately, that you were in danger."

"And you believed him?"

Wilson rubbed his face. "If he did that to Taggart, I wasn't taking any chances. We've been trying to call you at home and on your cell phone. I called Burt, and he told me about Colin renting this place." He handed me a cell phone after pressing a few buttons. "Here, talk to Taggart. He's been calling every minute to see if we found you. He's going to work himself into a God-blessed frenzy."

Thank God. That meant he was all right. I took the phone and held it to my ear with shaky fingers. "Aidan?"

"Thank God," he said, mirroring my thoughts. "I was going out of my mind." His voice sounded low, and his words came out slow, but he was there.

"He's dead."

"Colin?"

"I killed him. I'm not sure I could have if he didn't have Luke in a stranglehold."

"Oh, Maggie. I wish I could have done it for you. I wish I were there right now to hold you."

"Me, too," the words squeaked out. Just his saying it made me start crying. I was still holding Luke to my side. Reality was beginning to crash in on me. "I'll come as soon as I can." I looked up to see several officers standing nearby. Onc was calling something in. Wilson, I'm sure, was waiting to talk to me.

Aidan said, "I can come there—"

"No, you stay. See you soon." Those last words came out a whisper. I handed the phone back to Wilson, who clipped it to his belt.

He reached out and took my arm. "Here." He helped me down the steps. I was glad for his support; my legs had gone rubbery, and I still had Luke holding on to me. His face was buried against my jacket, and I could hear his muffled crying.

This time we'd go to therapy together. We'd work everything out. He would be different, too, afterward. We'd never be able to go back to the two people we were. But we would be better, I vowed. Better and stronger.

EPILOGUE

ONE MONTH LATER

I sat on the deck, even though the temperature hovered just above forty. I wanted sunshine, wanted to feel it on my face and my hands. I watched Luke down at the lakeshore, trying to skip rocks. He'd never gotten the hang of it.

We'd both been seeing a therapist in Keene for the last three weeks, working through feelings of guilt and fear of trust. Luke didn't quite believe that I still loved him as much as I had before he'd "taken up with the enemy," as he called it. With time, he would come to believe. I'd made mistakes, too. I'd trusted Marcus. I'd distrusted Aidan.

It was hard to admit, but Colin had done some good. He'd helped Luke through the sexual abuse by teaching him Tae Kwon Do, which had given him a sense of control. And Colin had wrenched us both from the bubbles we'd been living in—and using to keep others out. We would never live in our bubbles again. We would embrace each other and life.

Luke looked over and caught me watching him. He turned away. It would take time. We had plenty of that.

I returned my attention to the small book in my hands. Only one page of writing remained. Dana's last entry:

> *I did a horrible, terrible thing. I betrayed the person I love the most. It was such an awful thing, I cannot even write the words down. Now I know that I deserve Colin. I deserve it all. I*

don't know how I will ever live with myself . . . or look Maggie in the eye again.

It ended abruptly. Maybe she'd looked up then and seen Colin standing there. I would never know. At least I knew why she'd said she deserved it. Why she'd taken her life. If she'd come back to us, she would have had to explain who belonged to the mystery DNA.

If I'd been the Maggie I was, I probably would have been angry. Would have maybe hated her for a while. I'd spent all my hate on Colin, though, with a healthy dose for myself. I had none left. As I'd read through the earlier entries, I'd seen a trace of envy that Dana felt for me, for my life. To her, I'd always had so much and she so little. I had once suspected that she had a harmless crush on Marcus. As it turned out, it wasn't harmless at all, though she couldn't have known the repercussions of her desperate act. I hoped I made my mother proud by forgiving Dana.

I had been spared the legal punishment I deserved. I'd met with the new county attorney and told him everything. After much deliberation, we made a deal. I wouldn't speak or write of Marcus's legal maneuvering, and they wouldn't prosecute me for perjury.

A horn blast sent me spinning around. The moving van pulled into the driveway and backed up to the front door. I got to my feet and walked around front. Luke ran from the lake, tossing his cache of stones over his shoulder like salt for luck.

The new owners would be arriving tomorrow, a family of five who'd fallen in love with the house just as I had three years ago. I hoped they would find the happiness in the house that I couldn't. I reached the truck as the driver stepped down to the ground and swept me into his arms.

I let out a girlish giggle. "I would have hired movers a long time ago if I'd known the service was this good."

"It's only this good for our special customers." Aidan kissed me quick and hard before scrubbing the top of Luke's head. "You all packed?"

"Yep. Everything but the dust, sir." Luke had been trying especially hard to please Aidan, who'd told him time and again to relax. I knew Luke was trying to make it up to him, as though Aidan's attack were his fault, too.

He raced inside, leaving me with a little ache in my stomach. I turned to Aidan. "It'll pass and he'll be a bratty pre-teen boy again."

"I hope so. Makes me nervous, a kid that age acting so polite."

Aidan still had scars in his scalp where the lamp had cut the skin and a red line through his right eyebrow. Sometimes I saw a tremor of fear when he couldn't remember a word right away. Overall, though, he was still the Aidan I had fallen in love with. I was amazed that he still loved me, despite the fact that that love had nearly cost him his life. I adored his grandfather. Jessica . . . well, she would come around eventually.

"You going to miss this place?" Aidan asked as we headed to the door.

"No. Yes. I love the area, but it was never home to me."

"I hope Boston becomes your home. I know you're going to love it."

I leaned into him. "I already do."

ACKNOWLEDGMENTS

Rarely can a book come together without the help of others. I always feel blessed to have the assistance of several wonderful people who help to make my books better.

Joe Veltre, who batted ideas back and forth with me and told me nicely when they stank.

Lt. Mark Pierce of the Rockingham County Sheriff's Office, who answered what had to seem like endless questions and did so cheerfully, thoroughly, and patiently. Oh, and thanks for the vultures!

A. D. Copestakes and Lt. Nancy Secord, who put me in touch with Lt. Mark Pierce.

Sharon Copestakes, who refreshed my memories of the lovely city of Portsmouth and collected maps and real estate guides.

Antonio "Tony" Sanchez, MSM, CLET, Commander, Investigative Services, Biscayne Park Police Department, for general procedural questions.

Marty Ambrose, my critique partner.

And the generous folks at NINC for never failing to answer research questions.